Lone Stars

Lone Stars

★ ★ ★

Justin Deabler

ST. MARTIN'S PRESS ◆ NEW YORK

First published in the United States by St. Martin's Press, an imprint of St. Martin's Publishing Group

LONE STARS. Copyright © 2021 by Justin Deabler. All rights reserved. Printed in the United States of America. For information, address St. Martin's Publishing Group, 120 Broadway, New York, NY 10271.

www.stmartins.com

Designed by Meryl Sussman Levavi

Library of Congress Cataloging-in-Publication Data

Names: Deabler, Justin, author.
Title: Lone stars / Justin Deabler.
Description: First edition. | New York : St. Martin's Press, 2021.
Identifiers: LCCN 2020040154 | ISBN 9781250256102
    (hardcover) | ISBN 9781250256119 (ebook)
Classification: LCC PS3604.E14 L66 2021 | DDC 813/.6—dc23
LC record available at https://lccn.loc.gov/2020040154

Our books may be purchased in bulk for promotional, educational, or business use. Please contact your local bookseller or the Macmillan Corporate and Premium Sales Department at 1-800-221-7945, extension 5442, or by email at MacmillanSpecialMarkets@macmillan.com.

First Edition: 2021

10 9 8 7 6 5 4 3 2 1

For my parents, and Mark, and our son

Contents

Lone Stars

Prologue

The cry rang out through time and space. It shot down the hallway and into the bedroom, past the cats wheezing on the bed, over Philip snoring through his mouth guard, and pierced the hazy bubble of Julian's melatonin tablet. He rocketed up to a sitting position, out of habit, and waited to see if it was a passing thing. Their son howled again.

"Your turn," Philip mumbled and pulled a pillow over his head.

Julian squinted at the blue spectral glow of the baby monitor, lowered to mute because Pablo had a real set of lungs on him. He stood at the edge of his crib, facing the camera with an omniscient stare, and shrieked. "Hang on," Julian sighed. He stuffed his feet in his slippers and hurried to the nursery.

The baby had worked himself into sorrowful hiccups. Julian picked him up, careful to bend at the knees and save his back, which could go out at any moment. He paced in a circle on the rug while Pablo fussed, and sang the usual songs. He couldn't help falling in love, he began, singing like Elvis, like they heard in the hospital cafeteria the day their son was born. They walked some more. The rainbow night-light cast shadows around the room—the stuffed bear looming on the wall and the origami birds hanging from the ceiling, undulating to the current of the humidifier. The nightmares were a new thing, over the last few weeks. They sent Julian scrambling to Google in his own daddy terror, like the colic and stranger danger had sent him before, back when they rode into town—and then eventually moved on, like everyone said they would. But Pablo wasn't everyone's baby. He was theirs.

His hiccups softened to the occasional whimper, felt as a tiny hot breath on Julian's collarbone. He went to the window and nudged the curtain open. The treetops in Prospect Park stood black against the cobalt sky, lit by a lonely moon. Julian's throat tightened. He had to pull back at times like these and not think too big, about climate change and the world Pablo would inherit, or raising a kid to be good today amid all the noise. Pull back, he told himself, because now, tonight, life was so great it defied logic. How was it possible—after all the struggles of growing up, and so much loss—that Julian could enter the nursery, and Pablo could gaze up under a halo of black curls, and suddenly everything that came before made sense?

Julian looked down at a book on the windowsill. *The Story of Pablo*, it said in round letters on the cover, with a smiling dark-skinned cartoon boy and two white cartoon dads. It had come in the mail the day before. He would soon be old enough to understand when they read it to him, about the mom who loved him so much when he was in her tummy that she gave him to her older friends Julian and Philip to raise.

"What will you tell him?" Philip had asked when they leafed through the book that afternoon, during the baby's nap. "About your family?"

"What do you mean?" Julian replied.

"Well. He sees mine all the time. He's met his birth mom. But your mom and dad. What will you tell him?"

"I don't know. Stories."

"But which ones?" Philip persisted. "History is about the future. What will you tell him about where you came from?"

A streetlamp flickered outside, on the park. Pablo shifted on Julian's chest, maneuvering his thumb into his mouth, and sighed peacefully. The world was silent again. Out of nowhere Julian remembered a painting he saw many times as a kid. It was one of his mom's favorites, a Magritte at the Menil Collection in Houston. He and his mom used to stare at it for what seemed like hours: a painting of a house in both day and night, a blue sunlit sky at the top, until the eye traveled down to the dark roof of a house, and shadowy trees, and a streetlamp in the nighttime.

Gently Julian kissed Pablo's head and looked out at the park. He thought about the night, and dawn, and his mom and dad and other people who were gone. And he wondered—which stories to tell?

I.

Love

1

The Man with the Muddy Boots

For the first time in her life, Lacy Adams paid attention in church. There was nothing special about the service that Sunday. Her dad sat beside her, blank-faced as usual. Junior doodled in the hymnal. Her mom fanned the wet Gulf air blowing in from Harlingen, while the familiar calls of green jays floated through the open windows. But that morning Lacy felt different. She had just learned the scientific method at the end of the school year, and her teacher said it applied to everything but the Bible. And ever since then Lacy had looked at the world with narrower eyes, tingling with a sense that asking questions, using her mind, could unlock mysteries around her. She sat forward in the pew and listened. The pastor told the story of beautiful Queen Esther, a Jew in a hostile land who loved her people and saved them from slaughter when she revealed herself as one of them. And now, today, the pastor preached, let us pray for the freedom-seeking people behind the Iron Curtain, under the soulless Soviet grip, who have to hide themselves like Esther to survive.

After the sermon, the congregation rose to pass the peace. Lacy and Junior hopped to their feet, but they could never reach any hands to shake. The Adams family had a pew reserved for them, front and center, and no one sat in the pew behind them—a distance the farmers kept out of respect, Lacy knew, to give her family more of God's light. She watched her parents lean over the empty pew, but when her dad stuck out his hand and said, "Peace be with you," a farmer with a thick beard just stared at it, keeping his own calloused hands on his belt buckle. "Not while you're still around," the man growled, loud enough to hear, and turned his back to them.

Her dad didn't blink. He turned to his wife and shook her hand, and then Lacy's and Junior's for good measure. The service resumed. Lacy could tell that her mom was seething, but she didn't speak as they filed outside and piled in the red Buick and drove home. She held her tongue while she warmed the pot roast and set the table. She led them sharply through grace. "The nerve," she huffed when they started eating. "The disrespect, *inside* First Baptist? After all we've done for them, to refuse to shake your—"

Lacy's dad lifted his hand for silence. The family watched him sweep the last bites off his plate and run the good linen napkin over his mouth. "They're blowing off steam, Mary," he said, standing up. "Two days and it'll be over." He had changed before the meal, out of the Sunday suit and snakeskins he got in Houston, into dungarees and work boots. He settled his Stetson on his massive gray head and went out the door without a look or goodbye.

"Pure white trash," she resumed, talking to no one in particular like she did at the table and in the car and whenever Lacy's dad wasn't around. She smoothed the blond hair she wore in a fluffed-up Grace Kelly style. "None of those fools had to sell to your father. Drowning in debt, and he bailed them out and gave them jobs. Couldn't grow corn in Eden. Do you see your daddy taking a day of rest? Ten years he's worked on the Plan—the feedlots, cattle, sticking *his* neck out—to change how America eats. Pure disrespect."

"Can I have some more—" Lacy began.

"No, ma'am." Her mom slid the bowl of potatoes out of reach. "You've got to reduce to look good for your Girl Scouts pageant. Junior, you want seconds?"

"Yes, please," he said, and shot a wary look at Lacy.

"Is your troop ready?" her mom asked, serving Junior a heap of mashed potatoes. "Y'all just got the one more singing practice, right?"

"I guess," Lacy said impatiently. "But first I have to turn in my family tree to get my Family History Badge. It's due tomorrow." She hated Girl Scouts. It wasn't her choice to go, and she never wanted to mix with the uppity town girls. But anything Lacy did she did full steam, and for two weeks her mom had put her off, saying some other day they'd do her tree. "I can go get it," she said.

"Manners, Lacy, not at the table." Her mom sighed irritably and stabbed her pot roast. "I already told you about my family. I was orphaned, working in a washateria in Laredo when your daddy came in on a business trip with a tear in his shirt, and I had a needle and thread. Then we got married and had y'all two blessings. The end."

"You were born in Laredo?" Lacy persisted. "I need your birth date, and your mom and dad's names, birthplaces, and birth dates, to finish—"

"Write 'deceased,'" her mom snapped. "Junior, how was Boy Scouts this week?"

"OK," he chirped. "Wanna see what we did?" He wiped his face on his sleeve and jogged to the foyer. Junior was as cute as a puppy, with blond hair as light as their mom's, not like the black mop on Lacy's head. He charged into the room, doing an elaborate fall-roll-and-point maneuver, and aimed a pretend gun at their mom. "Kill the wetbacks!" he shrieked, spraying the table with rounds of fire.

"Junior!" their mom scolded. "Get up. Don't say that word again."

"What word?" he asked, rising in confusion.

"Wetback. It's ugly. And no running in the house."

"But that's the name of the operation," he objected. "Operation Wetback. We met the Border Patrol in Boy Scouts. They're doing sweeps now. They started in Brownsville. Now McAllen, up the river to Laredo, all the way to El Paso."

"And *we like Ike*," their mom pronounced. "We always support our president. But." She straightened her place mat. "Not all Mexicans are bad people, Junior. Some of them don't want to blend in and be American, speak English or eat our foods—"

"Animals," he barked. "That's what the patrol man said. Live like pigs and send our money to Mexico, and we gotta get rid of them. He asked the Scouts what we think. I said build a big wall. With swords on top to stick them if they get all the way up."

"Get rid of them?" Lacy said, slightly disturbed but masking it in the superior tone she had to take with her brother sometimes. "Listen, nosebleed, your patrol guy is talking about *us*."

"Excuse me?" her mom blurted. "What on earth are you talking about, Lacy?"

"Our farm?" she said, suddenly filled with doubt at her mom's tone. "Daddy's business. His workers are Mexican, aren't they? Like Xavier, he's from—"

"Oh," she sighed. "Yes, a good number of them."

"Because one of the town girls," Lacy muttered. "In Girl Scouts." She bit her lip, unsure if she should continue but needing to test hypotheses. "She said Dad's filling up the county with cow shit and Mexicans. And ruining everything."

Her mom watched her and then leaned forward and asked, in a not-friendly voice, "Do you know what a pioneer is, Lacy? The man with the polio vaccine? Henry Ford? Thanks to your dad we're going to be rich. We are rich." She put a finger to her lips like they had a secret. Her eyes blazed. "But this week we'll be really rich. Junior, you, me—the three of us. And we'll move into town where we belong."

"Mommy?" Junior asked softly. "Is the Border Patrol coming here, for our men?"

Lacy watched her mom's knuckles whiten as she squeezed the napkin in her fist. "Don't worry about that," she replied. "Your daddy's got it all worked out."

★

Lacy's mom had been talking about the Plan for as long as she could remember. Her mom kept to herself and didn't have friends, so when her dad was away, which was most of the time, Mary Adams talked to her kids in a low, steady stream, like a faucet left a little on. For years their dad had been buying up the farms near McAllen and clearing the crops and trees to build the feedlots. He shipped cattle in, fattened them, and sent them to slaughter, and after ten years he hit the impossible number: a hundred thousand heads, with the facilities and staff to sustain them. He met his target—her mom always talked targets during meals—and could sell to a company in Chicago, and they were finally leaving this stink patch for a big brick house her mom had picked out. Because that's how America works, she would say as she cooked or folded laundry—you get rich and stay that way, and your kids stay that way, your grandkids, on down the line.

Lacy had nothing against McAllen, with its grand paved streets and palm trees reaching for the sky. But she and Junior didn't share their mom's excitement, or really believe they were moving, because the farm was what they knew and it was fun. As soon as Junior could walk, he and Lacy played together. After school and summers they spent side by side, climbing the fence posts to watch the cattle storm the troughs at feeding time. Or they'd play their favorite game, seeing who could get closer to the bank of the manure pond before one of them gagged and ran away, coughing and giggling in a sick ecstasy. On clear days they climbed the only tree for miles, a cottonwood beside their house, and surveyed the dirt squares stretching to the horizon, full of cattle barely moving as the sun beat down. Lacy told Junior what she learned at school as they perched on a branch, photosynthesis or the Boston Tea Party, so he'd be the first to know in his class. They were best friends.

But the last few months, something seemed to change between them. Lacy knew for sure on the day they saw a calf being born. One morning at the end of the school year, their dad woke them up and they ran to the barn to watch. For an hour its head peeked out of its mom's rump, waiting as the sun rose, opening its mouth silently like it didn't know the words yet. The cow lowed as her calf's legs cleared and it fell into a bright new world. It staggered to its feet. Lacy held her breath, scared to interrupt the sacred scene. "How long till it's fat enough to kill?" her brother asked.

"Junior!" she cried. Because it was the last prick of what had been building for a while. From the moment their mom signed them up for Scouts, her brother started acting like another person. He didn't want to play with her much, and when they did, all he talked about were boys in his troop or killing things. Or he'd lecture Lacy, fresh out of first grade while she was through fourth, and when he got things wrong and she corrected him he'd cut her off with the same line—"You're a girl"—and ride away on his bike or shut his bedroom door. And that was how things stood between them soon after, on the Sunday Junior fired at their mom in the dining room.

Lacy couldn't put her finger on it, but something didn't sit right when their mom said stuff got worked out with the Border Patrol. Lacy didn't make a habit of questioning her parents. She loved them. Her mom was the prettiest lady she knew, with a big twang and bigger smile—a real Texan woman, a teacher told her once. And her dad had muscles, even though he was old, and a face as strong as Mount Rushmore in her history book. But there was a look in her mom's eyes at lunch that Sunday, a sound in her voice, that made Lacy excuse herself from the table to go find Xavier.

Next to the barn she saw the truck he used to shuttle workers from Chilitown to the feedlots every morning and back again at night. Xavier came out of the barn carrying a couple of cattle prods. Lacy knew she'd find him. He was her dad's right-hand man, and if one of them was working, so was the other. Xavier was a good guy, her dad said, and there was something Lacy trusted in his mellow voice and the pressed dungarees and clean white shirt he always wore. He smiled as she approached, his hair so black in the sun it shined a little blue.

"*Muchacha.*" He dropped the prods in the flatbed. "Want to drive the big truck?"

"Hi, *muchacho*," Lacy replied. Junior's recent indifference to Lacy had left her with more time on her hands, and lately she spent it tracking down Xavier and talking to him about Mexico and his wife and daughter there.

"Your dad's not here," Xavier said. "He drive out to the west lots."

"I'm not looking for him." Lacy climbed in the flatbed and watched him load tools.

"The Border Patrol came to Junior's Boy Scouts," she announced abruptly. "They're rounding up Mexicans. But Mom said Dad worked it out."

"Yes."

"He did?" Lacy asked.

"He get us all papers." Xavier stopped working. "Why? Why the sad face?"

"Nothing. My mom seemed . . ." Lacy didn't put words to many feelings. They weren't those kinds of people. "Weird," she mumbled. "What papers?"

"Papers. To say the government knows you and you can be in America."

"Why does the government have to know you?" she asked.

Xavier shrugged and loaded the truck.

"Why did they leave Mexico?" Lacy asked.

"Who?"

"The men in Chilitown. The workers."

"Because." He sighed. "Not everybody can live where he's born."

"How did they get here?"

"In trucks. Or walk and follow a star."

Lacy looked down at the dress her mom made her wear, a stupid frilly thing from a shop in McAllen, and thought this over. "I was born here, but we're moving to town."

"Yes," Xavier said. "I know."

"Can I come see you after? You're not moving, are you?"

"No. Your dad's buyer, they buy the men and equipment, everything, so we stay. Your dad needs all the men now. He hires a one-leg man if he can hop here." Xavier stopped and smiled at her. "And you can come visit."

"Is that why you left Mexico? You couldn't live where you were born?"

"I come to work. So I send money back and Xiomara can go to school like you."

Xiomara was Xavier's daughter, a year older than Lacy. She had long black hair and was good with horses. Her name meant "warrior," Xavier told her once—"a tough girl like you."

Lacy was still thinking about papers as she lay in bed that night, watching the moon cast wavy shadows of cottonwood branches on her wall. The details were murky, but she figured her dad was a hero for getting papers for his workers, and she drifted to sleep. In the morning when she went down to breakfast, the table was set but Junior ate alone. "Where's Mom?" she asked.

"Attic," he said, his mouth full of toast. "Packing. He works her like an ox."

"Who does?" Lacy asked, pouring a bowl of corn flakes.

"Daddy. It's not right. That's what Mommy said. Don't tell Daddy."

Lacy contemplated this as she ate her cereal. Their mom complained sometimes about not having a maid. Lacy asked her once why they didn't, if they were rich, and she gave Lacy a surprised look and said their dad was thrifty and everyone had a job to do. The words stuck in Lacy's mind, connected vaguely to how her parents never gave each other love kisses like the pastor and his wife did, and how their dad was hard on their mom. He never hit her. But he put his fork down when he didn't like dinner, and said a bad job was no job at all, and waited until she scuffled like a whipped horse back to the kitchen to cook him something new.

Lacy heard her dad coming downstairs as she slurped the milk from her bowl. He wore his Sunday suit and snakeskins on a Monday. He sat at the head of the table, poured coffee, and sipped. "Where's your mother?" he asked Lacy.

A crash from above startled Lacy and Junior in their chairs. Their dad looked at the ceiling. She heard her mom's footsteps on the half flight, then the second floor, and as she descended to the foyer Lacy could make out her words. "Too cheap for hired help," she grumbled, "like a slave, the blood from my—" She caught herself when she turned into the dining room, meeting their dad's gaze, and looked down. "I thought you were gone."

"Heading out," he said and stood up. "How's the packing?"

"Dusty. I think I'm getting sick."

"I heard a crash," he said sternly. "The house goes with the sale."

"I know that, James. That's why I'm packing. Lacy, put on your uniform. We're leaving for Scouts in ten minutes."

"I'll drop her," he said, putting on his hat. "Get back to packing. Pork chops tonight. And when you're done in the attic, iron my blue shirt for the closing tomorrow." He walked into the foyer and stopped with his back to them. "I give orders once," he said. "You hear?"

Lacy and Junior locked eyes as the silence thickened and grew unbearable, until their mom wiped her hands on her apron and said quietly, "I heard you."

★

Lacy could count on one hand the times she'd been in her dad's giant black truck. The smell of corn feed wafted from the flatbed as they bounced down the dirt road to the highway connection. Tools jangled on the floor. The seats weren't soft like her mom's Buick, and Lacy felt a mixture of nausea and awe at the whole situation.

"Where's y'all's practice at?" her dad asked.

"McAllen High. Where the pageant is tomorrow. Are you coming?"

"I got a meeting in the morning, and then we're all coming. Free lunch, right?"

"It's a lunch pageant," Lacy said. "Where are you going now?"

"To meet with our congressman. You know what Congress is?"

"The Senate and House of Representatives." Lacy considered his errand. "Does our congressman give papers?"

"Do what?"

"For our workers. Does he give the papers to protect them from the patrol?"

Her dad gripped the steering wheel. "He helps out. He

wants me to be happy and keep all the men I want to keep here. Do what's best for the area. When I sell the business tomorrow, the buyer's building a plant outside town so we don't have to ship the cattle away for slaughter. That's more money for the county and more jobs for everybody. Texans, Mexicans, whoever."

"Why does the president want them out?"

"There's no one mind on the Mexicans." He shook his head. "Senator Johnson sees it like I do. If folks want to work for my price, do what I say, no backtalk, what do I care if they're from Mexico or Timbuktu?"

Lacy's chest tightened. She hadn't finished her family tree. She yanked it from her knapsack and spread it out on the dashboard. "What year and place were you born?" she fired off. "And your parents. It's for my badge."

"Nineteen oh one, Galveston. Clarence and Eugenia Adams, Angleton, 1874 and '75."

"Are they alive?"

"I expect not. They gave me to a home. Dirt farmers. Couldn't feed us all." He turned to see a furry corpse on the side of the highway, one of the cougars that had been popping up lately. "Solitary beast," he muttered. "Roadkill now. The dead feed the living," he explained. "We feed cattle, cattle feed people. A cycle. I worked my way from an orphanage to A&M." He stole a look at Lacy. "They didn't let girls into the ag school in those days."

"And Mom?" she asked. "She was born in Laredo?"

He yanked the stick shift. The truck shot forward. "That's where we met. Write that in for her, and 1928."

"And her parents?"

"Write 'dead.' Or 'deceased.'"

"You never met them, right?" she asked. Lacy sighed and shook her head. "She didn't even know their names."

"Don't bad-mouth your mother. She's a hard worker. Knows how to make a deal." He drove. "A man and woman come together," he said. "A man needs a family too. One with no wife and kids draws attention. But a man with them—goes to church, kids in Scouts—folks do business with that man."

"So you never met—"

"No, never met her parents."

Lacy looked out the window at the landscape of Chilitown, where the workers lived. Tin-roofed shacks patched with cardboard, smoke drifting up from the cook pits, a row of wooden outhouses at the far end. Bones and bread wrappers and trash scattered around. She passed it every day on her way to school, but that day each object jumped out sharp in her eyes. She thought for the first time that one of those shacks was Xavier's, where he slept at night.

"Do they like living here?" she asked. "The workers?"

"I expect so." He worked a toothpick around his mouth. "Down here together, living their own way. They got it good. The company I'm selling to is giving money for a wing on the hospital just for Mexicans, so they can go there when they're sick and be with their kind, and get better and come back to work."

"Mexicans have souls, don't they?" she asked.

"Sure."

"But they don't have flush toilets in Chilitown like we do at home," Lacy noted. "They have outhouses."

"Flush toilets are expensive."

"But yesterday didn't pastor say thou shalt love thy neighbor as thyself?"

Her dad cocked his head. "Smart girl." He looked her up and down. "Not sure what the return is on you yet, but I doubt it's marrying some boy in town." He turned back to the road. "Your mom wants one of the new TVs with the color picture.

They're televising Miss America. She says you need to see. I said you're going to college. Studying science would be my bet."

Lacy flushed with pleasure. Always her mom talked of Junior's future—he'd be an Aggie like his dad someday—and not a word about Lacy. Except that she'd be a mom. Her life would start when she got married and had a baby, a boy if she was lucky, and she'd pour herself into her boy and her love would feed his dreams. It made Lacy's skin crawl every time her mom said it. But her dad thought she was smart.

"Till then," he said, frowning, "keep wearing the dresses like your mom says."

Her dad didn't walk her into the Scouts meeting. He left the car running when he pulled up to the high school, until Lacy got the hint and hopped out of the truck. "Hey," he called. "I'll be late. Have Mrs. Melton give you a ride home."

"Dad," she whined.

"Tell her it's coming from me." He yanked the door shut and drove off.

Lacy was anxious the whole meeting and kept to herself. First they went around the circle and showed family trees, and in front of twenty girls the scoutmaster asked Lacy why hers was missing information. She shrank to nothing in the spotlight, praying she wouldn't lose a badge over this and fall behind the other girls. Then she fumbled through practicing their song for the pageant. By the time Lacy approached Jenny Melton and her mom for a ride, she felt low. Politely she said her dad was hoping they could bring her home, at which Mrs. Melton nodded and walked away.

Jenny and her mom chatted the whole drive in the front seat, ignoring Lacy in the back. She looked out the window, recalling a time when the farmers' wives were nice to her but unable to pinpoint when it changed. Mrs. Melton took her as far as the highway connection, stopping the car at the foot of the road to the Adamses' house. She turned and looked at Lacy with unkind eyes. "I wish your mom and dad a fond farewell," she said, like she didn't mean a word of it.

Lacy walked the mile home in the blazing sun. The sharp, familiar smells of cows and manure swirled in the breeze. Red dust coated her saddle shoes. The armpits of her Scouts uniform were soaked, and she was sure, walking in the front door, that her mom would say what a burden Lacy was making her run a new load of wash. But inside it was empty, and she called out to no answer. She didn't like surprising her mom. Lacy had peeked in the parlor once, unannounced, and saw her sitting on the couch staring off at nothing, her face unforgettably sad. Or another time Lacy heard the radio on and thought her mom was talking to Junior, only to discover her alone in the wing chair repeating the words from the news program in a turned-up twang, like she was practicing how to talk.

She heard her mom's steps above her, leaving the attic, and then a knock came at the front door. No one ever came to the front. They never had guests, and if Xavier needed her dad for something urgent he used the back door. Her mom hurried downstairs. Lacy retreated to the dining room and watched, shadowed by the buffet. "Last trial of my life," her mom muttered. "Hold your horses!" She opened the door. A man in a frayed shirt stood there. He had a dirty beard and looked like he hadn't washed in weeks. It was nothing new. Mexicans showed up looking for work on the lots pretty often, yet her mom froze like she saw a ghost.

"Maria?" the man said hoarsely. His chapped face opened in a joyous grin. He reached out as though to touch her golden hair. "Maria Elena—"

"No work," her mom said, stepping back.

The man erupted in Spanish while her mom tried to shut the door. "*No trabajo*," she repeated, "go away." But before she could close it the man reached forward and stuck a letter in her hand. He turned his head as he was reaching and saw Lacy. He laughed in surprise and waved sweetly at her. Her mom followed the man's gaze. "Out!" she shouted, slamming the door. She locked the bolt, closed her eyes, and leaned her head against the door.

The grandfather clock ticked in the parlor.

Her mom stood up straight. She clenched her jaw and raised a cautionary finger at Lacy. "Not a word," she said.

"Doesn't Dad need workers now?"

"I said not a word."

"Who is he?" Lacy asked.

"He's a man with muddy boots!" she exploded. "Disrespectful girl! To your room. Now." Her mom grabbed her by the shoulder and escorted her up to her bedroom. Lacy went in but stuck her head out into the hallway as her mom hustled, letter in hand, to her bedroom. "Shut the door," she called back to Lacy. "You're grounded."

Lacy shut it. She turned and caught her reflection in the mirror she tried to avoid. She saw her wild dark hair and potbelly, all the things a husband would never love, her mom said, so how about trying to look nicer and talk less? Lacy didn't understand anything, why she was disrespectful, or why the man kept repeating a word Xavier had taught her: *madre*.

She slid her window open, crawled onto the roof, and shimmied along a branch of the cottonwood until she reached the trunk. She scanned the road for the man with the muddy boots, but he had disappeared. She spent the rest of the afternoon watching for him, as her mind wandered in miserable confusion. There was no method to her mom, scientific or otherwise, no clear way to please her that Lacy had ever found. As the sun began to drop, a memory floated back to her from when she was little and walking was still sort of new. She sat at the bottom of the stairs while her mom knelt before her, sliding on her socks and tying her shoes. She looked at Lacy with love in her eyes when she finished. "Go on," she said, "stand up on your feet." A nice memory before all the corrections began, the disappointments she brought her mom for not being ladylike or as delicate as her name.

The sound of Xavier's truck snapped Lacy from her daydream. She watched him park by the barn and go inside. She crawled back into her room and opened the door a sliver. She heard her mom rustling in the attic and Junior downstairs playing with his Roy Rogers figures. Quietly Lacy crept down the hall to her parents' room, where kids weren't allowed but Junior slept every night when their dad was away. She shut the door behind her. She knew what she was looking for but not where to look. Under the brass bed? In the hope chest? She paused in front of her mom's vanity. Its legs bowed elegantly, its lacquered front glowing in the early evening light.

She opened it on instinct and turned over its contents. Creams, tiny scissors, colored powders. But no letter. In the last drawer Lacy found a box of Miss Clairol Golden Apricot dye. She pulled out two more. Her mom's hair. It never occurred to Lacy that she wasn't blond. Then, below the dyes, at the bottom of the drawer, Lacy spotted it—a grimy envelope. She opened it and a bead necklace with a cross fell out. Lacy unfolded the letter. *Maria Elena*, it began, continuing in scratches that Lacy was sure were Spanish. She had a sudden rush of feeling like she might be sick, a hunger to know and a sinking fear that it couldn't be good if her mom hid it. She closed the drawer, scooped up the envelope and beads, and ran downstairs.

"Where you going?" Junior asked, but she ignored him and took off to the barn.

"Xavier?" she called, running past his truck and into the dim doorway.

"Hey, *muchacha*." He walked by her with a grain sack on his shoulder and heaved it onto the truck. "Now is not good. I have to get back to the men and drive them home before dinner."

"I found this," she said when he returned to the barn. She held up the necklace. Xavier stopped, watching it twist in the golden sun passing through the barn boards. Dusk approached. He laid his hand gently under the cross. "Is it for church?" she asked.

"*El rosario*," he said. "To pray. Protect. Where do you get it?"

"With this." Lacy handed the letter to him. She studied Xavier's face while he read, her heart nearly bursting as his eyes widened. "What's it say?"

"How does it—" Xavier stopped reading and took the envelope from Lacy's hand. "There's no stamp, where it comes from, how does—"

"A man came to the house and gave it to her. She sent him away."

"Away?" he said louder.

"She shut the door. I don't know. I climbed the tree but I can't find him."

"*Pocho puta*," he said, shaking his head.

"What does it say? *Madre*, I could read that, but what else?"

"Your mother's mother," Xavier said angrily. "Your grandmother. She is very sick in Mexico and needs money. Doctors."

"No," Lacy corrected, "she's dead."

"You ask me and I tell you what it says."

"Lacy?" Her mom's voice pierced the air, outside the barn. Her feet crunched swiftly down the gravel path.

"Take it, take it!" Xavier hissed, thrusting the letter and rosary at Lacy. But she had already taken off across the barn, toward the secret loose board she and Junior had found behind the grain sacks. She shoved the board and wriggled out of the barn. When she turned around and peered back in, she saw Xavier stuffing the letter and necklace in his pockets—a length of beads still hanging visibly down his thigh. And just before she ran away, Lacy saw her mother's silhouette in the middle of the barn door, dark against the fiery sunset, blocking his way out.

★

Lacy's mom barely spoke at dinner that night, as the three of them ate. Lacy breathed a sigh of relief when she asked to be excused early, promising to run her own bath, and her mom nodded. For hours after she got in bed, Lacy could hear the creak of her mom's footsteps, pacing the floor of her bedroom. Around ten she heard her dad come in and go upstairs, and then the muffled sounds of their talking—hers high and nervous, his cool and brief.

In the morning Lacy woke up late and came down to a feast. Junior and her mom sat before piles of bacon and pancakes drenched in syrup. A stack waited by Lacy's place at the table, with a glass of chocolate milk. "Come on, sleepyhead." Her mom smiled. "Better eat a big breakfast before your pageant. Get your energy to sing."

Lacy sat down and ate fast, shooting looks at her mom in case she changed her mind.

"Good news!" her mom said. "Your daddy telephoned from his meeting. All the papers signed. Done." Her chest heaved as she breathed. She smiled like she might cry and touched her eyes with her napkin. "Ten years." She laughed. "We did it!"

"Daddy sold his business?" Junior asked.

"The land, cattle, machinery, men. Well." She paused. "All but one. You were right, Junior, about the Border Patrol coming. They came last night and took one of our men. Xavier."

"What?" Lacy cried.

"Sad." Her mom shook her head. "After all your daddy did for him, I caught Xavier stealing from us. Jewelry of mine. A necklace." She watched Lacy serenely. "We couldn't have an enemy among us. Your daddy couldn't give a man like that papers, so the patrol took him. Xavier and one other man. A vagrant they found in Chilitown. Maybe that one that came to our door, Lacy. I don't know. Listen to me, children," she said, fixing her eyes on her daughter. "We are very rich now. We ruffled a few feathers along the way. That means we have to be careful of people—everyone, everywhere—who want to take what's ours any way they can. We have to cast out threats to the family. Understand?"

She hit the word "family" hard, like it was hers to open the gate and let you in or not. Lacy was hot with anger but muddled, confused how truth was a threat and lies were safer, and at the table in front of Junior she asked her mom, "Are you Mexican?"

She saw it in her mom's eyes briefly, a light flashing and shutting off. A cruel, sad thing she couldn't name, but whatever it was, Lacy sensed something change between them. A terrible feeling like she was outside the family her mom talked about, even if she slept under the same roof and ate at the same table.

Junior turned his head from one to the other, watching.

Her mom laughed. "What a thing to ask! Are you feeling all right?" She pressed her hand to Lacy's forehead. "I wonder if you're running a fever." She watched Lacy. "What I am," she said slowly, "is a mother who takes care of her children and protects what's theirs. You and Junior are the future." Her eyes shone with unfallen tears. "I washed your uniform. Go get dressed."

The whole drive to the pageant Lacy thought of Xavier. She wondered where he was as her troop paraded past the school cafeteria toward the stage. The Scouts assembled on a set of bleachers behind a gold velvet curtain. Lacy could barely keep from crying as it opened. She was blinded at first by the footlights, and in the whiteness she thought of the calf being born a few weeks ago. She could make out the cafeteria full of round tables with families eating lunch. She saw her mom and dad and Junior, front and center, a circle of mostly empty tables around them, and the families of the farmers she knew sitting farther back and to the sides. And it dawned on Lacy that it wasn't like she thought in church. It wasn't out of respect that the farmers gave her family space.

The scoutmaster swung her baton, and the Scouts around Lacy began to sing:

> *America, oh land of plenty,*
> *Light of hope around the globe,*
> *Send a dream to all our sisters*
> *Who are hungry, sick, and cold.*
> *Open your heart and your hand,*
> *Do what's right, take a stand,*
> *And together, America*
> *Will heal the world.*

2

A Day's Work

In a week Aaron Warner would leave his podunk town for Houston, to join the thousands of politicians, tycoons, and common men with tickets to the opening game at the Eighth Wonder of the World. The Astrodome! Aaron had memorized every detail about the place from the newspaper: eighteen stories tall, the dome a miracle of engineering can-do, and a scoreboard that lit up at each homer with a show of steam-nosed bulls and fireworks and cowboys shooting pistols. Mickey Mantle was playing the home team. LBJ and Lady Bird would be there. And Governor Connally would kick the whole thing off with the first-ever pitch in an air-conditioned stadium, chilled to a pleasant seventy-two degrees.

This trip to the modern Colosseum foreshadowed other journeys ahead, to college and the world that would soon be his oyster. Aaron didn't leave for UT for a few months, but a wave of psychic goose bumps told him that his old life was ending and a new one was about to begin. All he had to do was give up one Saturday and tag along with his dad on a day's work.

★

His principal, Mr. Richards, called him to the office a few days before, during seventh period, and surprised him with the tickets. The jackpot moment played out for Aaron in a kind of slow motion: Richards rising from his desk, tugging the lapels of his blazer until they crossed manfully over his tie, and fanning out the tickets in his hand. "The As-tro-dome," he said with quiet reverence. "A graduation gift to Midland Robert E. Lee High School's best running back and favorite senior." Aaron's jaw went slack. "Thank you, sir," Aaron said in the charming voice he reserved for life at school. "I'll talk to my parents. Thanks so much."

Aaron stayed on campus until the janitor locked up that evening. On the walk home he pictured his family at the dinner table, around the centerpiece of plastic apples and grapes. His brother, Wally, would be slouched on his elbows, a freshman at Lee still playing with trains in the basement. Next to him all two hundred something pounds of their mom, holding on to the table edge to keep her hands still. And at the head would be Ernest, eyes shut as he said grace in a strained voice like Kermit the Frog. When he got to the house, Aaron took a breath on the porch. He retracted each sunbeam that had glowed from him that day—every boy he glad-handed and girl he teased, every tired teacher he made laugh—and once he had shrunk himself down to a hard, silent coal, he went in.

Nobody spoke as Aaron slid into his seat. Forks shoveled meatloaf and fluorescent mac and cheese. His mom smiled at him and chewed absently, tracing a chubby pinky along the rim of her prized Fiestaware. His dad rattled the ice in his sweet tea. "Stuck in traffic?" he said.

"Principal Richards got tickets to the Astrodome," Aaron blurted.

"The Astrodome!" His mom's tiny blue eyes twinkled above her flushed cheeks. "It looked huge on the TV."

"The Yankees next weekend?" his dad asked. Aaron nodded. "Well, that's fine," Ernest murmured, his face opening in a rare smile.

"He invited me to go. As a graduation gift. Mr. Richards has a brother in Sugar Land we can stay with after the game, and come back Saturday morning, if . . ."

"Richards." His dad munched a green bean with vague suspicion. "He fight in the war? Europe? Pacific?"

"Um," Aaron mumbled, "he was maybe thirteen back then?"

Ernest shook his head. "Not the fighting type."

Aaron felt like saying how Richards lobbied the UT scout to come watch his game against Permian, or how Richards fought for the scholarship he needed to get the hell out of nowheresville, but he held his tongue.

"It sounds like fun, Ernest," his mom said quietly.

"Gertrude," he snapped, "I'll let you know if I need your—Sure!" He turned to Aaron. "I wish we could all drive to Houston for the big game, but some of us have to work six days a—"

"I work," Aaron said. "I work my tail off at school and practice."

"Fine." He set his fork on his plate. "If you want to go to the Astrodome next weekend, show me how hard you work this Saturday. I got two big jobs I could use you on." He watched Aaron. "Deal?" Aaron nodded. "Well, Gerty." Ernest sighed irritably. "You happy?"

"Yes." She patted her mouth with her napkin. "Meatloaf came out real juicy."

★

So, early that Saturday morning, Aaron stood before his dresser in white Jockey briefs. His thick blond hair stuck out porcupine-style from his head. He nodded at the mirror, admiring the mercurial blue of his eyes, and yawned and studied the contents of his drawers. He was a careful keeper of his clothes. He thought of the dirty work ahead and, after real deliberation, chose to sacrifice a pair of old jeans and a Rebels sweatshirt for the sake of the Astrodome.

Through the bedroom door Aaron heard his mom's high yet resonant voice, a bird trapped in a buttery chamber down her throat. In the hallway he could make out words broken up by Wally's silences. "Doesn't it take your breath away?" she asked. "Isn't it amazing?"

"What is?" Aaron strolled into the kitchen. He hated the pauses, waiting for his brother to speak. It made him cold and angry to watch Wally's mouth twitch as he tried to get the words out. "What's amazing?"

"This machine." His mom held up a copy of *Life*. "'Astonishing Revolution,'" she read aloud from the cover, her hands trembling at the weight of the magazine. "'Ultrasonic waves show a baby in womb.' I wish I could've seen *you* back then," she said and patted Wally's arm. He sat beside her, spooning Cap'n Crunch. "I didn't need to see Aaron," Gertrude reflected. "I could feel him kicking, trying to get somewhere else. But you were so peaceful I wondered sometimes if you were still there."

"Mom?" Aaron said casually, sliding bread into the toaster. "I was thinking, since I'm giving a speech at graduation, maybe I'd buy a new shirt to wear. If you guys don't have the—There's my pocket money for UT that you've been saving."

"Well," she sighed. "You're with your dad all day. Ask him." His mom played dumb about money, even though she ran the numbers for the business. She took a bookkeeping course after high school, the only one of his parents to do something beyond what Aaron was about to achieve. But he had to ask his dad. A guy who didn't know the first thing about how the world works or why the Roman Empire fell. He spread peanut butter on his toast with indignant precision and sat down at the table.

"You coming?" Aaron said to Wally. "Say goodbye to the seniors?"

"If-f-f-f'm here."

"If you're here?" Aaron laughed and took a big swagger of a bite. "Busy schedule this summer? Busy train schedule in the basement?"

Wally's face clouded. He shot an ugly look at their mom. "Driving to—"

"Shush," Gerty scolded, her mouth wrinkling into a frown. Then she gave Aaron a strange bright smile. "Your dad found a speech therapist to help Wally—express himself better. A good doctor, in Dallas, not like the ones here, so they have to drive there every week."

"You're coming, right?" Aaron asked her. "To my graduation?"

"I hope so." She pushed her special chair back from the table. "But with my ailments . . ." She shrugged, muttering quietly to herself, "Have to see how I feel that morning."

Aaron studied her as she settled back into the chair Ernest had customized for her. It was green metal with industrial casters on the legs so Gerty could roll where she needed to around the house, rising to cook, get in bed, or make the short, mysterious transit from chair to toilet. Aaron knew better than to talk about her ailments, so he rose and put his plate in the sink.

"Could you fix my bike?" she asked as he left. "The rope's jumbled up. And, Aaron?" He stopped at the door and turned back to her. "Congratulations," she said. "If I don't make it."

On the front porch Aaron put up the hood of his sweatshirt at the unseasonable chill and knelt beside the bike. He didn't know where his dad found an oversize kid's tricycle with a giant seat, but every day at three o'clock Gertrude Warner mounted her red set of wheels and budged cautiously down the driveway to get the mail. And though there was barely an incline, her husband had tied a rope to the handlebars that stretched as far as the mailbox, and no farther, to help pull herself back home when her feet needed a boost.

Aaron untangled the rope and stared at his dad's truck, a burnt orange '61 Econoline pickup. He could never decide which was worse: the color or the logo. The day his dad drove it home Aaron said, "Orange." Ernest launched into some rigmarole about the color reminding clients of how dirty their carpets used to be, "The Before," but Aaron was pretty sure it was the only one he could afford at the used lot outside of town. Then came the demented logo on the doors—KLEEN KARPETS—in a circle of white letters. Inside the circle was a blue vacuum cleaner with eyeballs on a smiling vacuum head and three pink tongues sticking out the vacuum mouth, ostensibly licking up dirt but really looking more like a trio of scrotums.

"Here," his dad barked, walking out of the garage. He threw Aaron an orange baseball cap with the same logo, one of the dozens sitting unworn in a box by the washer/dryer. "Take off that Longhorns cap and try this on for size. Let's load up."

★

"He's halfway to Odessa!" Ernest cried as they bumped along a desolate patch of Route 80. "Wake up! Almost there!" Aaron cast a sidelong glance at him. He was tan from working in the sun, an even nut color except for where the skin cancer had been. The doctor had done a cheap graft there, and afterward Ernest walked the world with a patch of Silly Putty–looking stuff on his neck the size of a half dollar.

"Bill's my oldest client," his dad began. "He closes one day a year and that's where we come in. It is a race. To. The finish. Every carpet, drape, and armchair in the place: get done with one and it's on to the next one, and the next one, and the—"

"Yup," Aaron grunted. He looked out the window at the oil derricks. The field ran to the horizon, an eyesore of drills bobbing in the earth like hungry insects. Here and there were empty shacks. He remembered the fields at night when he was younger, the ghostly sunrise color as the rigs burned off gas they couldn't hold. All the wasted potential burned up here, Aaron thought, and sank into his hood.

"Funny thing is," Ernest resumed quietly, "the first day you ever come to work with me, and it's right before you leave. Weeks, isn't it? Till you go?"

"July," Aaron mumbled. "Football orientation."

"That's what I said. Eleven weeks. First time we did this. Doesn't have to be the last."

Aaron caught the scent of a lecture. In the thousands of meals and hallway passes that made up their relationship, his dad had two modes—saying no and lecturing—and it was too early for either. But, sure enough, Ernest launched into the wonders of the family business again, how Granddad, rest in peace, started it with a wet vac and a vision, and built it up to two vacs so father and son could work side by side, the American way. Aaron tuned out. He'd heard the rumors about monster-jugged cheerleader Carrie Trills, like if a guy got on her prayer list she'd kiss his willy, and he was spiritually beating off to the possibility when he heard his name.

"Aaron!" Ernest repeated. "You listening? Did I tell you or not?"

"What?"

"How I met your mom. Me and Granddad were doing a job, and I took the upstairs, and in the last bedroom there was your mom in an armchair doing her correspondence course. Plump and pretty as a doll. She ignored me till I said, 'Ma'am, I gotta clean your chair.' 'But where will I sit?' she asked. I was twenty. She was the older woman." His eyebrows did leaps of naughty joy. "Kleen Karpets isn't just a family business—it *brought me* my family. Who knows?" he said ponderously. "Maybe you'll find you a wife today."

Aaron squinted to hold down the smirk tugging at his lips, real sure the girl of his dreams wasn't in Midland and for damn sure he wasn't cleaning her carpets. Ernest put on the blinker. A dark sign loomed on the highway. BLACK GOLD MOTOR LODGE, it read in light bulbs and flaking metallic yellow letters. A cartoon derrick shot up between the words and sent a gush of oil to the top of the sign, also in a trail of bulbs. The motel was a shabby, low-slung set of rooms covered in faded yellow siding. Black doors caked with dust opened onto the parking lot. Drills the size of elephants surrounded the motel on three sides, pumping a few feet past a dainty black picket fence that ran around the place.

"Lord," Aaron mumbled, "who stays here?"

"Nobody today," Ernest snapped. "That's the point." He stared at the steering wheel and then turned to Aaron. "Try and keep your mouth shut." He got out and slammed the door. "Nutter!" he called to a gray-haired man smoking and making his way down the rickety office steps. "How the devil are you?"

Through the windshield Aaron watched them shake and slap at each other. Ernest play-kicked the oxygen tank the man had dragged down the steps behind him.

"And who do we have here?" the man rasped when Aaron got out of the truck.

"My son, Aaron Warner. Shake the man's hand," Ernest ordered.

"Bill McNutt," he said in the scratches of a former voice, "but friends and fools like this one here call me Nutter. You going into business with your dad?"

"I'm going to UT," Aaron replied. "I'm a freshman this fall."

"A college man!"

"Well, Bill," Ernest said, chuckling, "we never got our heads stuck in any books and we made it this far, didn't we? Aaron and I better see about cleaning some carpets."

They unloaded the vacuums and carried them to the porch. Aaron followed Ernest through a door with a gold 1 on it and hit a wall of stale air. His dad threw back the drapes, releasing a Big Bang of dust. There was hardly space to move between the bed, a wing chair belching stuffing, and a liquor cart with chipped golden goddesses at the corners.

"I'm thirsty," Aaron said, retreating to the bathroom, tiled in a dizzying shade of mustard. Aaron turned the faucet on and leaned down to drink, but brown water pulsed out. "Jesus!" he muttered. "How are we supposed to clean anything if the—"

"Let it run," Ernest bawled from the other room.

"Here's your basics," his dad began in lecture voice after they filled the vacs with water. "Three-and-three system: three kinds of stains, animal, vegetable, mineral . . ." On Ernest droned. So much talk about vacuuming reminded Aaron what a master of small things his dad was. Ernest could give driving directions for days, or jabber about gas prices at this or that station. Aaron beamed his brain elsewhere, leaving his body behind to show Ernest he could handle the wet vac and not pull down the drapes when he cleaned them. And the moment his dad stopped for two seconds to take a breath, Aaron blurted out the truth.

"I'm ready," he said. "To try this on my own."

Ernest cleared his throat hotly. "All right." He turned his back and put the vacuum on. "Guess we'll see," he shouted over his shoulder.

Aaron dragged a vacuum along the porch to the far end of the motel, its wheels chattering over the hum of the drills. He stopped outside room 13 and squinted down the highway at a cloud of dust. A truck shot by the motel, the first car Aaron had seen since they got there.

Inside he vacuumed and avoided the mirror. He told himself that life now was temporary. But he couldn't shake the thought of his dad's smallness earlier, insulting college. It was the kind of thing his teammates and their dads saw—the way Ernest never came to football games, or left right after when he did come, never staying to talk to folks. Or his smallness on Sundays. They were the only family in town that didn't go to First Baptist and instead, thanks to Gerty's ailments, were parked on the sofa at home with their Bibles in their laps. A tiny world where Ernest was the preacher. Until high school, that is, when Aaron started going to church alone after home prayers. His dad wouldn't look at him when he got back those Sunday evenings. Sometimes Ernest wouldn't say a word to him until Tuesday.

"Ready, huh?" Ernest's voice startled Aaron from his thoughts. His dad stood in the doorway. "*One* room to my *twelve*?" He chuckled and shook his head. "Dump your dirty water and let's get some grub." Aaron turned to the bathroom. "No," Ernest scolded, seizing the vacuum. "We dump off the porch."

"I got it." Aaron yanked it back and dragged it outside, tipping it over the front of the porch.

"Not the parking lot!" Ernest cried. "Over the side, *side*; give it to me." Ernest grabbed at the tank, but Aaron was too strong as they struggled over it, and his dad slipped and fell into the gush of dirty water. Ernest froze on his hands and knees. His Dickies and shirt were soaked with greenish vacuum juice. Narrow rivers of it crawled along the porch, dropping between the planks. Aaron held his breath. But Ernest just stood up without a word and walked away.

"Sorry," he whispered and trailed his dad to the motel office.

Aaron loaded the truck while Nutter counted out a wad of bills. He dropped them distractedly into Ernest's hand. "Well, sir," Nutter rasped when he finished paying, "we done business a long time. I wouldn't even mention it except there's another man who's paid me three visits already. A carpet man, like you. He got a GI loan to go buy the newest vacuums—"

"Government handout," Ernest barked. "I didn't take one of those when I came back."

"New machines," Nutter continued, "and a team that can do the motel in half the time it takes—under an hour is what he said." He adjusted his oxygen tube beneath his nose and cast a furtive glance at Aaron. "He's a colored man."

Ernest's face softened from the anxious mask it had frozen into. He guffawed. "Negro?" he said, chuckling. "That's good! You got me, old devil!"

Nutter lit a fresh cigarette. "Half the price, too." He blew out a column of smoke for a little too long. "That's what he offered."

Ernest laughed again, but tighter. "You trying to Jew me down? Negroes coming around the place? Word getting out? With that agitating going on in Alabama now—are you reading the paper? You want that on your hands?"

"Course not." Nutter sighed. "No. The man's persistent is all."

"Persistent." Ernest's voice hardened. "We had some Negroes in the Eighth Infantry. Served our country alongside each other in France. But when we were under fire, and a Kraut bullet ripped my throat open—" Ernest touched the Silly Putty spot on his neck. "And I lay there, not knowing dead from alive, was it a Negro who came to my aid? No, sir, it was not."

"Forget I said a word, soldier." Nutter reached out a bony arm and solemnly shook Ernest's hand. "We gotta stick together."

★

Ernest didn't talk on the drive back to Midland. Aaron watched the passing wasteland, floating somewhere between disgust and resignation to the man his father was. The way he lied about getting shot. About seeing any combat, actually, a fact Aaron learned one night when Gerty was ailing too much to cook and Ernest stepped in. "Good chef, isn't he?" she mused to Aaron afterward. "It's what he did the whole war, cooking in the mess hall." A loser, Aaron thought, such a sad old sack he had to lie to compete with a colored man.

"Burgers?" Ernest said. He pulled the truck into a Sonic decked out in shiny chrome.

Aaron didn't answer. His mind was overtaken by a buxom waitress roller-skating toward the truck. She was a real grown woman, maybe even thirty. She had long dark hair, his favorite, and wore the blessed uniform of curve-hugging red dress, white apron, and striped socks pulled high on her sun-kissed legs. For a minute, Aaron was in love. "Afternoon, gentlemen," she said, gliding up to Aaron's window. "I hope you came hungry today."

"Seeing as I'm buying," Ernest said, "maybe you can skate over here and take our order."

"Sure thing." She winked at Aaron and made a smooth arc to Ernest's window. He watched as she jotted down the order. Her name tag said CHRISSY! She skated off. The truck sank back into silence.

"It's how you build a business," Ernest said after a while. "First rule is you keep the customers you have. Then add new ones. We got a new one after lunch. That's how you keep the money rolling in."

"Dad?" Aaron seized the opportunity. "I'm giving a speech at graduation, and I figured I'd get a new shirt. There's a sale at Fedway—one ninety-nine—so if I could have two dollars out of the money Nutter just gave you, or . . ."

"Did you ask your mom?"

"She said to ask you."

"Well." Ernest exhaled dubiously.

Aaron waited. He grew angry at the bind he'd put himself in: studying and practicing after school instead of working at the Dairy Queen, knowing he was meant for more than scooping ice cream but still penniless today, reduced to asking Ernest for money.

"Gentlemen." Chrissy skated up with a tray.

"Great!" Ernest said, counting the food at top volume. "Two burgers, one fries, two Coca-Colas. Thank you, ma'am." He unwrapped a burger and stuffed it in his mouth. "Eat up." He chewed. "Gotta get on the road."

Aaron felt a sudden twinge, imagining the days his dad ate lunch in his truck, between carpet jobs in a town he'd never leave. He thought of his shirt again. "Fine. If it's not from your work money, take it out of my pocket money for UT. I'll be needing it soon anyways."

Ernest took a savage bite. When he pulled back, the innards came loose and an avalanche of pickles and meat tumbled down his shirt. "Shit!" he cried. He wiped at the mess and sighed and set his burger on the tray. "The pocket money. Your mom and I needed it to pay for the—"

"You spent it?" Aaron asked in disbelief.

"No. Not—Some of it. Wally's speech doctor bills ten sessions up front, and he'll need more than ten, or could," Ernest rambled, "but if it helps him talk like a normal—and then we'll put some money back in for you. Real soon."

It was the one thing his parents had promised for his future. When the UT scout came to his game, lightning fast his dad said they had no money for college. But then came the day Aaron got called to Mr. Richards's office, and the scout was there to congratulate him, and Aaron could go home and tell his parents he got a scholarship. His mom's face lit up, but she hid her smile at the sight of Ernest turning blood red. "We got pocket money for you," his dad said. "You think we had nothing to give you? Well, we do. Pocket money, for the odds and ends."

But they didn't have the one thing after all.

"Real soon," Aaron said, turning a dead stare on Ernest. "Where's the next job?"

★

On the seat between them Aaron left his burger uneaten. They drove to the east side of town, where the rich oil kids lived. Soon they were passing gigantic houses and green lawns that cost a fortune to water. Aaron shrank down in his seat. He couldn't risk being seen in the Orangemobile. At school he did a comedy routine about Ernest and his truck, which had expanded since freshman year to include Gerty's tricycle, Wally's trains, the whole scene at the Warner house. It left his classmates in stitches. But as he rode shotgun down the fancy street with Ernest, Aaron knew in his gut that what was funny to tell wasn't funny to see.

"Sit up straight," Ernest snapped. "Slouching like an old man. Now, keep your mouth shut, and clean." His dad parked in front of the most incredible house Aaron had ever seen. It had pillars like the White House, glass going up two stories, and a curving staircase you could see from outside. Its splendor made Aaron stumble as he rolled his vacuum to the porch. Ernest wiped his finger on the leg of his Dickies before pressing the bell.

A blond woman about his mom's age opened the door. She was thin. Her bra made her jugs torpedo-shaped under her white silk blouse. "Y'all must be from Kleen Karpets," she said, her eyes lingering imperiously on Aaron. She turned to Ernest and winced. "And what a dirty business that must be. It's cold out. Come on in."

It was like stepping into heaven. At church the pastor said human eyes couldn't take in its beauty, and he was right. From the moment he entered, Aaron was blinded by wealth. A grand piano, crystal chandeliers, white carpet everywhere like angel clouds. He squinted and stole looks around while Ernest prattled away about the job.

"But before you start—" the woman said tensely when Ernest reached for his vacuum. Aaron could feel her gaze on him again. He met her eyes and saw the same look, the sex hunger, as when she came to the door. He imagined reaching from behind and grabbing her jugs, her bra popping open in front like a barn door. She frowned and turned to Ernest. "Well," she said in sudden exasperation, "I don't want the carpets *dirtier* on account of y'all." She waved her hand at the soiled mess covering Ernest from shirt to shoe. "Hang on."

She disappeared down a hallway and returned with armfuls of pink fabric. "My aunt was a full-figured woman, so I think these'll fit." She handed them women's bathrobes trimmed in lace and pompoms. "I was about to donate these to the Salvation Army."

"What?" Aaron sputtered. "No." He turned to Ernest. "You can't let her—"

"Never mind," the woman said. "I try to assist men who show up unprepared, in a dirty uniform, but I think it's best not to waste any more of your time."

"No, ma'am." Ernest grabbed the bathrobes. "I was just telling my son Aaron here the first rule of business: the customer's always right."

"Dad?" Aaron said, instantly ashamed of the pleading tone in his voice.

"I had some accidents earlier," Ernest continued. "Doesn't matter. This job is what *you* need." He handed a bathrobe to

Aaron. "Take it," he said coldly. "Ma'am, I do downstairs, my son takes upstairs, and we'll get the carpets looking good as new."

"Tie those robes tight, gentlemen," she instructed. "And shoes off. Thanks so much."

Aaron grabbed his vacuum and flew upstairs. It was mercifully empty, no one around to see him in the pink lady bathrobe. He dreamed up ways to destroy the woman but couldn't think of one that had him coming out ahead, so he shampooed her carpets in angry lines, as neat as his penmanship.

He felt the vibration of Ernest's vacuum go off first. Aaron couldn't look at the woman, so he busied himself on the landing at the top of the stairs, winding his vacuum cord, while his dad settled up with her in the foyer.

"Mr. Warner." She handed Ernest a check. "No tip, of course, with your son speaking out of turn like that."

"Yes, ma'am," Ernest muttered. "Of course not."

"Did you say you do drapes, too?" she asked.

"We do."

"I think we understand each other. I'll have to call you about those drapes."

"Anytime would be a pleasure, ma'am. Aaron?" he called upstairs. "Let's go."

★

They were a block away from home when the truck stalled. Ernest must have turned the ignition ten times before he mumbled, "Give it a sec." The sunset dwindled in the rearview. The air had turned frigid, and what little heat the truck puffed out was gone. He tried again.

"You need a new truck," Aaron said, putting up his hood.

"I need a lot of things, son."

"Good luck, letting a woman talk to you that way."

Ernest took off his glasses and rubbed his eyes. "You know how much a tip is on that job? Ten percent. One of Wally's speech lessons. And the truck, and your mom's medicines." He laughed strangely and shook his head. "I been taking care of you since I was your age. Half my life. Best day of my life the day you were born, right up there with meeting your mom." His voice dropped low. "You're ashamed of your family. Worship without us, like God don't know who your people are. You think I couldn't build this business if I had a partner? You know how much it cost when Granddad got sick?" He turned to Aaron, and for the first time his son could make out the fear in his eyes. "You think there's nothing else I wanted to do? I brought you to work *one day*. The rest of the time you study and play football. I left you alone."

Ernest hit the ignition right. They drove the last block home. He parked and went in the front door, lingering a moment on the threshold. "Take the hose," he called to Aaron, "and rinse the vacs and attachments."

"It's freezing," Aaron protested.

"I know how much the Astrodome means to you." Ernest shrugged and shut the door.

Aaron dragged the hose around and cleaned the equipment while defaming his dad in his head. Twice Ernest came out and twice pronounced the vacuums dirty. Gertrude watched from her chair at the window, pressing her hand to the glass anxiously at each inspection. Aaron's hands were red after a third scouring, and by then the house was dark. He went inside, his head throbbing in the warm air. He sneezed once, and again. He saw a covered plate on the stove, but he was so tired he trudged to his room and dropped into bed in his wet jeans and sweatshirt.

He fell asleep and had wild dreams. He was drowning in a steamy jungle, and beyond it was a mountain but the mountain was his mom's silhouette, he knew, from the squeak of her chair rolling into his room. He felt a hand on his head and heard the high nervous murmur of her voice. He was freezing. It seemed like day but it was dark again and he was back in the jungle, and he looked up past the treetops at a sky full of stars—a constellation in the shape of a baby, the line of its cord trailing out from its belly and ending in darkness, untethered.

★

Aaron woke up in a sickly white light. He didn't know where he was or how long he had slept, only that he'd lived whole lifetimes that disintegrated in the waking air. His head was heavy, but with effort he lifted it and saw machines around the bed. In a corner Ernest rocked on the edge of a chair. He made a noise and ran from the room. Someone else entered. Aaron turned and saw a man he knew, in a suit. "The Astrodome," Aaron croaked.

Principal Richards smiled. "They played already. You've been here a week. The good news is you're graduating and things with UT are fine."

"Where am I?"

"The hospital. Pneumonia. It came on fast. Maybe something you were breathing with your dad. There was—uncertainty at home, about your symptoms. But the doctor says you'll be OK. Your dad's getting him."

"How was the game?" Aaron whispered.

"Astros won in extra innings. Turk Farrell was on fire. I saw it on TV. Didn't feel like traveling with you in here." Richards held up one of the tickets that had seemed flecked with gold a few weeks back. "Keep it," he said. "Like you were there."

"Thanks."

"Thank your dad. He's here every morning and evening when I swing by. He's getting the doctor, did I say?" Richards smiled tightly. He leaned in over the bed. "It's hard knowing what to say to your kids sometimes, Aaron. Maybe you'll have a son of your own someday and understand. You're a real joker at school, but I bet you care a lot about your dad, so try to—"

A doctor in a white coat knocked and entered, reading a clipboard. His dad peered out from behind the doctor, and the whole ordeal came washing over Aaron again: Ernest on his hands and knees on the motel porch, his dad passing him the bathrobe. Aaron felt the weakness in his bones and wondered vaguely if this moment would be his life, if for the rest of his life he would be the guy who almost got to the Astrodome.

He nodded deferentially at Richards. But deep inside him, in his blood coursing hot with penicillin, Aaron knew it wasn't in him to forgive Ernest, or to forget.

3

Pen Pals

Lacy sat alone at the window of her dorm room, watching the street below awaken from its long summer nap. Cars parked and doors slammed. Teenagers dragged suitcases ahead of parents loaded with boxes. Everywhere families completed the Labor Day ritual, settling in their young Longhorns and then, after hugs and tears, driving away with empty cars. Lacy scoffed at the maudlin scene. She opened her copy of *The Return of the King* to a dog-eared page and rejoined Gandalf and Pippin at the siege of Minas Tirith. But the midday heat left her languid. She fanned herself and gazed out the window again, down the street and up to the Tower, where Charles Whitman had opened fire her sophomore year. Thick clouds were rolling in. And like Sauron's darkness creeping across Middle Earth, Lacy sensed a portent in their weight.

A knock startled her from her reverie. "Miss Adams?" a voice drawled. "It's Miss Clifton, from down the hall?" Lacy waited. She hadn't had a single visitor her first year of grad school, or the whole summer. She chose this dorm, with ten black girls and tons of vacancies, precisely because it was a ghost town. And what was the point of lying to her mother about living in a mixed hall, Lacy groused as she opened the door, if not to get some peace and quiet?

"Hello," the dark-skinned girl began, "I'm Helen Clifton." Lacy watched her through the narrow crack. "A junior? Sorry to interrupt. My fiancé's stationed in Da Nang, north of Saigon, and in his last letter he mentioned a soldier in his company who has no one to write home to. A white gentleman. And I thought if you had the time—"

"He wants a pen pal?" Lacy asked. "Any old stranger for a pen pal?"

The girl stared at Lacy and handed her a slip of paper. "His name is Aaron Warner, from Midland. That's the address, if you want to do something for our troops in-country."

Lacy shut the door and threw out the paper. For the rest of the day, as she lay reading in her underwear, she thought back to the intrusion. She didn't want to be reminded of what was going on over there. Nobody wanted to see it on the news— piles of bodies, or monks in flames, forests stripped by chemical plague down to ashen netherworlds. Then twilight came. Lacy imagined the night ahead. Trudging to the hall kitchenette for her TV dinner, with the foods in their separate squares. Eating at her desk, not talking to a soul, reading Asimov or Bradbury until she tired her eyes out enough to sleep. Loneliness gathered into a cold spot in her chest. She found her hand reaching into the trash. Slowly, almost indifferently, she took her best fountain pen and a sheet of the monogrammed stationery her mother insisted was a hallmark of proper ladies—even lost causes like Lacy—and composed a letter.

September 1, 1969
Dear Mr. Warner—
My name is Lacy Adams. I received your name from the fiancée of a gentleman in your company, who thought you

might like a pen pal. She suggested your family were not the best correspondents. I'm no stranger to those sorts of things. I was raised on a farm where we fattened our anger and resentment right beside the cattle. I am pursuing a PhD in chemistry at UT Austin. I know nothing of yours, but I am of a serious disposition.

As an organism, there are two ways your tour could end—1. You could come home, or 2. if not, your valuable carbon, nitrogen, and sulfur will be returned to the earth to create new life. (That's a joke.) In seriousness, I appreciate your sacrifice. Whatever anyone thinks of this war, your service is something our country never asked of me, or any woman, and for that you have my gratitude. If you ever need a friend on a long night, my address is below.

Very truly yours,

L.A.

In the morning, as the mailbox swallowed the letter, the thought crossed her mind of whether Aaron would respond and what she might have gotten herself into. Lacy shook it off. She'd had twenty-three years of being herself, and all the good that did her, and she figured she could scare off a guy halfway around the world as fast as she did here at home. In stockings and cashmere twinset, she marched to the chemistry building, popping a stick of Juicy Fruit to calm her nerves.

It was the moment Lacy had worried about all summer: would she finally get placed in a lab with faculty, like the rest of her cohort, and launch her career? She entered the office with jaw clenched on her gum and took the envelope from her mail cubby. By letter from Department Chair Wallace, she learned instead that for the third straight semester she would grade undergrad problem sets if she wanted to keep her fellowship. Tears swelled, threatening to blow her meticulously serene exterior.

"Miss Adams." A hand patted her shoulder as Wallace hurried through the office. He turned at the door and smiled blandly. "Always a lovely sight."

They watched each other. In his face Lacy could recall every expression she had cataloged since her freshman year—his bemused smile when she declared her major, the wrinkled amazement when she said she applied to the PhD program. The man who controlled her fate, who gave her money to live so she'd never have to ask her mother for anything again. Gone, out the door. She sank into a chair, pressed a Kleenex to her eyes, and told herself for the millionth time that there was no problem, she wasn't a problem, and science wasn't for the fainthearted. She checked her watch; she was late for biochem. And without a better idea of what to do, she rose and soldiered on to class.

★

One Monday evening, while Lacy sat grading in her room, she heard the labored steps of the housemother distributing the mail. For the first time in more than a year her feet paused at Lacy's door. Under it whisked a letter with Private Warner's name and hers printed on a dirty envelope. She tore it open. *Dear Lacy* was scrawled in a wild hand, followed by words and dark boxes all over—phrases blacked out with a marker, whole lines at a time. She squinted, looking for a full sentence, as random bits dashed into view: *dying clock ticking . . . people in the trees . . . losing my mines . . .* and near the bottom a repeated stream of *look ma no hands!!!*

Lacy stuffed the letter in her desk drawer and locked it. But after one look, Aaron's words had already begun mutating in her head into a voice she could not quiet. For days she barely slept and stumbled through her classes, imagining the man who wrote them. And then, on Friday evening, the housemother paused again and four more letters shot under her door. *He's writing me every day*, Lacy thought with a shiver as she locked them away, unopened, that week, and the next. Yet with each letter her fear was gradually inflected with mystery. Why did he keep writing? What lay behind the redactions? What if Aaron was trying to tell her something and she'd done nothing to decipher them after promising friendship?

She held out until late on a Saturday night. The girls down the hall cranked their Motown and sang along, turning gray skies blue, their voices echoing off the walls of the empty dorm. At the stroke of midnight Lacy took Private Warner's ten letters from the drawer. She laid them out on her yellow silk duvet, cautiously, reverently, like tarots, and opened the second one.

Aaron began with an apology. His last letter was crazy talk, but when he got hers it was like a ray of light blew up a dam and he couldn't help but gush, and just knowing she's out there reading this means the world, it's life and death so please keep reading. Lacy continued. She sensed a hint of crazy in this letter, too, despite the square, manly handwriting—some nonsense about how he was really supposed to be in med school and not over there. But then he told her he laughed out loud when he read about the cattle on her farm growing up, the anger and the cows, and how her family must be like his. Suddenly it seemed as if Aaron was in the room beside her, whispering hot words in her ear. He had to sign off, but he'd talk to her tomorrow.

Her pulse skipped as she tore open the remaining letters. *Are you the disfavored one?*—the next letter began without a greeting—*Lacy, are you the black sheep in your family too?* She read these words and instantly knew him. Not from data or thoughts in her mind but through her very being, the way Legolas and the Elvish knew rocks or the souls of trees.

Aaron wrote his life story on letterhead scrounged from the Red Cross. He told her about his brother with the stutter, and the parents falling over themselves to praise the average one.

And to Aaron, who got straight As and a full ride to UT, did his dad say congrats? Still he put his head down and strived, because that's the American Dream. *But how does it work anymore? Twenty-three years you believe things matter, school, jobs, to end up in the jungle? To see it slip through your fingers halfway around the world, in a hell so deep you start wishing for death. You dream of it and wake up cursing your eyes for opening. So, thank you, Lacy*—he closed his last letter—*if you're there.* There wasn't much left of Aaron Warner to write home about, but when he thought of her reading, *it's like God said let there be light and it shined on these chicken scratches* of what he used to be. He heard it took five days for mail to go from A to B, and maybe in five days he'd be dead but could she send him a sign?

The last words were smudged where her tear had mingled with the blue ink. Lacy wiped her eyes and breathlessly paced the room, rereading each letter. The Tower bells chimed twice, vibrating through the now silent hall. A night curled in on itself and gone to sleep, she thought, while she had been with Aaron.

She sat at her desk and, hours from dawn, wrote with a focus as sharp as hunger. She didn't believe in God, she told him, so she wouldn't pray for him, but she'd send a letter every day, so that he'd know someone at home was willing him not to die. To keep writing back. She could hear him in his letters, she said, a man of substance in dire straits. *Hold on, Aaron, every day until the next one.*

In the morning Lacy rose with purpose. She didn't linger over her doughnut at the diner, picking at the Formica counter and fretting over school like usual. She returned to her desk and wrote another letter. Aaron wasn't alone in his loneliness, she assured him. Her two best and only friends from UT were engaged before graduation, married after, and launched on their husbands' vectors to Tulsa and Corpus Christi. And if Aaron wanted to talk family, well, she hadn't spoken to hers in thirteen months, so, yes, she was a black sheep too. She wasn't the girl her mother wanted. How she looked, or talked to men, or had a brain full of more than beauty secrets—no detail was too small to escape her mom's eye. And one day, after Lacy beat her head against that wall enough times, she realized it could kill her. And stopped trying.

She mailed the letters on her way to class Monday morning. In the evening, as she sat to write again, Aaron's next letter flew under her door. Thus began their system: writing across continents and each other, their words like ships passing daily. They talked about themselves. They asked questions that went unanswered, or responses lagged for days or weeks, appearing out of nowhere to forgotten queries.

Lacy wrote about the dissertation proposal she submitted early—silicon etching on CMOS wafers—and how cool computers were and maybe someday they'd be more than big calculators and be like our friends, too. Aaron wrote that the cigarettes were awful lately, and he had some fungal thing on his chest. She confided that the last time she went home her mother invited an old classmate of Lacy's to dinner. Heir to a funeral home chain, recently divorced—her mom whispered during cocktails—*very* eager to remarry. And when Lacy left the table after the boy shushed her, her mother trailed her to the foyer and asked, "Who do *you* think's going to marry you, Lacy? You're not like other girls, be smart!" Aaron said in his nightmares a vulture kept ripping his eyes out. But a week later he wrote, *Never marry? Shushed you? God forbid Lacy Adams patents a computer chip and makes a million dollars—I hear the sky falling already!*

Lacy knew then that he was listening. He'd been listening all along.

She shared more. Things she could never say aloud flowed from her pen. The awful memory of being pulled from class in fifth grade, when her dad died, and the red-hot unfairness of her mom's house, where she had no place. Her feckless brother who could do no wrong, who totaled a Stingray at sixteen and got the whopping punishment of a purse-lipped "boys will be boys" from their mother. Lacy's words were sharp and controlled; she liked who she was in her letters. Some days she recalled a turn of phrase, a curated intimacy mailed to Aaron, as she sat in class. She started raising her hand more and kept it up until the professor acknowledged her. Her grades, always good, turned excellent.

On Halloween, an undisguised Lacy made her way to the chemistry building through students dressed as Popeyes and Jeannies. She delivered a typed memo to Department Chair Wallace describing how each day of biochem had begun that semester: a compound listed on the chalkboard—PCB or resveratrol—that a male classmate would diagram and always coincidentally looked like a pair of breasts. She noted the professor's response every time—"hubba-hubba"—and asked if this lived up to the academic standards of the University of Texas. Lacy never heard back. But for weeks Aaron ended his letters with *Give 'em hell, Lacy!*

And then, around the time Aaron's vulture stopped visiting his sleep, a nightmare of her own came true. One evening the housemother didn't stop at her door, and again the next night. For a week no letters came. Lacy couldn't eat. She bought a pack of Virginia Slims and took up smoking. At night she was plagued by the same sliver of a dream: the housemother paused at her door, but when Lacy opened it a duty officer stood there with a somber face. Each night Lacy awakened, sweating, to the reality that no one would come tell her if Aaron died. To the world outside they were nothing. The word entered her mind as though for the first time: *Love?* She pushed it away. But harder to subdue was a bittersweet truth of their letters—that the world they created there, together, was better than where either of them was fighting.

A letter arrived on the eve of Thanksgiving. Aaron was sorry for the gap. He tried not to talk war stuff, but he was a minesweeper and his partner tripped a partial dud while they were scouting. Aaron was laid out, exposed and bleeding. He thought of letting death come. A bullet from anywhere any second. But he thought of Lacy, the way she dotted her *i*'s, and he dragged himself to cover. He had a letter to write. *You're a cherry lifesaver*, he said.

Soon their letters bore flashes of open affection, twinkling like the lights going up around the shop windows on the Drag. Lacy wrote that Willie Nelson just played the Armadillo, and of course she didn't go, but when his song came on the radio she thought of Aaron. He was always on her mind. She hadn't even asked what he looked like, she wrote, but she saw him in places—in the face of a cook at the diner, or Charlton Heston in *Planet of the Apes*. Aaron hoped it wasn't too forward, but could she send him a picture? To put a face to the beautiful words? She didn't have any of herself, she replied, but she'd get one.

After her last exam of the semester, Lacy was skipping down the steps of the chemistry building on her way to the Sears photo booth when Professor Wallace called out to her. He led her to his office and shut the door. "Is this about my dissertation proposal?" she asked. "Or the biochem memo? I'm in town the whole break if you—"

"It's about everything." Wallace rubbed his eyes behind his horn-rims. He told her how proud he was of her, how much he enjoyed the experience of having her in the program, and how he thought it best if she finished out the year with her master's and left. Lacy's mouth went dry. She asked if her performance was substandard. No, he said, flicking his hand at the question, she was near the top of her cohort, but science isn't strictly about results. Lacy objected that science is precisely about results, to which Wallace replied irritably that scientists worked with others, in labs and companies in the real world, and Lacy had proven a distraction. Her fellowship was a resource better allocated to a student with a real future, surely she could understand? But with a master's why not teach high school chemistry? Wallace knew a number of elite private schools that would be happy to have her.

It happened fast. Lacy couldn't remember if she said goodbye or if she thanked Wallace as she was leaving, out of habit. Instead of Sears she found herself a few minutes later at the diner. She ordered a Coke and a Frito pie in the bag. "Make it two pies," Lacy called out, too shell-shocked to care about her hips. She devoured the first one and was turning to the second when the waitress leaned over the counter. "When's your friend coming?" she asked. Lacy stared. The waitress pointed to the second pie.

"Oh." Lacy's eyes watered. "Soon, I hope."

But he didn't. No letter came from Aaron that night, or the rest of the year.

★

The dorm cleared out for the holidays. Inside her room, Lacy heard the thumping of suitcases down steps, and silence. She was alone again, but the ache of it was different now. She had tasted something she learned too late was love, she had made shelter with Aaron, and now nothing could protect her from the emptiness. Time was too big, and her imagination terrible. She filled the void with Tolkien, studying every passage about Aragorn, a humble man risking his life to fight against evil. One night she was tracing Aragorn's path on a map of Middle Earth when a passage from one of Aaron's letters came to mind. A dream he shared before he went silent. He was a diplomat traveling the world—*like the beginning of* Casablanca, he wrote, *that map of Africa?*—ending wars, on missions of peace, with a strong woman at his side. And not some trophy wife. A lady who brought science and progress along with peace.

No letter.

Another night Lacy smoked at the window as a storm rippled nearby. Carols played on the radio, fading on the hour so the DJ could wish everyone out there a very merry Christmas. Nat King Cole came on, imploring her to hear the angels' voices. Lacy pressed her cheek to the windowpane and tried to hear like the Elvish, like Arwen for her human king. She listened for any sound. The patter of rain, or the Tower bells. A car on Guadalupe. But no sign of whether in a faraway jungle Aaron had turned into valuable carbon, nitrogen, and sulfur.

★

"Private Warner, can you hear me?" Aaron opened his eyes and saw her. His angel, Lacy. "Merry Christmas, Santa's here!" She fiddled with his arm. "High as a kite now, huh? And I've got another present." She leaned down to his ear. "The doctor says we're gonna get you good as new. Almost." Then she was gone. She would stop by to fix his pillows or give him sips of water. Every time she said his name so sweet. One time she asked if he remembered what happened to him, and that's when he heard it for sure—an accent, like how the New York mobsters talk in the movies.

"You're not Lacy," he mumbled.

"Nope, I'm Nurse Maureen. Is she your sweetheart?"

"I have to write a letter," Aaron croaked. "I need a pen and paper."

"Stay still." She pressed his shoulders down. "You're broken all over. I don't suppose you're left-handed?" He shook his head. "Well, the good news is you got four working limbs. First we lower the morphine, and then you can dictate your letter to me."

"It's private."

"Easy." She dabbed his face with a towel. "Relax."

Aaron drifted in and out of sleep. With each awakening, time and place slowly reemerged, carving at the soft oblivion with questions he couldn't answer. How long had he been here? Where was here? Not a field station, judging by the ceiling fan, but a real hospital. It was OK. He lifted his head and saw a mummy body, a cast from ribs to feet and another on his right arm. That was OK too. He repeated the nurse's question in his head, *What happened?* until he could uncoil the memory of that day.

He remembered the sun and the dirt road, and giant banyan trees on both sides. He and Peanut were at the front of the company with their headphones on, listening for clicks as they swept the road in slow arcs. Peanut's walk was weird, off-balance. He stumbled forward and the ground exploded and things went black. Aaron woke up to Peanut screaming and rolling in the dirt with no legs. Big Boy tried to drag Peanut behind the jeep, but he got picked off, and then Aaron watched the company shot down one by one as they tried to save him—Dash and Gorey and on and on. Aaron tried to yell it was a trap, but no sound came out. The snipers shot Peanut last and it was quiet again. He remembered the hard tree roots pressing into his back, and the heaviness in his eyes. *Stay awake*, he thought, *stay awake stay awake.*

But that day seemed far away to Aaron as he watched the hospital fan turn. Happening to people he used to know, distant like the body attached to his head. Things were OK. The only thing that wasn't, that nagged at him through the haze, was the thought of Lacy out there not knowing that his heart was still beating and hers to keep.

★

"Morning, Private," Maureen said gruffly. She busied herself between his legs. "We switched you over last night. No more strong stuff, just old-fashioned Tylenol now. You'll be feeling more," she said, wiping him down there with a moist towel. "You'll tell me if you gotta go number two? You'll help and call us when you get that feeling?"

"Can I have your pen?" His face burned. "And paper?" She paused. Then she came around his left side and turned a page on her clipboard and settled it below Aaron's hand. He gripped the pen, aching at its cumbersomeness. He raised his head as best he could and wrote *Dear Lacy*. Maureen sighed at the childish scrawl. Aaron's eyes watered.

"How'd you think you'd do that with your right arm in a cast, huh?" she scolded. "You're a hero. No crying like a baby. Give it time."

"How am I supposed to write home," he snapped, "to let her know I'm alive?"

"Private Warner," a voice boomed. A square-jawed officer stood at the foot of the bed. "Major Colin Hanford. Don't worry about contacting your parents. My staff notified them by phone that you're alive and receiving the honor that brings me here today. The United States Army has awarded the Purple Heart to you and Private William Gorey of your company—"

"Gorey's alive?" he rasped.

"He's doing fine. I'd present you with the medal today, but we're holding a ceremony here at the hospital soon. Stay tuned."

"What'd they say?" Aaron asked. The officer furrowed his brow. "My parents?"

"They said 'thank you' and—they said 'thank you for calling.' Rest up."

Aaron tried to sleep after the major left, but Maureen was right. He was sensing everything. Lysol and rotten smells. He was itchy under the casts and pain throbbed in his core, jangling a thousand new points in his hips. The once quiet air teemed with breathing. "Hey," a voice called, "welcome to Special Surgery." Aaron glanced sideways and saw a freckled ginger waving at him with a thumbless hand. Nineteen, tops. He scanned the room and counted maybe a dozen beds, bodies in traction or threaded with tubes. "They had you doped up for weeks," said the voice. "I'm Rob." And Aaron, who had always made friends as easy as breathing, pretended not to hear. Panic flooded his veins until gradually it subsided, leaving behind a cold residue. A whisper of nothingness ahead.

In the afternoon Maureen said she had a surprise for him. Aaron shut his eyes and pondered how he ever could have mistaken her—an old bottle blond with ham-hock arms—for Lacy. "OK, look," she said, returning a moment later. A black typewriter sat on a stool beside his bed. "Now you can write your girl and keep busy till the casts come off and we get you walking again." She guided Aaron's free hand to the keyboard, but he couldn't reach, so she moved the stool and stacked books under the machine, but the keys were always just past his fingertips. "Mother of God," she grumbled. "Hang on." She came back and handed Aaron a chopstick. "You got it? Hit *S* for me? Do it," she ordered. "Now *L*? Hit return? There you go." She loaded a sheet of paper. "Call me when you're done and I'll mail it out."

At last Aaron began the task he'd pined for from the moment he returned to the living. But after all the waiting, his mind felt blank. Each keystroke was a shaky effort. An hour and three near drops of the chopstick later, he had typed:

dear lacy, im alive in hispital in saigon. im ok, ten fingers and roes.

write me at address on envelope. your loving aaron

"Done?" Maureen asked later, on a round past his bed. She pulled the page from the typewriter. "This is it?" He nodded. "Well," she muttered, "I'll get it out today."

Aaron fell back on his pillow and rested his neck, sore from craning as he poked at the keys. He thought of their letters in the fall, toppling over each other in the mail. How he'd written her every day and found a place where he was still alive, where he could redraw the outline of himself that was breaking into dots. But the terror he'd been outrunning had finally caught up to him. A mummy trapped in a bed. He knew it in the cold sweats that woke him up at night. He was different now.

He would lie in the darkness and think of who he once was. Because of all the things that returned to him—his mind, pain, shame at being wiped like a baby—the fire inside had not. He remembered the kid who left his redneck town and fought his way to UT, who pledged Sigma Nu with the rich sons of Dallas and Houston, who entertained them and drank with them and maybe someday would work with them and be rich too. He thought of the hours of study, politics, history, grinding toward grad school and, the minute the war was over, the foreign service. The intense new study when the deferment rules changed and he went premed, two years of bio and chem in one so he could apply by senior year and never risk getting sent to the jungle. Topped off by the Monday last spring, when he went to the post office after no response from ten med schools, not even rejections, and learned that a shipment of mail was lost right around the time he sent his applications. All that work, to save his own life, flushed down the drain by the US mail. He remembered the cold rage at his luck. The world laughing at him.

He saw it all in a flash that day at the postal counter—how he would graduate and be drafted and rather die than give his dad the satisfaction of hearing he dodged.

Aaron revisited these places at night, as he lay in the wheezing dark of Special Surgery. He marveled at the kid he used to be and mourned the flame that had burned in him. He thought of the escapes he'd imagined just a few years ago, and the dirtier trick the world had played on him—coming inside his mind and extinguishing it, so there was nobody left to escape. Aaron Warner. Not missing like a thing to be found, but dead.

Then one morning he got his first letter in months. Lacy's handwriting was bigger and bolder than before. *Right when I gave up on miracles*, she wrote, *your letter comes? Do you know I blew a fuse on the army switchboard looking for you? Do you know I thought of you every night, and cried and dreamed your dream— the two of us, diplomat and scientist, saving the world? I have a list of questions a mile long, Aaron! What happened? When are you coming home? What can I do? Please tell me what I can do!*

Your Truest Love, she signed it, Aaron would remember until the day he died.

He didn't wipe away the tears. He let them run down his face in joy, and fear. Maybe he had no fire or a family who cared if he lived or died, but he had Lacy. He couldn't lose the one good thing in his life. If she still wanted the diplomat, he'd have to fake it. Anything Lacy wouldn't want, the broken, unworthy things inside him, she didn't need to know and he wouldn't write them down. *i have to keep this short*, Aaron typed in his next letter, *with the chopstixk and all. we hit a mine, company mostly dead, im in casts but will walk and be fine, pls tell me aboit you, how is school?*

And with this they resumed their pattern of daily letters, hers in pages of chatty script and his in a few terse lines. Lacy wrote that she was leaving her program to teach at a private school in Houston, which was a good thing in its own way, and did Aaron think a lot about the day he was injured? *i lost my partner on that mission*, he typed a few days later. Aaron didn't mention his recurring dream of Peanut screaming *get my legs!* or the guilt he bore, knowing Peanut had been snorting heroin cut with Saigon's garbage ever since he tripped that first dud a while back, but having no idea what to do about it. *so*, Aaron typed in closing, *leaving the phd? before you get your patent? good for you but good how?*

Lacy wrote that the pay was generous, and believe it or not she wasn't one of those girls burning bras at Miss America, and even with her degrees maybe she wondered about living on her own, not in her mom's house or some man's, so good in that way, a new challenge. *welcome to the wirkforce*, Aaron typed, *you will be a great teacher. so much i want to tell you when im out of my casts.* But Aaron didn't put into words his strongest desire, to be enveloped in her safety. To have someone take care of him, plug the hole inside and love him. Aaron had always sensed Lacy's safety. Not just her soon-to-be-generous pay, but her background. The stationery with her initials on top, her brother's Stingray, or the way she wrote—a way no one did from an average farm, so Aaron knew what kind of business her family must have owned.

When will you be out of your cast? Lacy wrote. *soon a week or two*, he typed, *im excited to walk.* He didn't tell her the former running back might have a limp. She wrote how wonderful it was that he'd come home intact and have a future, didn't he think? Aaron knew the truth about the future but couldn't share it: that it was a myth once you looked chaos in the eyes, saw a dozen men die taking a Vietcong road, only to find the next day it's been replanted with Australian mines. Things didn't move forward. Destruction in circles, yes, but no future. Still, when he dreamed of himself lying on the roots of a banyan tree, a helpless child in an enemy land, someone did reach out her hands to lift him up. It was Lacy.

when i come home, Aaron typed, *i want to meet you.*

★

Albino raisin. It was his first thought when the doctor sawed off his casts and exposed his shriveled limbs. "Daylight's wasting," Maureen said as soon as he was free, working a pair of scrubs up his legs in no time. "Got to get you on your way." She swung him around, angled crutches under his armpits, and hoisted him to his feet. Aaron gasped and fell back onto the bed, clutching his hips in shock. "Oh, Mr. Baby." Maureen sighed. "Fine. A pain pill to tide you over, but we're going for a walk today. We are winning this war. You're not going home in a box, and not in a chair either if I have any say. You're a lucky one, so set an example."

Lucky. For weeks this was her refrain on their walks around the hospital, no matter what Aaron lobbed at her. He had no filter. At first he yelled it was a sick joke, and he could barely feel his legs so what the hell were they doing? "You're lucky you got them at all," she would mutter, balancing him with a squeeze to his stringy biceps. But the more weight he put on his legs, the more he felt things inside them, odd pressures, objects that he bellowed at Maureen for the doctors to remove. "You're a survivor," she said, unfazed. "Those pins are a point of pride to some men." Aaron was left to distract himself from his woes. He focused his mind on the heat of Maureen's body and her smell, of talcum and old-woman sweat. On many walks he yearned for his casts again, and all they had kept at bay—the proximity and contact.

Do you wear perfume? he wrote Lacy when he was strong enough to sit up and use a pen. Other parts of him were sitting up too, and he sorely wished she'd sent that photo of herself before he got blown up. *I wear Chanel No. 5*, she replied a few days later, *do you like it?* That was all she wrote. Her first and only short letter. Aaron checked the envelope to be sure, and his heart nearly stopped. Inside he found a sweet-smelling picture of Lacy Adams. Black hair to her shoulders, curled out at the bottom. Smoky eyes with a hint of defiance, full lips and cheeks, but the cheekbones—almost a Mexican shape going on in her face. For the rest of the day Aaron looked at her, and kissed her, and put her away and repeated it again, waiting for cover of night.

The next morning, as Aaron studied the photo with exciting new memories, Maureen led Major Hanford into the ward. "Amazing," he said, approaching Aaron's bed with a smile. "A new man, Private Warner. Healed and on your feet, I hear."

"Soon, sir."

"Very soon. Next week is the Purple Heart ceremony. Two public affairs officers will be there to take your photo and get some background information."

"My photo?" Aaron asked.

"There are naysayers back home, Private," the major explained, "saying this battle isn't worth the price, and we don't have what it takes. What better way to change hearts and minds than a story like yours? A young man broken head to toe, who survives to stand for God and country."

"We're winning this war," Maureen interjected.

"With men like Warner we are." The major looked Aaron over. "And when you get back home? Have you thought about it?"

"I'm just thinking about my next walk," Aaron said.

"Complete the mission, right, Private? See you next week."

The major wasn't the only one talking to Aaron about his plans. Hardly a day went by that Maureen didn't remind him of how many soldiers never left, or never left the same, so how would he use his second chance? Lacy set in on him too. *Are you*

going back to school when you get home? she asked once. He ignored it. But letter after letter she kept at it with the questions,
in passing at first, until she pressed right on the button. Did he
need more school to take the foreign service exam? He'd mentioned med school once—did he want to be a doctor in the service? *I'm thinking about a lot of things for when I get back*, Aaron
wrote eventually. But he only thought of one thing, truly, one
devouring numbness that he couldn't tell her about, that whispered, *we'll all be dead soon*, and no one, not even Lacy, could
tell him a single thing he could do with his life now that would
matter in the least.

One afternoon Aaron got two letters, the usual from Lacy
and another from Ernest Warner, stamped in Midland, Texas, a
week before. He opened the letter from his dad—the first one
he'd gotten since he deployed. *Dear Private Warner*, he'd written, *We didn't expect to hear you'd be coming back, the way this
war is going, but we are so very glad you're alive and we salute you.
There's a job waiting for you here in Midland if you want it. Two
veterans working side by side could make a real go of it, swapping
stories and making money. Keep in touch.*

He opened Lacy's next. Her voice seemed different, sad
maybe. She was graduating two weeks from Thursday, she
wrote, but she hadn't told her family. *What's the point? Days like
that never turn out to be what you imagine, anyway, as happy or the
big deal you want.* But she'd be thinking of him when she turned
her tassel, like she had been all year.

Aaron felt a vague stirring inside him, almost forgotten, to
get up and go and do.

By the morning of the ceremony, he could walk for ten minutes and stand in place for fifteen. He dressed himself slowly but
without assistance. When Aaron was ready, Maureen nodded soberly and escorted him without touching to the hospital courtyard. Aaron stepped into the sunlight and thought of Gorey,

the only other guy left who was there that day, and wondered where he redeployed and if he was still alive. Aaron lined up with a bunch of strangers. Somebody talked into a megaphone about sacrifice, and the major went down the row and pinned medals to their chests. Aaron stood up as straight as the rods in his legs. The PR men took photos. One of them asked Aaron, what was the first thing he was going to do when he got back to the USA?

"A surprise," Aaron said. "You can print that."

★

The speeches were over. Graduation had wound down to a blur of names. Lacy stood in cap and gown, waiting at the edge of the stage to be called. She thought of school ending, her world changing, and smiled tightly to control the doubts flickering within— whether she should have fought harder to stay in the program, or if her dreams were too big to begin with. At the sound of her name, she held her breath and crossed the stage. Professor Wallace took her hand a moment before presenting her diploma. "A tremendous mind," he said, smiling wistfully. Lacy opened her mouth, trying to find a sound for all the mixed-up thoughts running through her brain, when she got a nudge from behind. It was the next guy's turn.

She descended the stage and wandered through the hubbub. Soon the families would go to lunch, laughing and quibbling together. She would go to her dorm and pack. A man waved at Lacy—for a second she thought she knew him—and asked her to take a picture. Lacy counseled three generations to move in closer, and snapped a photo. She felt so old that morning looking in the mirror, going on twenty-four, but handing the camera back she had a premonition of how long life could be. It struck her that the grudge that had separated her from her family the past few years had become something definite. A milestone missed. And it turned out Lacy wasn't as good at congratulating herself as she hoped.

Wallace found her in the crowd and asked when she was leaving for Houston. Tomorrow she'd be out of his hair forever, she replied with a faint smile. As he said goodbye, Lacy noticed someone behind him, watching. A tall, handsome man, gaunt-faced, in jeans and a white T-shirt. His golden hair buzzed down to chick fluff and his square jaw covered in stubble. His blue eyes never strayed, and when Wallace left he started toward her. She caught a slight limp in his stride and knew for sure. It was the impossible, standing before her. The love she read about in books. She was flooded with care and relief at a vigil ended. And desire.

"Lacy Adams, master of science." Aaron handed her a cluster of bluebonnets.

"You came," she said. "You came home."

"I came for you. Don't cry, Lacy!" He wiped a tear from her cheek and took her in his arms. She held him close, her hands searching the hard angles of his frame until he let out a small cry. "Nothing," he mumbled apologetically. "My hips still give me trouble." He kissed her timidly. Their faces lingered close. "Nice to meet you, Lacy," he said. "You hungry?"

They went to lunch. Lacy's diner would take them, on graduation with no reservation, so there they settled in a booth. The conversation was halting and factual on the walk over: when and where Aaron processed out, how he bought an old truck and drove forty hours straight to get there in time. He gave her hand a squeeze on the table. She smiled. He squeezed again. "So," he blurted.

"It's a little weird," Lacy offered.

"A little bit. Yeah. Because, the thing is . . ."

The thing hung in the air as Aaron searched for words. Maybe it was their presence revealing the nakedness of their letters, and leaving them bashful. Or the unmet expectations hovering like a chill mist—Lacy heavier than her picture let on, Aaron holding his water glass in a rough way she never imagined. Maybe the thing was that their letters were letters and nothing more. A few months of scribbling at a hard time. A civic duty. A situation that was over now, no matter their words or the places her heart had been.

"The thing is," Lacy declared, "we have to order." Firmly she discussed the ups and downs of the menu with Aaron. She analyzed his Reuben when it came, and her cottage cheese salad and a lot of nothing, while Aaron nodded with a lost expression on his face. He finished his sandwich. She stopped to take a bite.

"What are you doing tomorrow?" he asked.

"Moving." Lacy sighed. "I should be packing now."

"This is your last night in town? Tonight?"

"Yes. The school found an apartment for me. They're training me this summer."

"Great." Aaron stared at his plate. "I could move you. Drive you there."

"Oh." She flushed. "How generous. But you must have plans. You haven't seen your family yet. Are you going to Midland?"

He thought of his dad driving around town, sucking dirt out of rich folks' rugs, feeling bigger as he made Aaron small. "No," he replied. "Nothing much for me there."

The check came. Aaron insisted on paying. He told Lacy one last time what an amazing accomplishment, and congratulations.

"Where are you staying tonight?" she asked as they were leaving.

"Hadn't thought that far ahead," he mumbled, "but I got a new old truck and—Lacy?" He turned to face her on the street and gripped her shoulders. His eyes were glassy and distant. "I don't know how to thank you for all you've done for me, but—"

"Are you leaving?" A wave of terror hit her. "Sleeping in your car? No." She threaded her arm through his and pulled him along. "You're staying with me tonight. We'll figure it out. If anyone sees you, you're my brother. Long-lost family here to help me pack."

And once they made it to Lacy's room, he did help. She packed her clothes while Aaron sat boxing her books. The activity relaxed them. They talked about their college years, a few of them overlapping on campus, and memories of childhood. They laughed and heard each other's voices again, even in the same room looking at each other. Lacy sat closer to Aaron on the bed. Letting go of the past seemed possible. So did having a future, stepping into a life that belonged to them and no one else. And gradually, by a conspiracy of glimpses, they were touching, and kissing, and loosening their clothes.

With hands and tongue Lacy explored the body she had long imagined, broken, marked with scars, but warm and manly too. She worked with a zeal that startled Aaron, especially as he made his way into her and confirmed, through her clenched jaw and eyes squeezed tight, that he was her first. They found a rhythm, and it calmed him. The first breath of true protection he felt in years. When he grunted with pleasure, Lacy asked if he was OK and was it his hips? Aaron nodded and beamed at her rocking above him. She slid her fingers into his mouth. They fell asleep around sunset, embracing, and slept through the long cool night.

★

In the morning Aaron awakened to Lacy watching him from the windowsill. She was smoking in a silky white bathrobe. She turned away and tossed him the pack of cigarettes. "Lighter's in there. Pretty day," she mumbled, pulling her knees up and looking out the window.

"Let's get married," Aaron said.

Lacy flinched. "It's 1970. We don't have to, just because . . ." Her eyes traveled over the duvet on the floor and the sheets scrambled on the bed.

"I know." He lit a cigarette. He grabbed *The Two Towers* off her nightstand and shuffled its edges. Carefully he inched his back up the wall, and smoked, and stared at his feet. "But," he said, "I've been alone my whole life. Maybe I don't have to be. Or you either." He looked at her with a raw intensity. "Maybe we could have a kid someday, and tell him about how we met and the day we got married, and protect him so he's never alone like we were. Maybe he'll grow up and change the world."

Lacy's eyes shined. She nodded. "Yeah?" he cried with a silly grin. "Right now?" She nodded bigger, and the tears started rolling. They didn't shower. They laughed as Aaron threw on his jeans and helped Lacy into the red crepe de chine dress that fell most forgivingly on her curves. She ran her fingers through her wild bed hair. As they were leaving, Lacy noticed an old black woman coming out of a room down the hall. She was hunched over, walking slowly.

"Ma'am?" Lacy said. "That's Miss Clifton's room, isn't it?"

The woman stopped and looked through Lacy. "Do you know Helen?"

"Yes." Lacy took Aaron's hand. "She put us in touch. This is my fiancé, Aaron."

"Ma'am." He nodded.

"He served with Helen's fiancé. I was sorry to hear about him. And for her."

The woman clutched her purse. "She tried coming back for the spring semester, for a few weeks. The university said, 'No rush picking up her things, nobody moving into her room soon.' So I came now." She turned to Aaron. "Were you there? When he died?"

"With Big Boy? Private Williams. Yes."

"It wrecked my girl. For now. Was it bad, what happened to him?"

"He died saving—" Aaron paused. "Trying to save a life."

"But was it painful?"

"It was quick. For him it was quick."

"Thank you." The woman touched their hands. "I'm Beverly Clifton. Marriage is a wonderful thing. God bless this marriage."

Somberly Aaron and Lacy walked to city hall. While they waited in line she thought of how modern they were, dispensing with the white dress and wedding, beginning a new life together that would be a serious one, about the right things. When it was their turn, they handed the paperwork to a woman with a frosted bouffant at the counter. She glanced over it. "There's another for name change," she said.

"Sorry?" Lacy replied.

"Another form to fill out. You're taking his name, right?"

"Not if I take hers first," Aaron deadpanned.

The clerk's face puckered. She worked in silence. "I would appreciate it," she said when she handed them their license, "if y'all didn't make light of God's plan."

They kissed and left a trail of giggles behind them in the hallway. At a deli they made a picnic and walked to Town Lake. Aaron and Lacy sat close and fed each other. They talked about the sunshine on the water, and the cheese, the nice breeze, everything immediate and in front of them. In quiet moments, their minds wandered to the things they didn't know about each other yet, and the drive to Houston, and whether God had plans. But mostly to what their lives would be like as Mr. and Mrs. Warner.

II.

Marriage

4

Escalate the Call

The phone had been ringing a lot at the Warner house. For weeks its brassy cries disturbed the kitchen air, startling Lacy every time. She would watch it a moment from the sink or stove, as the beige handset jiggled on the wall and the cord swayed like a long, rangy tail. But when she picked up there was often no one on the line—or rather, there was a breather who wouldn't speak.

It happened again one morning while Lacy was making breakfast. She picked up and said her usual bright hello. After three hellos she heard the breathing, and she decided enough was enough. She craned her neck toward the pass-through and confirmed that Julian was still in the bathroom, his little legs dangling from the toilet as he bore down with a focused look.

"Go ahead, make my day," Lacy hissed, cupping the mouth-piece fiercely. "But have the balls to say who you are, sicko." She slammed the phone down, adjusted her T-shirt around her hips, and scooped cottage cheese onto her grapefruit.

"Who was that?" Aaron entered the kitchen and poured himself coffee. He looked sharp in his suit and paisley tie, blond hair parted neatly at the side. Fifteen years, Lacy thought with an ache as she studied him, nearly over the hill and still as fit and fine as the day they met.

"Same prank caller." She sighed. "I'm getting tired of it."

"Let's get the number unlisted."

"No," she said decisively, wondering as soon as she did who in the world might be trying to find her, or be unable to if they unlisted. "Sit down. I made you eggs."

"Can't." Aaron scanned the newspaper and sipped at the counter. "Early meeting today, the whole HR staff. You need cash for groceries?" He took four twenties from his wallet and set them on the leather Post-it station by the phone.

Lacy waited to see if he'd look her way, but he passed into the foyer. "Thanks," she said, following him. "I'm going shopping later, after his lessons and lunch with Bonnie. She's filling me in on the latest at school."

"Do you care?" Aaron asked, putting on his coat.

"Well," Lacy muttered, a little tender and shrunken, "if I'm going back to work I guess I should know what I'm getting myself into."

"See you tonight." He gave her a dry peck on the cheek and left.

Lacy stood in the foyer, listening to the rumble of the Taurus as he pulled away, until a flush and a cheer from Julian brought her back to life. "I didn't hear the faucet!" she called out reflexively. "No Cheerios till those hands are washed."

★

When Julian was almost three, Lacy passed his room one afternoon and heard him talking at an odd, deliberate pace. He sat in the wicker rocking chair where she read to him, wedged between his stuffed bear and bunny instead of on her lap. He held a picture book upside down and was saying the words. Lacy was startled, unable to discern whether he'd memorized it or was really reading, so when he stopped and looked at her, she turned the book right side up—"Try that," she said—and left. The next day she heard him again, so she put a new book in his hands, one they had never read together, and Lacy lost her breath to see that her son had taught himself to read. This was the beginning of Julian's lessons.

By the morning Lacy went full Clint Eastwood on the phone breather, she had crammed Julian's head with heaps of schooling and knowledge far beyond his years. He read the Narnia books, some Orwell, Dickens, and all of Twain. He could rattle off Linnaean taxonomy and was on track to start his multiplication tables that very week. After Julian rinsed his cereal bowl, they sat beside each other in the breakfast nook that Lacy called the dining room, and she announced the plan for the day: language arts from eight to nine, focused play for thirty, an hour of math, snacks and manners for fifteen, and ninety minutes of science before lunch.

The lessons began well. Smoothly Julian read aloud from *Great Expectations* and, upon quizzing, knew the meaning of "consternation" and "augment" and every other vocabulary word Lacy flagged. She shifted to critical thinking, as she liked to, and asked why Pip in the story would want to help a convict he met in a graveyard. Julian pondered this. His chestnut hair tilted like a shining bowl on his head. A fervent intelligence lit his hazel eyes. Lacy noted the slight rise in his posture, the influx of poise that filled her son as thoughts turned to words. He opened his mouth.

And the phone rang. Julian stopped short and watched her. "It's OK," she said. "The machine'll pick up."

But the caller didn't leave a message and instead kept trying, cutting off Julian twice more as he tried to answer Lacy's question. "Are you gonna get it?" he asked. "Can I go play?"

"Not till we're done with language arts."

"We have all day and all week and all year." He sighed with a vague air of superiority. "I always answer *my* phone. You never know who's calling." Lacy had recently bought him a red and yellow Fisher-Price phone, on which he spent most free play-time chatting with Isaac Newton or Mr. Belvedere, the British butler from his favorite sitcom.

"Julian," she said in her serious, bordering-on-displeasure tone. She shut the book and waited for the gravity of the moment to sink in. "We've studied together for a long time. Next week we're going to a school and you'll take some tests. If you do OK on them you'll go to kindergarten, but if you do well you can skip a grade or two. Or three. Isn't that exciting?"

"You teach me," he chirped. "Why do I have to go to school?"

"Because you're old enough. We're both going. Mommy was a teacher before you were born, remember? Now when you go to school, I'll be a teacher again and you'll have new ones."

"At the same school?"

"I'll be next door at the high school, so I'll drop you off and pick you up every day."

The phone rang.

Julian watched her with troubled eyes. "Can I go play?"

"In your room. I'll be right there." Lacy waited until he was down the hall before snatching the phone off the wall. "Enough!" she snapped. "I don't know what kind of dirty kicks you get harassing a woman at home with her baby, but I'm calling the cops!"

"Good morning," said a cheerful voice, "I'm David, a customer care specialist for Lone Star MasterCard. Can I please speak to Aaron Warner?"

"He's at work," she said with a cringing defiance. "This is his wife. Can I help you?"

"Is there a convenient time when I could reach Mr. Warner at this number?"

"I'm sure there is," she replied hotly, "but I paid the full balance like I do every month, so what's the problem? My phone's been ringing off the hook all morning."

"Ma'am?" The voice paused. "I think there's some confusion going on. I'm just now trying this number after the primary—I tried the primary phone for the account, but I was told Mr. Warner is no longer working there."

"You called him at work? At Enron?"

"Yes, ma'am. They said he's no longer employed there, so if there's a new work number where I could reach Mr. Warner, I'd appreciate—"

"No," Lacy barked. "No, no, escalate the call." She pressed her hand to the mouthpiece and shut her eyes. "Nothing personal," she resumed, "but you're not making any sense, so just put me through to your supervisor and we'll take it from there."

"Please hold."

Wait music blasted. Until that day she'd never endured a full listen of Carly Simon's "You're So Vain," which irritated her and now plagued her anxious mind. She remembered the episode of *L.A. Law* where she'd heard the phrase, "escalate the call," and how the blond woman partner said it, oozing with power, to a congressman's chief of staff. Lacy had to be powerful. She had to get a supervisor and tell him he was wrong and that Aaron was at an early meeting of the HR department. She thought of lunch with Bonnie, and going back to work after years, and Julian's lessons sitting undone right before his tests while she waited on hold. She stretched the phone to the living room until she could hear Julian having a conversation of his own.

"Mrs. Warner?" said a new man's voice. "This is customer care manager Robert. I'm sorry to bother you, but it seems we're having trouble reaching your husband."

"It is a bother," she snapped. "He's in an important meeting, and I have a busy morning myself, and now I have to take time from my day to give you his work number because you must have it wrong in your system, you ready?"

"That won't be necessary, ma'am. We did reach his former employer."

"Well, obviously not," she faltered, "because he just left for—I hope my call with David was recorded before," she shifted gears imperiously. "I probably asked him five times what the problem was, but he wouldn't say."

"Unfortunately, we can't speak to persons not listed on the account."

"It's a joint account, Robert! Just escalate the call." Lacy's face flushed. "Go on. Put me through to your supervisor."

"There's no one else to speak to here."

"Whoever's up the food chain, your higher authority."

"Ma'am, I manage this center and you are not listed on the account ending 7602."

"For God's sake, do I have to read it to you?" Lacy stretched to her desk where she paid bills, a rolltop oak veneer hulk that looked more elegant on the floor at Sears, and grabbed their last card statement. "Here we go, I'm looking at—" She ran her eyes over the account number once, and twice. It was like a truck hit her.

"A Popsicle, Belvedere!" A bit of Julian's chatter floated into the living room.

"Ma'am," the voice said gently after a time. "I do see you listed on an account with Aaron Warner, ending 5733, with a current balance of zero. I think I understand. I am not authorized to give you details," he continued at a pregnant pace, "about this *other* account, with a high credit limit, that you are *not on*."

"I see. With a high balance?" she asked tremulously. "The other one? Like, three-digit balance?" She waited. "Four-digit? Or. Five?"

"Yes, ma'am."

Lacy laughed. "It wasn't that long ago your company wouldn't even let me on a credit card of my own, remember that? Women?" She brushed away the beginnings of a tear with her knuckles. "Now I'm on one I didn't even know I had, how about that?"

"Technically you're not."

"But." Lacy felt her head spinning. "What am I supposed to do?"

"Mrs. Warner, when I've had a hard day and really need to talk, I go right past my friends, right to the source, and talk to God. And when I pray to my Lord Savior Jesus Christ, things never seem as bad as they—"

Lacy hung up. Immediately she started dialing Aaron's office, but she paused before the last digit. A freeze set over her. She stepped out of time, numb to everything but a pain in her chest. The beeping of the untended phone drew her back to the kitchen. She returned the handset to the cradle. She made her way to Julian's room in a daze and stopped in the doorway. "You may live here, Belvedere," he said into his phone, "but you work for me." She knocked. Julian turned, his dark eyebrows arched at the interruption. "Are we doing math?" he asked.

"No." She put on a smile. "Today's special. Free play all morning."

"OK. I have calls to make." He turned back to his phone, but then abruptly he stood up and came to the doorway. "All morning?"

"All morning!" Lacy pulled the door shut.

She went to the garage, where Aaron spent hours lifting weights. He had a bench and secondhand dumbbells he used sometimes, but mostly he put on tiny nylon shorts—that even for a man of his fitness made Lacy shake her head—and did deadlifts. It clanged and shook the floor when a red-faced Aaron hoisted the bar to his chest, then overhead, and threw it down savagely on the concrete. Lacy popped out some evenings, after eight or nine impacts, to see him finish his set and drop his lifting gloves in a cardboard box of workout gear. He would look at her when she joined him. "It's not every man," he said once, breathing hard and giving her a deadly earnest stare. "Not every man can get that up."

Lacy headed straight to the box now and pulled out his gloves, bottles of protein powder, a notebook with *GOALS* written in Aaron's square script on the cover. She flipped through the journal, past clusters of weights and reps, and felt crazy. What was she looking for? *Answers*, her heart cried. Where was Aaron that minute? Fired? Since when? Where did he go every day? She shoved the box aside and went into the house. For hours Lacy combed through the newly foreign realms of their shared space, searching the medicine cabinet for suspicious items, nightstands, closets, every box of Aaron's dress shoes and the pockets of every suit. She toggled between crying and refusing to, because maybe nothing was wrong. The whole time she cursed Aaron's power to take the most real things in her life— their home and family—and make them feel unreal, as though they were incidental or imaginary.

She was tired when she got to his dresser and paused to look at the framed picture on top. It was a photo of Aaron getting his Purple Heart at the hospital in Saigon, with crutches hidden and soldiers discreetly propping him up. He was a kid, Lacy saw now, in the picture. When they met. "HR is a dynamic profession," he said to her the first time he changed jobs after they got married, and then said versions of it all the other times until she lost count. She plunged her hands in the drawers, through piles of white briefs and dark socks, and felt nothing strange buried within. "I give up," she sighed. How did she do it? Marry a man who lied and hid things, like her mother. The woman she spent her whole life getting away from, yet here she was digging through drawers like when she was a girl. Or maybe it was all in her mind.

Shutting the sock drawer, she caught sight of a paper corner sticking out from beneath Aaron's medal case. She tugged, and up came a new MasterCard bill with Aaron's name, a balance, over eleven thousand, and rows of purchases. Restaurants she had never heard of. A hundred here and there at Kay Jewelers. But mostly two recurring charges: cash advances every Tuesday, the day before she went grocery shopping, and every week a couple of charges for lodging at the Candlelight Inn. She shivered at the sense that her marriage wasn't what she thought. Not the loving fairy-tale destiny from one of her books. She and Aaron were molecules that randomly brushed under the right conditions, a perfect storm of loneliness and romance and war, now left to deal with the product of their reactants.

"Mommy?" Julian called. He stood in the doorway. "What are you doing?"

"Nothing." Lacy crossed her arms over the bill. "Cleaning." She followed Julian's eyes as they moved across the ransacked bedroom.

"What about Miss Bonnie?" he said. "Isn't it lunchtime?"

★

McNuggets, Lacy repeated in her head as she drove. *Chicken McNuggets.* She turned the car out of their subdivision onto Lake Houston Parkway, a long, piney cleanse of a road at the end of which lay a shopping center with Bonnie and fried food. Lacy had spent a lot of time trying not to think about them the last few months, but ever since these new McNuggets came along she experienced insane cravings for them, followed by guilt at the example she set for Julian. But on that day Lacy had other things not to think about, or talk about, or never, ever consider telling Bonnie about—unless she should tell her?

Bonnie was her best friend, though Lacy had never said those words. The first time they met was soon after Julian's lessons began and Lacy took him one muggy afternoon to the pool in Bonnie's nicer subdivision, where there was real landscaping and the plastic straps on the chaise lounges weren't broken. As they tanned beside each other—Lacy mostly covered in a sarong—Bonnie started chitchatting in her bendy bayou drawl. She was from Baton Rouge and taught English at Royalwood High, and Lacy was a teacher too, or had been before Julian was born and they moved out to the suburbs. Bonnie's boys were older than Julian, and whenever Lacy was with Bonnie she got a hint of something maternal, like her friend saw a younger mom and it made her happy.

Lacy confided things in Bonnie, secret stuff she never told anyone, and somehow it was OK. Within a week of their poolside conversations, she had shared the whole history of her sex life, beginning and ending with Aaron. How it stopped with the first miscarriage, like he broke her and she couldn't be fixed with any talking or touching, and having to beg for sex after that, tactically, in the words of motherhood and not just because she wanted it. How she tried to think rationally when they lost the second baby—a natural release of an unfit embryo—and resist the lure of signs. Fears their marriage could make nothing grow. After the two strikes, they only had sex on Lacy's birthday, she told Bonnie, the one day a year when Aaron approached her that way, pushing through it like he cleaned the storm gutters. Their efforts were brief and, following Julian, stopped for good. The irony settled on Lacy that the more Aaron starved her of sex, the bigger she got, and through all that happened—the grief, a hard pregnancy, forty unshakeable pounds—she learned to stop asking Aaron about sex and lots of other stuff.

"Why this again?" Julian crowed from the back seat. He had been humming quietly to himself on the drive to McDonald's—he could hum for hours, such a marvel in the car—but he suddenly started fidgeting against his big-boy car seat. "You said we were done with this thing."

"Sorry," she said, "I wanted you safe and—Golden Arches, here we are!" She checked the side mirror before turning into the parking lot. She saw in her reflection what she usually did around then: the heavy cheeks and round tortoiseshell glasses, her lustrous black hair starting to thin despite the textured bob meant to hide it. She tried smiling, but it looked more like an upset-stomach face.

The fried atmosphere enveloped her soothingly as they pushed inside. Bonnie waited at the back of the order area, cracking her nicotine gum and reading the menu with a look of focus. She had the sweet, labile face of a girl from Dr. Seuss, and permed corn-silk hair and a willowy frame. They both wore patterned legging-and-sweatshirt sets, but Bonnie was so lean that the clothes hugged and hung just right on her—like a pretty flapper mom, not the marshmallow profile Lacy cut.

"Hey, y'all," Bonnie called and hurried over to hug Lacy.

"Hi, Miss Bonnie," Julian said with exceeding poise.

"Do you know what you want, Julian?" Bonnie asked. "I'm buying today."

"Noooo," Lacy protested. "Why?"

"Happy Meal, please." Julian waved goodbye. "I'm off to the bathroom."

"Why?" Bonnie grinned. "We're celebrating your new job! I know what *you* want and I'm getting you the nine-piece and fries, no arguing. Go grab us a table, would you, hon?"

Lacy found a booth. She slid in but quickly discovered she couldn't be alone with her thoughts and got up. She moistened a wad of napkins and gave the table a series of increasingly intense wipe downs.

"You OK?" Lacy heard and turned around. Bonnie stood waiting with the tray of food. "The table's clean, but your color—it's like you saw a ghost. I noticed as soon as you got here."

"I'm fine." Lacy smiled with a dismissive shrug. She couldn't tell Bonnie about Aaron, she decided on the spot, because what did she know for sure at that point? Nothing. "How are you?" Lacy asked. "How are things at school, since . . ."

"This gum." Bonnie tossed her purse in the booth and set down the tray. "It's supposed to help me quit, but I'm wired. My students? Ever since last week it's like they forgot what I've been teaching them all year. I said it. Again. Today. Miss Bonnie's Cardinal Rule of Writing: do not start a sentence before you know how it ends. Same with paragraphs: don't write the topic sentence till you know the concluding sentence. But." She covered her face with her hands. "After what they saw."

"It's not your fault."

"How could anybody know?" Bonnie pleaded, dabbing her eyes with a napkin. "The whole school, every class watching live on TV when it caught fire and fell to pieces. The space shuttle! I didn't know what to say."

"Nobody did," Lacy murmured. For months she read everything about the upcoming launch, and then the *Challenger* exploded and nothing made sense. She devoured every word about Christa McAuliffe when the papers named the lucky teacher joining the shuttle crew. She envied her bitterly. Lacy Warner, with a master's in chemistry and knowledge of computing—who hauled her son down to Clear Lake for Space Camp—she was at home, but this teacher was going to space? Except that Julian still had a mom today, and the McAuliffe kids didn't. Lacy read that NASA engineers told their superiors about the very risk that caused the explosion, but the powers that be didn't escalate the call. And nothing made much sense.

"Well." Bonnie blew her nose, finishing with an angry pinch. "Between the *Challenger* and Reagan giving amnesty to the Mexicans, I don't know what the world's—They're saying he's gonna sign that bill! Anybody who's been here four years can stay, just show the receipt for the inner tube you floated over on, and if says '1982,' well, now you're a citizen. I swear you can't watch the news today without something terrible happening."

"The bathroom's clean!" Julian declared as he approached the table. "Toilets flushed. Towels in dispensers. I give it a seven."

"That's a better score than Applebee's last week," Bonnie said, "isn't it?"

"Ugh," Julian recoiled at the memory. "The floor was so sticky it made noise." He scrambled into the booth next to Lacy and opened his Happy Meal.

"What do we say?" Lacy asked.

"Thank you, Miss Bonnie," he recited through a mouthful of fries.

"Today's about good news." Bonnie sinuously unwrapped her fish filet, took a bite, and got a down-to-business look on her face. "You know the principal loves me. And I reminded him what a fancy new teacher he's getting, used to work at St. John's Episcopal downtown and so on and so forth, and he better treat her right."

"Thank you," Lacy said.

"Oh, if you only knew the old geezer you're replacing? You tell him to find something on the periodic table and it's like pin the tail on the donkey. Anyways, the principal's giving you the three-year tenure contract"—Bonnie beamed—"and the district isn't handing those out much anymore. He'll call you later today."

Lacy sat back while her friend rambled on about the tenure system and health insurance plan. Her mind wandered to the first time Bonnie suggested she go back to work. It had dredged up unexpected feelings in Lacy—about not getting her PhD, taking the easy road spooning out high school science—but over time, with each of Julian's lessons, her doubts diminished. She was the mother of a gifted child, witness to the miraculous possibility of one human to shape another. And it was teaching, after all, that made her rethink being a mom. Nervous as she was starting out at St. John's, she saw a few girls awaken to chemistry on her watch—and then they left, and the next ones left, and she started wondering what it would be like to have a baby that was just hers. So, yes, she told Bonnie about a year after her friend broached the idea, she might go back to teaching at some point. But as Lacy dunked her third McNugget in barbecue sauce that day, thoughts of her career were dwarfed by the planetary weight of newer questions. Did she have a partner at home? Was she going back to work just to throw money down a bottomless pit named Aaron? What other future was there?

"And that's the whole deal," Bonnie finished, smiling with a hint of confusion in her eyes. She waited. "Well, don't look so happy! It's what you wanted, isn't it?"

"Yes," Lacy said, sitting up straight. "Sorry. I'm a little tired today."

Julian finished his first phase of eating and crawled under the table to Bonnie's side. "What do we have here?" she cried and pulled him onto her lap. "You want a Pound Puppy?" Bonnie was a collector of various toy memorabilia, samples of which she hooked to her purse strap—one of many cool teacher notes she hit like a pro.

"No, Rubik's cube."

"My Rubik's key chain? OK." Bonnie dropped it in Julian's greedy hands. "You got two minutes to solve that." She studied

Lacy's face. "Don't apologize. I get it. After five years together at home, it's hard to say goodbye to your little Einstein. Sad. Headphones for Julian, incoming!" Bonnie flew her hands around his head and pressed them to his ears. "He may have some issues separating," she said softly, "but he'll be fine. Maybe he won't, who knows?" She lowered her hands from Julian's ears. "But there's whole chapters of your life you haven't seen yet, Lacy. I promise. I've been there. And I think—" Bonnie patted her friend's hand and continued in a confidential tone. "It's good for us girls to make our own money. You know?"

"Sure."

"How's Aaron?" Bonnie asked.

"Fine. How's Bill?"

"Fine. Traveling, always traveling. He was home two days last week, and I said to him, 'If you're just the accountant, why does Shell have to send *you* to Venezuela and Saudi Arabia and everywhere else?' But the job's the job."

Bonnie carefully lifted a fry to her mouth without disturbing Julian. Lacy took in the whole picture—her generous friend and her son placidly turning the cube—and her heart nearly burst with love and grief at the secret she kept. "Yeah." Lacy sighed. "The job's the job."

★

Lacy waved goodbye as Bonnie got in her Camry and reversed, and kept waving until her friend had pulled onto the parkway out of sight. "Come on," she said to Julian and held his hand while they walked to a pay phone at the 7-Eleven next door. She pulled out the metal-bound yellow pages attached to the booth. "Can you be a tree?" she asked. "Put your arms up?" She set the book on Julian's hands and flipped to Hotels, scanning with her finger until she found the one she was looking for. She scrounged in her purse for a quarter and dialed.

"Candlelight Inn," said a low scratchy voice.

"Oh," Lacy fumbled as though she was the one who got called. "Are, y'all open?"

"It's a hotel, ma'am, we're open twenty-four hours."

"Yes, I guess! And if—how would I get there, going down 59?"

"Take the Tidwell Road exit, make your first right. There's a big sign."

"That's easy! Then we'll—I will be there soon."

Lacy strapped Julian in the car seat and drove, past the green medians of Royalwood and onto the highway headed south. As they passed the strip malls in Humble, she saw the Fingers Furniture where they bought their first bedroom set, when they left the apartment on Westheimer for the suburbs. Lacy always wanted a brass bed, she told Aaron, but it cost more so they went with the pine set he liked. And what did a bed matter, she thought as she paid for it, when they had a child? Who cared about saying goodbye to city life, and moving to the cookie-cutter whitest place on earth, if Aaron thought the best schools were out there? He was focused on their son, the future, and everything after would be more loving.

It had dawned on Lacy, when lunch with Bonnie was winding down, that she might go crazy if she tried to carry on with her day as usual. So she hit the road with a destination and no plan. Had she never thought Aaron was cheating, in a five-year sex drought? Could she deny, during Julian's subtraction lessons, that she tallied the pros and cons of their marriage, with her thumb pressed habitually on the pros? Like how she never had to pick up after Aaron, who was so tidy? Or when her skin would crawl at the St. John's faculty parties, how Aaron taught her to make small talk without feeling fake, and laugh off the slights she was so prone to see in the words of others? No marriage was perfect, but theirs worked. They had their TV shows, and they went to the movies on Saturdays—*Weird Science* for her, those *Police Academies* for him—and laughed and repeated the best lines for days.

But this was too much, Lacy thought, and pressed her foot on the gas. The rows of CANDLELIGHT INN on the bill had seared her brain. She needed answers. She would summon her best Loretta Lynn and carry Julian through the inn like a woman whose man would not be taken. She'd set him on a plush chair, tell him to look for shapes in the crystal chandelier above, and approach the tuxedoed concierge. He'd be slick, hair slicked like the rat enabler he was, and feign ignorance when Lacy asked if he'd seen the man in the picture she took from her wallet. *When you do see him*, Lacy would reply and point at Julian, *tell him you're taking that boy's college money as you deliver that champagne.*

Lacy was startled from her planning by a sign for the exit a mile away. She looked at the feeder road and, with a wrenching sense of déjà vu, knew exactly where they were. It was a part of 59 just before the loop that Aaron and Lacy joked about when they went downtown. There was a megachurch, followed by a strip club, then another church and strip club all in a row, a jarring ode to the city that would not zone. "Sin-Repent-Repeat," Aaron named it one day when they were taking baby Julian to his first Oilers game, and they chanted it every time they passed by even after Julian started talking. In this wasteland, the butt of their private joke, Lacy noticed for the first time a gray billboard for the Candlelight Inn with an arrow pointing to the exit.

It was easy to find and nothing like she pictured. The block was full of potholes and strewn with trash. Lacy parked down the street and scrunched low in her seat. When she peered out the window, it wasn't a romantic inn she saw but a fleabag motel. Gray shingles, black with mold in spots, a slide-open cashier's window with security bars, and a pink neon VACANCY sign flashing above. The place looked empty except for a scrawny woman in cutoffs struggling with the door of an ice machine in the parking lot.

Why had she imagined chandeliers? To gild the sordidness? Because of the enormous balance on the MasterCard—built up over years, it now seemed, blown in a dump like this—or was it something deeper and more messed up about her? A black man emerged from the motel and berated the woman in cutoffs, who skittered into a room. Lacy hadn't thought of the motel man as black. He didn't sound black on the phone. She winced, thinking of her mother—how she spoke of people in generalizations, especially Mexicans, and how Lacy had to teach her own child to think critically. From some pocket of her mind floated the memory of a black man in Aaron's company in Vietnam—Williams, she thought, but she never met him— and his pretty fiancé, who passed Aaron's address through her dorm room door years ago.

"This isn't the grocery store," Julian observed behind her.

"No." Lacy sat up and turned the ignition. "We're going a different way today." She scolded herself brutally as she got back on the highway. She had endangered her son, lost track of the one soul who was never out of her mind, not for a minute since he was born. But there he sat in the back seat, a sponge soaking up the air of vice, prop to some vague revenge fantasy of hers. "Jules," she said, "name the five kingdoms of life." The whole drive back she quizzed him on biology, amping up her voice with praise and speeding like a NASCAR veteran.

When they reached the main entrance to their suburb, Julian craned his neck to see. It was marked by a wooden welcome pillar emerging from a man-made turquoise lake, with the community's logo of trees and deer and the motto beneath: ROYAL-WOOD—A LIVABLE FOREST.

"Home sweet home," Julian sang.

Lacy's eyes welled up. It was three o'clock. She couldn't go home. There was something toxic inside her that she couldn't say to Bonnie or the motel guy but also couldn't keep inside without imploding. Up the block she saw the stone spires of St. Martha's, the prettiest church in Royalwood and the only building in the suburb that looked remotely royal.

"Just one more errand," she said and turned into the church parking lot.

It was dim and smelled of incense when Lacy and Julian entered. She smiled at an old woman in the lobby and asked, softly in her ear, if it was a good time for a confession-type thing. The woman furrowed her brow, trying to place Lacy, and said Lacy should take her time while she and Julian had a tour of the organ, and maybe he could guess the number of pipes in it.

"OK," Julian said after getting the nod from Lacy. "Is there candy if I get it right?" he asked as the woman led him into the sanctuary. "My mom teaches me. I'm pretty smart."

Lacy followed them in. She approached the carved wooden box at the far end, a cross between a phone booth and retro time machine. She drew back a maroon curtain and sat down inside. She waited. She thought of a rosary she'd found as a girl, and felt afresh a guilt she had carried with her since that time—a sense that she'd harmed the foreman on her dad's farm, Xavier, got him deported without meaning to. She wondered if her marriage was some cosmic payback for that sin, or some sin of her mother's, who turned away her family when a man came to their door. A shadow flickered across the grate in the booth. She waited for something to happen.

There came an irritable sigh and a deep voice: "My child?"

"Yes?" Lacy whispered.

"Do you seek forgiveness for your sins?"

She knew some words to say from TV confessions, but her

gut told her honesty was the best policy. "I need someone to talk to. Someone to listen."

"About what, daughter?"

It was the priest's warm tone, or the rush she got at his fatherly diminutives, and though she wasn't sure she could even speak the words, Lacy opened her mouth and out they tumbled: "Someone's been calling our house but won't talk. I found a credit card bill of my husband's. I think he's having an affair. Not for the first time, or maybe one for a long time, I don't know. I think he lost his job again. We're in debt. He's lying to me, about all of it." She squeezed her eyes shut to keep from crying.

"You are being tested as Job was."

"I'm so ashamed," Lacy mumbled at the grate.

"Does your husband come to services with you?"

"Services?"

"Here at the church."

"No," Lacy said. "We don't—No, he doesn't."

"You let him stray? We must bring him back."

"OK." Lacy didn't know how they got there, or what to say.

"If he has sinned he will need his flock around him, to guide him."

"But. What about me?"

"You," the priest replied, "play the biggest role in his salvation."

"I don't mean about his—He betrayed me and our marriage and son. Am I supposed to keep sleeping next to him?" She could hear her voice rising. "Living with him? Just forgive and forget, and he'll keep doing whatever he wants?"

"You don't think of dissolving the union, surely. You have a son? Think of him. A broken home that will shape his character for life?"

"Yes," Lacy said haltingly, "but if it weren't for Julian I—It's for him. Partly. He needs a stable home where there isn't—"

"A stable home has a mother and father. You're a wife and mother. These are the roles God has chosen for you, and the challenges He presents for a reason."

"But." Lacy pressed her hands against the sides of the booth. "That doesn't make sense. It's not fair."

"You came to speak to God. The Almighty speaks to you through me. Trust in His plan. I hear the kindness in your voice and know God loves you. Think of this when you go home today and see your husband. Ask yourself: where will you ever find a greater love than His?"

★

On the drive home Lacy talked a mile a minute. She told Julian how he charmed the old lady at the church. He was so polite, the woman reported to Lacy when they met back in the lobby, and could you believe after he guessed within ten the number of pipes—a record!—and she offered him a candy, Julian said, "No, thank you, ma'am, the organ was enough of a treat."

"Butterscotch is gross," Julian announced tensely from the back seat. "What about the grocery store?" he asked as they turned onto their block.

"Tomorrow." She parked in the driveway. "You want pizza tonight?"

His face lit up with cautious wonder. "But. It's not— Saturday?"

"Pizza tonight—*if*. Nap time now. One hour. No books, no phone."

"OK," he said. "I just have to check my messages first."

Inside Julian shuffled to his room. She stood in the foyer, surveying the three-bedroom two-bath owned by Aaron and Lacy Warner as tenants in common. She plopped on the couch and shut her eyes, so tired of seeing. Defiantly she seized on a new thought, a true memory of Aaron from years ago. It was

Halloween night, after the second miscarriage, and he said they didn't need trick-or-treaters knocking, so he took her to the Shepherd Drive-In for a sci-fi double feature, and bought popcorn and held her hand through *Close Encounters* and *The Andromeda Strain*. For a few hours she lost herself in the pull of stories, with Aaron by her side. And maybe the priest scared her that afternoon, she thought, maybe fear had made her stupid, but what if it wasn't just delusions that kept her with Aaron for this long? He knew how to care for her in her darkest hour, a care he never learned from his own parents. She had seen it. The moment she spotted him in the crowd at UT? The one person to show up for her graduation? She had no rhyme or reason for it, knew he'd never be consistent one day to the next. But there was good in him to root for, wasn't there? Worth working at, for everybody's sake?

She sat up straight on the couch. She needed something, Bonnie's gum or a stiff drink. Soon Aaron would return from wherever he went. She didn't know how to look at the beautiful stranger she once felt so lucky to marry. She flipped on the TV. It was local news, a city councilman screaming about Reagan and amnesty and illegals coming out of the woodwork, all of them criminals and rapists. Quietly Lacy started to cry. About how cruel people were, and about the many things she didn't know. Like when her mom crossed over into Texas, or how, or what she dreamed she'd find. Or her best friend's views on Mexicans, unknown to her until lunch that day. It felt so unkind, she wanted to go out in the street and scream *No!* to the sky. But who was she? A mom in the middle-of-nowhere suburbs. Wasn't her first duty to her child? To raise him, not fix the world? What if they never moved here, she thought, what if St. John's gave faculty kids free tuition and they never left the city and things were different? Lacy and Aaron had promised each other once, the day they married, never to bring a child into the world only to leave him alone. And here she sat crying, imagining terrible new solitary futures.

"Are you sad?" she heard a whisper. Julian stood timidly in the hallway, peering into the living room with his toy phone cradled in his arms.

"I'm OK!" Lacy replied, too loud, wiping her eyes. "Are you sad, Jules? What do you do when you're sad?"

"I call my mommy." He watched her. "You should call your mommy."

"My mommy is hard to reach."

"Call me. Brrring-brrring!" Julian crossed the room and handed her the red receiver.

"Hello, Lacy Warner. Who is this?"

"It's Julian. Why are you sad?"

She watched him, her greatest creation and the love of her life. She remembered the moment she saw him in the hospital, shrieking and wet and alive. A shot of absolution and pure joy, as strong as a drug. "Well." Lacy felt a tear crawl down her cheek. And without a sense of where she was headed, she broke Miss Bonnie's Cardinal Rule of Writing and said, "Well, Jules, it's about your daddy."

5

The Dragon's Egg

There were few events Aaron loathed more than the Saturday each fall when he carted his family to the Texas Renaissance Festival. It had the awful inevitability of tax day mingled with the quiet embarrassment, since he turned forty, of a prostate exam. Every year around mid-September the Warner house trilled with terrible British accents as Lacy and Julian mentally prepared for the outing, swapping "cheerio"s and "pass the sowlt"s and the occasional random "g'day, mate." Aaron remained mute to these provocations. "Speak English," he would say when he hit his limit, "no, American English," until his wife and son stopped bothering him altogether and treated him like the third wheel and driver on their Renaissance date.

But this year was different. The day arrived and Aaron felt good. When he steered the family minivan out of Royalwood, not a thing could spoil his mood. Not the accents, or Lacy's big peasant blouse, not the loud plan of attack she and Julian were brainstorming over a preordered map of the festival grounds. None of it could drag him down because this year he had Crystal on the brain.

It didn't strike Aaron as ironic, while he drove, that the route to the festival was the same one he took to see his girlfriend.

If that's what Crystal was. Mistress, side piece—he didn't talk about her to anyone, so he'd never put her into words. Aaron pretended he was heading to her place as they passed the Hot Biscuit Diner and other familiar sites on 99, and the pretending made him smile. He knew a point would come when he had to turn the van toward the festival, while his heart would keep fluttering up I-45 to her. But he trusted in the image of Crystal at the fridge in zebra panties to keep him at attention the whole day through.

"And what would *you* like to see?" Lacy asked. She had stopped gabbing with Julian in the back seat and turned to face Aaron. "At the RenFest?"

"Y'all are the experts," he replied. "Don't want to mess up the plans."

"We have plenty of time," she said with a soft hint of resignation. She patted his hand on the gearshift. "So?"

Aaron nodded. Sometimes his wife touched him and it felt like a hand reaching from a crypt or raw meat. He never winced or pulled away, just nodded, and it usually helped. There was a deep-dish pizza Aaron ate at the festival every year that he hadn't found anywhere else, despite some looking. "Lunch," he said. "When do y'all want to eat?"

Lacy sighed. "Twelve. One. I don't know." She shut her eyes and conjured an epic silence, as though the day was pre-ruined courtesy of Aaron. "The court jesters!" she cried, and whirled around to the back seat. "We forgot the comedy show."

"Omigod," Julian chirped in his girliest tweenage voice. "This changes everything."

Aaron nodded at the road ahead.

★

The festival grounds always impressed Aaron. Gray stucco walls with muscular turrets, a real-looking drawbridge out front, the pine-scented acres inside done up like an old village with dirt paths and thatched-roof cottages—it was truly something to look at. And for a moment as he neared the entrance, the majesty of its construction distracted Aaron from the loser freaks they were about to encounter in droves.

"This way!" Lacy cried, and the Warners plunged into the dense human river flowing through the grounds. It was the usual mix. Grown-up drama club rejects decked out in costume, kids in black with pierced noses and mascara, leering for maximum effect as they passed, a few Asian tourists taking pictures. Through the moving bodies Aaron monitored Julian going in and out of sight ahead of him. On the drive over Lacy instructed them to watch for her Wonder Woman hand fan if they lost visual contact, and Aaron saw it shoot up over the crowd and gesture at the sign of a cottage, THY KINGDOM'S CLAY.

He followed Julian into the dim cottage. It was packed with fairies, gnomes, and other ceramic doodads, and a crystal ball in the middle where Aaron saw his distorted reflection come and go. Lacy was ogling something in a display case by the counter. Right away Aaron knew the drill. The festival had shows and food, but it was really a shopping mall in the woods, and every year the same Lacy who brought a Ziploc of coupons to Safeway would splurge on a big-ticket item—a giant bubble wand or the dulcimer she strummed once at Christmas. But no purchase could ever be consummated without the husband-wife dance first. Oh, she couldn't possibly buy it, she would say for the whole shop to hear, until Aaron insisted she had to and he was going to buy it for her, which she always refused just sharply enough to remind Aaron he wasn't much of a contributor to their household, before she bought it herself.

"A work of art," Lacy whispered to Julian, pointing at the case. "Can you take that one out?" she asked the shopkeeper.

"What're you looking at?" Aaron asked, coming up behind them.

"The dragon's egg," Julian said in a hushed voice.

The shopkeeper laid down a purple velvet cloth and set the sculpture on the counter. It was a dark blue-green ceramic egg the size of a football. At one end the shell was cracked, and a terra cotta dragon's tail and hind leg were pushing out of it, emerging into the world in scaly, taloned glory. Lacy ran her fingertips along the shell and turned the price tag. She flinched. "No," she murmured, "lovely, but no." She shook her head and said loudly in the shopkeeper's direction, "I wish, but there's just—no—way!"

Julian let out a sigh of support. Aaron knew his cue. But the sunny new Aaron—the one with Crystal on his mind and proverbial fingers—decided it was time for a new move in their money politics.

"Nice egg," he said, and said no more.

Lacy watched him. Aaron nodded vaguely at it. She waited; he nodded.

"Y'all come back anytime," said the shopkeeper, bringing the silent standoff to a close. "We're open till eight."

Lacy didn't look at Aaron as she went out the door. And something changed in her browsing after that. The rest of the morning, when she and Julian would have normally plunged into one cottage after another, Lacy glanced absently from the path and barely touched the wares. She didn't stick her hands in the Merlin and Arthur puppets or tickle the wind chimes into song. By the time they finished their initial loop and reached the food stalls, Lacy seemed preoccupied and restless.

"Over there!" Aaron seized the moment and pointed at an open table and chairs. "Grab those. Let me guess: turkey leg for mom, chicken fingers for Jules?"

"I'll get lunch," Lacy objected in surprise.

"Nope," he said. "Go get those seats. I'll be back."

The past few years Lacy always bought lunch, and Aaron liked flipping the script again. He got in line for food, inching up the field of trampled grass and pine needles and squinting to see if it was the same line for beer. This was why Crystal was good for his family, he thought as he waited. He'd had terrible bosses at every job, real bad luck, and he couldn't deal with them for longer than six months or so before he had to move on. His current boss was no exception—John the Baptist, Lacy nicknamed him, always pushing his megachurch on everybody in HR—but Aaron had kept this job for more than a year, and it was all because of Crystal. If he didn't have to travel around laying off folks when a Texaco field ran dry, he wouldn't have an excuse to go see her. So Aaron was providing for his family like never before, paycheck after paycheck, working down his debts, shrinking his affairs to one girl—Crystal, at the fridge—and feeling more alive than he could remember.

"Lunch is served," he said, arriving at their table. He smiled at Lacy, and as he passed her a weapon-size turkey leg he had a revelation: he was buying her that egg, and there was nothing she could do about it.

When they finished eating, Lacy stacked the food containers and Julian spread out the festival map. "The afternoon joust starts in twenty minutes," Lacy instructed, tracing her finger along a cartoon path. "This is probably the fastest route from here."

"You mind heading over solo?" Aaron asked. "Me and Jules have something to do first, but we'll meet you there." Lacy and Julian stared across the table at him in blank unison. "It's a surprise," he said.

"Allllright," Lacy eked out with suspicion. She nodded at Julian, whose face had gathered every drop of twelve-year-old outrage within him. "How long do you think it'll take y'all?"

"Ten, fifteen minutes, tops. Save us seats. Come on, Jules."

"I'll be near the front," Lacy called as Aaron hustled them out of the food court.

"What are we doing?" Julian asked sullenly, slowing down to walk behind Aaron.

"I'm buying your mom that egg she liked. So? How's school?"

"Fine."

"Fine?"

"Can I get something, too?" Julian asked.

"Yeah."

"I got a ninety-five on my algebra test and a hundred on my vocab quiz, and my world history teacher said my poster was the best in the class, and . . ."

Julian recited his accomplishments like a tubby Energizer bunny while Aaron retraced their steps to the shop. There were things about his son that only allowed Aaron to listen or look for so long—the high voice, the love handles and boy tits, or the way he swung his hips. Still, he didn't agree with Crystal's view of things. The last time they met she dropped a bomb on Aaron and said she wanted a baby with him. And when he shook his head at the idea, Crystal unloaded her theory of his family: Lacy holding Aaron hostage in their marriage with the miscarriages, years of Lacy grieving, baby crazy, pregnant again, then the whole thing on repeat until Julian was born, and if Aaron didn't want a kid with Crystal it was because he was too beat down by Julian not being the kid he wanted—a real red-blooded boy—so why was he closing his mind to the other boy he might have someday?

"Good, Jules," Aaron interrupted his son's monologue at no particular juncture. "Sounds like you're at the top of your game."

"Well," Julian informed him, "being valedictorian as a stepping-stone to Harvard is a plan that starts in junior high. Or else it's simply too late."

And this was something Crystal didn't get. His son was the smartest kid Aaron had ever seen, and Julian brought plenty of smart friends home. He had given his son a good school in a good suburb, where a few kids went off to the Ivies every year. Julian was growing up around flower beds and oil money, not panhandle dust and white trash like Aaron, and his son would get out and go even further in life with a mind like his. If the world didn't fuck him up first. So, yeah, Crystal was sexy and let him be the man he couldn't be with Lacy, and it was great. But Crystal was a single woman, and before she started demanding babies she had to understand that families are complicated.

"Here we go," Aaron said. He opened the shop door and guided Julian inside. As they were entering, Aaron noticed a couple watching them strangely from a women's clothing shop next door—a rough guy with full-sleeve tattoos, and a grizzled Stevie Nicks type smoking a cigarette.

"Hello again!" Aaron called to the shopkeeper.

"I thought I might see you later," the man said, scratching under his ponytail.

"That's one irresistible egg," Aaron smiled and turned on the charm for Julian's benefit. "How much is it gonna set me back?"

"*Birth*?" said the shopkeeper.

"What?"

"*Birth* is the name of the piece. The dragon?"

"That one there." Aaron pointed at the case.

"Originally three hundred, but I'll give it to you for two fifty."

"Let's do it." Aaron whipped out his Visa. "Jules?" he called and waved him over. Julian was studying a group of mermaids, but he needed to watch his dad in action: presenting the card, the growl of the carbon-copy machine rolling over it, the signature and gift wrapping. This was learning.

"Sorry," the shopkeeper said, rummaging under the counter,

"I can't find my machine. One sec." He disappeared behind a curtain.

Julian sighed dramatically. "I'm going outside."

"Hang on. He'll be right back."

"Mom liked the egg. You're buying it. Big deal." Julian rolled his eyes, threw open the door, and sauntered out.

"Hey," Aaron shouted, "shut that! There's AC in here." An infuriating wave hit Aaron, of Julian's willfulness and all that it triggered. The way his son thrived on Lacy alone, leaving no role for him. The way one glance or word from Julian could twist every good quality of his son's from a reflection of the father into his negation.

"Found it," the shopkeeper said, popping out from behind the curtain. "I'll box this up and get you out of here."

"You like working these festivals?" Aaron asked.

"I've got a studio in Nacogdoches. And the RenFest—it's good money fast."

"I don't know why folks come to these," Aaron mumbled.

"Make-believe, you know. Go somewhere else. Be somebody else."

"I guess." Aaron sighed. He heard a tiny primal sound that his ear alone picked up. Julian in distress. "*Stop!*" Aaron heard again through the open cottage door. He dashed outside to see his son being mauled by the tattooed guy next door. Julian was covered in pale netting and ribbons as the man grabbed violently at his head. They turned, struggling, and Julian saw Aaron.

"Dad?!" he screeched, his voice as piercing as his infant cry.

"Get off him!" Aaron bellowed, and shoved the man into the path. He grabbed Julian and pulled him against his hip. "What the hell is the matter with you?"

"That faggot was trying on my wife's veils!" the man yelled back, unrelenting. "Posing in the mirror, blowing kisses like a little bitch." He aimed a finger at Julian. "*Bridal* veils. For *girls*. Not faggots."

"He's a kid!" Aaron shouted. People had gathered and were watching. Whose side they were on Aaron couldn't tell. He grabbed Julian by the arm and tore off down the path.

★

It took Lacy the rest of the weekend to decide where to put the egg in the house. Her first instinct was somewhere private, to protect it, so she set it on the mantel of the faux fireplace across from their bed. She tried the top of her dresser and other places in the bedroom. She would leave the egg in a spot and go do chores, to cleanse her eye palate, and each time she returned she got the same joyful rush as when she first discovered it. The moment she saw it in the shop she had a flashback to reading the Dragonriders books as a teen—the memory of young Lessa approaching her hatchling, and the bond that forms between rider and dragon, a lifelong telepathic bond that will save humankind. It was during one of these dragon reveries, while Lacy did laundry, that she changed her mind about the egg. It couldn't be kept private. It had to be in the living room on the coffee table, where guests could be inspired by its magic. And on Sunday night, in a ceremony of one, she put it there for good.

Other thoughts crept into Lacy's head as the week wore on. More than once at school, while lecturing a drowsy classroom on covalent bonds, she found herself playing back snippets from the RenFest. Something had been off about Aaron, in the shop and at lunch. It wasn't like Lacy didn't want a husband who provided; she'd been cursing his financial failures since they married. But after getting cheated on and sponged off of for so many years, Lacy at least knew where she stood when she was the one buying things. Was the egg about Aaron's pride in having his own money, or was he feeling guilty about some new woman? She couldn't say. In her head she repeated the mantra that kept her pride half-intact: she was strong, could handle anything for Julian's sake, but the day Aaron hurt their son? The end.

Aaron was still acting weird when he sat down to dinner later that week. He barely gave Lacy their usual show-peck and didn't look Julian's way at all. He talked rapid-fire nonsense about work when Lacy asked how his day was, only stopping to breathe after he spilled a pile of Hamburger Helper on the table. "I was thinking," he said, slower, while Lacy rounded up the mess in a paper towel. "It was nice being outdoors last weekend, wasn't it?"

"Weather was good," Lacy called from the trash can.

"How about a camp for Jules?"

"Like summer camp?" Julian perked up. "There's a high school debate camp at Baylor that accepts middle schoolers, and it's kinda sorta expensive but totally—"

"Not summer," Aaron corrected. "We don't have to wait till summer. A getaway camp on long weekends. Fresh air. Columbus Day weekend, maybe?"

"But with his activities?" Lacy sat down and rubbed her eyes to think. "Speech and debate Fridays, symphonic band and—do you have piano that Monday, Jules? *On* the holiday?"

"Well," Aaron said, louder. He reached into his briefcase and produced a pamphlet with a gold cross on the cover. "I saw this and thought it might be nice."

"What is that?" Lacy snatched it from him.

"What kind of camp?" Julian asked cautiously.

"It's a Christian camp," Aaron began, "where they teach young men Christian—"

"Where did you get this?" Lacy asked. She could feel Julian's stare on her.

"Someone at work."

"Did John the Baptist give you this?"

"He did," Aaron said with intensifying diction. "John, my boss, thought Julian might enjoy it there."

"Why was your boss thinking anything about—" But before Lacy could finish, disturbing scenarios flooded her mind. She folded the pamphlet in half and pocketed it. "We'll talk later," she said softly to Aaron.

"Let's read the materials," he persisted. "We're all here."

"*Later.*" She put a smile on for Julian. "Tell us more about this Baylor camp!"

"It's six weeks," he mumbled. But it was too late. Lacy watched her son's eyes lose their sharpness and his neck wilt forward. "I'm full," he said to no one. "May I be excused?"

"Sure, sweetie," she said. "Clear your plate." She could tell Aaron was itching to talk, but she refused to look at him until she heard Julian's door close.

"I think you're overreacting, Lacy."

"I'll talk to you," she said with quiet purpose, "in the bedroom, when I'm done cleaning up the kitchen."

"I'll help," he said, rising with his plate. "Pass me that bowl over—"

"I don't need your help."

Lacy went to the sink and rinsed the dishes, on edge until she heard the creak of the bed and Aaron flipping on the TV. The faucet wouldn't get hot enough, or maybe she needed it to scald her out of the fog enveloping her mind. What to say to Aaron? She didn't believe in enemies, but she was living with one. A man who could think of sending their baby to the woods to be changed? Did Aaron think it was easy for her? How many hours had she tried to reason like a scientist about the evolutionary basis for homosexuality, supplemental caregivers for the clan and so on? Or all the times she held her tongue and didn't talk about Jules being a father someday, so he wouldn't feel pressured or abnormal? But in the end she didn't need Darwin to justify what her heart knew. Julian was growing before their eyes, the rarest light in a terrible world, and while she breathed no one would put out his candle.

Lacy waited in the bedroom doorway, thumbs tucked in the waistband of her sweatpants, until Aaron noticed and muted the TV. "I know about those camps," she said, shutting the door behind her. "Don't pretend you don't."

"We always said we wanted to expose Julian to ideas, right?" Aaron sat up and leaned toward her at a supportive angle. "Here we could expose him to—"

"I have something to say." She steadied her voice and looked him square in the face. "I used to believe you loved him enough to put aside fitting in and people's opinions, for what he needed. But I was wrong about you—"

"Fitting in? He could've killed him, Lacy! Get off your high horse."

"What are you talking about? Killed who?"

"At the festival," Aaron muttered. "A guy grabbed Julian and shook him—"

"Someone touched Jules?"

"I didn't want to have to tell you."

"Who? Why?"

"He tried on this girls' head thing and the shop guy ripped it off him."

"Where were you?" Lacy charged toward the bed. "You left him alone?"

"He walked out while I was paying."

"And you weren't planning on telling me? Was he hurt? *Julian?*" she called.

"Leave him be."

"You said you got in a fight and that's why he was quiet the rest of the day."

"We did. Before that."

"Before our son was attacked? Anything else you left out, Aaron? Why was he alone?"

"I wasn't there. Neither were you. We can't be there every minute every day." He rose from the bed and dropped his voice. "You didn't see that scumbag call Julian a faggot while the crowd watched. He wanted to kill him. I saw it in his eyes. He's not the only one out there like that. We've got to toughen up Julian, or else . . ."

She hid her face in her hands.

"Lace," he said softly.

"Not that camp."

"Are you hearing a word I'm saying?"

"That's a different way of killing him."

"What then? What's in your bag of ideas?"

"He's not going anywhere." She shook her head grimly. "It's not happening."

"Fine." Aaron gave an angry shrug. "Sports. He could use some exercise. He's been getting a little . . ." He looked her body up and down and finished the thought.

"Fine." Her eyes watered at his ludicrous timing. "He likes swimming."

"Football."

"No. Too dangerous."

"He needs a real team sport. He needs to be around other boys, not—"

"Me?" she said.

"Those band girls he's always running around with."

"And me."

"Well. You think it helps with the movies you take him to see?"

"What movies?"

"The, the AIDS—*Philadelphia*?"

"That's Tom Hanks," she cried. "So this is my fault?"

"I'm not saying it's anybody's fault."

"Because there's nothing wrong with Julian. Is there." She waited. Aaron stared at the floor. "*Is there*," she repeated.

"Soccer. It's safer than football. A lot of running. It'll be good for him."

"Soccer?" Lacy took a breath, but the teacher who never blinked at the crudest behavior from her sophomores suddenly found she had nothing to say. She watched him, the father of her son, before going into the bathroom. She locked the door, and ran the faucet, and cried.

★

Lacy couldn't sleep that night. Neither could Aaron, apparently, and it was past one before his snoring picked up behind her. She got metaphysical like she did lying awake in the dark, asking the big questions. How had she done it for twenty-odd years? How does anybody sleep beside a liar? By living separate lives, she figured, with their backs to each other and the focus somewhere else.

Ever since Bonnie coaxed her back to teaching and got her the job at the high school, Lacy's world had grown. She was a cool no-BS teacher, one who kids came back to visit. And the kids? From around the world now—India and China and Korea—because the suburb was changing. She listened to their histories, asking how they got from there to Texas, and tried to make them believe they could do anything. The way Bonnie told her that her own life had a next chapter. At times it struck Lacy that the new kids were mostly the "good immigrants"—as their principal said—not the Hispanic or black ones filling up crumbling schools a half hour south on 59, and Lacy suspected larger forces at work. But she tried to do good where she was. Like last week, when she had enough of the chatter in the teachers' lounge—"Why do the Mexicans need algebra to push a lawnmower?"—and Kim Powter from Math said, "Isn't it funny how black kids have fancy names like presidents, like Jefferson?" Lacy smiled and replied, "So you think Thomas Jefferson *didn't* have black kids?" And sure Kim was still trash-talking Lacy, and Bonnie had to run damage control, but Lacy hadn't felt so alive in years. Grown. Standing her ground. A farm girl who learned right and wrong in church and then became an atheist. That's how she slept at night, worried over lesson plans but sensing the fullness of her life, too.

Aaron's snoring crested. Lacy thought of Lorena Bobbitt on the talk shows, the respect she had for that nighttime snip—unthinkable, yet so simple. Bonnie had given her the number for a lawyer years ago, when Lacy broke down and talked about Aaron's affairs. She dreamed of calling it sometimes. Some nights she dreamed of the Mexican man who came to their house when she was a girl, and her mom let him in, and in the dream she married a man with black hair. Lacy kept the lawyer's card tucked away in her purse but never called. Because every time divorce crossed her mind, her mother's voice echoed after it, and though their bond was dead before her mom was, she could hear her from the grave saying, *What did you expect from a man if you let yourself go like that?*

★

The next morning, when Julian saw his mom and dad smiling at him from the kitchen table, it was like that episode from *The Twilight Zone* where the boy's parents get replaced by droids that talk like real people but aren't. His mom slid two extra Eggo waffles on his plate, and as soon as he sat down his dad gave a speech about the wonders of sports, and some guy Pelé, and how he—Julian—would be trying out for the soccer team in a few weeks. He looked at his mom to make sense of the bizarro things coming out of his dad's mouth, but she nodded and smiled like a robot.

"And," his dad finished, "to get ready for tryouts, we're building a soccer goal in the backyard this weekend, so you can practice."

"Oh," his mom said, scrunching her face, "we didn't, uh-hh—"

"A little project," he mumbled. "PVC, miter saw, easy. So"—he gave Julian a serious look—"you're making your first trip to Home Depot with your dad tomorrow."

His mom returned to nodding. *Don't I get a vote?* Julian wanted to shout. *To not waste my life kicking some stupid ball around a field?* But he didn't. He thought of the pamphlet at dinner the night before, and the muffled sounds coming from his parents' bedroom afterward, and he knew he didn't get a vote.

For the rest of the day Julian mused over the possibility that he might die and not have to go with his dad to the hardware store. Not an imagine-your-own-death thing, more of a not-existing thing, his body dissolving from family photos like he never was and the world moving on without him. But when he opened his eyes to a gray light on Saturday morning, reality sank in like an iron blanket.

"Jules," his dad called from the other side of his bedroom door. "Leaving in ten. We'll get a men's breakfast on the road."

It wasn't the first time Julian had been bribed with a McMuffin. Hash browns, chalupas, Jack in the Box egg rolls: if his dad got stuck taking Julian somewhere on a weekend, there was usually a drive-through involved. But the "men's" part was new, and the word struck dread in his heart. For as long as Julian could remember, his dad's whole being made him uncomfortable—the connection to his mom's sadness, the way the two of them fought—but he'd never felt afraid of his dad until he brought home the Christian pamphlet. Julian had heard of those camps. His best friend's older sister at the high school had a friend who was friends with a guy, Nathan, who sucked dick on the bike trail, or that was the rumor, and he got sent to a camp and never came back to Royalwood. Where he was now no one seemed to know.

"Best thing about Home Depot?" his dad said when he pulled out of the Burger King drive-through. "The men. Not just employees. Customers. Experienced guys, getting their hands on the right tools. Because the pride you get from building something? A soccer goal? It's like building a house, putting a roof over your head—you wait and see."

"But you didn't," Julian said, nibbling a tater tot. "We're not building a house."

"It's metaphorical. You can learn a lot from guys at Home Depot."

"Like what?"

"Like what?" His dad chuckled and shook his head at such a silly question. Then he frowned. "Like how to be a guy."

"Who taught them?" Julian sat up with a quizzical look. "If they teach other guys how to be guys, who taught them how? How'd they get to be the ones to—"

"So?" his dad barked. "How's school?"

In the upturn of his voice, Julian heard it was time to speak his dad's language, talk in numbers and percentages, forget anything he might actually be thinking because his dad only half listened anyways, and tell him the praise people piled on his son that day. Normally Julian played along so his dad would leave him alone. But driving to Home Depot, Julian thought of what the man at the RenFest had called him and wondered if his dad thought he was a faggot too. "What do you care?" Julian snapped.

His dad didn't say anything. He cleared his throat and

flipped on the radio and fiddled until he found Kenny Rogers. And for the rest of the ride, Julian tried to ignore the excruciating sight of his dad mouthing the words to "The Gambler."

★

"Look for a gentleman in an orange vest," his dad said when they parked. "They work here." Through the sliding doors they crossed from the heavy Gulf air into AC land. Julian had been to the local True Value with his mom, but this place was different: aisles thirty feet high, with heavy things that could crash on you, tools and metal bits everywhere to cut or snag you if you weren't looking, men with guts pushing carts around like zombies in the blue-white light. He followed his dad to Plumbing and helped him stack PVC onto a dolly. "Now," his dad said, "where's netting?" He strolled to the end of the aisle and squinted. "Hold down the fort, Jules."

"Where are you going?"

"Watch our stuff. Be right back."

Julian sat on the edge of the dolly and ran through his to-do list for debate club: research on universal health care, memorize a new oratory about the evils of date rape, and—

"Shut the fuck up!" A voice jolted him from his thinking. Two redneck guys came around the corner, grinning. One of them smacked the other on the head. They strutted down the aisle in baggy jeans and a cloud of tobacco stink. The smacker gave Julian a hard stare as he passed and pulled up the sleeves of his thermal, revealing forearms covered in tattoos.

Julian held his breath until they were gone, but when he let it out he found he couldn't breathe. His pulse raced. He could see the shop at the RenFest again, where he'd tried on the veil. He was always so careful not to act like a girl, or stare at boys or try to hold one and be held. But that day he made one slip. He'd just seen a rerun of Princess Di's wedding with his mom, and when he found the veil at the shop he felt a million miles from school and life. Until the shopkeeper's tattooed arms came down on him, yanking his hair and twisting his neck, and too late he knew the moment had come. He would die. He had announced himself to the terror that was everywhere, and it had come for the faggot.

"Jules?" His dad was shaking his shoulders. Julian looked around. He was in Home Depot, on the floor by the dolly with his knees pulled to his chin. "What's the matter?" his dad pressed. "What happened?"

"Nothing," he sputtered. He tried to stop crying, but when he noticed a guy in an orange vest waiting awkwardly behind his dad, the tears started raining harder.

"Come on." His dad helped him to his feet. "Let's get out of here." His dad struck up a conversation with the Home Depot guy and steered the dolly out of the aisle. Julian followed, watching his dad through blurry eyes. He told Julian he was special once. His dad said it one time, and not about grades. They were in the car driving home from a party one night, where his dad drank liquor, and he told Julian he was smart and that he came from both of them—his mom and dad. It wasn't that long ago. But when his dad stopped and turned in Home Depot to see his son lagging behind, it was only shame and disappointment Julian read on his face.

★

The saw was nightmare scary. In the years it sat gathering dust in the garage, Julian never paid it any mind. Then they got back from Home Depot, and his dad wiped it down and set it up on the back patio, and the gleam of the circular blade sent a chill down Julian's spine. He lined up the pipes on the lawn, the way he was told. But when he tried listening to his dad's instructions for the saw, he couldn't think. He was going to lose a finger over a soccer goal.

"All right, Jules," his dad said. "Your turn."

"You do it."

"I already did. This last bunch is yours. It's easy, come on."

"I'm going in," Julian mumbled.

"No," his dad ordered, "you're cutting pipe." Julian put on goggles and gloves and approached his fate. His dad set the pipe and turned on the saw. "Go on," his dad shouted. Gingerly Julian touched pipe to blade. His dad hollered something, but he couldn't hear over the shrieking noise. The saw made a grinding sound. His dad planted his hands on Julian's, shoving the pipe clean through, and turned off the saw. Julian retreated to the lawn.

"Good." His dad examined the mangled edge of the pipe. "Go faster this time." Beyond his dad, Julian saw his mom watching at the bedroom window. He felt a splash of something on his neck. The rain hovering all day had finally come. Thunder rippled. "Forget it," his dad said. "Lay the cut pieces inside there. I'll do the rest."

By the time his dad finished, Julian was watching TV. Every other channel was news about the Branch Davidians and the survivors soon to stand trial. His dad came in, soaked from the sudden downpour. "All right," he said, rubbing his head with a towel. "We're improvising, but we're finishing. We'll put it together in here—"

"What are you doing?" His mom appeared. "In the living room? Why not the garage?"

"Because the backyard's right—We'll put a few pieces together while it's raining, and then—Could you leave us men alone?" His dad ignored her until she left. "Grab me two joints, would you, Jules? We'll do the front frame first, get that screwed tight, then the sides and back."

Julian handed him the joints and flipped channels. He stopped on his favorite local access preacher, a lady with a waist-long perm and cauliflower bangs. *Mr. Koresh had the true faith*, she preached, prowling around her blue satin stage. *But the Davidians were different. And what does our government do if you're different? It destroys you.*

"Can you help, please?" his dad said, a little huffy. Julian looked up and saw the frame of a soccer goal rising. His dad stood there holding pipes like he was playing Twister, one leg swung around to hold a side piece, shoulder tucked in a joint, an arm lifting up the top, and the far side swinging with every jiggle of his body. "Stand there and steady it," he ordered, "so I can start screwing it together. And turn off the Bible thumpers."

"Whatever." Julian got up and flipped the channel. "Where do you want me to go?" he asked, eyes still locked on the screen.

"The other side," his dad barked. "Turn it off!" He leaned down to snatch the remote, and the frame buckled. In a strange, relentless slow motion, pipes came loose from joints and tumbled down with a crack, taking out a lamp and coming to rest in pieces on the couch and floor. Julian looked around and noticed a dark thing on the carpet. The dragon's egg, swept off the coffee table. He knelt down to pick it up, but the dragon's foot and tail, once hatching from the egg, had snapped off in the impact.

"What happened?" his mom called, hurrying into the living room.

"It . . . ," his dad began. "Fell."

Julian held up the egg and foot and tail. His mom stared at the pieces. Before he could think to say anything, she grabbed her purse by the front door and bolted. The minivan revved and pulled away. He turned to his dad, but he was already heading to the garage. The door slammed. The clank of weights on cement vibrated through the house.

Julian sat still on the carpet, until inspiration struck. He ran to the kitchen for superglue. It wasn't in the craft cabinet, so he tore through the pantry and drawers, all the while thinking of his mom's face when she left. He'd seen that look before, seen her storm into the bedroom when she and his dad fought, but she'd never gone out the front door. The glue appeared in a tray of pens. Julian ran back to the living room, set the egg on a magazine, and prepped for surgery. He uncapped the crusty tube and squeezed, but nothing came out.

Julian flopped on the couch and listened to the rain. His mind drifted over the past week. And he knew for sure. Something was broken in their family, and it was because of him.

6

The Swimmers

Aaron?" Lacy called from the kitchen. "I need you home by six."

"Yup," he barked from behind the bathroom door. He stood at the his-and-hers sinks and studied the shape he cut in the mirror, checking out different views. He threw his tie over his shoulder, pulled up his shirt, and pondered the slight yet unmistakable gut sheathing his forgotten abs. He sucked it in and let it go. He tilted his head to everyday angles, reassuring himself that only a hawk-eyed giant could find the bald spot in the blond still amply covering his crown. And for the first time since they'd met one afternoon two years ago, at a lonely diner by Lake Conroe, Aaron wondered what Crystal saw when she looked at him. Naked and in clothes.

"Not six like six thirty," Lacy blathered. "Six like five forty-five. We're carpooling crosstown with the Andersons, and we have hotel check-in, dinner, and bed by ten. Jules's first relay is at eight in the morning—"

"I got it!" he shouted. He retucked his shirt, buttoned his blazer, and stared deep into his eyes. "Fuck Machine," he growled. He unlocked the door and strutted from the bathroom.

"I mean it," she resumed when he reached the kitchen. "I

know it's your job, but I need you on time." His wife stood at the counter in her house uniform of saggy T-shirt and sweats, not a blob exactly but a familiar thing sort of fuzzy around the edges. Lacy kept talking while she spread jam on an English muffin, but Aaron's focus had shifted to Julian wolfing down cereal and reading at the table. His amazing son had turned thirteen and in a handful of months shot up before their eyes to six feet of lanky muscle, as lean and hard as beef jerky.

"Jules!" he said. "Y'all gonna win your relays tomorrow?" Over the tops of his glasses Julian scrutinized Aaron and returned to his book. "If I was a betting man," Aaron continued, "I'd say y'all take the medley and you set a record for the fifty breast."

Lacy sighed and put her knife in the sink. "He'll do his best," she muttered.

"Course he will. Our big boy dives off that block and he's way ahead of the other guys. Jules, see you tonight?" Aaron waited in vain for him to look up. "Carb-load at dinner, and then protein in the morning, right?"

"Bye," Julian said irritably and flipped a page.

Aaron donated a peck on Lacy's cheek and slipped past her out of the kitchen.

"Hey." She followed him to the front door. "He's nervous," she said quietly. "Coach says he's ready. It's good you've been showing interest this summer, in him and his teammates, all the swimmers, but he doesn't need more pressure on him or—" Lacy watched him a moment. "Six o'clock. Or we're leaving without you."

"Yes, ma'am." Aaron clicked the heels of his wing tips together and saluted her. But as with the rest of his jokes, she had stopped laughing a long time ago.

★

People always thought it was easy being Texaco's angel of death out in the field—easy, they'd say when Aaron told folks what he did, because you're never the one getting fired—but they hadn't met his born-again boss or clocked all the miles he drove. The first time he had to do a round of layoffs was in Conroe, a few years back, when the natural gas dried up like the oil had before. It was a marathon trial by fire. One after another, field techs and mechanics trudged into the trailer-office in their Timberlands and soiled jeans. Aaron sat at a folding table, the single-breasted picture of a mature gentleman from the Macy's sale circulars in the paper, his hair only slightly ruffled by the AC blasting in the window. He was manly and never beat around the bush. He made a listening face when the guys swore about wives and babies, or ranted about the money the company sucked out of the ground on their watch. He wrote down questions and made no promises. He ended every meeting with a speech about how many jobs he left because of a bad boss or whatever, but look at him now—he found another! And after six hours of ruining lives with no lunch break, Aaron was tired.

He left the trailer and hurried to his car through the hot-jelly air. He drove toward the lake. A few miles up the highway, in the middle of piney nowhere, he came across a chrome-wrapped diner shaped like a caboose. He pulled in and adjusted his tie knot in the rearview mirror. Door chimes announced him with a jingle when he pushed open the frosted-glass entrance, and instantly he spotted her sitting alone at the far end of the diner—a petite blond thing, as fresh as a cheerleader, in a tight khaki uniform and hair done up like Farrah Fawcett's. She was eating a piece of cherry pie. Smoothly Aaron slipped off his wedding ring and approached her booth.

"I thought it was doughnuts that police like," he rumbled. "Not pie. Did I get that wrong?"

"Good thing I'm not the police." She scanned Aaron skeptically with huge blue eyes, flicking her mascaraed lashes like moth wings.

"Pardon the intrusion. Must have been that uniform that led me astray."

"Prison guard. Food services, up in Huntsville. Polunsky Unit." She sipped her coffee, watching him over the rim of her plastic mug. "Death row?"

"Is that right?" He chuckled. "You make their last meals?"

"I bring them. A man's gotta eat." She took a wet bite of pie. "Ever been up that way?"

"I have." Something in her slow, lippy bite made the invitation. Aaron sat down and told her about the first trip he made to these parts, to check out Conroe Field when the layoffs were still a rumor, and how he missed his exit and ended up in the national forest, almost driving off the road when he got to that Paul Bunyan–size statue of Sam Houston right on the edge of I-45, like he was fixing to step onto the highway, and when Aaron came out the other side of the forest, there he was in Huntsville. Home of the electric chair. It turned out she lived a few minutes away on the lake, in a cabin she was staying in year-round with real nice views, and of course he wanted to see her views and yes he did come to a diner but no he didn't need any food.

"I'm Crystal," she said as she wriggled out of the booth. "And you are?"

"Blessed." He gave her his hand. "Lucky. Aaron."

He fucked her three legendary times that summer day, twice in her bed and once on the screened-in porch by the water. The first year of the affair was incredible. Two or three times a month, anytime he had to fire somebody north of the city, Aaron found his way to Crystal's cabin. She always had a cold beer waiting, but it was the food he remembered. She made elaborate meals in his honor, from scratch, chicken-fried steak and pecan pie. They drank and fucked and he ate, and they fucked again, sometimes twice, once his food settled. Afterward Crystal curled up in a rocking chair on the porch and smoked her Misty menthols, still naked at his request, until he wrapped her in his arms, and dotted her jugs with gentle kisses, and whispered to be a good girl and put that out. During those afternoons into evenings, gone from his mind was Lacy's nagging, bills and debt, the dog peeing on the rug, and there in front of him was a pretty woman with desire in her eyes. Aaron had carried on with other girls before, little snatches at motels or cocktail lounges, but never had a woman looked at him with such desire. By the time summer rolled around again, and Crystal smoked in her rocker and abruptly said, "I love you," he found himself repeating the same three words in joyful surrender.

But somewhere along the line, things changed. Crystal started talking about her mom. Every time Aaron came by she wanted him to meet her mom, who lived in Tomball. "I showed her a picture of you," she said one night, passing the corn bread with a glimmer in her eye. "She said you could be her traveling man any day." Crystal giggled and sipped her Bud Light. "The Dolly Parton song? It's a compliment. Mama's a big fan of yours."

They still had sex right off the bat when Aaron visited. Usually. But in the fall the baby talk started, and then every conversation led to babies. Aaron didn't get it because he was fifty and had a kid, Crystal insisted, but she was thirty-three, driving off a cliff with no time to waste, and if he loved her like he said, then the rest was details. Aaron kissed her brow at these dead ends, and through the winter and spring he nodded at her like he did with the guys he fired. But she didn't understand what he couldn't put into words: he already had a family and wanted more—more fun, not more problems.

Things blew up between them on the day of OJ's car chase. In the morning, Aaron had to call the police when a mechanic he fired started whacking a wellhead and screaming, "Piece of shit corporate bitch," and he was worn out by the time he got to Crystal's for dinner. She acted funny, barely talking and letting him get his own refills at the table. He beached himself on the couch to digest her brisket and grits, and when he flipped on the news and saw that white Bronco zooming down the highway with the LAPD in pursuit, he hollered for Crystal to come see. "I'm right here," she said, leaning against the wall where she was watching from behind. She muted the TV. "If we did have a baby," she said, moving in front of the set. She picked at her nails. "Hypothetically. Would you leave her—Lacy?"

Aaron smarted at the sound of his wife's name, rarely uttered in the cabin. *Silly girl*, he thought. *What if I grew a third arm?* But he must have taken too long to respond, because before Aaron could say anything, Crystal opened her mouth and made it namesake clear to him and her neighbors that he should get out of her goddamn house.

So back to his home life he went, to Lacy's bustling summer schedule of errands, his weight set in the garage, fish sticks for dinner, and Julian's surprise thrashing of all swimmers with his first foray into sports. And in a new twist to their relationship, Aaron's calls to Crystal went unreturned for over a month.

★

Lacy didn't need to order Aaron home in time for Julian's swim meet, which he wouldn't have missed for the world. And he didn't need her pressuring-our-baby hint that morning as he was headed out the door either. He didn't pressure Julian. He asked questions and predicted his son's races because he cared. For a minute last year he thought soccer was the sport for Julian, but things got messy and Aaron resigned himself to Lacy's swim team idea. Then Jules shot up a foot and took like a fish to water, and the rest was the amazing history of that summer.

Every Saturday morning Aaron was at the pool, pushing sunscreen and reminding Julian to stretch. He roared his son's name when Julian mounted the blue wooden starting block and towered over the teenage competition, his chestnut hair shining red in the sun. At the gun pop Aaron whooped, following up and back along the pool until his son slapped the wall in victory. Jules was the same kid he always was—same voice, a little girly, legs longer but still crossed when he sat. Yet to watch him swim breaststroke, rising and plunging as lethal as a shark, born to move that way, it reminded Aaron of playing football at UT. Before the war and all the shit that came next. The feeling of his muscles and the rush of freedom as he sprinted for the end zone, running toward something. The years got mixed up in Aaron's head as he cheered at the swim meets—memories of Lacy finally getting past the first trimester, and seeing the ultrasound of their baby, a girl they thought, and telling Lacy to pick the name because he knew how much it meant to her. Julia. Then out he came a Julian, *a king of kings!* Aaron cried that day, and now he understood at last. His son, his marriage, sticking around, it all made sense. The dreams that passed Aaron by were Julian's now. Because his boy would win his swim finals, go to Harvard, and conquer the world.

When the eve of the finals arrived, after weeks of buildup and sweltering Gulf heat, Aaron had much to do. In the morning he was finishing the last of the layoffs in Conroe, and then he had to get to Crystal's place to smooth things over—and squeeze in some gymnastic makeup sex—and be back home by six to carpool to the swim meet. Aaron felt a tingle when he pulled into the oil field and parked by the red-starred Texaco trailer for the last time. Acres of drills, once bowing to the earth in perpetual homage, sat still and ghostly. He had managed a two-year bloodbath, mopping up the latest human spillage in a cycle of booms and busts, and his final duty was to hand out paychecks to the tiny staff left—and, in his mind at least, to make a kind Mother Teresa nod when the last scraps of money hit their hands. But even with a skeleton crew some folks couldn't be found, and Aaron didn't finish his exit interviews and padlock the trailer until half past two.

He jumped in his Taurus and floored it to Crystal's place, stopping at the gas station for flowers and a couple of the Milky Ways she liked. When he pulled up the dirt road to the cabin, after weeks away, something felt different. The sun still peeka-booed through the pine trunks, the same green paint flaked off the shingles, but the place seemed shabbier than he remem-bered. He took the cracked cement pavers one at a time across the yard, planning his opening line. Aaron tapped on the door. Absence must have done a number on his heart because Crystal appeared looking prettier than he'd ever seen. Her skin had a rosy glow in the porch shade. Her hair was thick and shiny. She wore it natural, not teased in the front like she had for years, and with her loose white dress she looked like one of the hot goddesses from *Clash of the Titans*.

"Come on in," she said.

"These are for you." Aaron handed her the flowers and candy. Crystal smiled and took the flowers. She turned into the living room and beckoned him to follow. As soon as he entered he saw mess everywhere: shoeboxes piled in corners, videocas-settes dumped in the armchairs, wire hangers tangled on the carpet like bramble patches. And nearly hidden in mounds of winter clothes on the couch sat an old woman. Crystal's mom. He'd seen a picture of her but didn't need one. She was an older version of Crystal, maybe Aaron's age but older-looking with her bake-tan and dry smoker's skin. A janitor at a hospital, he remembered when he saw her pink teddy-bear scrubs. Aaron smiled tensely and looked to Crystal.

"Sorry about the mess," she said, not seeing or ignoring his stare. She passed into the kitchen and searched the cabinets for a vase. "I'm cleaning out the guest bedroom."

"The famous Aaron!" The old woman stood up. "We meet at last."

"You must be Mrs. Connors," he played along in a singsong voice.

She cackled. "I haven't been Mrs. Connors in years," she said, picking her way through the mess. "If I ever really was. Call me Tammy."

"Tammy." He shook her hand. She smelled like cigarettes and White Diamonds. Crystal arranged the flowers by the sink, unhurried, singing Johnny Nash to herself like a soft little bird while Aaron made nice with her mother. "Great to meet you, Tammy." He tried to let go of her hand, but she wanted more shaking. He thrust out his other arm. "Sweet tooth?" he said, unclutching the Milky Ways.

"Quite the gentleman," she called to Crystal. "Thank you, sir. I never mind a taste of sugar." She took the bars and ran her eyes over him like she was memorizing. She reached a hand up and patted Aaron's cheek, sending a chill through him. "Y'all got fat to chew," she said. "I'm gonna head out."

"Bye, Mama," Crystal said, entering with a vase of flowers and a plastic bag. "Dinner's in here," she said and handed her mom the bag. "Chicken-fried steak and mashed potatoes. Write yourself a note, OK?"

"Thanks, baby." Tammy gave her daughter a long, loving look. She dropped the candy in her purse and dug out a pack of Camels. "Goddamn," she mumbled, poking in it. "Chrissy, you got any smokes to tide me over till—oh Lord!" She laughed.

"Of course you don't!" She slapped her head, grinning ear to ear, and shuffled out the front door.

"Come here," Aaron growled. He grabbed Crystal and kissed her hard on the mouth.

"Mama's been getting so forgetful," she said, pulling back. "The last few years? I swear she won't eat if I don't make it and hand it to her every night and say 'write it down.'"

"That's a lot of cooking," Aaron said. "Did my good girl quit smoking?"

"I did." She smiled. "It's fine. I just make double everything."

"You trying to go cold turkey on me too?" He tightened his arms around her waist and squeezed. "A whole month and no call?"

"Ooh." She pushed Aaron away. "Little girls' room, sorry, be right back. Coronas in the fridge!" she called, scooting down the hall to the bathroom. *Mi casa su casa.*

Aaron grabbed a beer. He swigged and tried to shake off the memory of Crystal's mom. He thought of Lacy's mom, the one time he and Julian met her at her mansion in McAllen. She was a mean woman but damn well put together, at least ten years younger-looking than she was, with smooth olive skin and hair dyed blond. Aaron remembered her fancy dress and antiques, and the steaks on gold-rimmed china. The toilet flushed. He downed his beer and felt a surge of anger at Crystal for springing her mom on him. He felt cheap and tricked.

"You hungry?" Crystal asked, entering the kitchen. "I thought we'd order Pizza Hut. Meat Lovers? Or whatever toppings you want."

"Your mom was just in the neighborhood?" Aaron said, more than a little testy.

"What? Oh, she came over to help me clean."

"The same day I was coming."

"Yeah." Crystal looked him dead in the eye. "She wanted to meet you." She opened the fridge and took out a beer and a bottle of seltzer. "Catch," she said, tossing the Corona at him.

"Jesus!" He caught it. "What the hell got into you today?" he asked, but she was already heading for the living room.

"Come sit." She swept the piles of jackets to one end of the couch. Her eyes welled up when he sat down beside her. "Cheers!" She tapped her seltzer to his beer.

"Hey, don't cry." He rubbed her knee through her dress, continuing up her thigh. "No big deal about your mom. I should've called ahead when I was leaving—"

"I'm pregnant."

He sighed. "I know. I know you want a baby, but we've been over this."

"I don't want one. I have one." She pressed her hands to her stomach and smiled. "Due in January. We're gonna have a baby, Aaron."

"How?" He launched up from the couch. "You can't—Whose is it?"

"Excuse me?"

"Well, we weren't exclusive, so how do you—"

"Not on your end," she snapped.

"But you're on the pill."

"I was, and then—"

"Was?" he barked. "You stopped taking them? On purpose?"

"No."

"You've been talking about it nonstop a whole year."

"Stop yelling at me," she pleaded.

"I'm not. I'm trying to figure out why you stopped taking them and didn't say a word."

"I ran out, and the doctor was out of town when you came by and—you could've worn a condom! Always have to have sex, never leave without it. If you're so scared of your swimmers getting in me, how about a condom?"

"Because you're on the pill!" He stepped in a pile of hangers, kicking them off his shoe, and paced in front of the couch. "Due in January? When did you know? Last time I was here?"

"I wanted to be sure."

"So you kept it secret?"

"I'm in my second trimester." She made a little gasp. The tears started. "Stupid me. Thinking we had something to toast."

Aaron scratched his scalp like a maniac and sat down beside her. "Sorry," he mumbled. "It's gotta be hard, with the hormones and . . ." He patted her hand. "OK. We got time. There's a nice Planned Parenthood in Spring."

"Yeah?" Crystal pulled away, her face wrinkling in disgust. "You been there before?"

"No. When Lacy lost the—I'll take care of everything, don't worry."

"It's a boy. I felt him kick yesterday for the first time." She wrapped her arms around her stomach and rocked on the couch like a little girl.

"Crystal."

"I'm keeping him."

"How would that even work, hon? Think about it."

"I'm setting up the nursery right now," she said, waving at the mess. "But the lease is up here in June, and by then I figured I'd be down in the city."

"In—Move to Houston?"

She nodded. "I know a guy at Jester Three down in Sugar Land. It's no death row, but he said if I put the transfer request in now it'd be ready in six months, tops."

"What time is it?" Aaron checked his watch. "I gotta make a call." He hurried to the front hallway. "Could you turn up the AC?" he hollered back at her. He picked up the phone and dialed home—which he rarely did from Crystal's, where Lacy could *69 him—but nobody answered, so he left a rapid-fire message that he'd be home early and hung up.

Crystal's dark outline awaited him in the entrance to the living room.

"What are you calling her for?" she asked.

"Crystal." He sighed.

"Aaron Warner." She smiled, approaching him slowly. "Do you believe in miracles?"

"Sure," he said and took a step back.

"The grace of the Creator? We didn't plan this. He did. The first time we saw each other in the diner? A couple that turns heads. You know we do! We would, if we ever went out. A little boy with blond hair and blue eyes? Coming up here, teaching him how to fish. Going to Disney for Christmas. There's a chapel in the resort so you can go to services before the rides. I checked." She took his hands. "Can you see it?"

"I got a two-hour carpool down I-10 to Katy tonight."

"Don't be scared." She held him fast as he tried to pull away. "Look at me. I love you. And you love me, like you said on that couch, and in that bed—"

"Crystal."

"So many times you said it's over with her, and you haven't loved her in years—"

"It's not happening!" he snapped. "What part of that don't you get? When was I not clear? I have a family. A wife and son."

"A girlyboy!" she blurted. "You said so yourself." Aaron grabbed his keys off the hall table. "Don't walk away from me," she ordered. "This is getting worked out today."

"Goodbye," Aaron mumbled and threw the door open.

"Did Lacy pick up?" she cried. "I bet she didn't."

He stopped.

"You know what waiting does to a person?" Crystal said

quietly. "Every day I go to work I see guys waiting to die. Waiting to live. It takes you over."

"What did you do?" he asked.

"I went back to church. You're not here on Sundays. Last time we read from Jeremiah: 'For I know the plans I have for you, says the Lord, plans to prosper you and not harm you, plans to give you hope and a future.' And I thought, I been taking care of people my whole life. Murderers and rapists. Now my mother. When's someone going to take care of me?"

"What did you do, Crystal?"

"I told her the truth. I wrote a letter. I put it in the mail yesterday. If you meant what you said, then it's time to stop lying. And if you didn't mean it, if you were lying, then you're not the man I thought and why should it be one long freebie with me? I can't wait. I'll raise this child fine on my own, like my mama did, but—isn't it nicer together?" She watched him. The desire was still in her eyes, he could see, and fear, and many things Aaron didn't know. "I think you did mean it," she said. "I got life in me, Aaron."

"Don't contact my wife," he barked. "Or me. Or you'll regret it." He took off.

"This boy needs to know you, Aaron," she called after him. "Aaron?!"

But he already had the Taurus in reverse.

★

Lacy Adams, who became Lacy Warner, was the smartest woman Aaron had ever met. He could tell from the very first letter she wrote him. Smarter than the girls he grew up with in Midland, or the coeds at UT, or the secretaries at Enron or Texaco. She had such energy, too, starting and joining things—PTA or the Royalwood High Science Club—and talking about it at dinner, because the only thing more intense than her joining was her talking. Or the way she was plain capable? Like the afternoon she decided the orange flower curtains looked too seventies, so she taught herself to use her friend Bonnie's sewing machine and took Julian to the fabric store, and by the time Aaron got home the windows had navy-and-cream-striped curtains that made their house look like a fancy resort. Because she had it in her, the power to change their world and make their son—hands down her best work—feel like a part of something.

Aaron reflected on Lacy's good qualities as he raced home from the cabin. Traffic was light. He thought of the many times he made this trip and the rounds of counseling he and Lacy did over the years, dating back before the Crystal days. Every time Lacy found a credit card bill, or some oopsie thing in his pockets, she cried again like that alarm clock going off in *Groundhog Day*, and back they went to the office of Gloria Harding, MFT, in a strip mall in Atascocita, empty except for a TCBY yogurt. Gloria waited for them, under her *Footprints in the Sand* poster, round and unfuckable, a no-judgments half smile on her face. Lacy would rant and rage and go quiet—Aaron's cue to say he heard her pain, and he was going to keep her in mind next time he thought about stepping out, because that's what a real partnership required.

But this time he meant it. Hope swelled in Aaron as he exited 59 and crossed into the bucolic green of Royalwood. It wasn't a sure thing that Crystal's letter had arrived yet. He mailed her a cutout from *Playboy* once, with drawings and a note on it, and it took three whole days to get to her cabin. Aaron resolved that if he got to the letter first, if he and Lacy made it over this one last hump, he'd treat her with respect and honesty for good. Because there was Julian to think about. And not just their son. There was Lacy, too. It hit him, as he sped into their subdivision, that he hadn't stuck around all these years for Julian alone. He loved Lacy. The only woman he ever really loved, longer than a fling or a few years. But inside he felt it, as dense as the knots churning his stomach; he knew that love was more than needing. More than his needs, or hers, not to be alone. He used to care for Lacy. He remembered taking care of her. And he couldn't recall when he stopped doing that and just took care of himself.

He pulled into the driveway at four forty-five p.m. The minivan wasn't there. He hustled to the front door, but when he tried to go in his key stuck and wouldn't turn. He pounded and rang. He ran to the living room window and peered in the unlit house. The mini-blinds smashed against the window as the dog attacked the glass in a flurry. "It's me, Muffin!" Aaron said. "Daddy." Muffin brayed in recognition and trotted off to the kitchen. Aaron stepped back, and only then did he notice it beside the porch bench: his suitcase, with a paper bag on top. It was tucked slightly behind the boxwoods Lacy pruned every summer into double balls. He opened the bag and found a Tupperware inside, along with a note in his wife's careful teacher handwriting:

Aaron—

I got a letter from your friend Crystal. But this was a long time coming. I changed the locks on the house, and our phone number. Please don't bother the neighbors.

I filed for divorce today. My lawyer's card is in here. Go through her to reach me. We'll schedule a time for you to get the rest of your things, when Julian is away. He doesn't know anything yet. I packed you work clothes to last a couple of weeks. I made a tuna casserole for you to eat. It's what was in the kitchen. There isn't much money to divide up but I'll be fair to you, even though you weren't fair to me.

Lacy

Aaron felt his heart pounding and dropped to the bench. Out of nowhere and a long time coming. When did she get a lawyer, to move so fast? The heat pressed down like wet cotton. He shut his eyes and leaned his head against the house. His mind rambled back to his church in Midland, high school days, when he started going to services alone. He remembered a sermon one Sunday on Milton, so powerful that he went to the library and found *Paradise Lost* and the image the pastor described—Earth, surrounded by darkness and chaos, suspended from Heaven by a thin gold chain. He wondered if that was what Lacy was, tying him to Julian and the world. From far away Aaron could see himself, unworthy as he'd always been, slipping into a place without light or sound. Disappeared.

The buzz of a mosquito brought him back to the porch. He blinked at the evening glow and took in tidy Sycamore Springs Lane one more time. The years of sprinklers arcing languidly over emerald lawns that led up to this moment. He had to find somewhere to lay his head that night. It settled over Aaron that he would sleep alone. And for the first time since the war, he covered his face and cried.

7

Free Markets

Julian couldn't find a song on the radio. Or rather, he couldn't find a song that would make his mom stop talking about the high school, and Royalwood, and the bubble they lived in and he'd be escaping the minute he graduated. It was the same stupid chatter every morning on the drive to school, until Julian ordered her to let him out before the main entrance, while she continued on to faculty parking.

"Did you hear the theme for homecoming?" she asked one muggy September morning, a few weeks into the school year. She checked her lipstick in the rearview mirror and shot a look at Julian. "Beauty and the Beast. You thinking about going?"

"No." The Alanis on Mix 96.5 wasn't working. He dialed to Oasis on Power 104. "Don't look back in anger," Noel Gallagher sang, so Julian mouthed the words with a powerful irritation.

"How come?" she persisted. "A little dancing could be fun, couldn't it?"

"There's a genocide happening in Zaire right now?" he said, ignoring his mom's jiggly impression of dancing in the driver's seat. "And you think I should devote brain space to boutonnieres and football-cheerleader 'royalty'?"

"Well. It's great you're thinking about genocide, but can't

you think about both? Going on a date? I'm sure there's lots of special—people, on the debate team that want to go out with the star debater."

Julian dialed to KTRU and blasted the volume.

"Turn it down!" she cried, flipping the radio off. "I'm try-ing to drive here. You want to run me off the road with that noise?"

"That was Björk," Julian lectured. "She was almost acid bombed by mail in Iceland. That noise could've been her last album." He turned and looked at her for the first time that day. "Why don't you go on a date? Take all that energy you're put-ting into questions and go find one for yourself."

"Maybe I will," she said quietly.

"I mean." Julian felt the flush of something nasty rising in him. "It's been two years."

That did it. They drove the rest of the trip in silence. He didn't have to remind his mom to stop at the last bend of Roy-alwood Drive, like he normally did. She slowed down, pulled into the turn lane, and put on the hazards.

"Do what you want, Jules," she said, staring at the steering wheel. "The most important thing is to be true to yourself. If there's a way to be true and go to the dance, with a date if you want, then—And if you ever want to talk about anything—"

"What are you talking about?" Julian snapped and shoved the door open.

"What time are you done today?"

"Late." He slammed the door and started froggering across the street.

"You need a ride home after debate club?" his mom called out the window. But lanky Julian rambled away up the bike trail, Discman and giant headphones on, in full sonic cocoon.

★

Be careful what you wish for. Julian had heard the phrase a million times, but he never understood the meaning of it until he came home from a swim meet a couple of summers ago and his dad was gone. Many times as a kid Julian daydreamed about his dad going away, of a giant pencil eraser coming down from the sky and rubbing him out of their lives. There'd be no more fighting or sadness for his mom to carry around, and the two of them could do their craft projects without dark clouds looming. But when his dad left for real—no warning, just gone—Julian realized things were never going to be as simple as he imagined. His mom changed, but it didn't seem totally for the better. She started hitting the Entenmann's at night, polishing off a whole cherry Danish during *Masterpiece Theatre*, one bite at a time. Mostly she was all over Julian, telling him again and again that she wasn't going anywhere. And the mom who had always been his best friend suddenly wanted more than he had to give—more time, more talks, more laughs than he could generate.

So Julian became a joiner. If a club kept him at school and his mom wasn't the sponsor, he'd probably given it a try. By sophomore year he was in bloom: first in his class, president of the debate club and titled at three lesser ones, in monthly contact with the guidance office about his college apps. The more he focused on the future, the less he thought about his mom watching TV or the insanity called Texas. The place was crazy. And when you're the misfit in a crazy world, he told himself, keep your head down and eyes on the prize. Because he knew, with a faith stronger than all the Tammy Fayes and Osteens put together, that one day he'd get out and go to Harvard. And there he would be free.

He was considering joining a new club on the morning his mom mentioned homecoming. Ever since the school year began, she stayed later on campus, too, in a silent arms race with him. The past few weeks he heard the swish of her thighs in the hallway like a sixth sense and knew exactly when her head would poke in the door to offer him a ride home in front of his whole debate team. It sucked. He needed a new hideout. And then, on his way to first period that morning, he noticed a flyer with an American flag border:

COLLEGE SCHOLARSHIPS
FOR PUBLIC SPEAKERS!
Join the Ten Pillars Club
& Protect Our
Free Markets from the
Evils of Big Government!
3pm—Room 115
Refreshments!

He pondered this.

At ten past three, Julian cruised nonchalantly by the classroom. Inside he saw two no-account freshmen from debate and a girl in a CAMPUS CRUSADE FOR CHRIST T-shirt.

"Welcome!" A sinewy woman appeared in the doorway, maybe older but with short jet-black curls. She wore a tailored pantsuit and Catwoman glasses. "I knew there was another voice for freedom in this school! Come in. I'm Samantha Monroe. Call me Sam." She led him to a desk. "Now, I hope y'all can chat over snacks later." She motioned to a desk spread with chips and a sweating bowl of Cokes. "But first, I want to talk about fathers. Our Founding Fathers."

Sam lowered her head. She rested a hand on an easel beside her, with a blank white poster board on it. "We are a nation in crisis," she declared, launching into a speech full of violent images and stiff hand gestures. "Our free market system is on the brink of destruction, and the soul of our nation is at risk—a country that next month might reelect a president whose wife tried to *socialize* health care? Is there any hope in this night-mare?" Sam brandished a pamphlet: *The Free Enterprise Center's Ten Pillars of Economic Wisdom*. The minds of the future would win the war for America, she explained, and that's why her center had started a speech contest, focused on ten simple truths, and she was thrilled Royalwood High had signed up this year. Julian's mind wandered to the shade of the Doritos, and whether they were Cool Ranch, when Sam announced that every winning speech got a thousand dollars, and the Houston-wide winner got an internship at the prestigious Koch Foundation in Washington, DC.

"And if that lucky winner is sitting in this room," Sam said, returning to the easel, "he'll follow the path of our most famous alum." She lifted the poster board, revealing a photo of a white guy in a suit. "Graduate of Harvard Law, Supreme Court clerk, and who knows, future president? Rafael 'Ted' Cruz!" Sam gazed proudly at the photo and sighed. "Because if there's one thing we taught Ted—if there's one thing I want y'all sons and daughters of freedom to take away today, it's that we fight for the freedom of every American. Every. Single. American."

Julian got home that night with visions of Harvard Yard in his head. He made a beeline for his room, but his mom called out as he hurried past the kitchen. She was in her sweatpants and a stretched-out Spuds MacKenzie T-shirt, writing on a notepad. The table was strewn with jumbo pill bottles and the discarded sleeve of a Hot Pocket. "Hungry, sweetie?" she asked.

"I ate at school," he mumbled.

"Listen to this." She flashed Julian a look. "Mature full-figured woman who loves to laugh, loves football on Friday and museums on Saturday, seeks companion for—"

"A personal ad?" Julian frowned.

"For the classifieds, in the *Chronicle*. I think you were right about me getting back out there on the market. Trying." She studied her pad. "You think it's too, toooo—"

"Too what? Just be true to yourself. Isn't that what you said earlier? I mean, if you're advertising yourself."

"And what part isn't true, exactly?"

"I don't know. You used 'love' twice in one—and once about football? What kind of guy are you trying to—whatever. What're all the pills?"

"Nothing." Her shoulders hunched. She gathered up the bottles. "A new supplement."

"Good night." Julian backed away. He shut his door and found some Hootie on the radio to block out his mom and her diet pills. For the next two weeks he holed up at night, skimming books on the gold standard and welfare state that Sam handed out, plucking juicy phrases for his speech. It was boring. But Julian knew what Sam wanted to hear, and that brought him one step closer to his future. Parroting didn't trouble him. Everyone in debate knew that words had no meaning. Unlike most of his classmates—drinking and screwing on Saturdays— Julian was competing at a high school on the north side, wearing a too-big suit his dad left behind and spinning words into winning designs.

On a mild October afternoon, he returned to the same classroom to deliver his magnum opus on free markets. He paced the hallway before his turn, thinking of the zeroes on a thousand-dollar check. "Julian?" Sam called. She led him in and introduced two men—board members of the center—who by their suits Julian knew worked in skyscrapers downtown and fired people like his dad. Sam nodded. He stood up straight. "Everything that government *gives* to the people," he began, slow and dramatic, "it must first *take* from the people."

Out came the words.

When Julian finished, Sam beamed like he'd announced the

Rapture and they were headed up. "Well," she said, "I don't think we need deliberations, do we, gentlemen?" Things happened fast. They shook hands and talked about Ted Cruz and men like Julian not coming around every day. Sam handed him an envelope. "You got a bank account, don't you?" she asked. They laughed. As they were leaving, Sam offered to prep Julian for the North Houston semifinals, and one of the men grabbed his shoulder, mock serious, and said, "Remember, son, behind every great man is a better half like this one nagging at him!"

Julian lay in bed that night with the envelope under his pillow, trying to savor his victory. But something gnawed at him. He kept replaying the man's joke about a better half. For as long as he could remember, Julian had known he was maybe gay—bi, probably—and not in the leather drag-queen way. In the quiet, reasonable way. In theory, at least. He'd never kissed anybody, but he'd long ago decided to figure it out when he got to Harvard, where people could be many things and not get beat up. Until then the maybe-gay stayed in storage, and Julian passed as a nerd only slightly up the food chain from fags but a lot less likely to get killed. And on those nights when longing overtook him, when he heard Erasure on the radio, Andy Bell hammering out an ABBA cover, and dreamed of following that powerful fey voice out his window and through the indigo night, past the stars, to a land where gay boys sang proud and free and maybe there was a boy for him, Julian would remind himself that there wasn't any guy to have sex with in his whole school anyway. Thus he stayed his own master.

Until a few weeks later, on a Monday before sixth period.

★

Julian left his chemistry book in his locker that day, and he was racing back for it when a girl called out, "Warner!" He didn't know her name, but he took in her Cure T-shirt and black lipstick and knew where he'd seen her—and with whom. "Julian, right?" she said. "Do you know Ben Cross? Like, know *of* him?"

"Yeah," Julian said, his chest tightening. "I forgot a book. I gotta go."

"We're hanging out later." She tapped an imaginary roach to her lips. "If you want to come. Side parking lot at three thirty."

"Um," he mumbled, and took off.

The whole school knew of Ben Cross. In September he returned for his senior year and came out, not as gay, but as Morrissey. He showed up the first day with his hair dyed black like the *Bona Drag* album cover. He wore Doc Martens and T-shirts with incendiary messages about God and meat. He painted his nails with whiteout and scratched *H-E-L-L* into his left-hand ones and *P-R-O-O-F* into his right ones. A lot of rumors were going around about Ben and gerbils and AIDS, and within weeks he had morphed from human into spectacle. The student body avoided him like a contagious thing—except one husky goth girl who sat with Ben at lunch and shuttled between Earth and Gayville making invitations for afternoon weed hangouts.

During his last class Julian calculated risks. He couldn't be seen with Ben or within a hundred feet of a car containing Ben. *And yet*, his mind pressed. A string of "yets" led the pride of the debate team to the parking lot at four p.m., long after Ben would have left. Trickles of smoke rose from the only car, a rusted silver Trans Am. Julian made a wide path around it, which meant nothing because he wasn't stopping, but as he passed by Ben sat forward and flicked a cigarette butt in a graceful arc. He trained his sharp blue eyes on Julian. "Hop in," he said. Julian did as he was told, squeezing past Ben into the back seat.

The goth girl shot a look at Ben from the driver's seat.

"I didn't get your name," Julian said to her. "In the hall earlier?"

"Chastity." Ben grinned.

"Shut up!" She floored the car out of the lot.

"She goes by CiCi." Ben patted her hand on the stick shift. "We don't choose our names, babe." He lit a joint and took a religious hit. "And you're Julian Warner." He handed it back, eyeing Julian in the rearview mirror.

"No, thanks," he replied. "More of a drinker." Ben passed it to CiCi. The whole ride they smoked and gossiped and ignored Julian until they turned into Sherwood Lanes, the only subdivision cheaper and more depressing than Julian's. "Where we headed?" he asked.

They stopped at a tiny peeling box of a house. "Home," Ben sighed.

"Later," CiCi waved as Julian crawled out of the car.

"Just the two of us." Ben yanked open the screen door. "The parents won't be back for hours." He led Julian into a cramped but tidy kitchen. "Drink?"

"Beer if you got it," Julian said, some super-butch spirit passing through him.

Ben handed him a can of lemonade. "The parents are Mormon."

"Oh. Does that—Are you a Mormon too?"

"I'm a fuckup. It's my own special cult." Julian followed Ben into a dim room, blinds closed in the high small window and musky from a bottle of Drakkar Noir lurking in the dark. Ben switched on a lamp with a blue bulb. A massive stereo system colonized one wall. The rest were covered in posters for Kate Bush, Siouxsie and the Banshees, other bands Julian didn't know but looked dangerous.

"Fuckup?" Julian said. "Like, no colleges picked out? You're a senior, right?"

"I don't know," Ben said as he loaded a CD changer. "The Art Institute, if I can scrape up the cash." He picked a song and flopped on his bed.

"Whoa." Julian's nose wrinkled reflexively. "Is that a water bed?"

"Fuck yeah." Ben made an aqueous pat beside him. "Take the plunge."

Julian lowered himself cautiously to the frame. Ben nudged him, and he splashed backward. The wave rocked them, and on the rebound Ben's T-shirt rode up to reveal a pale white six-pack. "Julian's a sophomore, right?" Ben said. "Not a fuckup. What else is he?"

Julian grinned. "I'm a master debater." Ben stared at the ceiling. "And Royalwood's North Houston candidate for the Ten Pillars speech contest."

"Wait." Ben grinned. "Those nut jobs with the Old Glory flyers a while back?"

"Nut jobs?" Julian objected, laboring to a sitting position. "Is it nutty to protect the freedom of every American? The free markets that allowed that stereo to be produced in a factory, and transported to a retailer, and sold to you for a fair profit?"

"Freedom's what we do with what's done to us." Julian stared at Ben, rapidly trying to place the words. "A little Sartre for the master debater." Ben smiled and rolled on his side, closer to Julian. "Do you get downtown much? Like, the bars in Montrose?"

"I don't have a car."

"Oh. You sounded like a big drinker, so I thought—Rich's? Heaven? The gay bars?"

"I know what they are," Julian mumbled.

"Mine Shaft's the best," Ben announced. "Speaking of markets—it's a meat market there. Live shows. Dildos the size of your arm? S-and-M daddies? But older guys are kinda my thing. Guys my age? *Boyfriends?*" he said with a condescending whine. "Whatever."

"So." Julian bit his lip. "You're, like—"

"Gay." Ben smirked. "If you say a word enough it loses its meaning. Gaygaygay."

Julian felt the shiver of goose bumps sprouting. It dawned on him that the sensation since he'd splashed onto the water bed, dizzy and pulsing, was sex in the air. Sex could happen. Julian stole a look at Ben and realized how handsome he was under the alt-rock trappings. Then the memory of his own image swept over Julian in crushing detail—round hoot-owl glasses, the acne, Gumby arms and legs—and he turned his face away from Ben.

"I gotta go." Julian struggled to his feet.

"Relax." Ben laughed.

He grabbed his backpack off the floor. "I've got a speech to—"

"Shit." Ben cocked his head and listened. "Yeah, go. Out the window."

"What?"

"What the fuck is he doing home?" Ben poked his head out the door of his room and slammed it shut again. "My dad. Trust me, go out the—"

"It's too high," Julian protested, "I can't—"

"I'll help." Ben yanked up the blinds and opened the window. He knelt and clasped his hands. "Come on!" Once Julian had his chest through, he felt Ben's arms wrap around his legs and lift him over the edge. He peered back into the house after he was out. "Let's meet again," Ben whispered. "Your place?"

"I can't. My mom."

"I'll be in touch." He gave Julian's hand a fleeting squeeze and was gone.

From that point on, Julian thought of nothing but Ben and

their future. How Ben would come with him to Harvard and do unspecified things in Boston, where they'd live in a loft and make spaghetti and have sex. After school let out, Julian met Sam to go over his speech before the semifinal contest. She listened inscrutably as Julian recited it from memory. Somewhere in the middle, he realized Ben was artistic and would need a big-screen TV and one of those VCRs with two tape decks. He ended his speech with the usual power nod. Sam smiled. "Everything OK?" she asked. "You seem distracted."

"Should I do it over? I'll do better."

"You'll be great. There's a twist to the format tomorrow. After each speech, there's a question from the audience. Just stick to the rules in the Ten Pillars, and you'll be fine."

"Who's the audience?" Julian asked.

"The North Houston Rotary Club!" Sam said, and laughed. He waited for the punch line. She pursed her lips. "Julian, our movement has a lot of parts. Our center is what you call the brains. A neuron, connected to think tanks and policy makers around the country. But a movement's got to have muscle. Bodies for the brains to direct. And tomorrow you'll meet some bodies. I talked to the principal and got your pass. I'll pick you up at eleven thirty, OK?"

The next morning Sam idled at the front entrance in a gleaming black Mercedes. The whole drive down Beltway 8 they had a great conversation. Sam was fifty-six and ran half marathons. Her expensive clothes fit. She had a career as a geophysicist, like her husband, before their daughter was born. She asked Julian hard questions about where he saw himself in ten years. It wasn't like talking to his mom, he thought as they chatted, more like talking to a fellow adult—a colleague he could brainstorm with about his future and professional things.

"Twelve years," Sam said at one point, when Julian asked how long she'd worked for the center. "It's been my life since my daughter left home." She turned to Julian. "Saved my life, you could say. But we're saving the country, so it's an even trade, right?" She smiled. "I've seen a lot of kids in that time. Hundreds. Most I don't coach, or drive to contests. But I haven't met a man like you since we found Ted. You can go all the way, Julian. You can go far."

He smiled. The blue-lit memory of Ben's bedroom hit him, the heat of Ben's leg against his. And in an act of will undetectable except around his nostrils, Julian put Ben back in storage.

Sam exited onto the feeder road, passed a Jiffy Lube and an Arby's, and turned into a Best Western that had seen better days. "We're in the ballroom," Sam said as they crossed the baking asphalt. "Tighten that tie, and smile now!"

In the lobby Julian sighed at the smell of mildew. Sam waved and hurried to her board members in their fancy suits. The rest of the men milling around the event room—not a woman there but Sam—wore khakis and clip-on suspenders, windbreakers with plumbing and electric logos, an occasional Astros cap or VFW beret. A man with tinted glasses and a gut sat alone at a table smoking a cigar, waiting for lunch. Across the room Sam punched a Rotarian on the shoulder. Julian caught her eye. She tapped her watch and motioned to his name placard at a table draped with patriotic bunting.

Waiters brought out plates of chicken and white lettuce. Sam stood at the lectern and made apocalyptic remarks about freedom. The contest began. At each mediocre speech, Julian's body hummed with adrenaline. His rivals fumbled softball questions about unions and taxes. When it was his turn, the hunger to win reached a trancelike state. Julian stood before the crowd at a cheap hotel, but it was a classroom at Harvard, too, and the floor of Congress. He owned them with his words, finishing to applause beyond that of any other speaker. A radiant Sam passed the microphone to the smoker with the gut.

"Before my question," the man drawled, "I got to say, the passion this young man has? Am I right, y'all? American passion!" The room clapped. "I salute your views on free markets. But conservatives don't stop there. We protect the Christian family. Now, President Clinton"—he paused for effect—"and today I'm saying something nice, y'all. He just signed the Defense of Marriage Act, but is it enough to protect from the homosexual agenda? Boys growing up with no mother and father? Predators recruiting our youth? *That is their plan.* Don't we need more than a law, Mr. Warner? Shouldn't God's word be right there in the US Constitution?"

"Well, sir." Julian's neck beaded. He knew the answer, had the words on his tongue, memories of the caterwauling preachers on the local access shows. He just had to say them. "I think," he continued, "the Ten Pillars we're talking about— they advocate *less* government in our lives, not *more*. James Madison described, in *Federalist* 39, this great laboratory of federalism, so Congress passed its act, but if we leave it to the states to work out, before taking more federal action, I think that lines up more with what our Founders meant."

The man stared at Julian, confused, and looked down. A fork settled on a plate at the back of the silent room. "Thank you," Sam said into the microphone. "We'll let our speakers get a bite to eat while we tally the votes. Let's give them one more round of applause, y'all."

★

Sam talked less on the drive back to school. Julian answered with a word here and there, unable to explain the complex lacerations he was inflicting within. When Sam got to Royalwood High, she put the car in park and turned off the ignition. "You're two hundred fifty dollars richer than you were this morning," she said. "And third place goes to the citywide finals, too."

"It wasn't my speech," Julian said. "It was my answer. I stuck to the Ten Pillars and that book on the Constitution you gave me."

"You were the best man up there," Sam said, stretching her fingers on the steering wheel in exasperation. "I want my favorite student to win. I've been talking you up for weeks." She sighed. "We are the leaders of this movement, Julian. But sometimes, to make the changes *you* want, you have to give the people what *they* want. Understand?" She straightened the lapel on his baggy blazer. "You're a work in progress. I'll see you next week, before the finals."

Inside Julian trudged to his locker. When he opened it, a note fell out with a drawing of stars above a forest path, and a message written in extravagant calligraphy—

Greenbelt trail by my house. Midnight. Xoxo B

Julian stuffed the note in his pocket and looked around, confirming no one saw it. His cheeks burned and his temples pounded. He longed to see Ben, and touch him. But the thing inside him that was Ben, them, two boys' hands brushing on a window frame, there were laws against it to run it out of good homes. There was the day Greg Louganis said he was HIV-positive, and the news kept running the clip from the Olympics when he hit his head and his blood spread in the pool, a crimson monster that had to be cleansed. Julian knew the meaning of that blood. He had a weakness, a defect he couldn't talk about, because speaking made it real. Was that who he was? Who was he anymore, and what was he supposed to be? Today he was a third-place finisher. And he didn't like it.

When Julian got home that evening, his mom waited cross-armed in the foyer. He stood in the doorway as she stared. "When were you planning on telling me?" she asked gravely.

"Tell you what?" His body rocketed into high alert.

"Where were you?"

"Debate club."

"Earlier today, during lunch? Driving off with a woman I don't know?"

"You mean the chaperone for a school-sponsored club?"

"Why do I have to find out from the principal that you left school?" She threw up her arms. "Who just happened to mention it, thinking I knew."

"News flash: I'm leaving sooner or later. Sure as hell not staying here."

"Why didn't you tell me you're in a new club? What do you know about these people? These political types, with their philosophies and—"

"*Philawsaffy?*" he snapped, aping her twang. "What's yours? Lacy's Big *Philawsaffy*. Let's hear it." He gestured that the floor was hers. "Please, enlighten me."

She searched his face. "I think." Her eyes welled up. "Every person deserves someone to love. Whoever it is. And they should take care of that person."

Julian's blood ran cold. "Right." He snickered. "Real philosophy there." He stepped around her and slammed his door without saying good night.

At a quarter to midnight, Julian stuffed his comforter and slid out his bedroom window. He ran the mile to the bike trail near Ben's house, scanning each block for cops with no higher purpose than to collar a kid out past bedtime. His heart sank as he approached the wooden entrance sign and saw no stirring of life.

"Warner!" a voice whispered past the pink haloes of the street lamps. A face leaned out from the trees. Julian followed Ben down the trail, a few paces behind. On either side, back-porch lights carried faintly over fences and through the dense pines. Julian was studying the cling of Ben's sweatpants when he turned around. Delicately he took Julian's face in his hands, like a glass full to the brim, and kissed him. Their tongues searched wordlessly. The vibrations of the crickets engulfed them, bending time to their rhythm.

For three nights they rendezvoused on the trail. Each time Julian's hands journeyed deeper into Ben's clothes, to the small of his back or a nipple that, rubbed lightly, made him exhale in crisis. On the third night, Ben lay Julian on the path and pressed on top of him. Julian felt gravel bite into his calves and Ben's hardness astride his own. They rocked on the ground, clothed and unhurried, bestowing kisses like precious gifts. Until a branch snapped nearby. "Who's there?" a man's voice boomed. A beam of light angled through the trees as a hand waved a flashlight over a fence. The boys ran for the trail entrance.

A few blocks away they slowed down. "This is crazy," Julian fretted, trying to catch his breath. "We can't come here anymore."

"So." Ben looked straight ahead. "Let's go on a date." Julian studied his feet. "I'd be making an exception," Ben added. "You're on the young side for me. People go on dates."

"Yeah," Julian mumbled, "but where?"

"I don't know. Homecoming? Are you more a Beauty or a Beast? I don't care."

"What?"

"Forget it." Ben ran his hands through his hair. "Applebee's? Our amazing planned community's got two. Take your pick."

"What about the Cheesecake Factory in Humble? We could borrow CiCi's car. Oh!" He grabbed Ben's elbow. "I heard about a place in Kemah where they don't card and—"

"Across town." Ben yanked his arm free. "Halfway to Galveston. I get it."

"We can't keep doing this!" Julian snapped. "Maybe this is you, but this is *not me*."

Ben took a step backward and watched him. "Come to my window tomorrow night." His voice hardened. "We'll finish what we started."

"What about your dad?"

"Come or don't. I don't care." He walked off.

The next night Julian tapped at Ben's window. Excitement made him nimble as a cat burglar as he climbed inside. The stereo lights twinkled in the dark. He opened his mouth, but Ben put a finger to his lips and pointed at a chair angled under the doorknob. "He has a gun," Ben whispered. He yanked down Julian's jeans and shoved him onto the bed. Before the shock had worn off, Julian felt Ben's lips at his navel, then down, swallowing him whole. Julian's hips moved with the bed waves. A tiny moan escaped, and just before he came Ben clamped a hand over his mouth. The room exploded in light. Instantly Julian understood the pain in his crotch lately, a tension to propel him here—a white nothing outside the world, past secrets and time and the endless scrabble to make something of himself.

"Turn over," Ben grunted and twisted his shoulders.

"Why?" Julian mouthed.

"To fuck you, what do you think?"

"No," Julian whispered, but Ben tightened his grip and flipped him over. "*No!*" he cried.

Ben's eyes bugged out at the sound. He crept to the door and returned. "What the fuck did you come here for?" he hissed, towering over Julian. "Get out."

"I wanted to see you."

"Go. Don't come back."

Julian got dressed. He waited for an assist to the window frame, but Ben wouldn't look at him, first fumbling with the stereo and then wiping his face on his T-shirt. Julian caught a glimpse of a large dark bruise on his side. "How'd you get that?" he asked.

"I said go."

Julian went out the window and turned to look for Ben's face, but it wasn't there.

After that there were no more notes in Julian's locker. He'd never really seen Ben at school, but now he was nowhere to be found. For days Julian was late to sixth period, trolling the hall where he'd run into CiCi, but he never saw her either. Every night he ran to the bike trail and returned home alone. He couldn't sleep. His gawky frame shrank to bones. A week into his suffering, Julian found Ben's number in the phone book and called his house, but he always got the same redneck voice twanging, "Who is this?" Then one evening the phone picked up on the first ring. "*I wish you were never born,*" Ben hissed. "We're done, got it? Stop calling or I'll call the police."

The phone went dead. Julian stared at the receiver as though it might tell him more. Then he shut his eyes, curled up in bed, and cried himself in and out of sleep.

★

"You feeling well enough to drive, Jules?" his mom asked the next morning on the way to school. She interrupted her regularly scheduled broadcast of chatter and watched him.

"I'm fine."

"You look tired." She pulled over before the main entrance and smiled at him. "I could call in sick and drive you down there. I could watch your speech. It's your last one, isn't it?"

"I can drive myself," Julian mumbled and slammed the door.

At lunchtime he got his mom's keys from the secretary and pulled out of faculty parking. Nothing seemed real as he tore down the highway, not the trucks blaring their horns or the domes of the megachurches. Near 610 the skyline rose like a glittering fortress, and for the rest of the drive Julian ran through the speech he hadn't practiced since the Rotary lunch. He got off at Sam's exit and pulled over to study the directions to River Oaks. The entrance to her street had fancy metal gates. He turned into a row of mansions and parked the minivan in front of Sam's. The front was stone and brick in a pattern Julian had never seen. Sam waved at a window.

"Julian!" she said, opening the door. Her smiled faded. "Are you sick?"

"I'm OK."

"You sure? Come on in. I've got some Blue Bell. We need to fatten you up!"

"Your house is beautiful."

Sam took in the wainscoted foyer. "Mr. Monroe works very hard. I'll grab my keys and we can head out."

"What does he do?" Julian asked as he studied the family pictures on the walls.

"He's in management now at Mobil," she called from another room. "Always traveling." Sam popped back into the foyer. "The center, and our friends in energy in Washington—we take care of our own. Maybe you'll have a house like this someday."

"Is that your daughter?" Julian asked, pointing to a photo of a dark-haired girl.

Sam hesitated. "Yes. That's Abigail."

"Does she live in Houston?"

"No. Abi left for UT, and then to San Francisco of all places. She doesn't like airplanes or the telephone!" Sam smiled, disappearing inside herself. "We can't have that brain drain with *you*," she said when she reemerged. "Go to Harvard, but come home. Texas needs her boys." She held him with her gaze. "I see you, Julian, the good in there. You can win this and go all the way to the Koch Foundation. Remember what I told you?

Give them what they want?" He nodded. "Follow me," she said. "The hotel's about fifteen minutes from here."

They drove to a Ramada this time, with a room full of chamber of commerce men. There were five other contestants, but Julian noticed little around him. He was sleepwalking, numb from the cold place inside where Ben used to be. He gave his speech when Sam called him, and waited for the microphone to reach the questioner. A bald man with wild eyes thanked Julian for his remarks. "Now," he continued, "I have to ask how our government, in the name of 'choice,' allows our women to murder the unborn."

As the man carried on about abortion, Julian found Sam's face in the crowd. Her brow furrowed anxiously. He thought of how she listened when he talked on their long drives, and the look of disappointment on her face when she fixed his collar in the car. The coldness inside him caught fire. He hated Ben. A guy who tried to flip him over and hurt him, a freak who almost ruined his chance at an internship and amazing future.

"It's simple," Julian said when the man finished. "If Congress can't overturn *Roe v. Wade*, what it can do is use the power of the purse to stop the butchering of the unborn. There are actually times when a libertarian *invites* government action. And with precious life at stake? Today's speeches are about free markets, but markets don't sell miracles. They come from the Creator. And we either respect His miracles, or we reap what we sow."

Julian felt the caress of applause again. Sam's face flushed with pride.

When the speeches were done, Sam hugged him and promised to call when the judging was over—and she had a good feeling. "Reap what we sow." She chuckled at him.

He got stuck in traffic on the drive back, inching along until he passed a cluster of wreckage on the highway. By the time he reached Royalwood, school was over, so he went home. He heard a gasp when he opened the front door. His mom flew at him, gripping him frantically. "Where have you been?" she cried.

"There was an accident on 59. I didn't go back to school."

"I know you didn't! All afternoon I was looking for you, everywhere, in the—"

"Why?" Julian wriggled away from her. "What's with you?"

"I couldn't find you! There was an incident at school. A senior was attacked. Benjamin Cross. He had problems with boys in gym class." She watched Julian. "Calling him a fag. He stood up to them. He said he was gay, and they—did things to him. He's in the hospital." She seized Julian's head. Her eyes were fierce. "I love you. You got a problem, *tell me.* Somebody bothers you, *tell me.*"

The phone rang. They froze.

His hand quivered as he picked up the receiver.

"Julian? It's Sam. You did it! You're our winner! I'm holding a check with a lot of zeroes here, and soon I'll have a ticket to Washington! Ready to take our fight to the Capitol?" She waited. "He's speechless," she said away from the receiver. "Julian? Hello?"

"I'm here."

"Congrats! What do you say? You ready to be our new voice for American freedom?"

Julian turned to his mom, watching him by the sink with her hands clasped around her waist. He studied her careworn face, the one he had always known.

He hung up the phone.

8

Let's Get Baked Tonight

And then he threw up on the carpet and started walking circles around his mess, and I called to him, *Muffin! Muffin!* but he kept circling, so now the vet thinks maybe he's deaf on top of the cataracts and irritable bowel, because Westies are prone to—"

"Uh-huh," Julian said, the phone dangling precipitously between his shoulder and ear. "I mean, if he's that sick maybe the compassionate thing to do is—" He leaned forward to check his desk clock. "I gotta go. I have to grab dinner before a meeting across the Yard in ten."

"Oh. For a student group?"

"Yeah. BGLTSA. I have an idea for campus activism. A big one."

"Interesting. You want to talk about—"

"No, Mom, I gotta go."

"Okey-doke. There's only one Julian Warner! Knock 'em dead, sweetie." She sighed faintly. "Love you. Same time tomorrow?"

His mom's last words hung in the air like melancholy music as Julian bought a wrap from the snack bar and hustled to Boylston Hall. If it wasn't one thing on their nightly calls, it was another. In the three weeks since Julian started college, his mom groused about the cable going out, the kitchen faucet leaking, and lately every call about his dog, Muffin, who was totally fine when he petted him goodbye in August. Julian hurried across campus, past buildings that caught the sunset more beautifully than the poster in his room back home. It was the way she rambled during their calls that bugged him—different somehow from her chatter in high school, the white noise he tuned out every day. On the phone, far away, he could hear her voice pure and clear. And as much as he loved her—more than anyone in the world—it turned out he didn't want to see the sad, lonely things inside her. Or know what to do with them.

Julian stopped at the statue of John Harvard and wondered if students really peed on him. He thought of the meeting ahead. Where there would be boys, yes, maybe cute nice boys, but so what? He stared down the statue and reviewed the opening lines of his speech. The idea came to him in the cafeteria when he smiled at a butch woman working the lunch line, and they started talking. The hardest part of Harvard was getting in, people said, so why not draw attention to inequality, rile up the school, get his name in the *Crimson* as a freshman? He had the whole protest planned, the demands, the change he would make, and the glory. And suddenly, in the midst of his fantasy, came a flicker of doubt. He wondered if he could pull it off. Not wilt in front of the group, convince them he could do it. He should run it all by his mom first, Julian thought as he turned back to the path. But then he remembered he'd just hung up with her.

★

On a balmy night still perfumed with summer, Philip Rosenblum thought about sex as he crossed Harvard Yard. The usual stuff, nothing exotic. He itemized his own history, which by sophomore year amounted to making out with three girls and wiggling his fingers on a breast. He thought of dicks and how he liked them, or the idea of them, dropping momentarily into a Freudian black hole. He thought of straight people and the pass they got for bad behavior. Their strip clubs, Hooters, Mardi Gras tits for beads—sex so comically bankrupt it left him scratching his head, but if it ends with a few shrieking kids down the road, all is forgiven, right? His mind raced the whole way to Boylston Hall, where he stepped into the landscaping. He hid behind a manicured spruce and watched students go into the building. Philip hated the fact that his internal conflicts manifested as psychic conversations with his mother, a fact all the more excruciating when the conflict was sex. But he had made a decision and would see it through. He stepped from the bushes and, eyes lowered, made his way into his first BGLTSA meeting.

He held his breath as he entered the lounge. A hundred heads, or maybe twenty, turned in telepathic vampire unison. "Hi!" said a blue-haired girl with a clipboard. He sat in the back. Across the room, Philip spotted two guys with bloodshot eyes whispering about him. He'd overheard them in the Science Center at lunchtime, joking about the annual tradition of getting high and hitting the first gay student group meeting of the year, to scope out hot freshmen. Let's Get Baked Tonight, they called it. For the rest of the afternoon, Philip judged them and mulled over whether to hit up the meeting he had studiously avoided the year before. In the evening he fortified himself at his desk, studying econ. But when the clock struck 6:55, in one frenetic burst he stuffed a joint in his pocket and a condom in his wallet and ran for the Yard.

And there, somewhat to his own surprise, he was.

The meeting began with introductions by the officers. For a terrible moment Philip thought they were going to go around and say their names, but the discussion turned to fall activities. He stole glances around the lounge. Not a single guy jumped out as an option—too skinny, or fat, or dressed to the Wildean nines on a Tuesday. He wondered if he was one of those asexuals in practice, or if asexuals were really a thing. He was stuck in his head again, any chance of getting laid doomed by the feedback loop of real-time analysis. He sighed and plotted how to exit unnoticed. It was the summer that drove him to this meeting, he thought grimly, a shitty summer at his dad's bank, around vulgar douchebags who talked sex 24/7 like it was Chinese takeout and frayed his nerves until he figured he should just do it and get it over with. So he came. He saw. He got depressed. Because no matter what words his mom used to theorize it—intersubjective recognition of the blahdiblah—at the end of the day he was pretty sure that there was no Santa, and sex was just fucking.

"I have an idea." A sharp voice broke through his thoughts. A guy Philip hadn't seen stood up—an elf-boy who looked all of fifteen, with olive skin, runway cheekbones, huge dark eyes flecked with something lighter, greens or golds. His hair was shaggy and copper in the lamplight. Israeli? South American? Definitely southern by his voice. "Has anyone seen the college's domestic partner benefits policy for staff members?" he asked. "That's where same-sex marriage and income inequality are intersecting in our own backyard. I did an interview with a food services worker, and I think Harvard's got a problem. Can we add that to the list of fall projects? I'll take the lead."

"Great!" the president said, jotting on her clipboard. "And your name is?"

"Julian Warner."

He said it, surname and all, like he was branding the collective mind of the club. He wore faded jeans and a black T-shirt. A revolutionary look, as much as any kid in the dorms looked like a revolutionary. But the low, piercing voice as he talked, and kept talking, the hang of his shirt on his boyish frame, they sent a chemical pulse through Philip that was one hundred percent not asexual. For the rest of the meeting he snuck looks at Julian, chubbing in waves, and fingered the edge of the condom. It occurred to him it might have expired. Condoms expired. He hadn't checked the date on it, and now was a sleazily conspicuous time to try. He made a mental note and adjusted himself. When the meeting ended, Philip waited for the progressive whiz kid to hoist his backpack in departure mode, and left a few minutes ahead of him, darting outside and stationing himself in the dimly lit courtyard.

"Julian?" Philip called when he exited. Julian squinted in his direction. "Sorry," Philip stepped into the light and smiled. "I liked what you said in there."

"About what?" Julian said, blank-faced and oddly provocative.

"About pushing the school to—we should know if Harvard's treating all couples equally. I'm Philip." He held out his hand. "Are you a freshman?"

"Yeah." He stared at Philip's hand a moment before shaking it. "Hi."

"Are you headed somewhere?"

"Widener," Julian said. "I've got a date with a study carrel."

"Did you eat already?"

"I don't have time."

"To eat?" Philip asked. "You're not eating dinner tonight?"

Julian patted his backpack. "Falafel. While I study. I've got a system."

"Wow. Could I come to the stacks and watch you? Learn secrets to a productive life?"

"I could give you some tips. What's in it for me?"

"Tonight, what's in it for—" Philip watched Julian, who

stood impassive and unusually hard to read. "Well," he continued, "I know Cambridge top to bottom. I can show you around. An unforgettable night on the town."

"Good to know in advance what's unforgettable. I'm from Texas," Julian drawled. "Things are slower there." He ran his eyes unabashedly over Philip. "What's your go-to place to impress? On the town?"

A surge of heat rose from Philip's lower chakras. "You want to go?"

"Is it impressive?"

"Follow me," he said, motioning gallantly toward the wrought-iron gate.

Julian hesitated. "Where are we going, Mr.—?"

"Rosenblum." He couldn't stop smiling. "Philip Rosenblum."

★

Julian's brain hurt from listening. In the weeks since school started, as long as two lifetimes, he felt terror, ecstasy, a million things about the world pulsing through Harvard. How much bigger than he dreamed! The wealth and ambition, new classmates who already seemed to know things and one another. In lecture halls and dorm rooms Julian told himself to *listen, listen before you speak* like his mom always said. But when the unknowns got him too keyed up, he'd fall into old habits and start talking like the state champion debater he was—with total certainty and a contrary flair. He was used to being an outsider. Gay in the rhinestone buckle of the Bible Belt. President of the three-member Royalwood High School Democrats. It was a role he knew how to play. A tough one, at times, turning up enemies where maybe there were none. But with each natty freshman he met from Exeter or Trinity, the more that chip snuggled comfortably back onto his shoulder.

When he heard his name outside Boylston, after the BGLTSA meeting, Julian looked around with his guard up. Philip came out of the shadows. Julian read the situation. A closet case, and a handsome one, but who has time for that? Julian had seen it all—brave people hurt, liars walking free—and he only had space for truth in his life. Yet something about Philip held him there, drawing him in as the library receded to the back of his mind. It wasn't the dark, loose curls or his muscles, though Julian noticed both. It was his easy confidence, and warmth. An urge to connect that Julian sensed might come from kindness.

He listened while Philip led him from the Yard and gave a walking tour of the Square over to a hotel by the river. Inside he waved at the concierge and guided Julian to a restaurant. "Rialto," he said, opening the door. "Purveyor of cocktails that may or may not impress."

"Um," Julian whispered, "do they card here?"

"Philip!" the hostess called.

"Beth," he purred, touching her lightly on the arm.

"How was your summer?"

"Great!" He gave her a blinding smile. "I was back home working for my dad."

"How is he? We haven't seen him in a while."

"He's great. Is that round booth free tonight?"

The hostess grabbed menus and winked. "Your favorite?" She waved them into the restaurant. It was low lit and airy, with white brick walls, a gleaming bar, sheer draperies that rippled elegantly to the central air. The hostess stopped at a booth upholstered in plush sage fabric, a three-quarter circle in the middle of everything, yet shrouded, intimate.

"Could we start with that champagne-elderflower cocktail?" Philip asked as they slid in. "Two of those, if my friend Julian doesn't mind?"

Julian nodded maturely. "Nice place," he said when she left.

"We're off to a good start, then." Philip ran his hand along the curving wall. "I like this booth. Nice and private."

"So," Julian said, "where's home?"

"New York."

"The city? I've always wanted to live there. It's where I'm going when I graduate."

"Nice. Have you spent a lot of time there?" Philip asked.

"Not a lot. I haven't been yet, but—where did you work? This summer?"

"I was interning at Goldman."

"Cool." Julian had heard of this mysterious Goldman the past few weeks. "And your dad? What does he do there?"

"Um. He's a banker?"

"He knows the hostess? Up front?"

"Oh," Philip said. "My dad went to the business school. He does recruiting events here."

"And your mom? What does she do?"

"She teaches."

"Really?" Julian said. "Mine, too."

"Yeah? Well, she's a therapist. Still in private practice, but now she's mostly running the postdoc program in psychoanalysis at NYU. Where's your mom?"

"Chemistry. She teaches chemistry, just, at the high school where I went."

"Interesting." Philip smiled. "While you were there, she was teaching?"

"Yeah. Siblings?"

"Oh. I do. A sister. How about—"

"Older?" Julian fired. "Younger?"

"She's two years older."

"In school?"

"Oberlin. And you," Philip leaned forward, "are a regular Barbara Walters."

"Two elderflower cocktails," the hostess said, appearing in their circle.

"Cheers." Philip clinked his glass to Julian's. "Do you answer questions too?"

"Do I—yeah. I'm from Houston, where I'm never going back. The plan is to graduate early and then it's law school, here or Yale, and long-term working at the ACLU . . ." On this went for some time, Julian informing Philip about his future, the clubs he joined, classes in his schedule and their place in the grand scheme. He talked for one drink, and another. By the end of their refill, Julian had planted his flag at the table. Philip was smiling. But something was off. There was nothing between them. Or had Julian's mouth run it out of the room?

"Should we order?" Philip asked, opening a menu. "Dinner?"

"No," Julian snapped. Two things had happened when Philip leaned over to order their second round: Julian traced the outline of Philip's glutes through his slacks, wondering for the first time if he was an ass man, and he ran his eyes over the menu and knew he couldn't afford a thing on it. His mom had given him some spending money for the semester, but Julian was budgeted to within an inch of his life. He smiled coyly. "Could we, like, hit up a dive?"

"Not impressed with this place?" Philip said.

"Very. But now we're testing your versatility. Take me to the diviest place you know in Cambridge. And if there's a real chance I might get sick, there we'll break bread."

"Hmm." He tapped his fingertips together. "You want to get down with the people?"

He looked Philip over. The gray-blue eyes and pale cheeks, flushed with champagne, his face as sweet as a kitten. "I am the people," Julian replied. And prayed, totally agnostically, that he hadn't fucked it up.

★

"I give you—Hong Kong Restaurant and Lounge!" Philip threw up his arms at the red Chinesey neon sign. It cast a pink glow on the street where Mass Ave. elbowed around the Yard.

"A real dump," Julian growled approvingly as they entered. "Be right back."

"I'll grab a table," Philip said. He parked himself on a vinyl banquette and ordered a drink. Julian was a talker. He got this look in his eye as he talked, like he could eat or destroy anything in his path, the kind of guy who might look up, mid–blow job, and start discoursing on systemic racism in the criminal justice system. This frightened Philip, and turned him on. His most revelatory sex to date happened last year, sneaking into an adult video store in Back Bay and buying a movie from the BelAmi rack. Back at his dorm he watched eggplant-size Czech cocks pounding mouths or baby-smooth assholes, an oddly wholesome version of the things he wanted to do. He was by himself then. Now he sat waiting for Julian in a faint mist of MSG—horny, tipsy, with a joint and a Trojan Magnum he yearned proudly to inaugurate. But at some point during drinks, he started to wonder what Julian wanted. And to ask himself if all the smack talk at the bank last summer, about sex—was it really about fear? Of this feeling, or whatever was happening tonight? And why couldn't he ever keep things simple?

The sight of two guys from his lacrosse team knocked Philip from his musings. He spotted them through the window as they were passing the restaurant, walking down Mass Ave., and he ducked under the table. He pretended to tie his shoe for an eternity, only rising when the waitress came with their drink. Cautiously Philip lifted his head and scanned the street, their dining area, and the next area over for anyone who might see him with his pretty new friend.

"My goodness," Julian said, approaching the table. "What is that?" He pointed at the coconut-shaped bowl with two extra-long straws.

"The Scorpion Bowl, a toxic blend of liquor and juice. Was the bathroom vile enough?"

Julian grinned. "I used to rate them when I was a kid and we'd go out to eat. A ten. Seven. Two. It was sort of my party trick. People started asking for it."

"What to do with that fact?" Philip laughed.

Julian sipped from the bowl, grimaced, and gave Philip a childlike impatient look. "Tell me about you. I promise I won't ask more questions."

"Questions are good," Philip said. "I like questions. And listening."

"I'm good at that. You wouldn't guess by tonight. So, you had a great summer working for your dad at Goldman?"

"Great?" Philip considered. "I don't know if I'd use that word." They sipped. When Philip looked up Julian was watching him, but it didn't feel bulldozing anymore. It was warm, inviting him somewhere solid. "I had a weird summer," he said, and with gathering speed and sips, he unraveled the whole neurotic mess beneath the Rosenblum facade.

He didn't even like finance, he told Julian, and the summer was one more bad decision in a string of attempts to be like other people, going back to high school lacrosse, dating girls, the tap lessons he never asked for because it seemed gay. None of which was his parents' fault, in a shocking Freudian twist, because despite their success they were both so disgustingly supportive of everything in his life. But what killed him, he explained with an emphatic suck, was the talking. Everything at home got analyzed. Eggs at breakfast, books on the nightstand, pre-analyzed, re-analyzed, until life was strangled and his sister—the righteous terror of Oberlin Hillel—fled to the Midwest, convinced her parents had ruined her life, and the lives of Mom's clients, and the American economy by way of Dad's insatiable greed. And Philip wished for once the four of them could just sit down to dinner and shut up and enjoy the food.

"Have you tried bringing them here?" Julian asked as the waitress arrived with their order. He swirled an egg roll contemplatively in mustard. "But seriously, that sounds pretty crazy. Family can get you so angry. And it's all you know. Till you talk to somebody else."

Philip took in this statement and thought the world of it. "Yes," he said. From there Julian talked about his family. The mom who was nothing short of a hero—a tenured thorn in the side of the school, always pushing for more ESL classes, giving the principal friendly reminders about the law. A teacher you remembered. In passing he mentioned the dad he hadn't seen in years, whom he couldn't bring himself to hate because he felt nothing for him. They ordered another Scorpion Bowl. In a flash of awareness Philip knew he wasn't stuck in his head, overthinking. He was living and being, a state he dreamed of but never talked to his mom about, for fear it would trigger blame and some door-slamming enactment. And it occurred to him, as Julian chatted away, that maybe this was a man who would let him coexist, be a safe home for him even if he was still figuring things out.

"So," Julian said out of nowhere, vacuuming up the remnants of the second bowl. "Like, what's your greatest fear? If we're being honest."

"Y2K."

Julian laughed. Then his brow furrowed. "Do you think, on New Year's, something—"

"Oh, pandemonium! I'll be out of banks, into gold, and tucked in my bomb shelter."

"Is it getting shot in public?" Julian asked. "Like some Mafia hit? You've been looking around the restaurant every five minutes since we got here."

"N-no," Philip stammered. He felt his face flush from the drinks, or the stab of Julian's words, or his flat, deadly affect. "No, uh, greatest fear would probably be . . . I guess maybe never finding the thing I'm passionate about? Who I'm supposed to be."

The waitress brought the check. Philip grabbed it.

"Hey," Julian protested. "I can't let you do that."

"Too slow. Fortune cookie?" He handed one to Julian and opened the other.

"Throw it out. The fortune, don't look at it." Julian watched him. His eyes were uncertain, with longing or sudden disgust, Philip couldn't tell. "Let's write our own tonight," Julian said. "If you could have anything you want, right now. First thought."

"I don't know. For people to get along," Philip said quietly. "It's juvenile."

"No it's not. I'm just skeptical . . ." Julian sighed. "Is it possible?"

"How are we doing?"

Julian smiled mysteriously.

"And your fortune?" Philip asked. "Where are you headed, Man with the Plans?"

"Maybe"—Julian fumbled with his napkin—"mine is not to have any. Past the next hour."

Outside the restaurant, the fresh air revived them and made their drunkenness plain.

"It's your lucky night," Philip said. "I got Sour Diesel and a single in Kirkland with—"

"I'm not going back to your dorm," Julian blurted. "We're not fucking."

"Oh. OK. I didn't . . ."

Julian stood in the neon glow of the sign and watched Philip, his eyes forlorn in his slender face. "I should go," he said and turned away.

"Sorry!" Philip cried out. "I didn't mean to objectify you or—I was nervous in there, but if I can make it up to you with a nightcap or coffee—I'm not a jerk, I'm just . . ."

Julian turned around. "What's the most romantic spot in Cambridge?" He waited. "Can you take me there? Are you ready to be there with me, in full view of everyone?"

"I . . ." Philip began, and froze.

"Thanks," Julian said. "For dinner and drinks. Nice meeting you, Philip Rosenblum." Then the boy revolutionary trudged over the cobblestones, until his willowy frame slipped through the gates to the Yard, and he was gone.

★

Julian was feeling guilty, late the next night, as he packed up his books and plodded out of the library. For the first time since he got to school, he skipped his call with his mom that evening—shifted his routine an hour earlier, grabbed his dinner from the snack bar, and headed to the stacks. By six o'clock he was deep in Plato's *Republic*, jotting notes in the margin and not thinking of a phone ringing in an empty dorm room. Or trying not to. He didn't skip because of Philip or their date, or whatever failed hookup it turned out to be. It was bigger than that. His mom always asked what he'd been up to, and he didn't like to leave stuff out. And he wasn't sure how that would work. How there could be room for three of them—his mom and him and a boyfriend, not some boy he kissed in the war zone of high school but a real boyfriend. How she would feel or sound on the phone when he told her, or what she'd eat after they hung up. So he went to Widener and studied until the sky was dark and his brain was fried.

"Julian?" He was halfway down the library steps when he heard his name. Philip leaped off a ledge by the entrance and hurried to him. "How are you?"

"OK," he replied. "Were you—"

"No studying. No books." He held up his empty hands. "Just waiting. Two hours, to be exact. Not to guilt trip! That came out wrong. I had to see you and—" Philip sighed. "Say I'm sorry. About last night. I've never done this. I do know the most romantic spot in Cambridge. The one I always imagined I'd . . . if you still want to go."

"Are you asking me out on a—"

"Date? Yes, well, the continuation of a previously unspecified hangout that I screwed up." Tremulously Philip offered his hand. With a shiver, Julian watched his own slide into it. Philip led them down Bow Street—their backs straight, heads forward, hands pressed together in an awkward grip—to a red house. They descended into a basement with checkerboard floors and pale yellow walls.

"Café Pamplona," he said, pulling out a chair for Julian. "Site of anguished journaling, full ashtrays, and romantic nightcaps." He ordered cappuccinos. "So," Philip began when the waiter left. "After we parted ways, I paced and thought and concluded that honesty is the only foundation for a—" He sighed. "I don't do that. Get stoned."

"OK."

"Much. I'm not like a serious—I have a delivery service back home. But I didn't want you to think I came to the meeting last night just to hook up. I heard these guys at lunch, talking about this thing they—"

"Let's Get Baked Tonight?" Julian said.

"Oh. You heard about that too."

"I'm a good listener." Julian flashed Philip an inscrutable look, to hide how much hinged on the next moment. And to buy a little time, assess how much of himself he could truly reveal before Philip would turn and run. "So you weren't trying to hook up last night?"

"No. Maybe?" Philip shrugged entreatingly. "If it happens, it happens?"

"This is the most romantic spot in Cambridge. Has that ever happened to you?"

"What? Like a one-and-done thing?"

"Like sex with a guy," Julian said.

"Uhhh." Their coffees arrived. "Not yet." He looked up sheepishly. "Have you?"

"Once. In high school." Julian blew on his mug. "We did up to oral, but then . . ."

"Then?"

"He wanted to go further than I—It wasn't assault. Guys can sexually assault other guys," Julian announced imperiously. "He stopped, but. Then he got sodomized by a toilet plunger in gym class, and I never saw him again."

Philip smiled tensely at him and wrinkled his nose. "Wait. You're serious?"

Julian nodded. "The one openly gay guy at our school of four thousand. He had to be taught a lesson. No one got punished. The principal couldn't figure out how a plunger got up him. His parents were Mormon, ashamed. He never came back to school."

"What was his name?" Philip asked.

"Ben." They sat together, in quiet. "It's how I came out to my mom," Julian resumed. "The day it happened. She was at school when the ambulance came. She couldn't find me and went nuts. She figured out that Ben and I had been . . . She was amazing. Is. She's trying to start a Gay-Straight Alliance at the high school this year."

"Fantastic."

"Yeah. After Ben, and—" Julian looked up with tears in his eyes.

"It's OK," Philip said gently, handing him a napkin. "After Ben and?"

"Matthew Shepard, last year. She had enough. She said, 'Jules, I'm sorry you can't live where you were born, but once you're safe and far away, somebody has to protect the outsiders.' I told her not to hold her breath. But she's determined." Pensively Julian stirred his cappuccino. "And you?" he asked. "Are you out to your family at least?"

"No." Philip ran his hands through his curls. "It's not a secret. Not *not* in the realm of possibilities. They'll be fine. My sister will finally have something controversial to love about me. But. Just imagining my mom talking about it? Asking questions? It feels like so little is mine. And it's not about a relationship, or justifying who you are, but—I've never met a guy I'd want to take home. Make it real. You know what I mean?"

"Yeah." Julian did know. And he wondered, with a pain in his chest, if Philip included tonight in that statement. Instantly he felt stupid, for building up drinks and Chinese and coffee with a closeted stranger into a future with what? A husband and kids, a white picket fence? But guys were getting married in Hawaii now, or they had been for a minute. And after the years of longing, wouldn't Julian know the feeling when it came? Didn't he deserve it? The arrival of the friend he always wanted as a boy, another boy he could hold close, to be big and small with, the superhero and sometimes the scared mortal too. Philip came back for him, didn't he? "Yeah," Julian said, "I know what you mean. How'd your parents meet?"

"In undergrad, in the city. But their first official date wasn't until they got here for grad school. Coffee in Harvard Square. My dad was at the B-school, and Mom was getting her PhD."

"How funny," Julian said. "My parents too."

"Yeah?"

"In college. They were both at UT, in Austin."

"Twenty-nine years together," Philip said, shaking his head at the vast riddle of it. He shot Julian a look of alarm. "I didn't mean to give the wrong impression about them, before."

"You didn't."

Philip smiled ingenuously. "Did you ever think about our parents as kids? Or, like, someday we'll be parents? And, no," he said, catching himself, "I'm not stoned at the moment."

The check came. The café was closing. Julian took Philip's hand as they climbed the steps. Their fingers laced together, the space between their words no longer filled with tension but a kind of peace. When they got to the Yard, Julian threw back his head and gazed at the sky full of stars, until Philip looked too.

"Can you get on the roof of your dorm?" Julian asked.

Philip's face lit up. "Yeah."

"I'll smoke your pot." Julian's eyes fell from the stars to his companion, searching his face urgently. "But we have to declare ourselves. Who we are and what we want. Come out or die trying. Every time the world says to us, *That's your defect*, we say, *No, that's my strength. My X-ray goggles. And now I see.*"

Philip watched him and nodded.

"And just so you know," Julian continued. "I'm wearing two corsets. I'm actually four hundred pounds, and there's no un-wrapping this big delicious package tonight."

★

Philip knew Julian meant it when they got to his door and, resisting the lure of Philip's new Napster trove, he chose to wait in the hall. Philip grabbed blankets. They climbed three flights to a disarmed fire door and onto the roof, a glowing stage of re-flective paint bouncing moonlight everywhere. The river curled below. Above it sat the beetle dome at MIT, with a hint of the Boston skyline twinkling in the background. Philip fired up the joint. He really wasn't a regular drug user, nothing hard, but weed for anxiety—his mom?—it went with the territory. He passed it to Julian, reclining beside him, who took a monster hit and started coughing.

"You ever smoke before?" Philip asked. Julian shook his head in terror. "Breathe," Philip murmured. "It's OK. I'm here; the stars are here." Julian rose and wandered to the edge of the roof, taking in the views, his face like an awestruck newborn's. Philip struggled to his knees. "Not to beat a dead horse," he said, "but I meant no disrespect when I approached you at the meeting. I like hearing your plans. I think you're amazing. And cute." Julian stared off into the night like he hadn't heard. "Why'd you come back with me?" Philip asked. "Here."

"You gotta let it all hang out sometimes." Julian turned to Philip and smiled. "Or else you'll go crazy in the head." He strolled back to the blanket and flopped down. "I'm stoned," he announced. "Why'd you intern for your dad last summer, if you didn't want to?"

"We'll need a double session for that. God, the other guys there? Money and fucking, all they talk about. Who made it, who made more, what did he buy? No readers. I asked one intern the last great book he read. He said, '*The Art of the Deal*. Donald Trump. The man's a genius.' I was like, that douchebag? And he says, 'To be that big a douche and still make shit tons of money? Genius.'"

"Is it sexist," Julian pondered, "to use 'douchebag' pejora-tively?"

"I think you'd like my mom."

"What?"

"Nothing," Philip said.

They lay beside each other and watched the stars. Philip could feel Julian's heat where their arms touched. He could've made a move but he didn't, because in the clarity of his high Philip knew he desired something more than sex—for the night never to end, and then another night, to be close to Julian always and maybe let the whole world see.

"What's your greatest fear?" Philip asked. "If we're being honest."

"Huh?"

"I told you mine at the restaurant last night."

"Oh yeah. I guess . . . I have this anger inside me that I think could save the world, or some part of it. Or it could burn me up first. I don't know."

"He who wills something great is in my eyes a great man." Philip's words floated up and away. "Not he who achieves it. For in achievement luck plays a great part."

"What is that?" Julian asked.

"Herzl. Jewish flotsam, from back in the day. We're human. We fall on our faces. I'll fail. You'll fail." He nudged Julian's shoulder. "The point is the fight, right? To die trying."

Julian lay very still. "Do you think anyone will—could ever love us as much as . . ."

"As much as what?"

Julian sat up. "I have to go." He was on his feet, zipping his backpack.

"Oh." Philip tore himself from the life he thought they'd been having on the blanket island and hustled behind Julian to the door. Julian took the steps double time, until Philip called out, "Hey, Jay? This is my floor."

Julian stopped and checked his watch. "Twelve thirty. Wow. Thanks for the coffee and cannabis, the highs and lows of Cambridge, the—"

"Do we have to sum it up?" Philip asked. And he could blame it on the weed, or blue balls, or the feeling of something precious slipping away, but he leaned in and went for the kiss.

Julian put his hand to Philip's cheek before their faces met, and held him there. They stared into each other's eyes. Julian gave him a cautious peck on the lips, slow and curious, and continued down the stairs.

"Are you going to get home OK?" Philip asked, leaning over the railing.

"Call me tomorrow to make sure I'm alive."

"You want to do something?"

"Yeah. I need to see what you look like in daylight." At the bottom of the stairs, Julian paused and looked up. "Really. Thank you for finding me." He disappeared out the door.

Philip gripped the banister with both hands. He heard his mom's voice in his head. The voice he spent his whole life trying to shake, but in the wee hours of this particular night, on the stairs of his dorm, he invited in. "Yeah, maybe," he answered her. "Maybe this is the one."

9

Around the World in Eighty Minutes

Lacy had been driving in circles for almost an hour, on a very short fuse. She knew every drab detail of Intercontinental by her eighth lap around the terminal. Painted fields of long-term parking, the disc-topped spaceship Marriott where once upon a time Julian had his debate club awards dinner, then back to baggage claim with the wreaths on the sliding glass doors, where she craned her neck for a view until police toting semiautomatics shooed her off. The security was overkill. Irrational, like so much of the response to these terrorists. How was she supposed to pick them up if she couldn't idle for a minute and look for them? Do it like the old Westerns, where the cowboy dives into the speeding stagecoach? *You used to go inside,* Lacy thought as she circled. *You used to be able to stay with your loved ones all the way to the gate.* She was at the gate a few summers ago, waving goodbye as Julian boarded a plane for Boston by himself.

But the world changed. And this year when her son came home for Christmas, he didn't return alone. Men were flying planes into buildings, America was suddenly at war, and Julian was bringing his brand-new fiancé home. "We get in on the twenty-third," he said on a rushed call. "Great news, right?

Philip can't wait to meet you. Now, what's your doctor saying?"
The longer she drove around, the more she went over the things
Julian had on his plate right then: graduating early because of
loans, the LSAT, law school apps. She listed his burdens and
knew this wasn't the time. Not the time to tell him the chemo
wasn't working, or that the doctor had shrugged and given her
the sad death smile. What it was time for was one more Christmas, and to get a good look at the man who wanted to marry
the love of her life.

On her tenth lap, while waiting at a stoplight, Lacy saw Julian from afar. She glanced at her skeletal face in the rearview
mirror, remembering all the years she cursed herself for not being thinner. She fluffed the wispy remnants of her gray hair
and inched the car forward. Her heart fluttered at the sight of
her baby, still boyish at twenty-one. His hair was shorter but
the same pretty chestnut. Julian ducked down to get something
from his bag, and that was when Lacy saw him—the New York
Jewish boyfriend. But Philip was no Jeff Goldblum. No glasses,
not the nerdy lab-coat type. He was handsome, as tall as her
son but the shape of a man, his clothes perfect like he stepped
out of a J.Crew catalog and not off a plane. Julian stood back
up and saw Lacy, she could tell by his eyes. His face, usually so
determined, was shaded with something else. A shyness or fear.
He grabbed Philip's hand. The other he raised timidly to her,
fingers extended, in a gesture that said hello or to stay where
she was.

★

Lacy couldn't remember when the pain started. It was in her
lower back on the right side. For a while she thought she slept
on it funny, so she started taking Advil with her morning Met-
amucil and went to work. It was a busy new school year. And
she'd had plenty of pains after fifty. Her knees, ankles, hips. She

was fat, and she was used to how people stared when she walked slowly or stopped to rest at Walgreens—like she deserved every pain she felt. But one day the pain got so bad that Lacy couldn't hoist herself up into the minivan, so she called in sick, and over lunch her best friend Bonnie took her to her PCP. He massaged where the pain was, the first time a man had touched her like that in years. He frowned. The rest was a blur.

First she went local to Royalwood Hospital, then to MD Anderson, where they found the cancer wrapped around her kidneys and other places, and then every Friday it was chemo downtown. Bonnie took half days off and drove her there. They were both in need that fall and had to rely on each other. Right after school started, Bonnie's husband told her he'd been having an affair with a colleague at Shell and left her alone in a big house with the ghost of her family. During the chemo visits, Bonnie would crack her nicotine gum and read *People*, gabbing about the latest celebrity breakups while Lacy lay back in the chair. She rubbed Lacy's arm when she turned the page. On most Fridays they stopped at the Rothko Chapel before the Medical Center. It was Bonnie's idea. She knew that Lacy was an atheist, and that her own God had done her wrong. Yet when they entered the muted brick octagon and arranged their cushions on the benches, there was no difference. They could gaze at the black canvases around them until the colors came. They could shut their eyes and drink in silence. It was their church beyond words or stories, injustice or revenge. Outside the world rocked with violence. Inside they sat together. Breathed. And survived.

Julian knew little of this, though he and Lacy were in regular touch. He called home twice a week. But they usually talked about him. The authors he was reading, his classes, how pretty snow was. He talked about the Rosenblums. Philip's powerful dad, their country house, the mom with the PhD—who'd have ten PhDs if she got one every time Julian mentioned it. She never criticized her boy at Harvard. On the rare occasion when he asked how she was, Lacy had about a two-minute window to say something interesting before he began to give her advice. She could hear it in his voice then. Not disdain, but his sense of the smallness of her life—her conflicts at the high school, worrying how to pay for the new roof—that warranted a kind of distant pity.

So after years of playing second fiddle to Julian's Proust and Marx and Jane Jacobs, when Lacy slipped in a comment about her diagnosis on the phone one night, she wasn't sure how to talk to him about it. It was a few nights before the terror attacks. Julian started calling her every day after she told him, pelting her with questions, but Lacy felt out of practice in the spotlight and paralyzed by the darkness of the world. And often so tired she wanted to cry. She decided the easiest thing was to tell Julian the dry bits the doctor told her: the plans for chemo, scans, more chemo. For months, with no added emotion, Lacy shared everything the doctor said and prescribed. Until last week, when she got the news she got. And now it wasn't just her son she had to talk to face-to-face this Christmas. It was a curly-haired stranger too, smiling and waving vigorously as she pulled the minivan up to baggage claim.

"Hi, Mom," Julian said, opening the shotgun door.

"Hop in, guys," she called. "This policeman's about to run me out of town."

"Mrs. Warner!" Philip said, buckling up behind them. "I've heard so much about you. Great to meet you! From the back seat."

"You too. Call me Lacy." She pulled into the exit lane, stealing glances at Philip in the rearview mirror. Dark curls, the jawline, milky skin. He had movie-star looks. The exotic blue-eyed guy who leads Israel to freedom in the old movies. "How was y'alls flight?" she asked.

"Crazy." Julian turned off the heat. "You heard about the shoe bomber?"

"The what?"

"Yesterday. A guy put explosives in his shoes and tried to light them on a plane."

"And now?" Philip said, appearing between the front seats like a Muppet. A push-up kind of guy, Lacy thought, unsure how she felt about that. "Everyone has to take off their shoes and walk through security in socks. We gave ourselves three hours to get from Cambridge to Logan and barely made our flight."

"A bomb in his shoes," Lacy murmured. She drove, and stayed in her lane, but the world went dark again. She could feel her eyes watering.

"Mom?" Julian looked at her for the first time since he got in. "You OK?"

"Will wonders never cease?" She brushed her eyes on the sleeve of her Santa cardigan. It had taken her two hours, but that morning she'd showered and put on makeup and dressed for the boys. And after all her fashion efforts, she was still swimming in clothes that used to fit. "Let's talk about y'all's visit!" she said. "Philip, we're having spaghetti tonight like we always do, and tomorrow my friend Bonnie's coming over. She says she has a surprise for us. On Christmas Eve we each open one present before bed. And on Christmas I thought we'd go see *Lord of the Rings*." Lacy squeezed the steering wheel in fierce anticipation. "I was waiting for Jules to come home to see it."

"Oh." Philip turned to Julian. "I didn't know you liked those."

"Tolkien?" she blurted. "Of course, we both do. Every Christmas Day we go to the movies. We saw *Evita*, and *Chocolat*; last year it was *Miss Congeniality*." She shook her head sarcastically at Philip. "What a bomb that one was, right, Jules?"

Julian's face went blank. He would not receive the memories. "We can go to the movies if you want," he said. "Are you feeling up to it?"

"Sure," Lacy said. "Only if you boys want to. No biggie."

She didn't hear much of the conversation after that. Philip asked questions about her and Houston and Royalwood, and Lacy answered them, unable to tell if he was being polite or didn't know a thing about her. But her mind mostly shut down after Julian disclaimed their movie tradition. *Get home*, she repeated as she drove, she had to get them home and then she could put on another sweater and rest for a bit.

"How pretty," Philip said when they pulled up to Lacy's house, where the holiday lights and window candles were on a timer and clicked to life at dusk. "The decorations."

"Come on in," she said, opening the door as they dragged their bags from the car.

"Oh, wow." Philip's eyes went right to the tree, and the stockings hanging on the brick fireplace, and the tiny crèche on the entryway shelf. "It's beautiful here."

"Mom's a Christmas nut," Julian said. "How many trees do you have?"

"Four," she replied gamely. "This is my Angel tree. There's a Santa tree, a Snowman tree, a Homemade tree. But a lot of the angels and Santas and snowmen are homemade too."

"Did you make this?" Philip asked. With his fingertips he lifted a cross-stitched angel from a branch and squinted. " 'Julian, '89'?"

"I've been making one for him every year since he was born. Badly, at first, but I got better. I made this for you, Philip." She took one of the stockings off its hanger and handed it to him. The back was mint green satin with a needlework front. Some of her best and fastest work, oddly, on the days the chemo knocked her flat in her recliner. There was a scene running up the stocking of Santa and his reindeer flying over the New York skyline. "I figured," she said, "since you're from there."

"Wow." He held the stocking in his palms like a sacrament. "That is so sweet of you."

"Did you design the pattern?" Julian asked. "You did, didn't you?"

Lacy beamed. It was everything she hoped for, the moment she craved but never came, when everyone saw you and your work, and it was right. Then she noticed something in Julian's face, an expression too upbeat and false. He was standing far from Philip and her, in the dining area, blocking the spot on the linoleum discolored by water damage. A patch she meant to fix—the whole floor she wanted to replace with nice ceramic— but hadn't gotten around to. And she sensed it. Julian was seeing her home, his own, through Philip's eyes. Focusing him on the decorations like paint on an old whore.

"I can't believe you designed this." Philip grinned and without warning reached over and hugged Lacy. "How long did it take?"

Lacy shrugged. "Just a hobby. Do you have any hobbies, Philip?"

"Dance," Julian fired off.

"Yes," Philip said. "I like dance and theater. My parents took me to Shakespeare in the Park every year when I was a kid."

"I love the theater," Lacy said. "Great theater here, downtown at TUTS? I saw *Phantom* three times and *Les Mis* twice, but right now my favorite is *Into the Woods*. Did you see it?"

"No." Philip smiled.

"It'll blow your mind. It mixes fairy tales like 'Cinderella' and 'Rapunzel' and 'Jack and the Beanstalk,' but it shows the dark side underneath the—"

"I'm really tired," Julian interrupted. "Philip, are you—I think we need to lie down before dinner. And probably shower too. What time did you want to eat?"

"Whenever," Lacy said, turning away and heading to the kitchen. "No rush."

"Give me a hug," Julian said, grabbing her arm as she passed by. "We didn't hug." Gently he folded his arms around her. He held her there, running his hands over her ribs and spine. His eyes were red when he pulled back. "You lost weight," he said. "It's this way, Phil." He picked up their bags and led Philip to his old bedroom.

Lacy tried to rest too, bundling up in a blanket on the recliner. It was where she spent many nights, once the chemo wrecked her sleep. Every morning around two a.m. a possum came scratching along the same branch outside the windows, eyes reflecting the porch light. He was ugly, like a thing from her sci-fi novels. She named him Lancelot. And while Julian dreamed big ideas, and Bonnie lay alone in a king-size bed, Lacy had a standing date with her night creature. She talked to him, in her mind, about things. The feeling of her life slipping away. Leaving for college and saying goodbye to her mother, who reminded Lacy to condition her hair. The years of city life with Aaron—the fun, going out to Ninfa's with such a handsome husband, and the doubts, marrying someone better-looking, the babies they lost and the sadness, mixed up in one sweet-and-sour time. She talked about Julian's birth and the early days of inconsolable crying, which she took so personally. She tried to talk about death but didn't know how, or how she didn't feel at peace. She pondered some nights if it was because she didn't go to church. Had she crossed an angry God, by not passing on a faith to Julian? Then she scoffed and readjusted on the La-Z-Boy. But putting God aside, she asked Lancelot a few times, did people of faith—in something, anything—feel peace at this moment? More than she did with her vivid, bittersweet reflections?

She awoke at the sound of water. Julian was in boxers,

hurrying down the hall to the bathroom, where Philip was running the shower. She wondered if they had sex. All the bad feelings the nap blunted came flooding over her again. Julian's embarrassment at his home and mom, the Texas rube. Her son had sold her out for better people. And what was so great about the Rosenblums? Did they raise Julian? Pick up the phone when he called? Lacy put years into her boy, so he could take on the world. Then he did what she told him to and left. To be safe, to build a life, fine. But did he have to put a knife in her back when she was already dying?

"Can we help?" Philip asked when they entered the kitchen, pink and fresh from the shower. Julian set three bottles of wine on the counter and started rummaging through drawers.

"I'm good," Lacy said. "Dinner's ready. Right there, Jules," she said irritably, pointing at a drawer. "The corkscrew?" She turned back to the slow cooker and stirred. "I didn't know you liked wine. A lot of wine."

"Yeah." Julian opened a bottle. "We know what we like, so we brought it down. Phil?"

"Sure, I'll have some. Let me get that for you, Lacy."

"I got it." She felt both of their eyes on her as she lifted the tub from the Crock-Pot and slowly made her way to the table. Julian brought over two giant glasses of wine and the bottle and sat at the place farthest from Lacy. "Philip," she said as she served the pasta, "big things coming up for you. For both of you."

"Yes!" he said brightly.

"It's your last semester too, right?"

"Oh." Philip frowned. "Yeah, we're both graduating. I'm not quite the speed demon this one is," he said, nudging Julian, "finishing in three years. Accelerated course load, a million extracurriculars, the journaling?" He grinned at Lacy. "Did you know he journals every night?"

"I did." She gave a proprietary nod. "Do you have plans for after?" she asked Philip.

Julian guzzled wine. Philip talked about going back to the city to work in finance, temporarily and not for his dad, until he figured out what he really wanted to do. She asked how long he thought that might take, and Julian shot her a dirty look. She asked for an update on Julian's law school apps, whether Columbia was still his top choice, and what if he got into a better school not in New York? He answered impatiently, refilling his glass. Was Lacy avoiding stuff? Running the clock on dinner? Maybe. But did Julian have any idea how bad she felt, living her greatest fear? She had sharpened her son's mind to a razor, refined his taste with a true moral sense, always aware someday he might return to judge her. Think less of her once he went off into the world, and looked back, and saw her in full. The day had come. Her son was home. And all she wanted to do was hide. Or smack him hard across the face.

"In other news," Julian abruptly turned the conversation, "we're . . . engaged?"

"Yes, I know," Lacy said to her plate. "Congratulations." She twirled the same bit of pasta around her fork that she'd been working the whole meal. It tasted like metal, like most things. "How's your spaghetti, Philip?"

"Delicious."

"We're pretty excited," Julian pressed. "We're thinking about doing it here, in the spring before it gets too hot."

"This spring?" Lacy asked. "Before your last exams? You've been together—is it two years now?"

"Two and a half," Philip said. "Since Jay's first semester."

Jay. Philip had his own pet name for Julian. Her son, the more ambitious of the two, who had a legal career ahead that he'd worked hard for—that she and Julian had both worked for. "I hear a lot of young couples these days are getting married later," Lacy said. "Take their time planning a wedding down the road, once they finish grad school and get settled."

"How long did you and dad wait?" Julian asked, emptying the bottle in his glass.

"Those were different times. But today?" She smiled. "What's the rush?"

"What's the rush?" Julian snapped.

"Well," Philip cut in. "We're glad you've got the great care here at MD Anderson, and we're optimistic, but I had an aunt with renal cell carcinoma like you and—you never know, so we thought, we know we're getting married and we really want you to be a part of it."

"Boys." Lacy sighed and rubbed at the pain her temples. "You shouldn't be making decisions like that because of me."

"Of course!" Philip's eyes flew open. "For all we know you've got ten years, twenty! And you'll be telling your grandkids about that awkward Christmas dinner back in the day. It was me, not Julian. Sorry. I proposed. I said let's speed it up. Edith was my favorite aunt, and maybe it triggered—I didn't mean to offend you or—"

"Did you get your last scans?" Julian asked. He'd been staring at Lacy the whole time Philip talked. It was terrible how well they could read each other. All the years of watching *Law and Order* together on the couch, spotting the red herrings and guessing the killers.

"Last scans?" she said.

"You were supposed to get them a week ago? You said the doctor wanted another radiologist to look at them?"

"Right."

"And did he?" Julian sat up straight. "Did you hit your target for shrinkage?"

Lacy nodded vaguely.

"That's great! See?" Julian said, poking Philip. "I told you."

He turned back to Lacy and smiled, his eyes shining. "So what's next?"

"Dessert." Lacy set her napkin on the table. "I made ginger-bread men."

"About your treatment?"

"I'd rather not talk about that now."

"OK," Julian persisted. "But it's good news. And it looks like the chemo's been hard on you. Did the doctor say how many more rounds before you can stop?"

Lacy studied her son's face, full of cautious hope, as though she were saying goodbye. "We're focused on pain management now," she said.

Philip sighed, sucking the air out of the room.

"What does that mean?" Julian asked. "Like until the next round?"

"We're not doing any more rounds. We're stopping chemo."

"Why? They got it all already?" She could feel Julian's eyes on her but couldn't look up. "Why stop if it's working?" he asked. "You said you hit your target."

"I—the other radiologist did look at the scans." She could hear each word coming out, slowly and distinctly. "It didn't shrink. It spread. To my lymph nodes. Lungs. They think it's past the point of treating, so for whatever time I've got—"

"Nope." Julian downed the rest of his wine in one swig. "That's one opinion. To stop treatment? One random Texas doctor? We have to get a second opinion."

"He consulted with others."

"Not here. New York. Philip's parents know lots of doctors. The best in the country."

"Jay," Philip whispered, laying a hand on Julian's arm.

He shook it off. "When did you find out? Were you planning on telling me?"

"I found out last week."

"How?" Julian shot to his feet. "How does it go from chemo and treatment plans to this? In a week? How'd that happen?"

"We caught it late. It was already—"

"You said you were fine." He wrapped his arms around his chest. "All semester he's been going crazy"—he thrust a finger at Philip—"talking worst-case scenarios. I told him you're fine. You said not to come down."

"Jules," she said.

"I said I'd fly down. Over and over! You said, 'Finish your midterms, law school apps, finals, I'm fine.' Lying the whole time."

"It's your most important semester of college," she said.

"*College?* Do you hear yourself right now?! Do you actually hear the words coming—"

"Stop yelling!" she exploded with a heedless force. "Taking! I'm dying, all right? And when I'm dead there'll be nothing left to take."

Julian froze, dumbstruck. And then, before Philip could stand and reach him, he took off out the front door. Philip waited in limbo a moment, halfway up and leaning on the edge of the table. He looked at Lacy. "I think I'll try and—"

"It's a dead end," she said.

"What?"

"It's a cul-de-sac. He won't go far."

Philip nodded. "I'm sorry."

She nodded as best she could, before he left too. Then she sat alone at the head of the table, her eyes traveling across the remains of the unfinished dinner.

★

In the morning Lacy was back in the same chair, trying to keep down some water. She had cleared the table, cleaned the kitchen, lain awake for hours, gotten up and made breakfast. Cinnamon rolls, eggs, coffee. None of which she would enjoy, like the Christmas cookies or the tree and decorations she'd hauled out from the garage. *Why bother?* she asked as she steeled her stomach and sipped. What was the point? Because it was living. Cooking, preparing for guests, marking time: the rituals remained the only game she knew.

She leaned over the table and adjusted a glass ball in her centerpiece. This year she'd cribbed from a Pottery Barn catalog—a mirror for the base, reflecting up glass ornaments and candles she had carefully arranged. Julian was right to be upset. He'd been a self-absorbed jerk lately, and still she had misled him. Told him every word the doctor said and omitted the reality of the situation. How the doctor looked at her, listing things they could do, technically, as his face waited for Lacy to say, *Enough*. She knew she was terminal at the first appointment. But how was she to live with death?

The coffeemaker beeped and turned off with a full carafe. She thought of a dream that plagued her lately, a memory of the one time she took Aaron and Julian to meet her family. She was nervous on the way to McAllen, yet hopeful too, wondering if her childhood home wasn't as bad as she remembered. Aaron whistled when they parked at the mansion in town, where her family moved after they sold the farm and her dad's heart gave out within a year. During lunch, Lacy ignored her mom's slights about her weight. Her brother Junior turned out fat too, and aimless and short-tempered, a man who never left home. His daughters barely spoke. At four years old, Julian was his chatty, irrepressible self, and during coffee, while he was still in earshot, Lacy's mother advised her to deal with that sissy boy before it was too late. Junior nodded like a drunk in church. She stared at her mother, a woman who spent her life in hiding, naming the weaknesses of others. Lacy felt the blood rise in her face, certain she never should have visited and risked the disease of her family touching Julian. She never did again.

Yet whom did her son have now? MIA Aaron? Bonnie? No one, she thought. A whole family in Mexico neither of them would ever know, that she never even mentioned to Julian because of the questions it stirred up about her own past—why she cut ties, and how do you do that to your own family? Through all that hadn't happened in life, a failed marriage and so-so career, she always had her son. But on Christmas Eve, Lacy didn't know if he'd be OK when she was gone. She wondered what her life amounted to. A pile of unanswered questions is what it felt like, jumbled memories, moments in time that faded like they never were. A wave of nausea hit her. And out of despair, or to keep from throwing up, Lacy resolved to make one last gift for Julian. She took the yellow pad she kept with her since the chemo brain set in, and started writing.

The creak of the front door startled Lacy from her task. The house hadn't stirred since she got up. She craned her neck. "Philip?" she called.

"Hi, Lacy." He kicked off his sneakers in the foyer. He moved for the hall, on the way to Julian's room, but stopped and looked at her.

"There's breakfast if you want," she said.

He wound headphones around a white gadget. "Thanks," he said, approaching the table. "If you don't mind me sweaty. I went running. It's pretty here. Royalwood. All so—planned."

She started to rise. "The food's on the—"

"Sit, I'll get it."

"Is that an iPod?" she asked. "Bonnie said the kids started showing up with them this semester, listening to music during class."

"Yeah! This tiny thing holds a thousand songs." He brought his plate and sat by Lacy. "I'm one of those Apple geeks who gets in line to buy it first. Every new gadget. Pavlovian."

"Must be nice," Lacy muttered. He paused, midchew. She

regretted her words, sort of. "So," she resumed, "I know a little about your parents. Jules mentioned a sister?"

"Older, yeah. She's out west. A labor organizer. We don't see her much. We're close," he blurted, glancing at Lacy. "A good family. But sometimes close means you have to go away. Did you ever—" He smiled and shook his head. "Never mind."

"What?"

"Did you ever think of having more kids, besides Julian? He always wants to meet my sister, like the sibling thing really excites him."

"I bet people open up to you. Tell you what you want to know?" She fingered the edge of her place mat. "I miscarried a few times before Julian. And then he was such a blessing and a handful—" Out of nowhere Lacy thought of the letter Aaron's mistress sent her years ago, the last straw in their marriage, all of it playing out in her mind like it happened to someone else. And of how Aaron was alive, she figured, figuring she would've heard somehow if he died. The man who cheated and spent, while she grew a baby inside her and worked and worried herself sick for their family, and then grew a cancer inside her.

"Lacy?" Philip said.

"No, Aaron and I never had any other children, after Julian. Do you think you will?" she asked. "You want to be a dad someday?"

"Are you kidding? My dad took me to the Natural History Museum when I was five—I've heard this story like a million times—and showed me the T. rex and said, 'Someday you'll bring your son here.' The next time we went, I brought my teddy bear and explained the fossils to him, the exhibits, elevators." He watched her. "Does Julian's dad know you're sick?"

"I don't know where he is." Philip's eyes were so blue, and keen, it took getting used to. It crept up on Lacy, the feeling that he was lovely to be around. She resented it. People like him with their money and poise. How easily things worked out, calling the shots like she never did, pretty like she never was, healthy like she used to be. But death had come quickly, outpacing her sensibilities. She clenched her jaw, pissed off at the world and how little her anger got her now. "That show, *Les Mis*?" she said. "Jules thinks it's some hokey musical, whatever, fine, but it's the story of—" She searched for the word. "Stewards, of a child. Cosette. The daughter of a prostitute, Fantine, who has to entrust her child to Jean Valjean, who protects Cosette until she meets the man she'll marry. Marius." She looked up at a sniffle from Philip.

"Sorry." He smiled. "I cry at commercials. But I love Julian so much. He's the most amazing person I've ever met. We Rosenblums are penguins: mates for life. All the lecturing and kvetching and just-a-suggestion-ing till death do us part." Philip put his hand on hers. "It's nice to meet you. He talks about you all the time. Like you're a hundred feet tall."

Lacy chuckled and shook her head, thinking of the Gay-Straight Alliance she started after Julian left, and how long he suffered and never said a word until the day Ben Cross was attacked. She imagined all the secrets her son must have told his fiancé by now. She nodded at Philip and pulled her hand away.

"Morning." Julian entered the kitchen. He was in boxers and a Harvard T-shirt, loping to the coffeemaker like the rumpled teen Lacy remembered. He came over without saying a word and leaned over to hug her. He kissed the top of her head and sat down at the table.

"Where'd you guys go last night?" Lacy asked.

"A playground," Philip said. "Julian's old school around the corner."

"His elementary," she said. "Where he went after our lessons."

"Yeah." Philip smiled. "He said you homeschooled him for a while?"

"I was his first teacher."

"Did the doctor . . . ," Julian began. He sipped his coffee without looking up. "Did he say how long he thinks, once you stop chemo, how long you have?"

"Hard to say. Six months. Maybe more." Slowly Lacy got to her feet. "Could you guys clean up? Bonnie said she'll be here at eleven, and I've gotta get a move on."

"Sure," Julian said.

For the second time in two days, Lacy showered and did her face, working some extra lipstick into her cheeks for color. She put on red slacks, a green sweater, and an Abominable Snowman pin she found at Big Lots and couldn't resist. She plumped the couch pillows and fanned out some gingerbread men, and the boys were just about ready when Bonnie rang.

"Knock-knock!" she said, coming in. She spotted Lacy, and her eyes watered. Silently she waved and put her purse down. Lacy had a sudden flash of the day they met, years ago at the pool, and of the person she was then. A woman convinced she'd measure her life by the people who died or disappeared or betrayed her, until she met Bonnie and for the first time knew the feeling of someone who was there for good.

"Aren't those cookie men precious?" Bonnie exclaimed, gathering herself. She hurried to Lacy and wrapped an arm around her. "How you doing?" she whispered. "Did you tell him?"

Lacy nodded. "What's this big surprise you've been talking about?"

"Wouldn't you like to know? Oh!" she cried as Julian entered the living room. "Doogie Howser, come give your Bonnie a hug! And this must be the tall, dark, and handsome fiancé!"

"Philip," he said, reaching out his hand.

"Bonnie. You're getting a hug too," she said, her bayou drawl stretching a little longer like she had a crush. "Nice to meet you, Philip. I was thinking about you and praying none of your loved ones got hurt on 9/11?"

"Oh. No, thankfully. My dad works down there, but we're all OK."

"Well, we've got plenty of our own troubles right here in Houston." Bonnie shook her head. "Enron? Families destroyed. Husbands of our coworkers, retirements just wiped out. Dark times we're living in. But it's Christmas."

"I'm sorry," Julian said delicately, "about you and Mr. Boudreaux."

Bonnie sighed. "It's with God and the lawyers now. And mine's got expensive taste. I hear congratulations are in order for you boys!"

"Thanks." Julian grinned. "You're invited."

"I wouldn't miss it!" Bonnie whirled around at the sound of car doors slamming outside. "All right, let's get your mama settled like the guest of honor she is." She led a bewildered Lacy to the couch and was tucking a blanket around her friend's legs when the doorbell rang. "Come on in!" Bonnie cried.

Through the door came a stream of Lacy's former students, mostly members of the GSA and a few Science Club nerds. Five, ten, twelve in total. First was Ralph Lee, who crashed in Julian's room for a few nights after his parents caught him on a Gay Korea chat site, until they calmed down and stopped talking exorcisms. Then came sweet butch Juana Rodriguez with purple hair and more piercings than Lacy recalled, along with a big girl Lacy couldn't place. Every one gave her a hug. Bringing up the rear was odd Calvin Washington, the only black kid in his class of a thousand that one hard year. He held up boxes of Krispy Kremes and coffee and smiled at Lacy. As the students settled in, time flowed back to her. The year of the principal saying no to the Alliance—the "homosexual stuff" was too controversial—years of hearing no from men in general, from grad school forward, until it became like a superpower how Lacy learned in time to smile nice and keep asking. And the victory she felt at that first

GSA meeting? Like anybody who ever had to hide who they were—her own mother, or Rock Hudson, anybody different—could come to room 214 Thursdays at three and be themselves. And then, while Lacy sat on the couch surrounded by young faces, it dawned on her that maybe her son had given her a little compassion for her mother—too late, but there it was.

Lacy's boys reacted swiftly to the influx of guests, Julian playing traffic cop with the seating while Philip ran to the kitchen for mugs and plates. Her house was filled once more with sound and action.

"Now, Lacy," Bonnie said after a couple of rounds of doughnuts and catching up. She went to the foyer, where she had left a large Kinko's bag. "We've been working on a little surprise. Philip!" she called to him across the room where he sat by the tree. "I think you're the only one here who doesn't know about Lacy's vacations."

"Vacations?" Lacy asked blankly.

"Look at her," Bonnie smirked, "trying to play dumb now. We taught together almost twenty years, and there was a point every semester, right past the halfway point, where Lacy would start talking at the end of each class, and I mean *each* and *every* class, about where she'd be on vacation right then if she were rich and famous."

"It wasn't that bad," Lacy objected. The room erupted in catcalls.

"Lacy, dear, one time I was doing morning announcements with Principal James—y'all know Mrs. Boudreaux likes her announcements—and he turns to me and whispers, 'It's started. Lacy's vacationing. Let's broadcast it so the whole school can hear where she's going.' It was a *thing*. So last week I got out the craft supplies and invited Lacy's old students over to help send her to all the places she planned to go on vacation."

Bonnie lifted posters out of the bag and handed them out.

One by one the students showed off their handiwork. Bonnie had cut out pictures of Lacy from yearbooks, or that news feature the *Royalwood Observer* did on her when the high school finally sponsored the GSA, and the students put the cutouts in the places they remembered Lacy talking about. A poster of the Eiffel Tower, with little Lacy on top. Lacy hanging off Big Ben like King Kong. Lacy riding a camel at the Pyramids.

"This is Mrs. Warner in Greece," Juana said when it was her turn, pointing at Lacy on a white cliff overlooking gorgeous blue water. Juana Rodriguez, Lacy thought to herself, family from outside Saltillo; she always asked, and never forgot, where the Mexican kids came from. "Also, I wanted to say—" Juana pulled in her lip and sucked on a ring at the corner of her mouth. "My first day at the club, you talked about Sappho, and how long women loved other women." She opened her eyes wide and breathed. "And I felt like you liked me when no one else did. Like you were on my side. I brought my girlfriend to meet you. This is Carmen," she said, touching the girl Lacy didn't know. They both went over and hugged Lacy, sitting in a throne of blankets at the center of it all.

"Um," Calvin said at the end. "I didn't do things like everybody else."

"Tell me something I don't know, Calvin." Lacy grinned.

"After I graduated, I got my associate's in graphic design at North Harris, and now I'm illustrating for some comics and a medical publisher. It's good. I made you this." He turned his poster around. It was a stunning drawing of a dragon flying through space with a woman rider atop—a skinny babe with gray hair and glasses and giant breasts breaking free from the tatters of a futuristic rag gown. "Dragonriders of Pern?" he said. "You gave it to me in Science Club, and the story, it got me—I started drawing. That's you, see?" He pointed at the babe. "Holding the graduated cylinder? I speak for myself, but I feel like for everybody, when Mrs. Boudreaux put out the word about you being sick, we wanted to come say Merry Christmas, Mrs. Warner. And get better soon."

Folks chatted a while longer, fueled by sugar and memories, until the students started to peel off. They stayed a little more than an hour. Bonnie stacked the posters neatly by the couch, where Lacy still presided.

"I'll call you tomorrow," Bonnie said, resting her hand on her friend's shoulder. "Boys?" She hugged Julian and Philip. "I've got my eye out for that wedding invitation. Don't forget."

Philip took the plates to the kitchen and loaded the dishwasher.

"That was nice," Julian said, sitting down beside Lacy on the couch. "What Bonnie did."

Lacy nodded. "She's a true friend."

"The Asian guy? He stayed in my room when his parents kicked him out?"

"It happened fast," Lacy said.

"No, I don't—it's great. I didn't know that happened. I'm sorry. About last night. And I'm sorry for . . ." Julian squeezed a throw pillow, trying to find the words. "I don't want you to die." He looked at her plaintively. His voice was sweet, full of urgent feeling like when he was a boy. "The world needs you. I need you."

"I don't want to die."

"Maybe—" Julian wiped his eyes. "We're supposed to fly back on the twenty-sixth, but I could stay longer. Just the two of us. We could watch HGTV. Stencil something, or whatever?"

Lacy smiled absently. "Philip is nice. He eats pork, right?"

"Yeah."

"I forgot some things for dinner at the store. I made a list. Could y'all go get them?"

"Sure." Julian stood up. "Thank you. For Christmas."

Julian and Philip went to the supermarket. Lacy needed a moment to herself after the excitement. She looked at the stack of posters leaning on the couch. She was on someone's mind, somewhere in the minds of her students. It hit her then, sitting alone, that it wasn't like her mother said when she was a girl. About her future. Her life didn't begin with Julian, and life wasn't either-or. She stood at the head of a classroom for years, at the private school downtown, but she didn't really become a teacher until she was a mom. She raised her kind, feminine boy, a book reader and football hater, a boy nobody wanted in those parts back then, and found herself astonished at what was inside him. And forever after she looked at her students that way, the lost causes and misfits and first-generation kids, like you never know what lies within. The way her dad looked at her once in his truck when she was a girl, and said she'd go to college. A tingle of pride ran through her. Because she could see it, she knew, after all the things that diminished her over her life—a fearful mother, marriage, men in charge of whatever— she had never truly given up on that girl who loved science and asking questions.

She pulled the posters close to her and studied each fondly rendered picture of her globe-trotting. Paris, Venice, the Great Wall of China. Places in the world she would never go, she thought. But Julian might, with a good husband. Her son had many places yet to go.

10

Reading

What was your resolution?" his mom asked over breakfast. "For New Year's?"

"I don't know." Julian took a long sip of coffee and guided the last of his eggs onto his toast. "I hadn't really thought that far ahead."

"Mine," she said brightly, "is to get this house organized."

"Seems pretty organized to me," he muttered. And he meant it. He noticed as soon as he arrived with Philip for Christmas, how the pantry looked like a strangely perfect IKEA ad, or the closet in his bedroom was practically empty, every nook and cranny of his childhood home pared down and somehow more than just holiday ready.

"Finishing getting organized," she conceded. "I've been doing a little every week. Purging on trash day, sending Bonnie to Goodwill. That's where you come in." Her eyes twinkled with impending mischief. "There's two boxes in the garage with your name on them. Literally."

"So that's where this was headed." He smiled wryly at her. "Free labor?"

"It's stuff I thought you might want, or want to see, before I tossed it. Do you mind?" she asked. Julian nodded as he carried his plate to the sink. "You might try forgiveness," his mom lobbed at him abruptly. "For your resolution."

He looked up at her, smiling cautiously beneath the stained-glass panel that hung in the pass-through—a fiery sun pattern that for years had filled the kitchen with a red-orange light. "Forgive who?" he asked.

She shrugged. "Whoever needs forgiving. Start with your mom. We're the beginnings of all problems, right? Moms? Plenty of time to think while you're cleaning out there."

"Yup." Julian raised his eyebrows in a show of confusion and headed to the garage.

It had been a weird, exhilarating week since Phil left. There was nothing new about how they spent their days. He and his mom did the usual things, time-killing pleasures of past visits. They went to the movies and saw *The Lord of the Rings*, and Julian nodded along as his mom critiqued woeful departures from the book. They watched home design shows until the same episodes reran, oohing at nice interiors and ridiculing bad choices. "Oh, come on!" his mom cried at one appalling misstep—text painted on a kitchen wall that said, *Today Is a Great Day for a Great Day!* "I couldn't get up in the morning," she declared, "if I had to read such empty words." During commercials they made vague plans for spring break and beyond. She fought him on coming home for the summer instead of doing an internship, but she agreed to go to South Padre Island in April. It was kind of like band camp reunions, Julian thought as they curled up on the couch, cramming in the good times without grazing old wounds. He avoided talk of the Rosenblums; she left unsaid how rarely he visited. They laughed a lot, sometimes until they cried. But it wasn't until they watched the ball drop in Times Square, the night before, that Julian began to comprehend the giddy feeling in the air. His mom was dying, not today or tomorrow, but soon.

She wasn't joking about the boxes. He entered the garage and spotted two large ones in the corner with JULIAN'S THINGS written on the sides. The space was immaculate, eerily more pristine than the closets. On one rack of shelving sat original boxes for appliances, the Dirt Devil and George Foreman Grill, while the other rack held four footlockers for her Christmas tree ornaments, each labeled by name. The floor was swept and mopped. And in the center of it, the only other thing left in the garage, was his dad's old weight bench with a handwritten sign taped to it: SALVATION ARMY PICKUP (1/5/02).

Julian slid the boxes over to the bench and started perusing. The lighter one was full of debate trophies from high school, the fruits of young ambition now coated with dust. He opened the heavier box, and under stacks of papers and school projects he found his childhood journals. His mom had kept them. But then she was the reason they existed at all. There were dozens, two or more a year until he left home, in various states of decay—edges frayed, tattered spines, pages hanging loose off metal spirals.

He took out his first one, with the Care Bears cover— *December 3, 1987*, scrawled on the top line—and remembered the day his mom gave it to him. He started school that year, and he lived for his turn at show-and-tell. The teacher said to bring an object about his dad, and he was determined to show the Teeth. He had discovered them not long before, snooping in his parents' room: four molars at the ends of a metal retainer, in the top drawer of his dad's dresser. He waited until his mom was paying bills that day to grab them. But when he snuck in and gazed upon them, he thought of the toothy killer plant from *Little Shop of Horrors*—he and his mom had just watched the movie—and fantasy got the best of him. He stuck the retainer in his mouth and put on his mom's lipstick to match the plant's lips. Then he grabbed a framed photo of his dad in a military uniform and serenaded him with "Feed Me Seymour," singing until his mom appeared at the door. She muscled the lipstick off with Kleenex, shouting that her son shouldn't be wearing makeup, and sent him to his room. She came to him there later and apologized and gave him a journal as an early Christmas gift. Sitting in the garage, Julian recalled every bizarre twist of the incident, summed up in three lines on the opening page:

> Mom says Dad was in a war.
> And I should write things here if I don't want to say them out loud.
> Or if she's ever not around to talk to.

He set his Care Bears journal on the bench and tugged up handfuls of others from the bottom of the box, taking desultory peeks inside, until a draft swept through the garage and made him shiver. He was still wearing the boxers and T-shirt he'd slept in. He grabbed his first journal of sixth grade, with a diva-feathered Annie Lennox on the cover, and went inside.

"You can get rid of the trophies," Julian called on his way to the kitchen. "But can you keep the other box for now? There's stuff in there I want to—" He stopped at the sight of his mom leaning forward in her chair, gripping the edge of the table. "Mom? Are you OK?"

She didn't respond. But as he started across the kitchen she turned her head slowly, like it pained her to move, and whispered, "I think we better call somebody, Jules."

★

Royalwood Hospital rang in the New Year and kept ringing. It was the first thing Julian thought when they finished the paperwork. They sat in the admitting lounge, his mom hunched over in a puffy jacket while he cast frantic glances around. Blue streamers hung off the intake desk. A Baby New Year sign was still pinned to a bulletin board, with his wide infant grin and jaunty top hat. It was tacky, wrong, to leave up old holiday decorations in a hospital. There had to be a policy against it. His mind raced in circles, criticizing the staff and space, because it had nowhere to go. His mom wouldn't talk to him. He asked a million questions driving over there. "Are you in pain?" "What's happening?" "What can I do?" All she said was that her stomach hurt; her back hurt. But she grimaced. And it was the frozen detachment of her expression that killed him as they waited to be seen.

His mom changed momentarily when Bonnie arrived. Julian had texted her when they got to the hospital, along with Phil, who immediately started looking for flights back to Texas. Bonnie threw open the door to the room they'd been parked in, and his mom's face softened. Bonnie hurried to her, still bundled in her jacket on the bed, and murmured something a long time in her ear. His mom nodded. "Well," Bonnie exclaimed, stepping back and smiling at Julian. "Here we are."

A doctor came in, not much older than Julian, he thought, and spoke to his mom about going over her oncologist's file and figuring out what was going on. Then it started: a process Julian had never seen before, of his mom hooked up to tubes, a catheter, a chest port he didn't know she was hiding under her shirt, pricked and drawn for blood, promised information soon. The whole time his mom nodded blankly, fingering the blankets layered over her body while her arms, now exposed in a gown, seemed to thicken. Or Julian's eyes were playing tricks on him. Bonnie dished the latest school gossip. His mom listened, maybe. She glanced up at times with a vague smile but otherwise stared at her feet, or farther out somewhere. They existed like this for hours, morning into afternoon, pieces of day shedding their character in the fluorescent light. Nurses came in and out to check monitors. Julian and Bonnie flanked the bed. They talked and were quiet. They didn't mention her legs clearly swelling under the coverlet.

When the doctor returned he brought a middle-aged woman, Eastern European by accent, devoid of any bedside manner. She spoke quickly, almost cheerfully, about how lucky that she was there, a nephrologist on a holiday, and creatinine and numbers going up or down, but the gist of it was that his mom, Lacy is her name?, had unhappy kidneys, just one working really, and now it wasn't, and soon her liver would stop too, organ dominoes, and then no more peeing and toxins would build up and make her very sleepy until she faded off. "A good death," she finished, smiling at his mom. "No pain, not the cancer. OK, bye." She nodded and left. The young doctor looked from them to the door, mumbled he was sorry, and followed her out.

"Hang on." Julian took off after them. "Doctors?" he called, squinting in the hallway light and quickly saddling his aggression. "I'm trying to—" The woman opened her mouth. "Not you," Julian snapped. "Good death? I don't know what you're doing in a white coat. You," he addressed the young doctor, "seem at least semihuman. My mom has cancer. She stopped chemo. Fancy doctors at MD Anderson gave her six months. We show up here and random stranger doctors say she's dead on arrival, so I'm just trying to get some answers."

"Her oncologist—" The doctor pressed his hand to his clipboard. "He discussed with your mom—she's been in kidney failure for some time, or close to it. They knew there was a chance this could happen. How it ended. I don't know if she told you?"

"You're not listening," Julian pushed. "You're the ones who keep people alive, not me. So do it. Dialysis, whatever you do, just do it."

"It's hours," the specialist said. "Maybe days more you get, but once the liver goes, that's it. Nothing to do. I see this every day. I'm sorry."

"Maybe hours matter," Julian said and stormed back to the room.

Inside Bonnie hummed and massaged his mom's hand. "I talked to the doctors," Julian began. "We can start dialysis to keep your kidneys going." His mom turned and smiled weakly, but something was gone, the usual flicker of self-consciousness or thought behind her eyes. "For more time," he said.

"No, Jules," she replied softly.

"Mom," he pressed, "don't you want to—" Before he could finish, Bonnie's other hand grasped his below the bed where his mom couldn't see. She squeezed it. And in one touch the situation revealed itself to him. They were having breakfast that morning when everything went sideways into nightmare. Yet however strange it felt, so impossibly unreal, he was the one who'd missed the rehearsals. Didn't even know about them until it was too late, and here they stood on a grand morbid stage. His elder knew her lines and told him kindly to stop.

His mom wiggled her free hand at him, to come closer. Julian took it in a daze, the three of them forming an impromptu circle. "I have the people I love most here," she said.

The doctors were right. His mom seemed good as she drifted into evening. When her eyes were open they talked and sang. She responded here and there with phrases or their names, those eventually breaking up into sounds without place or time. A smile settled over her, or her face upturned in a way that looked peaceful. Night fell. Inside Julian wrestled with all he didn't know and needed urgently to ask her—*What are you thinking? Where are you? Are you scared?* Each time he nearly gave in and opened his mouth to speak, he thought of Bonnie squeezing his hand. And reminded himself that the things his mom didn't say weren't his to demand. That he had to let it be.

★

Close to midnight, Philip texted that he was descending into Houston. His mom wasn't waking up anymore by then, just breathing rhythmically with her arms tucked under the covers like a child. Bonnie stepped out to get coffee. Julian went into the bathroom to cry and wash his face. When he turned off the faucet he heard a voice. He opened the door and found a nurse at the foot of the bed. Not someone assigned to them, a woman he saw in the hallway that morning pushing a cart and wearing a pair of 2002 New Year's sunglasses. She was reading: "'Don't be alarmed! You are looking for Jesus the Nazarene, who was crucified. He has risen! He is not here. See the—'"

"Get out!" Julian cried. The woman looked up, stricken like she'd seen a demon. "Get the hell away from her!" He charged at her. "Now!"

She hurried out of the room. Julian approached his mom, ran a finger down her cheek, and whispered he was sorry. "Quite a commotion out there," Bonnie said when she returned a few minutes later. "A nurse crying about something. Here's your coffee." She shot him a look as she passed the cup. Her eyes were red. Julian could smell the smoke on her.

"Me, probably," he mumbled. "She was reading the Bible to Mom. I went off." He glared at Bonnie, angrier as he put it into words. "An atheist her whole life, and they come try that shit when she's lying here helpless?"

"Listen to me." Bonnie sat down and stroked his mom's leg. "My mama drank herself to death. By the end she was swollen and tender as a buster. I went home to be with her, and—" She looked up at Julian and sighed. "You are still here, OK? When it's done? Alive like the rest of us, getting up, making breakfast in the morning, even if it's just for one." Softly Bonnie petted his mom's hand. "This one here made me a better person. Yes, you did, Lacy. Her way with students. All of them. Mexican, or from wherever. She could see what they wanted. She liked seeing different people getting things. Being proud. She made me think. Me and everybody at school." Bonnie fluffed her blouse and wrinkled her nose. "I made it sixteen years and Mr. Boudreaux leaving without a cigarette, but *this*?" She wiped her eyes. "I'm gonna wash my hands again." She hustled into the bathroom.

The young doctor knocked at the door. "Mr. Warner? How's she doing?" Julian stared. "I think there was a misunderstanding with one of our staff."

"The nurse," Julian rifled back, "reading my mom the Bible without her consent?"

"Yes. I apologize. I asked one of our orderlies to stop by and suggest you read to your mom, and when she didn't see anyone in here—she keeps the Good Book in her pocket. She was trying to help. You should try it," he said. "Reading to her. She can still hear, even if she can't respond. So she knows you're here."

"I didn't bring anything," Julian mumbled, "to . . ." He nodded at the doctor to go. He waited a moment, alone with his mom and the tick and burble of the machines. He picked up a stack of used magazines by the bed, *Texas Monthly* and *Car and Driver*. He opened his backpack in a futile gesture. And he saw it. The Annie Lennox journal he was holding when he found his mom in pain, that he had no recollection of tossing in with his wallet in the commotion to get to the hospital.

"He's probably right," Bonnie said, emerging from the bathroom. "About reading to her. What you got there?"

"An old journal. I was cleaning out the garage when she . . ."

"Scintillating stuff." She blew on her coffee. Julian opened the cover and paused, scanning his words, editing, trying to control who knew what. "Go on," she said softly.

So in the middle of the night Julian sat beside his mother, like he had countless mornings as a boy, and read to her:

September 23, 1993

Mom was supposed to take me to Amy's house for a sleepover with the Woodwind Girls. She knew it was Crucial (a French horn hanging out with flutes and clarinets?) even if I couldn't stay overnight. But she got a migraine and made Dad take me. He asked her why I was the only boy going. They took forever fighting about it (like I can't hear in the living room?!?!) so I got three sticks of gum out of Mom's purse. I found a business card in the pocket next to the gum. *I wasn't snooping.* Deborah Epstein, Esq.—Matrimonial + Divorce. Everyone's parents are divorced these days. Might as well join the club.

I was the last one there, thanks to Dad. I ditched him at the lame "Parents Party" downstairs. I did our secret knock on Amy's door, but when she opened it, it wasn't just the Woodwind Girls. Faith Felton crashed the sleepover. Lame Faith with her Keds and stupid scrunchies. Amy rolled her eyes and we all ignored her. I told the Girls about Mrs. Cooper's nipples doing a jailbreak in Earth Science, poking through her bra and shirt and everything. They laughed so hard. Mandy and Tina played Uno. Amy passed me a note that Faith was only there because Amy and Faith's moms are BFFs and Faith and her mom are staying at Amy's house because Faith's dad TOUCHED HER and her parents are splitting up. Then Faith flipped out and yelled at me Why Are You Here? Are You G——? Amy told her to shut up, but she grabbed my journal and asked if that's where I wrote down my G——boyfriends. I pulled it back, but she yelled Do You Even Have a Dick? and grabbed my belt and tried to undo my pants. I screamed at her to stop and ran. I hid on the stairs. She's going to spread rumors that I'm G—— on Monday. I can't go back to school. I'll tell Mom I'm sick. But the algebra test. And I can't be sick forever . . .

I heard Dad from all the way on the second floor. He was laughing and talking too loud. When I came downstairs he had his arm around another man. He said Come meet Gorey. They did a shot of liquor and we left. Dad couldn't walk straight on the path, and he went the wrong way in the car until I told him. Dad said Mr. Gorey is Amy's uncle, visiting on his way to Gulfport. He's the only other guy in Dad's company who didn't get killed in Vietnam. Dad was a minesweeper in the war. He tried to show me with his hands, but the car swerved. He was driving fast. He said what kept him alive in Vietnam was his mind and Mom's letters. He said I'm smart as hell and I got that from him and Mom, and everything I am is from them, so fuck (he swore) anybody who says I'm going to hell or can't hang out with girls. Then he missed the turn onto Rustling Elms Drive and hit the brakes, but we hit a mailbox. It swung around. Dad put his head on the steering wheel and just sat there. He asked if I wanted to drive the rest of the way. I asked if I should, and he drove home. What's wrong with him?

Julian had never reread this journal, had long ago buried the incident. He looked up at his mom, certain she'd have opinions, that she heard every word and couldn't resist waking up to comment on the mysteries of their family and time. But she didn't. His mom lay still, her chest rising and falling, undisturbed.

★

On the afternoon of Lacy Warner's memorial, Julian stood at the mirror of his high school boys' room. He barely recognized the face staring back. He knew he had to get away from everything for a moment before the service started—from Bonnie, the hundreds of people who came, even Philip—so he ran to the bathroom. To be alone and let something out, get out a good pre-cry before the ceremony if he could. He opened his mouth, silent and fishy at first, but right as a wheeze began to trickle from his lips, he heard a shuffle. He turned and saw feet in the far stall. A toilet flushed. Julian swiveled to leave when out walked his dad, Aaron Warner.

"Julian." Aaron said his name to the reflection in the mirror, casually, as though they had seen each other now and then, or even once, in the eight years since he left. His gut pushed out, and he looked shorter. His face was hardened with age. "I ate something funny last night."

"I have to get in there," Julian mumbled and slipped out the door.

He hurried down the hall toward the auditorium. Every moment since he stepped inside the school was like a dream watched from above. Since his mom died. Time had warped. She was supposed to have six months after she stopped chemo at Christmas. He was supposed to be in Cambridge finishing school. Now his vanishing act of a dad appears? A worthless man who did nothing to raise him was here, alive, but his mom was gone? At the door of the auditorium he stopped and turned, thinking he saw a glimpse of her down the hall like he used to in between classes. He remembered how he ducked to avoid her in those days, and suddenly he wanted it all back—all the time, every hour he pined to get away from her and home.

Julian went in and stood in the shadows. The smell of chilled dust wafted from the navy velour curtains. The stage was done up exactly as his mom had written. After Christmas Julian noticed her scribbling on a yellow pad she carried around, but it wasn't until he was back from the hospital that he looked at it on her nightstand and saw notes she had made for her memorial service. *Not in a church*, she wrote, *At the high school, where people know me. Pots of daisies and bluebonnets. The stage lit like a rainbow. No readings, just songs.* No mention of a picture or people to talk about her, which didn't surprise Julian. He had to take care of those himself.

In the front row Philip and Bonnie craned their necks toward him. The principal gave a nod, and the memorial began. Julian stepped onstage, past a blown-up photo of Lacy teaching at a blackboard, and crossed to the podium. He squinted at the outlines of people and thanked them for coming. He told them a story of Lacy Warner that he knew to be true but didn't understand, of a strong woman who didn't mention her cancer was terminal until her son finished exams and came home the other week. Because education was the most important thing. He didn't share what he witnessed a few nights before—the person he knew best in the world rendered silent, unreachable, by the ruthless efficiency of death. A young teacher spoke after him, of how she wouldn't have survived her first year without Lacy stopping by with Kit Kats and the way she listened, like your problems were hers. Bonnie spoke last. Even in the darkest times, she said, she knew there was a God because she lived half her life, past forty, when one day at the pool He put her there, Lacy, in a pretty sarong in the next lounge chair. Another smart weirdo living undercover in the suburbs, who taught her the meaning of friendship. The girls' choir came onstage in red satin gowns and sang "Coat of Many Colors."

There was a reception in the cafeteria. Bonnie must have hugged every guest. Philip stood beside Julian as he shook hands and nodded at condolences. All of his old teachers came. The skylights in the cafeteria let in a brilliant winter sun that made Julian squint as they talked. Occasionally, through the numbness he felt the weight of disbelief. *This is it?* the question turned inside him. *This is how we remember?*

"Eat something," Philip insisted when the first wave of people subsided. "What do you want? A cookie? Cold cuts?"

"Just coffee," Julian mumbled. "I'll stay here." He watched Philip zigzag through bodies and remembered the sight of him coming through the door at the hospital. The love mingled with fear as he took in Julian, and his mom's face stretched out in the death rattle.

Aaron appeared out of the crowd. "Real nice day, Jules," he said.

"You made it." At Philip's urging, Julian had sent an email to an AOL account he found under "Aaron Warner" in his mom's address book, with details about the memorial. And got no response.

"Did you do all this yourself?" Aaron asked. "The service and whatnot?"

"It's what she wanted."

Aaron nodded. "She didn't tell you she was sick till last month?"

"I didn't know she was dying. We talked every week in the fall, about her chemo. I thought it was going well. Did you?" Julian stood up straight, taller than his dad. "Know she was sick?"

"We didn't keep in touch." He fiddled with the program in his hands. "Quite a woman. Lacy. The good ones die young." He shut his eyes and leaned his head back, like she might be up past the skylights, sending down a little winter color. "How long you in town for?" he asked.

"Philip and I fly back to Boston tomorrow."

"Philip?"

"My fiancé. Here he is." Philip handed him a paper coffee cup and smiled widely. "Philip, this is my dad, Aaron."

"Nice to meet you." Philip held out his hand. "I'm sorry it's under these circumstances."

"OK." Aaron let his hand be shaken. "What're y'all doing later?"

"Today?" Julian said. "Miss Bonnie's hosting a thing."

"Oh."

"But I don't know if that's a good . . ."

"OK." Aaron nodded at his feet. "We could get a coffee after that, if you want."

"Um." Julian felt Philip's laser eyes burning into his head. "I could step away. Briefly."

So later that afternoon, as Bonnie's house warmed up with wine and stories of Lacy, Julian left alone and took Roy- alwood Drive to the Starbucks across the pond from Kro- ger. Anger stirred as the occasion of the memorial wore off and Julian's nerves receded. He didn't want to see his dad. He was only going because Philip pulled rank as the thera- pist's son and insisted it was the right thing to do. Who was Aaron to suggest coffee? A guy who leaves while Julian was at a swim meet—he had somewhere else to be, was all his mom said—never to be heard from again? Not one call on a birth- day or graduation, and he and his mom had done just fine, thank you. And now at the worst moment of his life, his dad wanted to lean on the manners of people he used to know and have a catch-up?

Julian straightened his collar and entered Starbucks. He swept the place with his eyes, but the only customer was a young mother nursing at a corner table. Then he saw the blazer his dad was wearing earlier, heaped over a chair next to a table cluttered with things—junk mail, an OTB receipt, two empty cups, the denuded bottom of a muffin slumped on its wrapper, a yellow Post-it with his dad's handwriting. Julian hovered over the table, twisting his head to read the list on it:

Zoloft (90 refill) Xanax soon
Beer, Swanson salisbury steak
Car wash—Thurs ½ price Platinum pckg

"Jules?" Aaron called.

Julian jerked up, one hand knocking the muffin off the table. "Shit, sorry," he mumbled. "I'll get you another."

"That's all right." Aaron approached with his hands on his stomach. "Bread's my friend today. How's life in the Ivy League?"

"Oh. Yeah, I'm at Harvard. How did you . . ."

"It was in the local paper."

"Yeah. Phil and I are both done this spring."

"You graduate this year?" Aaron said. "I could've sworn you got one more to go."

"I'm doing it in three. When you're paying for it yourself, you go as fast as you can."

"You want a drink?" Aaron asked.

"I'm good."

"We're here. Let me buy you a drink. Coffee, latte, whatever you want, you want one of those caramel—"

"A small coffee's fine," Julian said. "Plain black."

"That's how I take it." Aaron smiled. "With eight sugars." He went to the counter.

Julian lifted his tidy Moleskine notebook from his coat pocket. He wrote down names for thank-you notes to send once he was back in Cambridge.

"Whatcha writing?" Aaron asked, returning with two coffees.

"A list. People who sent flowers and cards."

"Is that a diary?"

"A journal," Julian corrected.

"What do you put in there?"

"Stuff to do. Stuff that happens. Jot things down and make sense of it later."

"Does it?" Aaron asked. "Make sense when you read it later?"

"Sometimes."

They sat quietly a moment until, apropos of nothing, Julian launched into his fabulous life. The Phi Beta Kappa thing, and getting into Columbia Law, and how Philip took an analyst position at Morgan Stanley because his dad's at Goldman and Philip didn't want any special treatment, and how much Julian respected him for that, and how Philip's parents wanted the Central Park Boathouse for their wedding but they weren't sure. Julian talked and talked like he used to, waiting for Aaron to say something. To tell him the things his boy wasn't anymore, all the people his boy wasn't like and never was. Aaron nodded throughout. At a pause late in the monologue, Aaron asked, "Do Philip's parents—"

"The Rosenblums."

"OK." Aaron nodded, and kept nodding into an unsettling zone between assent and nervous tic. "Is his being—do they know why Philip turned out to be . . ."

"To be what?"

"Homosexual. Is it the same, or, like how you did?"

"Huh." Julian strapped his journal shut. "I think people would like one explanation. Some things are bigger than us, you know?"

"Is that legal?" Aaron asked. "You two getting married?"

"It will be. Sooner or later."

"Well, that sounds real nice. Congratulations."

"Thank you," Julian said.

Aaron stared at his coffee. "It's a damn stupid policy," he mumbled.

"Policy?"

"This Don't Ask, Don't Tell business. Perfectly able-bodied

homosexuals want to serve their country, but draft-dodging Clinton and now this 'Air National Guard' sack of shit Dubya say they can't. The idiots running our military." Aaron's eyes welled up as he studied his son's face. "But, hey, if it spares you the—" His hand reached across the table and patted Julian's. Just as fast he pulled it back into his lap, like a crab darting for a hole.

"How are you?" Julian asked, after a time. "You're still living in Houston?"

"Yeah. I got an apartment off I-45, by Greenspoint Mall. I get my medical at the VA. I make out all right. In a couple of years I can take Social Security early."

"Oh. You're—thinking about retiring?"

"Retire," Aaron said grimly, and laughed. "Stop working. Checked out. Pick a year. Turns out the corporate thing wasn't for me. The rat race, the people. Two decades. Not getting those back. I'm working security now."

"Like, a security guard?"

"A manager. At a skyscraper downtown on Fannin. There's a big law firm there, Vinson & Elkins?" Aaron offered. "See people coming in and out all day long. Talk, say hi."

"Good. That's good. Do you have anybody in your life?"

"What do you mean?"

"People," Julian said. "Like, anybody you see every day?"

"Yeah. The guys at the VA. I started sticking around there in the fall, after the doctor. We hang out in the lounge. Watch TV. Take trips. The Vietnam memorial."

Julian's mind filled with visions of wheelchairs and amputees, insane screaming people, people lost to the system and their loved ones if they had any. He thought of poor people. How poor his dad looked in his suit. "You have friends," he said. "At the VA."

"Pretty good doctors too," Aaron said. "This one guy, served in Desert Storm, he got his jaw blown off hunting, but they put it back together and made him custom dentures. He's eating ribs today."

"You had fake teeth, didn't you?" Julian asked. Aaron stared blankly. "Not like that guy," Julian continued, "with the jaw, not a whole set. Those four teeth? That retainer? In your underwear drawer, under the picture of you in Vietnam. Remember?"

"Oh. That, yeah."

"I always wondered how—did you lose them in combat?"

"Combat?" Aaron frowned. "The teeth? That wasn't the war. Football, back at UT."

"Oh." Julian sat up straight. "I must have—never mind."

"Those teeth." Aaron grinned. "They sure gave your mom the creeps."

"Are you seeing anybody? Besides your friends, like, dating?"

"I am officially off the market." Aaron shook his head and chuckled. "One marriage was plenty trouble for one lifetime. Sure as hell not doing that again."

Anger flared once more inside Julian. But almost as quickly as it came it died down. Aaron sat across the table, folding empty sugar packets, and it was as if Julian could see him for the first time. Past the things his dad never did, the failures that cluttered Julian's mind, to the things Aaron managed to do, that took up all his energy, taking care of himself. Remembering his pills. Eking by at the supermarket register. Forgetting himself at a double feature, some day when the ticket lady wasn't watching for folks jumping theaters. The way he taught his son to do years ago. Julian groped inside for the hatred as familiar as an old pair of jeans, but it had faded at the sight of his dad. How much he needed and how little he had.

"Why'd you leave?" Julian asked. "Why did you leave us?"

Aaron watched his son as though he had whole chapters to share behind his eyes, if he felt like it. Or Julian was imagining things. "You're better off," Aaron said. "I promise."

Julian flushed, ashamed that he went there. "I should go."

"When's your graduation?" Aaron asked as they were leaving.

"The first weekend in June."

"Right around the corner. Maybe I can make it up."

"Oh," Julian said. "OK."

"Keep in touch."

"OK. Keep that email address."

"Yup," Aaron nodded. "That's my email."

"I mean, it's the only thing I found for you in Mom's stuff. To reach you."

Aaron hugged him, finishing with a quick pat on the back. "You got good in you," Aaron mumbled, looking away. "Like your mom. Take care, Jules." He got in the old Taurus with its low-hanging muffler. Julian waited beside his mom's minivan. He waved, but his dad didn't see him as he pulled out of the parking lot.

Julian drove back to Bonnie's house. She was waiting in the foyer when he came inside. Guests milled around chatting and laughing in the den behind her. He pushed the door shut and leaned against it. Slowly she approached Julian and rubbed his shoulder like she knew a thing or two, and in her soft, bendy drawl asked, "How's your daddy doing?"

III.

A Baby

11

Stuffed

Through the leaded glass window, Julian looked out at the postcard view of Stockbridge. The October colors were otherworldly. They got the double Berkshire blessing for their wedding day—a good leaf season and sunny skies. From the parlor of the B and B, past the other mansions set back from Main Street, Julian could see the sprawling white outline of the Red Lion Inn and the start of the commercial district, where Norman Rockwell painted America. Over their long engagement, the wedding was going to be in a lot of places. Houston, when his mom got sick, but Julian planned her memorial instead. New York for a minute. In the end they settled on Massachusetts because that righteous colony stepped into the future and legalized them. And because Gerald and Ruth had a farm in Lenox—the gut-renovated kind with a red barn and no animals—and when Ruth Rosenblum had a preference it was well-known.

But mostly because it felt right. For a year Julian and Philip watched President Dubya campaign for reelection on their backs and win, twanging about God's plan and constitutional amendments, giving beady-eyed cover to statehouses across the nation to do violence to gay people—which they did. Every week a new bill demonized love. Hate was in the air. They kept their heads screwed on straight through the madness, never conceding it was too much to ask to be able to open the *Times* at breakfast and not feel assaulted by their own leaders. So when the Bay State swam against the tide and did the right thing, Julian and Philip agreed about where to have the big day.

That piece of the American Dream, for so long incomprehensible and then out of reach, would be theirs. And aesthetically speaking, Philip went all in. He had an artist paint them as *American Gothic* for the wedding invitation, a tiny replica with Julian and Philip as farmers, pitchfork, gabled roof, the works. The drawing room, where the ceremony would be, was forested with purple and yellow mums, pumpkins, and what Philip called rustic-chic squash. Deer heads hung above the fireplaces on wood-paneled walls. Programs nestled in a red wagon by the front door. Here Julian sat in a movie set of a house, at his perfectly appointed wedding that was really legally happening. Yet he was down. Not about Philip. Of all the sadnesses and regrets the day dredged up, none were about Phil. He was sad about death, and the permanence of things. Stupid, he knew, when he could just look at leaves and mansions and be happy.

"Did you know," Philip said, poking his head in the parlor door, "the big one with the pillars—across the street—is a nuthouse?"

"Huh?"

"What are you doing in here by yourself? That one, see?" Philip laid a hand on Julian's shoulder and pointed out the window. "The Austen Riggs Center for the Study and Treatment of the Psychoneuroses. Mom said all the biggies came through. Anna Freud, Erikson, Bollas. Some messed-up people over there. I think we're in the right house." He smiled, waiting, and frowned. "Jay, are you OK?"

"Yeah." Julian rose swiftly. "What's up?"

"Everyone's here for the final-final run-through. Ready?"

Julian followed him into the drawing room. "Hey, people?" Philip began as they turned the corner. They spotted Ruth. She wore a plum-colored suit and cream blouse, her salt-and-pepper hair disheveled in a style she hit with precision, at once suggesting hard-core thinking, carelessness, and an expensive curl specialist. She was at the chuppah, talking alone with the middle-aged lesbian rabbi/spiritualist Philip had chosen after much vetting.

"Mom, what are you doing?" he asked, rushing to them. Julian waved at their parties—Phil's sister, friends from Harvard and Columbia—but the place was packed with uninvited family of Gerald's and Ruth's. It was the same scene as the rehearsal dinner the night before, a crasher situation Philip treated as normal. He and Ruth carried on in hushed tones about some entrance for the ceremony, gesturing their discord. The constructive suggestion was the story of their wedding. Ruth's good boy tended to share their plans, big and small, which Ruth always found wonderful and always knew how to make more wonderful. One night Philip passed along a message from her about how healthy it would be for Julian to invite his dad, Aaron—a fresh choice, letting go of the reenactments, a choice worthy of Julian—and would he reflect on it?

"No," Philip said audibly, smiling at Ruth, and turned from the chuppah. He clapped his hands and addressed the room. "People? Thanks for coming early for one last truly final—look, if the parties get their cues right this try, we'll be out of here in no time. Ready?"

They did a speed-through of the ceremony: entrances to Glass, Plato's *Symposium*, Torah, Gilgamesh, Chopin interlude, a sermon on Saints Serge and Bacchus, vows, circle each other, break a glass, recess to Purcell. Done. The extra rehearsal left Philip chewing his lip, but he grudgingly released the group.

Ruth immediately descended on him, touching his arm in the same incorporating way her son did when he wanted something. He shook his head and kept walking. Julian saw her canvassing the room with her eyes and tried to duck out.

"Jay!" she called. He flinched at her bright smile weaving through bodies, and waved, fortifying himself for her arrival. Ruth was all-around intense. Intensely loving and warm. Intense with her opinions, about a place setting or the BDS movement, and with the confidence she exuded, of knowing exactly how to order the world if she had the chance. Scarier still was what Julian had witnessed for years at dinner parties and gatherings: the boundlessness of Ruth's analytic mind, the sense that nothing—not her marriage, or Phil's adolescent nonsexuality—was shameful or off-limits for group discussion.

"My son," she said solemnly when she reached him, lightly gripping his elbows. "Here we are. The big day. Can you believe it?" Julian smiled. "I was chatting with Phil earlier, about care and support. The joining of peoples, not just grooms. You have us, the Rosenblums and Bergmans, all of us. You know that, right?"

"Thank you," he said.

"So why don't we walk down the aisle together—you, Phil, Gerald, and me?"

"Ruth." Julian sighed. They were back to this, the one opinion she couldn't let go.

"Gerald and I can give you both away," she said, nodding at the obviousness of it.

"We went over this," Julian said to Philip with a tense smile as he approached.

"Mom, we're on a tight schedule."

"I know, but, Jay?" she implored. "Somebody should give you away, don't you think?" She watched him through her gold wire-rims, as guests chatted and laughed around them. He was surrounded by people on a joyous day of union. And he felt alone. The way he had traveled the world for years, even with Philip by his side—like a baby in a basket, floating downstream, the clouds above his only company.

★

Life had been looking backward since Julian's mom died. It didn't appear that way on the surface of things. To the outside world, Julian moved relentlessly forward. He finished college early, sorting out his mom's affairs from Cambridge between finals and his thesis defense. In one tight week after graduation, he enlisted Bonnie's help to sell his childhood home, put stuff in storage, and get him back to New York in time for an internship at the ACLU. He worked long hours that summer, commuting downtown from the walk-up he and Phil rented near Columbia, far from the Rosenblums' West Village town house. Julian started law school and crushed it. He dominated moot court, edited the law review, surprised his professors when he turned down a clerkship to get scrapping as a civil rights lawyer. His passion was written everywhere: on his résumé and cover letters, in his eyes if you were looking for it.

But flowing under all of this, like a dark river, was the life on the inside. The Julian who knew the rat race was a distraction, to hide from the truth that nothing mattered. The Julian only Philip saw. That Julian brought his mom's pain pills back from Texas—two ninety-count bottles of Dilaudid some doctor had incongruously prescribed—and for months, every moment he wasn't studying or changing the world he was high on the couch, incoherent, while Phil babysat the man-child fiancé. When they had a scene over the holidays, Julian's first year of law school, the pills got flushed and he found other numbing agents to keep his head above water: wine, weed, bareback porn. At some point each semester, in a chemical oblivion, Julian imagined throwing it all away, every pointless success of his life, which he would have traded in a heartbeat for another day with his mom. To hug her and talk about what happened.

When he graduated from Columbia and they started the wedding planning in earnest, Philip demanded Julian see a therapist. Julian found an older woman unconnected to Ruth, who in a recent session shared that the grief of losing her own mother stayed with her until the birth of her first child. Great, Julian thought. Because the problem he couldn't solve, three years later, was how to find meaning anywhere when his life's purpose was to be a good son. Therapy dug up memories, not answers—like the childhood lessons at the kitchen table, how his mom framed their life as the Grand Mystery of Julian and what he'd become, every day put to him as a question. Only after she was gone did it occur to him that the drive that got him out of Texas, to the Ivy League and beyond, was fueled by something simple. Not ego or glory. Just the wish to please her. That was over now, and the world seemed empty. The future a lie.

This was the cloud Julian lived under, that followed him and hovered over his wedding day, when Ruth suggested she and Gerald walk him down the aisle. He faked a cough as she stared at him, waiting for him to bless her idea, and then mumbled he needed water and took off. When he returned from the kitchen, a few minutes later, he walked into a surprise photo op. Ruth had commandeered their photographer and arranged a tableau of Rosenblums and Bergmans around the dining room table. Phil smiled wearily at Julian, from his spot next to Gerald, while Ruth reviewed digital stills.

"Jay, there you are!" She beamed and waved him over to look.

"Ruth," Julian replied, carefully screwing his water bottle shut. "We're not doing photos until right before the ceremony, when we're dressed."

"Yes, three thirty." She sucked on the Fresca that was her constant companion. "We took some quick family shots. It's so rare we're in the same place anymore, all the generations. We waited in position—will you join a few?" Julian stared. "No? OK. Thanks, folks!" Ruth called to the room. "Oh, Jay?" she said, turning back to him. "Could you stay a minute? Bubbe Bergman has something she wants to give you and Philip."

She motioned to her frail, white-haired mother, stationed in a wheelchair at the end of the table. Julian never really knew Philip's only surviving grandparent. By the time they met at Harvard, Sura Bergman had already sunk into the soft dementia that left her smiling and quiet, emitting "oh yes" and "oh no" in accordance with no particular logic. Julian thought of that Joan Baez song "Hello in There" whenever he saw her, the blank face with the intense biography—escaping Berlin as a girl before the war and making it to Brooklyn, a life of work from the time she was a teenager, moving with her husband to a row house on Church Avenue, the lap of luxury in her day, raising her little joy Ruth. All of this narrated heroically to Julian by her daughter, as Sura's intentions had been for years.

"Have a seat." Gerald smiled benevolently at Julian and patted the chair beside him. He looked crisp as usual in a navy suit and rich red tie. He ran a hand through his lion's mane of gray waves, an older version of Phil's hair. The light caught his cuff links, golden compasses, and Gerald—warm, taciturn, socially subdued—gestured for Ruth to take the stage.

"Julian," she began in a confidential tone. She took her mother's hand and leaned into the half-circle they made at the end of the table. "Bubbe Bergman gave Philip his favorite gift as a boy—his stuffed bear, Coco. He fed Coco, bathed Coco. They were inseparable. Now she has another gift, for both of you." Her lips puckered with feeling. She slid an envelope across the table. Philip opened an investment statement from Goldman Sachs with a hundred-thousand-dollar balance. "A college fund," Ruth said, "for your firstborn."

"Oh," Julian exhaled.

"Mom? Dad?" Philip gushed. "Thank you!"

"Thank Bubbe," Ruth said. "Gerald has agreed to manage it until the baby's eighteen. We all know your sister has expressed ambivalence about marriage and children, but you two—the parents you'll make!" Ruth reached over and rubbed their hands. "I've explained the whole surrogacy thing to Bubbe, and she understands."

"What?" Julian blurted. "Surrogacy? What are you talking about?"

"If you decide to go that route," Ruth said. "Then you remove the uncertainty, the baby's yours, you pick the sex, pick whose—"

"This is—" Julian shot a look at Philip. "We haven't decided, for sure, if we're even going to have a—"

"We talked about adopting once, remember?" Philip volunteered anxiously.

"And that's lovely," Ruth interjected. "Something definitely worth exploring. And then there's blood. Keeping the line, using Phil's materials. Yours too, Jay. Have two, three! The more the merrier."

"I don't know why we're talking materials, *anyone's*—" Julian rose from his chair. He couldn't believe Ruth's gall. Or the gall of the universe, letting Philip's grandmother go on living half-dead, while his mom died in her prime, badly needed and missing this day. Instantly he felt ashamed at reducing Sura's life to his private misery, convinced it was a sign he was unstable, unworthy of marriage, a generally disgusting solo guy. "What gives you the right?" he said to Ruth.

"Jay?" she cried in surprise. "We're family. We're talking."

"How is it OK to dangle a check with strings like that today? To tell me what family to invite? How to walk down the aisle at my own wedding?"

Julian took off for the backyard. The smell of mountain air made his eyes well up at the wish to be happy. He crossed the lawn to the creek at the edge of the property, winding its way to the Housatonic and into something larger. He had an anger he didn't know where to put. At Ruth, and life not working out. He breathed and tried to calm himself. He knew in his head that she meant well, that no woman made it through a PhD at Harvard in the sixties without being a fighter. Without a cost. But in his heart, it felt like every other time he got too close to Ruth over the last few years—like regret, and a wrenching guilt at the memory of phone calls home to his mom from college. Long calls while he carried on about the Rosenblums, enamored of their lives and Ruth's many accomplishments. Julian turned away from the creek at the smell of cigarette. Two waiters were smoking by the back door to the kitchen. Through the French doors to the ballroom, he could make out Phil's silhouette, adjusting centerpieces. He resented that Phil didn't come find him. He didn't know what to say to him, or if he wanted to say anything. But he felt less lost at the prospect of bickering with his fiancé than annexed to a random smoke break, so he plodded back to the house.

"Hey," Julian called, entering the ballroom. His voice echoed across the two-story space. A wooden staircase led to a mezzanine, where the DJ was setting up. On the far wall, some rich eccentric had painted a mind-boggling floor-to-ceiling mural of a Japanese landscape. Julian had yet to take in all of Philip's reception prep, the asters and black-eyed Susans exploding out of pumpkins on the tables, but it hit him as he wove between them: after all the planning, they were here. Two twentysomethings, babies in gay years, getting married. "Phil?" he called again.

Philip futzed with flowers before replying. "Hi."

"You need help?" Julian asked, navigating toward him.

"Now you take an interest?"

"Um." He waited as Philip moved on. Julian was being avoided. "What are you doing?"

"Make sure—" Philip sighed and studied the centerpiece. "I want an even distribution of flowers around the circumference of the pumpkins. Can you do that?"

"Yeah." Julian followed him, mimicking the way he massaged them. Philip didn't apologize for Ruth, or the situation, or speak at all. "So," Julian began. He shivered with loneliness, yet his words came out hot. "Did you know? About the whole—Bubbe's gift?"

Philip stopped and shut his eyes. "Of course not."

"It felt a little like a sneak attack in there. I didn't mean to yell, but the—walking down the aisle, pictures, the baby shit?"

"I didn't think you meant to," Philip muttered.

"What?"

Philip ran his tongue along his teeth, scratching the stress ulcers he'd been getting all week. "I want a day about us. Not her."

"I know." And he did know, about Phil being her favorite yet always under her thumb. Or how he still hadn't figured out what he wanted to do with his life after three years at Morgan Stanley, and how this day had become everything. The one thing to look forward to. Julian also knew Philip needed to cut the cord. "So, you're not mad?" Julian asked.

Philip shrugged. "Mad? I'm . . . embarrassed."

"Excuse me?"

"It's not about her. You really can't see it. I listen to you," Philip continued in a slow, practiced tone. "I told you I wished your mom was alive and here with us today. I asked you to get help."

"I did! I've been seeing Maxine for months. Sorry it's not the therapist Ruth wanted, so you could pick up your Batphone and get the inside—"

"Stop it," Philip snapped. "Stop wasting time. I've been kind to you. I'm here too. Not just the times you're up. The times you're down. Who are you going to be, Jay? Who do you want to be in this marriage? The future? You're stuck. Do you want to be the drugs? Escapes? Work, hiding—"

"Call it off, then!" Julian bellowed. "Send them home. Everyone. If I'm so bad, why do this? Why would you ever want to marry me?"

Philip glanced up at the mezzanine, where the DJ had stopped unpacking. "Because," he said quietly, and shrugged. "You know how to say no. To stand up for yourself."

"Oh. Like I just did with your mother?"

Philip sighed. "And all the other reasons I wrote in my vows."

Softly Phil cupped the flowers in front of him and looked at Julian. Philip was the kindest person he knew. And as much as Julian circled in darkness around the question of whether he existed at all, there at that moment he stood, he was, in Philip's eyes. He dropped his head and nodded at how painful it was to be seen by someone else, really seen and known.

"I don't have anybody," Julian mumbled.

"What do you mean?"

"People. At the wedding. It's like a hundred of your family. Mom, dad, sister, aunts, uncles, a grandparent. I supposedly have two uncles in Texas I don't even know and that's it."

"And a dad."

"Please," Julian said. "Not again."

"Knock-knock!" Bonnie stood at the door of the ballroom, beaming in a shiny blue suit that set off her blond dye job. Her skin looked younger than the last time Julian saw her, years ago. She had come out the other end of her divorce OK, or hadn't given up yet. "Jules! Philip!" She hurried over and hugged them. "Sorry I couldn't get here till late last night. The family I took in after Katrina, they've got a dog and there was a situation with my cat, but I changed my flight and everybody's snug as a bug in a rug back home with my son there helping out! How y'all doing? You ready?"

"I think so." Julian smiled and startled all three of them when he reached out and hugged her again. "It's good to see you."

"Sweetie." She laid a hand on Julian's cheek. "Your mama would be so proud of you. Can I do anything? What are y'all up to?"

"We're about to put on our tuxes," Philip said. "Some alone time before the ceremony."

"Go on, then," she smiled. "Jules, you know how to tie your tie?"

"I do," he said.

★

Julian found a lot of old objects the week he went home to clear out his mom's house. Some he had seen going through boxes before she died, report cards or macaroni collages, while others triggered new memories. In the back of a closet he found a faded poster—WELCOME HOME JULES! with shapes of Texas and crimson *H*s—that his mom held at the airport the first time he came home from Harvard. She wore jeans that day, he remembered, which she never did because they didn't make them for fat women, or not nice ones she said. But she had slimmed down. It wasn't until years later, while moving his mom's life into trash bags, that it occurred to him that maybe she fit into jeans on that visit because she missed him.

In the rush to throw things out, Julian almost tossed the gift. He was working on her bedroom, dumping stacks of old *National Geographic* from a basket by her nightstand, when he noticed a shallow box mixed in with the magazines. The wrapping paper was pale blue and silver, folded tight at the corners but without his mom's usual curly ribbons on top. He lifted a paper square and saw her handwriting:

To Julian, on his Wedding Day.

He brought the present back to New York and hid it in his closet, in an empty Yahtzee box. He never told Philip. He wanted something of his mom that was just his. Something he could hold close and private, a wedding dance they'd never have. He took it out some nights when he was drunk and alone in the apartment, shook it, speculated on its contents. They shifted end to end solidly, a book maybe, or a last picture album. Many times he thought of opening it before the wedding but resisted, returning the box to the closet. Until two days ago, when he packed his suitcase for the wedding.

He sat alone with it in his lap now, in their bedroom upstairs at the B and B. Its once glossy paper looked faded against the shiny slacks of his tuxedo. Philip had decamped with clothes and toiletries to another bedroom, to make sure they didn't cross paths in the run-up to the ceremony. Julian was almost ready. He had twisted his hair into the short messy points he liked and put on his clothes. There was only his bow tie left, and the gift his mom had left him.

His fingers fumbled as he tore the wrapping from the plain white box. Inside he waded through blue tissue and found not a book or album, but papers. He unfolded printouts of search results from Ancestry.com, thirty-odd pages of links to birth certificates for dozens of Maria Elena's in Laredo, Texas, and a bunch of Mexican towns he never heard of, gathered over several years, he could tell by the print lines. Below them, tied with a ribbon, was a bundle of letters his dad wrote his mom at UT, from a military base in Vietnam. And at the bottom of the box, or maybe the top, was a letter from his mom written on yellow lined pages. Julian recognized the paper, from the same pad on his mom's nightstand where she wrote the instructions for her memorial service years ago.

Julian—

Happy wedding day. I would've made you a gift like I did for Philip for Christmas, but you didn't tell me you were getting married until right before you came home. The Rosenblums probably bought you some overpriced blender or latte machine. I don't know when we'll say goodbye, but if you're reading this I'm gone and this is what you're getting.

I've been rereading Tolkien on nights I can't sleep, the trilogy and *Silmarillion*. There was a time you loved Tolkien, too. Aragorn was a Ranger of the North, you may recall, a remnant of the Dúnedain of Arnor. They were split from their ancestors to the south in Gondor, three thousand years ago, and their numbers dwindled until they were just a wandering pack of men without people or land. All they had was a history inside them. Your dad and I had problems, but you were made in love. You can see it in these letters we wrote, helping each other through hard times. That's where you come from. I never knew your dad's family, and you only met my mom once. It was for the best. She was Mexican and didn't want to be. A man came to our house once from Mexico when I was a girl, a relative, but she turned him away. In the closet, you could say. I always wanted to find her family. I looked for her on one of those family tree websites but didn't get far. It probably doesn't feel like it now, but you have people somewhere. Not all those who wander are lost.

Remember Valinor, the Undying Lands where the immortal Elves returned to live? And took Bilbo and Frodo to spend their last days in peace and beauty? Can you imagine it? Nothing about our world is fair. It's a cruel sick place most of the time. And when you're different it's worse. The world wants you invisible. But you never really could hide and you never did. Don't let it happen, Jules. The Elves were warriors, with good aim. Do what's right for the invisible people. Raise hell. Never shut up. It's all over before you know it.

Love,

Lacy Adams Warner

Julian stared at the pages. It was the intensity pulsing through her words, the heat, that was unfamiliar. Things his mom apparently couldn't say in person, or all the ways he hadn't been listening when she was alive. He wondered about the anger that burned in him, that drove him and sometimes kept him apart—had it been passed along like some inheritance?

"Julian?" A knock came at the door. "It's Ruth. Are you dressed?"

"Yeah."

She poked her head in. "Do you have a minute?"

"Sure," he said, tucking the box under a pillow.

Ruth puttered to the walnut sleigh bed and settled at the foot of it. Julian watched her, recalling the first time he and Philip hosted the Rosenblums at their apartment uptown. The grief of losing his mom was still raw, and Julian channeled it into an elaborate dinner—beef bourguignon and a chocolate soufflé. Ruth barely touched her food, and when he offered her more salad—the one thing she deigned to eat—she smiled grandly and said she was stuffed. And years later, their relationship had never really moved past that night.

Julian fiddled with the tie undone around his neck. "I'm glad you came by."

"I tried Phil's room first," Ruth started briskly, "but he

wouldn't let me in. I haven't seen you in months! Congrats on the new job. We donate to the ACLU, and I happen to know they don't hire much right out of law school."

"I got my own funding"—he smiled—"so I'm free."

"Julian." She adjusted her glasses and sat up straight. Her floral perfume wafted lightly toward him. "At the rehearsal earlier, and with my mother, I upset you. It was not my intention, but it was the effect of my actions. Try as we may, we're all Freudians. The gift is excrement. I'm sorry."

He had never heard Ruth apologize. They hadn't had many one-on-one conversations over the years. Julian tended to avoid them like any potential ambush, mindful that analyzing him was one of Philip and Ruth's favorite pastimes.

"I got carried away," she continued, talking into her lap. "I think—you adjust to things, in life. Phil came out, OK, I love my child, so he won't marry a Jewish girl, he'll marry a—and then he met you. The One. What does it even mean, to keep a line going? I don't know. But. Around the time Bubbe stopped making sense, she asked me every day when she was going home. To Berlin, I think she meant. After decades, and what happened." She looked at Julian. "Phil's my baby. Take care of him. And go run your own lives. You'll do the best job of it."

"I'm sorry too, Ruth."

She pressed her hands together. "Gerald and I will walk our son down the aisle, and give him away. We'll walk you down as well, if it feels right. But I—I kept asking because you're precious and deserve to be given away. That's what I meant to say. Because you are loved. Nobody turns out like you did unless he was loved very much."

It occurred to Julian that for all of her controlling ways, and the totemic shadow she cast across Philip's childhood, Ruth was sometimes just trying to be nice. "Did you and Gerald have fun?" he asked. "At your wedding?"

"I think so. Memory fades. You lose things." Ruth looked out the window, studying a brilliant red treetop. "And gain. Much holds us together. Family. History. Our daughter. You boys." She smiled. "Grandkids someday. I digress." She scrutinized him, but in a way that wasn't unwelcome. "I wish I could have met your mother," she said. "What kind of amazing woman was there at the beginning, to shape you into this? The stories she could tell."

The light shifted in the window, and suddenly Julian remembered the sun falling through the curtains in the breakfast nook one morning, when he was a boy. It was during a lesson at the kitchen table, the day his mom told him he would go to school and have other teachers. "Ruth?" he said. "I think I'll have Miss Bonnie walk me down the aisle."

"Wonderful." She put a hand on Julian's shoulder and smiled warmly, and with the other smoothed out the points he had carefully twisted in his hair. "Shall I find her and let her know?"

"Yes. Thank you."

Ruth got up and turned to the door. "Oh!" she cried at the sight of the deer head over the fireplace. "We are not alone." She took a few curious steps toward it and raised her fingertips to tease the fur on its lower neck. "Funny," she mused. "The ways we hold on to things." She smiled at Julian. "See you downstairs."

Julian put on his shoes, twisted his hair into new points, and did a last check in the mirror. He thought of Philip, in the bedroom down the hall, and how he struggled with bow ties. For the first time that day, Julian smiled naturally. He was marrying a good guy. He was alive. And maybe parts of his mom were too. Because she did it, didn't she, on his wedding day? After all the tiptoeing around and putting him first, she finally did what she never had his whole life. She told him what to do.

12

The Shakes

Philip leaned back in his ergonomic chair and took in the view one last time. Thirty floors above Times Square, he let his eyes wander wistfully uptown. The green bathtub of the park. The towers of Central Park West jutting up toward Columbia, where they used to live, and down to the sleek Time Warner Center. A black plug reaching for the bright blue sky. It was a sunny June day, dry with a kiss of heat, and Philip had quit his job. He dumped his few personal items in his gym bag, carefully laying on top the custom bobblehead Jay had ordered of him, and zipped it shut. He grabbed his spare suit from the back of the door. He would miss the view, and a few assistants. The rest made him want to gargle and spit.

Heads turned as he walked by the bullpen on his way out, but none of the guys spoke. What was there to say? He didn't wake up that day planning to quit his job at the bank. But as he returned from the Keurig machine with his second cup of coffee that morning, he stopped to grab a deal deck off the printer and mistakenly grabbed a printout of an email chain as well, from a fellow VP to everyone on their team except Philip. *Soliciting better deal names for Davenport 2008-1?* he wrote about the deal they were marketing that week, *Best one gets shots on me*

@ *Flashdancers*. Every analyst and associate replied, weighing in with new names for their deal. *Toxic Shitbag*, one wrote. *Subprime Flesh-Eating Virus*. But the winning stripper shots went to *Mike Tyson's Nuclear Mortgage Holocaust*.

Philip read the email standing at the printer. A switch flipped inside him. He marched straight to his boss's office and handed it over. Martin Hogenkamp, who would sell his mother depending on the spread. Martin read it, smiled wearily at Philip, and told him it was important to let the guys blow off steam with the hours they're putting in, and Philip was a manager now, so try to let a joke roll.

"The American economy falling apart?" Philip said. "That joke? You brought me on to figure out exactly what we're selling in these deals, and I told you. Garbage." He tried to keep his voice down. "People losing their homes. Evicted. Thrown out with their kids' Pokémon cards on the lawn. Now we're joking about it? That works for you?" Philip offered the last drop of generosity he had left in him, waiting for a look, any sign of humanity or remorse.

His boss stared blankly. "Are you finished, Phil?"

"Yeah." He sighed. And in a strange rush he kept talking. "I am. I'm done." He took his ID from his wallet and dropped it on the desk. "Give me ten minutes," he said, heading out the door. "Actually, five's plenty."

He was true to his word. Five minutes later he made his final pass by the bullpen, where he'd spent the last six years before rising from the swamp of pitch books, Nerf hoops, free weights, flat-screens, and man-boys, and graduating to an office with a view. He walked fast, keeping his hands and face steady until he got to the elevators. As the doors shut and he dropped down to earth, it started sinking in what he had done. What his dad would say. Gerald would hear about it and start blowing up his phone in thirty minutes, max. He had to call Jay, he told himself, get in the car and call. But when Philip stepped out to the street, into Dante's tourist level of hell on Broadway, two things occurred to him: he was leaving work in daylight, and there was no Town Car waiting.

He hailed a cab. "Going to Brooklyn," he said, tossing in his bag and hanging his suit. "Prospect Park Southwest." He started to call Jay but stopped. It felt wrong, selfish to interrupt him and demand his time right before his first big trial. Philip texted instead:

```
Sorry 2 bug u
I quit my job
I'm very dumb but just
not evil enuf 2 cut it
Going home-getting drunk
Still love me?
        ☹
```

He shut his eyes and slumped in the vinyl seat. He felt exhausted at noon. He thought of the ocean, and life since college. Spent in the company of thieves and bandits. Not everyone at the bank. That was too broad a brush. But inside he cringed because he knew one depressing thing for sure—he had spent most of his twenties, crucial years he'd never get back, in a place devoid of *chesed*. Kindness. Human kindness that evokes God's own. He'd been reflecting on his bar mitzvah a lot the past few months. Now he wondered how he ended up here, on a nice summer day, leaving a job like that with no plans for the future.

"It's a bad accident!" the cab driver cried from the front seat.

"What?"

"On the West Side Highway, going south, all lanes shut. I go local."

"Yeah," Philip mumbled. "I've got all the time in the world."

★

On a mysterious cloudy day in fifth grade, Philip visited his dad's office for the first time.

Instead of taking the 2/3 with his mom to go to St. Ann's, he got to play hooky and follow his dad into the black car that waited at their house every morning. It whisked them down to Broad Street, on the tip of the island. The office was a fortress of reddish gray stone outside, with shiny elevators and white guys in suits. His dad made introductions. The men shook his hand and called him mini-Rosenblum. The women touched his hair without permission and told him how handsome he was. Now and then they passed other father-son pairs, and the boys watched each other like one dog to another at the vet. After the tour, Gerald got two sticky buns and they sat on the maroon velvet couch in his office. "Not too shabby, huh?" he said, gesturing regally at the harbor view. "Pop quiz," he said. "What is Goldman Sachs?"

"A bank."

"And what do banks do?"

"Keep money," Philip replied.

"We *lend* it." His dad wiped a smudge off Philip's face. "When people need to make things, big things, skyscrapers or bridges or stadiums, we help them find the money so they can do it. We're doers. Problem solvers."

Elegant ones. That was a takeaway from the visit. His dad didn't look like a construction worker, or one of the guys in the *payot* and black hats on the way to school. The men wore silk ties in his dad's world, and raised skylines without breaking a sweat. Got things done. It was a sense Philip internalized, and why his dad loomed large in his mind as he neared thirteen and had to choose his mitzvah project. His mom praised him when he picked *chesed*—the rest is commentary, she said—and told him he was on his own to come up with a project. He badly wanted his dad to like it and waited nervously when he shared his plans: a food drive at school to benefit a local shelter. His dad said how proud he was and then asked what would happen the next time that same homeless man came back to the shelter for food, and was there a way to teach him to earn his own food? He mulled over the profundity of his dad's question. One that to this day Philip—nearly thirty and newly unemployed—couldn't answer.

He daydreamed about his dad the whole cab ride downtown from the bank. Both his parents had a profundity to them—kids of immigrants who met at City College and rose to dominate their fields—but where his mom exuded warmth and talk and diagnoses, his dad could be reserved. Gerald's love flew off his lips, yet respect was something else. His whole life Philip watched for things that pleased his dad—being good at sports or math—and did more of them. Lacrosse, majors, internships. He pleased Gerald without being asked. And one day he finished college, started as a fixed-income analyst, and had no idea what he was doing. Lost. He lived vicariously through Jay for years, watching him finish law school and join the ACLU. He hid behind numbers and got paid. Numbers never hurt anyone, he often thought, and tried not to think too much.

Then last fall he got promoted. He got the office and an invitation to the CDO structuring desk. They needed a VP with quant skills to drill down, loan level, and check their risk analyses. Martin promised insane upside. Ambitious Martin knew who Philip's dad was. Philip said yes. For months he dug into the numbers, and they told a story: Americans borrowing like there was no tomorrow, borrowing for nothing, without signatures or jobs. Every week he warned Martin about the numbers, default rates crawling up the tranches, and chatted about the Hillary-Obama primary slugfest to keep things light. Weekly he faced a more unsettling thought: beneath the numbers were real people in trouble, feeding the beast of their bad deals. Martin thanked him and never reported his concerns. In January Philip got his bonus number, four hundred thousand dollars for a partial year, which he deposited and didn't touch. Through winter and spring he went to work, chewed Tums, and kept his mouth shut.

Until that morning, when he found an email chain on the printer. His colleagues—every one except the bleeding-heart gay quant guy—laughing at the sick joke of it. And soon his dad would know he was a quitter, if he didn't already.

"Almost there," the cab driver cried through the partition. "Bus lanes. It's slow."

Philip looked out the window. They were inching to the fork at the bottom of Broadway, a few turns from the tunnel. He watched tourists crowd around the bronze bull statue, kneeling to smile and cup its balls while cameras snapped photos. His phone vibrated as they headed underground. He ignored it. By the time they reached Brooklyn, Philip had two messages and three texts from his dad. The first voicemail gave off a strained but friendly "hard day?" vibe, but he sounded anxious in the second, asking about misunderstandings at work. His texts were more direct:

```
Where are you
Is your phone on
Turn your phone on.
```

They pulled off the expressway onto the leafy streets of Windsor Terrace. At the sight of their neighborhood, bright at midday, Philip was overcome with nostalgia and a scary feeling of failure. Or freedom. He remembered discovering the neighborhood when they were looking to buy their first place, and falling in love. The funky old frame and brick houses. Epic inflatable lawn displays at the holidays. Cops nursing to-go beers and laments outside Farrell's on Friday nights, alongside artists and writers—that white girl who directed *Paris Is Burning*?—or the random MSNBC anchor browsing the farmers' market at PS 154. It was lovely. Their home life was real. So why did his days in the city feel like holes punched out of it?

The cab stopped at their building, an Art Deco beauty on the park with turrets like a castle and a courtyard full of trees. Philip ducked into the Palestinian family bodega on the corner. He had a vague notion that if he got drunk and had pizza, and ate too much and smeared it on his face, he might feel relatively less disgusting on the inside. Amina, the chubby oldest daughter, sat at the cash register. She had spread out her makeup kits on the counter, and her iPhone was balanced on a box of Slim Jims, filming. Half her face was painted green like the *Shrek* princess. Philip grabbed a six-pack, paused, and grabbed another one.

"You subscribe to my channel yet?" Amina asked when he put down the beer.

"Channel?" he said.

"On YouTube. My tutorials. I do dragons, aliens, Bollywood, DC, Marvel, and X-Men. And Jessica Rabbit. I told you last time. I'm trying to monetize. You OK?" she asked.

"Yeah." Philip smiled. "Why?"

"Starting a little early." She bagged the beer. "AminaMagic. Don't forget to subscribe."

Philip went upstairs and ordered pizza. He put on gym shorts, climbed on the fire escape overlooking the park, and started drinking. He was considering whether the number for the old pot dealer still worked when Jay finally texted back:

    FREE AS A BIRD!!!
    WE HAVE TO CELEBRATE!

```
I'd call but I'm in a moot
for my opening statement.
Call you later—proud of YOU
            ☺
```

He smiled sadly at this. Of course Jay was proud. He'd been telling Philip to quit for years. Jay was the original trigger for all these feelings in Philip—the disquiet with his life, the sense of being outside watching it. The night they met, at a BGLTSA meeting in college, Jay was already advocating for some cause, and since then Philip had yet to find any kind of passion to match his husband's. Jay wasn't nice about it, either. "White, Harvard, rich parents," he listed on his fingers lately when Philip complained about his job. "That's called options, Phil. Work it out." So he did. He quit. And now, three beers in with the sun tickling his face, he was still waiting for someone to come tell him the purpose of his life.

The door buzzer went off. He climbed inside and pulled on a T-shirt. But when he opened the front door it wasn't the pizza. It was an old guy in a rumpled suit. Jay's dad. Philip quickly recognized him—he was sure though they only met once—but his brain froze in denial.

"Mr. Warner?"

"Philip!" His hands were stuffed in his pants pockets. "Nice to see you again."

"You too. Wow. I didn't know you were here. In New York. Does Julian?"

"I didn't tell him." Aaron winked. "Did you?"

"Oh no. No, so that's a real hundred percent surprise. Come in?"

"Thank you." He shuffled slowly into the apartment. A faint unwashed smell floated from his suit as he passed by.

"Have a seat," Philip said, leading him to the living room

couch. "Relax. You want anything to drink, water or—" He noted the bottle in his hand. "Beer?"

"What's that you're drinking?"

"Blue Moon? A—wheat beer?"

"Yeah, one of those."

"OK. I will grab that and let Julian know you're here." Philip started to leave but hesitated. Aaron looked frailer than he remembered. "You're good? Alone here while I—" Aaron nodded. "OK." Philip smiled. "Be right back." He hurried to their bedroom and called Jay but got no answer. He texted:

```
Your dad is in our apt—call me!
```

Immediately Jay texted back:

```
Do not engage.
Let in but don't talk.
But don't leave alone in apt.
Be there ASAP
FML
```

Philip took his time in the kitchen, opening a beer. "Here you go," he said as he entered the living room. Aaron wasn't on the couch where Philip had left him. He stood at the oversize windows looking onto the park. The sun lit up his thick white hair.

"Pretty," Aaron mused. "The lake." He turned around, eyeing the room from coffered ceiling to Persian rug. "Y'all got it all here."

Philip instantly saw their home as Aaron might—a big, swanky, old-school New York apartment. But bought at Jay's insistence without help from Gerald and Ruth, strictly from their earnings and the little money Lacy had left Jay. "Aaron!" Philip said warmly, buzzed and always keen to normalize. He handed Aaron the beer. It almost slipped from Aaron's hand, but he grabbed it in time. "Sorry!" Philip cried with a jolt of adrenaline. "Was that—I'm a klutz, sorry. Cheers." Philip took a long swig. "I haven't seen you since—I met you, at Lacy's service. How have you been?"

"I'm alive." Aaron smiled and sat down on the iron radiator cage by the window. He pressed his beer into his legs. "What time does Jules get home?"

"Lately? He's got his first trial as lead counsel next week. Working around the clock. He flies to San Diego this weekend for it."

"The ACLU, right?" But before Philip could answer, Aaron continued: "Staff Attorney, ACLU Immigrants' Rights Project. What's it about?" Aaron asked. "The trial."

"Prison conditions, where ICE keeps undocumented folks waiting for deportation. Sick conditions. Men and women stuck there for years, Central Americans, Mexicans, people who got on the terrorist watch list for some unknown—"

"Lacy was Mexican," Aaron blurted. He took a slow, careful sip, watching Philip. "Jules's mom. Half Mexican, she thought. On her mom's side. Not sure if he knew that."

"He does," Philip said. "I think it's a lot of what drives him now. His work." He noticed Aaron held his frame like Jay did, and despite Aaron's elder gut, Philip could see where Jay got his lankiness. The sexy long limbs he loved. And, yes, Jay told him not to engage with Aaron, but how did that work when your father-in-law was in your home?

"So he does well?" Aaron asked.

"Jay?" Philip furrowed his brow. "Yeah. He's a superstar."

"He has a good career."

"A great career."

"Helping people," Aaron muttered at the bottle pressed firmly into his thighs. "What about you? I saw you in a suit earlier."

"Oh."

"I was on the park bench, across from the building, when you got out of the cab."

"Right." Philip sucked on his beer. He liked being a good host and chose not to dwell on the creepy image of Aaron watching from the bench. "People like to sit there, nice view of the—I work at Morgan Stanley. Banking. Worked. I quit my job today."

"There's always another. Enjoy your freedom while it lasts." Aaron sat forward. The sunlight caught a moth hole in the sleeve of his wrinkled, and once fashionable, gray chalk-stripe suit. "Your family does well?"

"I'm sorry?" Philip said.

"You're from a—stable family. Well-to-do."

"You could say that."

"Jewish."

"That too."

"Did y'all ever go there?" Aaron asked. "Israel?"

"No. My mom wrote a paper and—we've been boycotting since Bibi came to power, done-to becoming doer, victim turned oppressor—" Aaron watched him, uncomprehending. "Never been," Philip said. "I hear Tel Aviv's nice."

"My dad had a thing with Jews," Aaron said with a nod. He'd been nodding the whole time Philip talked, rhythmically, like the Hasidic guys praying on the subway. "But my dad was an old country fool." Aaron smiled. "I say, look at the things we have in common. Brisket? You like brisket?"

"I do."

"See? You're an honorary Texan."

"Maybe you're an honorary Jew," Philip quipped.

"What makes you one? Not your mom, I mean, like deep down?"

Philip opened his mouth and paused. It was a harder question than he thought. He shrugged. "Circumcision? Guilt?"

Aaron considered this. "One of those."

Philip thought of Julian's cock, the first time he held an uncut one his sophomore year, and wondered if he came off as more neurotic than he imagined.

"Is Julian?" Aaron asked. "Jewish now?"

"No. We—It never came up."

"But you're married? You guys got married?"

"Yes. Three years ago, in Massachusetts."

The buzzer went off. Aaron started up from the radiator cage.

"Pizza," Philip said, heading to the foyer. "Are you hungry?" Aaron responded with an indeterminate grunt. Food would tide them over until Jay got home, Philip thought as he paid the delivery guy, and in the meantime maybe Aaron would loosen up and talk about his son's childhood. Shed some light on the world behind that Texas twang—the one Philip was crazy about when they first met, and had by this point slipped out of Jay's speech except when he was drunk or angry. He plated two slices and returned to the living room.

"I should head out," Aaron said, setting his beer on the windowsill.

"Before Jay? He works downtown. Out of the tunnel it's ten minutes. He'll be here any second." Philip checked his phone. Five new texts from Gerald, none from Jay.

"Well, I've got a flight to catch."

"Today?" Philip said. "When did you get in?"

"This morning." Aaron stood up. "It's a red-eye home, but I figured I'd give myself time to get to the airport, not knowing New York from Adam and—"

"Why did you come here?" Philip asked. "Why did you come?"

"I wanted to see—Julian's life."

"But not him?" Philip stood in the entrance and crossed

his arms. "Why come all this way without telling us, for a few hours? After staying away so long. Why stay away?"

"That's an old can of worms. Expired." Philip stared at him, waiting. Aaron chuckled to himself. "Would you want me?" Aaron asked, clasping his hands tightly. "As your dad?"

"I—have a father, who is by no means perfect, because no one is. But if I didn't have him I would want a father."

"I don't bring good where I go."

"But here you are," Philip said.

Aaron stared at his hands. "When I was serving." He looked up at Philip. "Was your dad in-country? Vietnam?"

"No." Gerald failed a vision test, or that was the story. Thirty years later he got Lasik, covered on the Goldman health plan, and overnight was twenty-twenty. "No," Philip stammered, "he had a—medical deferment."

"Well. Whatever happens with these Democrats, McCain's got my vote. Real patriot. The day my company was killed over there—I was younger than you are now—I lay at the side of the road, hips and legs broken on the roots of a tree. And the tree said, *No one is coming, You'll die here alone, You will die.* I've always known. We know." Aaron unclasped his hands and let his right arm float up like he was doing a magic trick. It trembled and started jittering wildly. "I got Parkinson's," he said. "The shakes. Agent Orange they think, probably. Sometimes it's genetic. I figured Jules should know." He put his arm down and clasped his hands again.

"Mr. Warner, Aaron, I'm sorry. Is there, are you doing treatment now?"

"I take my combo. I get worse if I don't. The doctors say I won't get better. But I got my friends at the VA. They pitched in and bought me my ticket here, and drove me to the airport so I didn't—Cabs in Houston aren't like here. Real expensive."

"Are you not allowed to drive anymore?" Philip asked.

"Oh no, I can drive. They adjusted my benefits last year, So-cial Security or disability whatever, and my monthly—it wasn't enough for the car payments anymore, so the dealership came and took it."

Philip had been to Houston twice, and Jay assured him no one but the seriously poor took the buses. "How do you get around? Like for food or doctors?"

"There's a convenience store on the feeder road by my place," Aaron said. "And my buddies pick me up to go to the VA."

The image of Aaron shuffling down the highway for a TV dinner was too much for him. Philip swigged his beer. A pas-sage from his mitzvah speech floated to mind—the parsing of *chesed* versus *tzedakah*. And here it was. Not in the abstract, a real opportunity to show loving-kindness toward Jay's dad. Ex-pressed through money, yes, but capable of improving his life in a time of need. "How much do you owe on it?" he asked. "The car. To get it back?"

"Nice seeing you again, Philip. I should go."

"Hang on." Philip hurried to the foyer and grabbed his checkbook from his Jack Spade attaché. "Don't be offended," he called, returning to the living room. "It can't be that much if it's a few months, and it's the least we could do to—"

"That's not why I came." Aaron shoved his hands in his pockets and stood up. The front door opened. They both turned to the foyer. Jay entered in his daily nonprofit uniform—fitted khakis, untucked button-up, red Converse high-tops—a mil-lion boyish miles from the profile he cut in the Ted Baker suits Philip made him buy for trial. He looked lean and handsome, always sexy to Philip when he was this focused, even if the focus lately meant Jay had no libido and just rolled over like a doll and let Philip fuck him.

"Hey," Julian said to Philip, and turned to Aaron. "Dad. Unexpected, as always."

"Hi, Jules," Aaron said.

"What are you doing here? Wait." Julian looked Philip over. "Why do you have your checkbook? Did he ask you for money?"

"No," Philip said.

"You're giving him money?"

"He didn't ask. He's sick. He has Parkinson's. He came to tell you."

"I came to say—" Aaron stepped toward Jay but stopped, like he wasn't sure what he came to say. "I came to see you."

"OK." Jay shut his eyes. "Maybe you're sick, or dying, or broke, I don't know—"

"Jay?" Philip interjected.

"But I've done a lot of work on myself. I promised my therapist that if this day ever came, I'd share some things with you." His eyes reddened. "Your disappearance when I was thirteen was harmful to me. Your lack of any contact for years, when I knew you were out there somewhere, was worse than if you were dead. Then you show up. At Mom's memorial. Now. There are ways to have a relationship. We can try to have contact, with boundaries. But this, out of the blue, I do not accept. You need to go."

"Julian," Philip whispered.

Jay shot him a primal, with-me-or-against-me look and turned back to Aaron. "I have to protect myself and what I've created. You need to go now, Dad."

"I never got in your way, did I?" Aaron said. His head bobbed. "All the things different about you growing up, the things you wanted to do, but it seemed like you knew what you were doing, so who was I to—I didn't get in your way."

"And that makes you what?" Jay asked. "A parent? Please go."

Aaron dropped his head. He loped around the perimeter of the room, avoiding them. "Goodbye," he muttered as he passed Philip. He went out the front door.

Jay stood fixed to the spot where he'd made his speech. Philip came over and hugged him. Jay kept his arms at his sides. "I've got to get back to work," he said.

"What?" Philip said. "No, take the rest of the day off."

"I'm going to lie down a minute, before I head back."

"Jay, they'll survive without you for one day."

"But my life doesn't change," Jay snapped. "It doesn't change because my dad decided to blow through it. So put away your checkbook and stop talking about things you know nothing about." He left. Philip heard him tread down the hall and shut their bedroom door.

Philip's phone vibrated at a string of new texts. His mom had entered the fray:

```
Where are you?
We're calling the police
if you don't call now.
Right now
```

He got another beer and lay on the couch. As his finger hovered over Gerald's missed calls, an image of his dad came to mind. At breakfast, when he was a kid. His dad would discourse on the headlines in the *Journal* as he peeled a hard-boiled egg, getting under the membrane with delicate breaks and nudges until the whole shell came off in one piece. He salted it, and then after minutes of calm talk and focus, Gerald would devour the egg in two bites.

"Philip!" His dad picked up at the first ring. His voice was warm and nervous.

"You can call off the National Guard."

"We were worried about you. You weren't answering your phone."

"We had our hands full," Philip said. "Jay's dad was here."

"From Texas? Here in New York?"

"It's a long story."

"I got a call from Samir Desai, the head of Global Fixed Income at Morgan. He said you quit this morning? No notice or anything?"

"Yeah," Philip said, "and I flipped a table on my way out." Regressing, he could hear himself regressing and it pissed him off.

"Samir's an old friend. Whatever it is, I'm sure we can fix it."

"No, Dad?" His whole career he never asked Gerald for help—avoided Goldman after college, was the first in the office and last out at night—but he didn't fall far from the tree so he never really needed to. He kicked the couch at his stupid illusions. "There's no fix. Ever since I got promoted and moved over to—I can't do it anymore."

"But what happened?" his dad demanded.

"An email. My group was laughing at how bad our deals are. For nine months I've been running around spraying perfume in a sewer, shouting, 'It's all gonna blow!' Nobody cares. You and Mom taught me to do the right thing, *tikkun olam*, but we're the problem! These bad loans keep happening because our banks keep buying them. Do you have any idea how bad it is?"

"Sure," Gerald said. "Sure, there'll be a correction."

Something in his dad's tone, the slight pause, set Philip's hair on end. And it occurred to him for the first time what his dad might have done. Gerald, always two steps ahead of the pack. "Dad," he asked, "are you shorting our deals?"

"Me?" He laughed. "Am I personally shorting your deals?"

"Is Goldman short RMBS? Are you betting this all goes to shit?"

"That's proprietary," Gerald snapped. "You know I couldn't say if we—and even if we were, we wouldn't be the only ones. With synthetic swaps"—his voice arced high—"there's an opportunity. A market for everything. You didn't hear it from me."

Philip wished he hadn't. He thought of the overblown things his sister used to say about their dad and his greed, and how she never came home anymore. He thought of the great things he imagined his father built, and the money Gerald bundled for Obama. It was confusing. "You bet against the country," Philip said. "For what? More money?"

"Phil."

"I gotta go."

"Hold on a minute!" Gerald cried. "This is complex stuff. You know how sophisticated these deals are. It's not a black-and-white—" His dad stopped talking. The phone went silent, muffled as though it was covered. When his dad spoke again it was slower, softer and mucosal. "Do what you want. Do something else. I didn't work this hard to have my kids feel stuck. I was good at one thing. Numbers. I got paid. But people like you. You help them see inside. You're strong like that, like your mom. It's special, Phil."

"Dad. I'm gonna go."

"Wait. Should we come over? Your mom and I can—"

"If I neglect this buzz any longer I can't get drunk. Hanging up now." Philip dropped his phone and stared at the ceiling. The apartment was quiet. He couldn't hear Jay in the bedroom, wrapped in his own misery. An agitating sadness swept over Philip. His head spun, less from the beer and more from the feeling that everything he knew—top and bottom, profit, loss, fathers and sons—seemed scrambled.

★

They were watching Rachel Maddow when the call came. The guests on TV chattered about Obama bailing out the banks, and what "too big to fail" meant, when a 713 number came up on Jay's phone. Philip watched the color drain from Jay's face as he gave short responses—"Yes. . . . Where? . . . Thanks."

He hung up. "My dad died," he mumbled. "It was the VA in Houston. He fell at home. He had Parkinson's, and his balance was bad and—" Jay wrapped his arms around himself and started to cry, silently, as tight as a turtle pulled into its shell.

The next day they flew down. Jay put on headphones and slept the whole time. Philip ate peanuts and replayed the day Aaron showed up at their place last summer. They never really talked about it. Not about the rude way Jay spoke to him after Aaron left, or about a question that still lingered with Philip: if he hadn't quit his job that day and come home early, would they have seen Aaron or known he was sick? He never put it into words because he knew it was that very thing, the not knowing, that had grown familiar but never safe for Jay. For months, Philip held the memory of Aaron's visit on his own. It seeped into him—Aaron's urge to see and connect that day—and placed him, he guessed, in a line of women going back to Jay's mom, who thought they might fix Aaron. He figured all the questions had been asked before: which were the preventable or inevitable disasters in the arc of a life. But Aaron's life was the first one Philip had ever seen close to playing itself out. And it haunted him.

Things had resettled after Aaron's visit. Jay handily won his trial, spanking the Bush administration. The *LA Times* did a story with a court exit photo of Jay and his clients, and a lofty quote from Jay about America treating immigrants like members of our human family. Philip meanwhile binged on reality shows, bought a guitar, and lived the unemployed life, until one morning he rolled over in bed and said he wanted more. "You should start your own thing," Jay said. "People like you." Philip heard echoes of Gerald, the day he quit, and wondered if what his dad said was right. Did he have a fundamental desire to heal, to listen and help, that he shouldn't ignore? He leaned into thoughts of Aaron, and in a week he had a modest concept sketched out: a nonprofit offering financial literacy to veterans.

Jay was supportive with his time, and an idea evolved into a business plan. It was how Jay showed love, more action than words. Philip used his last bonus from the bank as seed money. For the first time he expressly asked his dad for help, to tap folks for the board, and he'd just had a meeting about a pilot at the VA in Manhattan when a caseworker from Houston called with the news about Aaron.

After they touched down at Intercontinental—"Bush Airport now," Jay said with a wry grin—they didn't head north to Bonnie's, where they were staying, and instead drove straight to the VA to catch the caseworker. She was a sweet older woman with gravity-defying hair, who thought Aaron was dapper, always dressed in a suit when he was there. She told them Aaron's friend found him soon after he died, when he came to pick up Aaron and no one answered. She handed Jay a bag of personal effects and apologized for not calling sooner, but he wasn't the emergency contact Aaron listed, and she just happened to see a son mentioned in Aaron's file yesterday. He was cremated, but his friends were planning a thing at Houston National Cemetery, and would they like information about it?

"We'll be in touch," Jay spoke for the first time since they sat down at her desk. He leaned forward. "Philip works with veterans," he began, and proceeded to pitch his husband—the years of experience in banking, the need for financial planning in veteran communities, the importance of agency partners. *These are the words Jay has right now*, Philip thought, *his way of getting through*. So he smiled and gave the woman his new business card.

Back in the car, Jay looked straight ahead as they drove to Aaron's apartment in a seedy commercial section of northwest Houston. The whole way there was the same ugly sprawl to Philip, but Jay seemed to know where they were going. They pulled off at an exit. "There," Jay said, pointing to a faded apartment complex on the feeder road. Philip saw a 7-Eleven where Aaron might have bought groceries. The caseworker had called ahead, and the property manager met them in the parking lot by the first-floor unit. He was a grizzled older dude, with tattoos on his forearms that Jay couldn't stop staring at.

"Warner?" he asked. He shook Jay's hand. "Sorry for your loss. Good man, Aaron. Funny as hell. Rent always on time. I got some boxes, if you need any."

"Just trash bags," Jay replied.

The manager let them into Aaron's place, a one-bedroom with almost nothing in it. A metal dining set in the kitchen. A wood veneer couch with polyester-wrapped cushions, like something out of a small-town airport. There was an indent in one of the cushions, opposite the little flat-screen TV sitting on stacked plastic crates. Nothing on the walls, Venetian blinds across the slider to the patio. It was sparse and clean. Neither of them spoke. They wandered toward the one door in the open space, to the bedroom, and that was when Philip spotted a patch of red-brown on the bathroom tile. He whirled around in the doorway before Jay could enter.

"Let's split it up," Philip said. "I'll take the bedroom, and you do the common areas?" Jay nodded. "Anything you want to keep? Clothes of his, or . . ." Jay shook his head and handed Philip a trash bag. He waited until he heard Jay open a cabinet and start pulling out plates before rushing into the bathroom and assessing the damage. It was definitely blood. An irregular patch the size of a mouse pad in front of the sink, maybe a body's length from the shower, he couldn't be sure. He wet a handful of toilet paper and scrubbed the tile clean to the clink of silverware in the kitchen.

Philip emptied the medicine cabinet and moved to the bedroom. The bed was tightly made, with military corners, no duvet, two white pillows stacked neatly at the top. He opened the closet and found a few dress shirts, ties, the suit Aaron wore when he came to New York. He bagged them and moved to the pine dresser, the only other furniture in the room. He ran through the drawers quickly, tossing undershirts and khakis and white briefs, but when he reached into the sock drawer his fingers touched something plastic at the bottom.

He pulled out a large Ziploc bag of papers. Underneath it, at the bottom of the drawer, was a children's book. *The Story of Ferdinand.* He opened it. On the inside cover, scrawled in messy green crayon, it said *Julian Warner's Book.* Philip set it on top of the dresser and opened the Ziploc. He pulled out a faded ticket to the Astrodome, from some Yankees-Astros game in the sixties. Then he pulled out a picture of a blond woman with big Farrah Fawcett hair, smiling anxiously at the camera with her arm around a blond-haired boy. The rest of the papers were letters from Lacy to Aaron, addressed to a base in Vietnam, one of them signed *Your Truest Love.*

"Jay?" he called. "I found the other letters from when your parents met. Your mom's half. Jay?" Philip stood upright and listened, but there were no sounds from the kitchen. He came out of the bedroom. The apartment was empty and the front door ajar. Philip poked his head outside and saw Jay sitting on the curb, hunched over. His shoulders were shaking. *It's the Parkinson's.* Philip panicked for a moment. An idiotic thought, he scolded himself immediately, a stupid, irrational thought. Julian was crying. He was shaking from crying. And a lot of the time it wasn't even genetic. Jay was young. They were young.

Philip sat down beside him on the curb. Jay leaned over and buried his head in Philip's chest, and Philip held him until his body stilled.

13

The Match Meeting

Julian and Philip were having a baby. Maybe. They were possibly adopting a boy who was definitely due in three weeks. They had been in this position before, or similar high-stakes insanity. For two years they'd ridden the adoption roller coaster—going to work and living their lives through constant upheaval, maybe having twins in LA in a month, then not, or getting in the car to drive to Philly for a match meeting when a birth mom they'd been talking to for weeks suddenly ghosted, never to be heard from again. Each time their hearts fluttered to their throats and plunged to their feet, destroying them for days, making them oversleep, until they got up a little more bruised each time. But this time when they got in a car—a red Dodge Charger at the airport Hertz in Houston—things felt realer.

"What have we got on the Sirius?" Julian said, attacking the radio dials and scanning intensely. "Whoo!" he hooted at the sound of R.E.M. He pulled out of the parking garage into the bright Gulf sun, quickly accelerating from mouthing the words into a lusty sing-along of "Losing My Religion."

"Do you think Marisol is ashamed of where she lives?" Philip asked, turning the volume down a few notches.

"Umm, I don't know. We barely know her. Why?"

"Do you think that's why she wants to meet us at a restaurant?" Philip shifted in his seat. "Have you noticed, whenever we Skype, there's—laundry?"

"Laundry?"

"Everywhere. Stacked on the coffee table. In baskets." Philip whipped his hand around. "Hanging on chairs. Laundry all over."

Julian considered this. In their calls after Marisol emailed them through their website—eight months pregnant with no plans—he did recall seeing a lot of laundry on her end of the computer. "Well," he reasoned. "Her mom, two sisters, Marisol, and her daughters living there. Six people. Lots of wash. Whoo!" He jacked up the volume. "Chumbawamba! I love this song. We should get Sirius for our car. What station is this?"

"Adult Hits."

"Oh." Julian readjusted his hands on the steering wheel. "We're adults. We're about to have a kid; that's how it works. God, the nerves! We've Skyped with her, but face-to-face—it's like a first date." He shot Philip a glance. "Remember ours?"

"Do I remember our first date? Both nights. You made me work for it."

"You wanted to get laid. Tell me it wasn't worth the wait. At your peril. I think it's normal Marisol wants to meet in public the first time. I feel good. Don't you?"

"Worried." Philip scowled. "From the moment she called. I worry every time with these calls, every woman. You know that."

"But we're ready." Julian grinned and hit the gas. "Aren't you ready? For this whole awful process to make sense? The coincidence-not-coincidence that we got a call from"—he shrugged dramatically—"*Houston*?"

"We said in our profile that you're from Houston," Philip mumbled.

"A *Mexican* woman? Who already gave birth to two healthy

kids? It's perfect. She could go into labor any day now. She wants this to work too. It's like the agency said, and then the lawyer said—you just know when it's right. Doesn't it finally feel right this time?"

"Don't ask me that," Philip snapped. "I'm a wreck."

Traffic slowed to a crawl. "This used to be 59," Julian observed. "The highway. They renamed it since we were here. Sixty-nine now." He looked out the window at a rusting bridge over the San Jacinto, connecting two forgotten roads. He nudged the car toward the next exit. "We'll go local the rest of the way."

Julian maneuvered the car off the highway onto roads he still remembered like the back of his hand, past taquerias and gun shops, guys selling okra out of trucks, falling-down houses one after the next, miles of rotting porches and chain-link fence. As they waited at a red light by a particularly run-down place, Philip gasped. He pointed past an old car on blocks at something swinging in the breeze. Julian squinted. At first it registered as a tetherball with some kind of fabric trailing from it.

"An effigy." Philip sat up straight. "Obama. Look."

Julian saw it. A basketball painted black, with a monkey face and two round ears stuck on, pointing straight out. A blue boy's suit and red tie rippling in the wind below the ball, all of it at the end of a noose. And a sign next to it, hand painted on cardboard and faded by the sun: HANGING AROUND ANOTHER 4 YEARS. A truck honked. Julian looked up at the green light and hit the gas with a shiver.

They had the Obama Talk so often it was like playing chess with the same person—the first few moves always routine. Julian was the skeptic. If Obama was more than a feel-good symbol, he asked, if he was real change, then why, after the people had spoken *twice*, were there still lynching scenes on Facebook or birther crap spewed by reality stars on TV? To which Phil always answered with a question: are you listening to our president? It's not about Obama the man; it's about the people who elected him, because no matter what came next, the genie was out of the bottle. People could change history, one vote and conversation at a time. But that day in the rental car, going local to Royalwood, they drove in silence. Julian thought of Marisol on their Skype calls—her dark skin, and the black guy she guessed was the birth dad, and what their baby boy would look like. He figured Philip had the same thing in mind when he put his hand over Julian's on the gearshift and gave it a squeeze.

Julian passed the back way into Royalwood, by his mom's old house, and drove toward the main entrance. It was closer to Bonnie's, where they were staying, but also something in him wanted to see it again—the wood welcome pillar emerging from the lake, which had such a grand Excalibur feel when he was a boy. It was smaller than he remembered, he thought as they approached, but what really hit Julian was all of the trees missing. Not the silver ones in the logo on the welcome pillar—they were still there above the suburban motto, A LIVABLE FOREST— but the real trees behind the lake. His whole life a thick wall of green stood between the feeder road and willy-nilly development outside the entrance, and the suburb within. It was gone now, thinned to a row of trees through which a new Whole Foods was visible.

Philip took a photo.

"What are you doing?" Julian asked.

"Posting to our Adoption Journey page. I haven't updated the blog in weeks."

"There are better angles. Prettier spots of Royalwood, if you're posting."

"It's not about the angle," Philip mumbled and typed on his phone.

The rest of the drive Julian mused on Philip's resiliency. As much as he agonized over the process, Phil documented every moment along the way. He blogged about birth-mom leads and heartbreak when they didn't work out. He posted photos of their vacations and cats to their adoption Facebook page and Instagram feed, fashioning the story of their lives for digital consumption, doing what it took to catch the eye of a young woman swiping on her phone. They had both reluctantly accepted that their lives were wide open on the Internet—for any Jane, Jill, or Nigerian princess to try to scam them—but it was Philip who single-handedly invented the Warnerblum family online.

"Here it is," Julian said, turning onto Bonnie's block in a fancy subdivision. As they rolled up to her stucco McMansion, he thought of the last time they stayed with her, when they cleaned out his dad's apartment a few years ago. This visit was different. About the future, not the past. He pulled into the driveway and parked behind a gleaming Lexus sedan. "Wow," Julian muttered, "that's the divorce that keeps on giving."

"And a new guy too," Philip said, "right?"

"Jeff. Christian Mingle Jeff. A year or so they've been together. Oh, a buzz!" Julian dug in his jeans for his phone. "A text from Marisol. She says—" His brain froze. He blinked, and blinked, couldn't blink away what he was reading. "Oh God."

"What?" Philip cried. "What's the matter?"

"Marisol." Julian took a long breath. "'Sorry, guys,'" he read haltingly. "'Don't know if I can do this. So crazy. Gotta think. I'll text y'all.'" He shut his eyes and leaned his head on the steering wheel. Dark thoughts crashed over him. Another baby slipped through their fingers. It was never going to happen. They weren't meant to be parents. And he might as well accept that it was just the two of them and their cats, and Sunday dinners with Ruth and Gerald, because that was all the family they were ever going to have.

★

Julian hadn't always imagined himself as a dad. Unlike Philip, who'd wanted kids his whole life, he'd had stuff to work through first. The lasting effects of the air he breathed in his youth, telling gay people they didn't exist or weren't a part of the story of life. The way his mom never talked about him being a dad. And his own parents? The hubris to look at each other one day and say, *Let's have a baby*? Bring a life into this fucked-up world, and stay together too long for his sake and ironically fuck him up in the process? And yet if they hadn't, where would he be? On and on his thoughts looped.

But with time and Phil's nagging, the doubts began to fade. New things seemed possible. He came to believe he was a good person and say it to himself like his mom once did—a person with something to offer a kid, maybe one who was getting born anyway, and maybe make the world slightly less awful? They reached a point, in their early thirties, when the self-focus started tasting like too much sweetness in their mouths. The apartment was renovated. Careers were good. Philip's nonprofit grew to ten cities. Julian rose to run his project at the ACLU. After many wasted nights on Ancestry.com, trying to track down his mom's Mexican family, Julian realized that finding a Maria Elena near Laredo was like finding Tony in Bay Ridge or Ira on the Lower East Side. So instead he searched for the warmth of family in the faces of his clients—from Mexico first, then El Salvador, Burma, Syria. When the police swept up men who were driving while brown, or schools turned away refugee kids, Julian never missed a chance to do battle. And each time he stood up in court, before he laid his watch on the table to time his argument, he turned it over to see the words of Lacy Adams Warner that he had engraved on the back: *Raise hell. Never shut up. It's all over before you know it.*

Things were fine.

And then one day Julian and Philip woke up, and all their friends had kids.

They went to showers and *simchat bats* and first birthdays. Julian saw the muted joy on friends' faces as they nuzzled babies. It reminded him of his mom, the years before school when it was just the two of them. He thought if those memories could move him to tears, there was power in what she did, and he felt not just gratitude but a new kind of awe. It dawned on him that being a dad might be the greatest thing he'd ever do, more than any court case or crystal award on the shelf. Maybe he could raise his head, he thought, reveal his whole imperfect loving self, and be the dad he wanted and never had. He shared this with Philip when he turned thirty-three, along with a lingering fear—that his mom was gone and he couldn't ask her how she did it, became a good mom. Philip smiled. "What if she couldn't tell you when she was alive?" he asked. "What if the answers are already in you?"

They tried an adoption agency first, sitting through trainings as social workers described typical scenarios in dreamy nonjudgmental tones. ("Birth Mom did butt shots at a party. Birth Dad held her head while she vomited, and is maybe part Cherokee. Thoughts?") They waited two years and never got a call. Then one morning a friend tagged Julian in a post with a message, *SOOO sorry*, and a link to a video from *Inside Edition*. Deborah Norville had a breaking story about the bankruptcy of a once-respected adoption agency and the shattered dreams of its clients. Just like that, their nascent family went up in smoke. Julian threatened a lawsuit. They cursed lost money and grieved lost time. They winced at sudden sharp memories of hopes—of who their child would be and what she'd become in America, where most days anything still seemed possible. For months they licked their wounds. Then they got an attorney, built a kickass website and Facebook page to show off their fabulous life, and joined the digital Wild West of private baby hunting.

That's when things got weird.

There were the financial scammers. The Slavic woman who used to run a day spa, soothingly named Russian Roulette, but was now a bounty hunter and obviously couldn't work in such a dangerous field while pregnant with their baby. Or the emotional flashers who took up an hour of their time on the phone, normal sounding at first until they started talking about being a sex slave to grandpa or hung by meat hooks in a barn, and abruptly ended the call. The emails from teens across Asia whose parents hated them. Calls from Uganda in the middle of the night. And just when it seemed there wasn't an honest woman in the world, when nobody was who she said she was and their sense of reality was coming unhinged and the only thing left was to fulfill Ruth Rosenblum's dream and jerk off in a cup and go all *Handmaid's Tale* on a surrogate, right then an email popped up on their website from a Marisol with a 281 number:

    hey im 39 weeks u guys look nice.
    i have 2 girls
    i cant keep this baby. OK call me if u want

They painted on their smiles again and gave "Marisol" a call. She was twenty-two, friendly, calm given the circumstances, with huge dark eyes and lustrous hair—they couldn't help but notice—and a sane mom who fired off legit questions when she joined their Skypes. She seemed like the real not-crazy deal for more than one conversation. The paperwork checked out with the lawyer. Julian and Philip wondered, one last time, if they could let the bud of trust open and grow. They lowered their shields. Which was why Julian was stricken mute, sitting in the rental car in Bonnie's driveway a week later, as he read and reread Marisol's cold-feet text. They never learned. Child-less fools who flew to Texas for nothing.

"Jay?" Philip whispered beside him. "We've got company."

Bonnie knocked on the window, bending down inches from his head. She was blond as ever in her late sixties, with her hair blown out and full face on. "Jules!" she called through the window. "What're y'all doing? Come on in!"

They hugged and followed her inside as she chattered. Julian glanced around the house. Something was different. He used to love coming to Bonnie's as a boy. Her sons were in high school and never around, and the place was like an empty castle where he could slide in his socks or tumble on the carpet while Bonnie and his mom gabbed. When he came home from college, af-ter Bonnie's husband left, she had redecorated—a Laura Ashley detonation that left no surface un-floraled. Now he scanned the living room, saw the couch, and put his finger on the change. "Your Beanie Babies," he said.

"Don't y'all make fun," Bonnie drawled. She hurried to the couch and grabbed a Beanie bear and elephant off the top edge, dropping them in a cardboard box on the floor. The past few times they were there, maybe a hundred Beanies covered the tops of the couch and armchairs, the mantel, an army of plush watchers arrayed around the room. They were gone. "You boys were laughing at my Babies on your last visit."

"No!" Philip protested.

"But I've been meaning to put them away, and y'all coming down was the kick in the pants I needed. After the divorce, I liked waking up to something smiling at me when I came out in the morning. But now with Jeff spending the night—I roll over and there he is. Enough about me." She clapped her hands. "Tell me about the bay-by!"

Julian sighed. They sat down at the granite island in the kitchen and spilled the tea, beginning with Marisol's text and rehashing the whole two-plus years they'd been trying. In the middle, Bonnie started fussing around in the kitchen. "Go on," she said gravely, "I'm listening." She set a bowl of Cheez-Its on the island, poured three Diet Cokes, and pulled out a bottle of Jack Daniel's from the pantry. She splashed it over their drinks. They didn't toast. Julian and Philip were crying by then. "Well," she said at a lull in the story, "your birth mama might text any minute now. I can't believe this is the end."

"Maybe it isn't meant to be," Julian mumbled. "Kids need families, and I don't have anyone to give."

"Y'all got me," Bonnie insisted. "And Philip's parents, right?"

"I know." Julian took Bonnie's hand. "You were there at the end, with Mom, and gave me away at our wedding. But kids should know where they come from. When your grandkids ask where your sons came from, your sons point to you. There, their grandma. I have some old letters my parents sent. A story my dad told me once about cleaning carpets with his dad. That's it. Their pasts died with them."

Julian's phone buzzed. Philip jumped to his feet.

"See!" Bonnie cried. "What'd I tell y'all? Is it Marisol?"

"No." Julian sighed. "Facebook message." He frowned as he read, his eyes widening. He shot a look at Bonnie and kept reading.

"What is it?" Philip asked.

"I don't know," Julian said. "He . . ." He turned his phone around so they could read:

```
Dear Julian—I almost wrote you so many times
you wouldnt believe. But I saw the post on
your adoption page today and your here in
Houston so now or never. Im your brother. Half
brother, the same dad Aaron Warner. Maybe you
didnt know, probly not. Its cool your having a
```

kid. I have a daughter, fourteen months. Any-
how just wanna say hi, if you guys wanna meet
up with me and Tasha my wife while your here
thats cool or whatever. But nice if you want.
Yours truly, Clayton Connors

Philip looked up, his jaw hanging open in amazement. Julian put his phone in his pocket. Bonnie sipped her low-cal Jack
and Coke.

"Bonnie," Julian said softly. His finger traced a pattern on
the granite island. "Mom cleaned out her house before she
died. Meticulously. You helped her. When we were cleaning out
my dad's place, we found a photo of a blond woman and boy."
He turned his courtroom eyes on her. "Do I have a brother? Is
that why my dad left?" She stared at her drink. "You're the only
one left who would know."

Bonnie pulled a Kleenex from the steeple of a little ceramic
church and patted her eyes. "It wasn't mine to tell you," she
murmured.

"So it's true?" Julian asked.

"That he got some woman pregnant?" She grabbed a fistful
of Cheez-Its and chewed. "Your mama got a letter saying so. We
didn't know if it was true or just meant to hurt her. She made
me swear not to say a word. She was ashamed. But y'all should
know," Bonnie declared. "I was always giving your mama advice, about work and being a mother, trying to help, but the
truth is—Lacy had something powerful in her. A strength of
conviction that I . . ." She wiped her eyes. "I miss." Julian rested
his face in his hands. Bonnie sipped. "So!" she said with a perky
lift. "Y'all gonna go meet him?"

"No," Julian snapped. He looked up and saw Philip giving
him the I-know-what-you-did-to-your-dad stare. "Why?" Julian said. "What's the point? We're grown. It's done."

"Jay?" Philip growled. "You spent all that time searching for your mom's family in Mexico, and now this falls in your lap? He's your brother. He reached out. We're here. Our afternoon cleared. I'm not waiting around for Marisol to call. Good enough?"

A few minutes later, Julian messaged with Clayton, settled on a Starbucks near his place in Missouri City, and they were back on the highway. For miles going down 69, Philip scrolled on his phone in ominous silence. "Well," he said as they curled around Minute Maid Park, "it seems we're not the only ones with it all hanging out online. No private settings for Clayton. He's twenty-two. A NASCAR enthusiast."

"Thirteen years younger," Julian said. "Makes sense, when my dad took off."

"In the military." Philip held up his phone to show a photo of Clayton in camo fatigues, holding a gun in some sandy place.

"Where is that?"

"Can't tell." Philip kept looking. "No pictures of a wife or baby. No Tasha in his friend list. Is this a setup?"

"If we die it was your idea."

"Don't you think it's weird? No family pictures?"

"No." Julian felt his eyes welling up again. "He was too old when you met him, my dad, for you to tell. But Clayton looks just like him. More than me."

Quietly they drove across the south side, each of them lost in thought. "It all looks the same here," Philip muttered at one point. "Ugly. Construction everywhere. Is that normal?"

Julian nodded vaguely. "We had this video project in school," he said. "Texas history. The library got a video camera, and we had to check it out and interview a parent about the city we lived in. My mom hated cameras. She said, 'Houston is a place where stuff gets torn down, but things keep rising up.'"

"What's that?" Philip asked, pointing out the window at an abandoned stadium.

Julian looked at the lonely husk of it and remembered one strange night in sixth grade, back in the toughening-up phase. His dad took him to the Astrodome for the wrestling match of the year—a showdown between Hulk Hogan and the flamboyant Macho Man Randy Savage. Aaron watched the WWF from the couch on Saturdays, and though they never talked about it, he must have seen Julian peeping at the muscles and pageantry from the kitchen table. They barely spoke on the drive downtown, so uncertain of how to be together. But inside the stadium they got Cokes and hot dogs, and the crowd hissed at the entrance of the villain in his sequined cape, and Julian was swept into the drama. The men locked arms in a violent embrace. Popcorn and Raisinets flew. Then he was on his dad's shoulders, chanting at the clotheslines and pile drivers until they bellowed with the crowd as one primal beast—*Ma-cho Man, Ma-cho Man*—screaming their throats hoarse until the Hulk dodged a body slam and the match flipped and goodness was restored in the form of a blond, Speedo-clad victory strut along the ropes. Afterward, as they walked to the car, Aaron asked what he thought of the Astrodome. He didn't know what his dad wanted so he said, "It was fun screaming with everybody." "Yeah," his dad replied, putting an arm around Julian, "You gotta let it out sometimes or else you'll go crazy in the head."

Julian didn't share any of this with Philip as they drove. "The Astrodome," he answered. "They warehoused Katrina folks there, kind of its swan song. Condemned now. Always a swan singing somewhere. And then somebody DMs you on Facebook, and you're driving crosstown and—" He signaled and swiftly changed lanes. "It's not a setup. Meeting Clayton. But could you do some recon? Go in ahead of me and just watch out?"

"Sure." Philip frowned. "He saw me, on our adoption page. I should wear sunglasses."

Julian knew Phil lived for this kind of stuff, but he was too nervous to have opinions about it. "It's fine, meeting him. Right?" He turned to Philip. "I don't know what I'm doing."

They followed the navigation off the highway, to a Starbucks in an empty shopping center. Philip put on his Ray-Bans, pulled his US Open cap over his curls, and went in. Julian stared at his hands on the wheel. A breeze drifted through the window, bringing a surge of pine and memories of the last Christmas he spent with his mom. He thought of how the years made the unthinkable happen, had allowed his mom to slip from his daily memory, until the dream of parenting called her back to mind.

Julian went inside and cautiously peered around. Phil was in the corner reading the paper. A skinny blond kid with a buzz cut jumped up from a table, a goofy grin spreading across his face. He looked even more like Aaron than the Facebook photos. Growing up, there was a picture on his dad's dresser—long ago lost in some move—of Aaron getting a Purple Heart, and except for the acne scars on one cheek this kid in a random Starbucks could have been standing in the photo. "Julian Warner?" he said.

"Clayton?"

The kid lunged at Julian. Philip shot from his chair, but he stopped when Julian raised his arms and patted the kid's back, returning the bear hug he was caught in. Julian pulled away. "Look at you!" the kid said, eyeing him. "Your nice clothes and—it's redder!"

"What?"

"Your hair. It's redder than the pictures. And tall! How tall are you?"

"Um. Six-one."

"I'm six foot. I'm Clay. I got us a table," he said, talking fast and beckoning Julian. "And coffees. I don't know how you like yours so I left it black but I can get you milk if you want, you want me to—"

"No." Julian sat down. "Black's great."

"And a chocolate chip cookie and Rice Krispie Treat and brownie. You pick."

"Thanks. OK. The Krispie, I guess."

"That's my favorite!" Clay said.

"Oh no, you take it."

"No, I—My bad. We'll split." Clay broke it in half, handed Julian a piece, and bit into his. He watched Julian as he chewed, grinning. Julian smiled back, a little unnerved. "Crazy!" Clay cried. "Tasha says sugar gets me wound up and I talk too much. Without sugar, too. Are you freaked out? I'm Clayton Connors," he announced, tapping out his points on the table edge. "Son of Crystal Connors. She met your dad in 1992 in Conroe, when he was working HR for Texaco, and—"

"It's OK," Julian interrupted. "I know. I mean, I didn't know about you, but I saw a picture of you and your mom once in my dad's stuff." He sipped his coffee, grasping for words. "Is she still in Conroe? Your mom?"

"No. She died. Lung cancer. A few months ago, right before the holidays."

"I'm sorry." He winced, and waited. "Mine too. Cancer. Were you guys close?"

"Yeah." Clay ate the last of his Krispie and started on the brownie. "Sorta. When she got sick, I graduated early and enlisted. It was good money, and the bills were—" He clucked his tongue. "Lots of doctors. I deployed to Afghanistan. We didn't see each other as much after that. We went to Disney World when I was on leave. Me and her and Tasha. Mom wanted to go so bad. No energy, because of the chemo. But we did some rides. Epcot. We were close."

Julian was watching Clay gather brownie crumbs and drop them in his mouth when he had a sudden rush of all the times he felt scared and less than growing up—in the closet in high school, starting at Harvard, meeting the Rosenblums. He thought of Marisol and Clay, babies having babies. He thought he might cry. Clay looked up, eyes full of anxious concern. "Don't get me wrong," he said. "It was hard being far away when she was sick, but I had a blast over there. Didn't kill nobody. Partied. Met Tasha. She was ROTC. She's a nurse. Here I go, talking your ear off. Y'all're adopting a baby. Congrats!"

"Yeah," Julian mumbled. "Trying to."

"Isn't that why y'all came down?"

"It is, but." He sighed. "The whole process has been harder than we thought."

"Why, because you're gay? You know what?" Clay swiped a napkin across his mouth and threw it down. "Wait, aren't you a big lawyer? Doing your civil rights?"

"Yeah. Courtroom combat, I guess."

"Then you know people are fucking ignorant. The other day Tasha and I were at Panera Bread with the baby, getting lunch, and this guy and girl are giving us the Look—Tasha's black, African American, whatever—you know, like they don't say nothing to you but they give you the Look? And then the girl knocks Tasha with her purse as they're leaving. So I say to Tasha: 'home girl with the big butt, twerking like we at a strip club, only God can judge, fuck the haters, somebody loves ya.'"

"Oh. Is that—something you wrote, or?"

"No!" Clay laughed. "Miley Cyrus. I couldn't write that. People are stupid."

"Yeah." Julian smiled. "I don't think it's because we're gay. I think adopting is hard for everybody. Our birth mom got cold feet, two hours ago."

"For real?" Clay watched him. "Wait, y'all came all the way down here for—" Julian shrugged. "Fuck." Clay reached over and patted Julian's arm. "Wanna come see our baby? Vanessa? She's cute. Maybe cheer y'all up?"

"I don't—That's very nice, thanks, but we're—"

"We're like ten minutes from here. Tasha wanted to meet y'all bad. I told her we're meeting at Starbucks because he doesn't know me from a stalker freak. I been talking about y'all ever since y'all put up that adoption page on Facebook. Your life, it's amazing." Clay snapped off a piece of cookie and chewed. "My mom—" he began, staring at the table. "She told me about our dad, and you, when I asked her once. Aaron cut her off. Mom and me. No nothing after she told him she was pregnant, is what she said. So when she was alive, it didn't feel right to try and reach out to you or . . . out of respect for her, raising me and stuff." He looked at Julian. "But I wanted to write you. Find you. For a long time."

"OK." Julian took a breath. "Yes. Let's go to your place."

"Yeah?" Clay hopped up and stuck his fist out for a bump. "Awesome! Tasha's gonna be psyched." He gathered their trash. "Hey, do you see a lot of Aaron these days?"

"Oh no," Julian blurted. "No, I haven't seen him since—he visited us in New York a few years ago, but that was—"

"He's like not even online. Like nowhere."

"I know." Julian nodded emphatically. "He never was, has been, um, I just—" He pointed to the corner. "Let me tell Philip where we're headed."

"He's here?" Clay whirled around. His oversize button-up billowed out of his khakis like a pirate shirt. Philip lowered a corner of his paper and peered mysteriously from behind his shades. "Get over here!" Clay cried, bounding to him and going in for a hug.

Julian watched from a distance as Clay laughed and slapped Phil's back.

★

"What's he like?" Philip asked as they followed Clay's boxy old Corolla. "He's cute."

"He's sweet," Julian said in a measured tone. "He's had a hard life. He joined the military to pay his mom's medical bills. She died last year. He thinks our dad's still alive."

"Did you tell him?"

Julian shook his head. "It was right at the end as we were getting up."

Philip whistled. "Classic doorknob syndrome. In therapy? Waiting all session till you're going out the door to drop the bomb. You have to tell him."

"It seems like so long ago. Clay would've been—sixteen when he died? All these years, thinking about our dad. You'll see when you talk to him. You want to protect him. Marisol didn't text you, did she?"

"No," Philip said. "You?" Julian shook his head and drove.

Clay turned onto a street of faded little houses and parked in front of a tan one with a scratchy yellowish lawn. There was a metal security grate on the front door. He jumped out of his car and gamboled to theirs like a puppy. "Ready?" he said. He threw his arm around Julian's shoulders and led them up the cracked sidewalk. "Tasha?" he called, poking his head in. "We got company!"

They walked into a tight living-dining space. Julian heard some musical racket as his eyes adjusted to the indoor light, and then he saw a baby from behind pounding on a toy piano in the shape of a smiling kitty cat. There was a huge flat-screen TV on a stand with a PlayStation, and an oily-looking couch and two folding vinyl lawn chairs filling out the room. Dolls and crayons and picture books everywhere.

"Oh my goodness!" a woman said, standing at a small kitchen peninsula. She wore glasses, and her hair short and natural, and pink velour athleisure wear. "Julian? Philip? Y'all came!" She rushed over and hugged them. She was shorter but definitely heavier than beanpole Clay beside her. "Hi! I'm Tanishia."

"Hi, Tanisha," Julian said.

"Ta-nee-shee-yuh," she corrected, a little bookish. "Four syllables. Call me Tasha. Get the baby, Clay. Come meet y'all's niece! It's a mess, sorry, if I knew y'all were coming or Clay called ahead to—*Clay, get Vanessa.*"

"No worries," Julian said. "We surprised you. It's that kind of day, full of—" Julian stopped short, speechless at the sight of Clay hoisting a gorgeous baby onto his hip.

"Full of surprises," Philip picked up the thread, "like this one—hello, Vanessa!" Tasha smiled as the baby reached for Philip's wiggling finger. "Good girl," he cooed. Julian could see the way Tasha looked at Philip, the way everyone did. He had lost the slight banker gut since his Morgan Stanley days and leaned down. "She's fourteen months?" he asked.

"Almost fifteen," Tasha replied.

"Watch this," Clay said. He swung Vanessa sideways and stretched her out and played her like a guitar. She shrieked with delight.

"Did you get the diapers?" Tasha asked. Clay's face clouded, mid-strum. "What did I tell you?" she blew up. "The one thing you're supposed to do?"

"I'm a little busy today!" Clay snapped, handing the baby to Philip.

"All week!" Tasha yelled louder. "I told you and now we're out! You want me to watch the baby, work, *and* get the diapers—"

"I want you to shut up—"

"—how would I—"

"—on the biggest day of my life!"

"I'm done!" She threw up her hands. "Gimme a man *who can bring home diapers!*"

"Fine!" Clay shouted. "Get yourself a Third Ward baller with a truck full of Pampers!" Over her shoulder Clay saw Julian and flushed red. "Sorry!" he cried, scratching his head and turning away. "Sorry, sorry. TV?" He grabbed the remote and turned to Julian entreatingly. "Y'all wanna watch something? A movie? News?"

"Oh," Julian said, stepping back onto a squeaking object. "I'm good."

"Toys," Tasha muttered, "all the freaking—excuse me." She knelt down, pulling a rubber duck from under Julian's foot, and started gathering toys. Clay turned on the TV, and in it drew him, a supplicant to some flat oracle. Vanessa played with the cord on Philip's hood.

"Y'all want some lemonade?" Tasha asked, crawling around the couch.

"Sounds great!" Philip said.

"Turn that shit off," Tasha muttered on her way to the kitchen.

"It's not shit," Clay scowled.

"It's Fox News," Tasha said, getting out cups. "I don't know about y'all," she called to Julian and Philip, "but I'm an Obama Mama, with a brain, and that's garbage."

"You're a nurse?" Philip asked.

"Sometimes," Clay cut in, "Fox News is asking questions nobody else is. Malaysian Air Flight 370? Disappears over the Indian Ocean? Two hundred bodies still missing? People don't disappear like that. A black hole? Conspiracy?" He shrugged like *probably*.

"Scary." Philip nodded.

"ER nurse," Tasha said. "I graduated from Booker T. here on the north side, and studied nursing at Texas Southern, then two tours in Afghanistan, where I met this joker."

"Do your parents still live in Houston?" Philip asked.

"No. My mom passed, and my dad's incarcerated, where he belongs."

"TSU." Clay sidled up behind her and wrapped his arms around her waist. "My college girl." He kissed her neck. "My cougar."

She rolled her eyes and poured lemonade. "I keep telling this one he should get his BA."

"I'm in school," Clay said, giving her a bite. "Getting my associate's in HVAC. Three semesters, quick, done. I'm IRR, so I could get called up anytime."

"That doesn't mean think short-term about your education," she persisted. "Just because you might get the call."

"There are benefits you can—" Philip smiled. "Sorry, I'm sure you know, but there are scholarships for veterans pursuing four-year degrees. This is what I do all day."

"What do you do?" Tasha asked.

"He runs a group," Julian jumped in, "that offers financial planning for veterans."

"Veterans Financial Network," Philip said, laughing as Vanessa explored his nostrils.

"Wait." Tasha took the baby and gave Phil a cup. "We got a thing in the mail—VFN?"

"Yeah," Philip said. "We just started working with the VA here in Houston."

"Damn." Clay's eyes widened. "You run the whole thing?"

"Come sit," Tasha said. "We got some talking to do. Clay, get those cups. Y'all take the couch; we'll take the chairs. We're renting this place for now, not forever. So, Philip, are you here for work, too, or just seeing y'all's baby mama?"

"Just—to meet her," Philip said. "To finalize our match."

"What's she like?" she asked.

"Tasha," Clay scolded.

"What?"

"It's OK," Philip said. "She's a little nervous today."

"She bailed," Clay said.

"No!" Tasha pulled the baby closer on her lap. "She's not—Y'all aren't gonna—"

"We're hopeful," Philip said. "That she'll call."

"She'd be crazy not to," Clay said. "Who wouldn't want y'all as parents?"

A wave of something bittersweet washed over Julian.

"We don't know a lot about her," Philip continued. "Which is crazy but sort of how it works. Her name is Marisol. Her mom brought her and her sisters over from Matamoros when they were kids, and they settled in Houston."

"Gulfton." Julian nodded. "Not far from here."

"What else?" Philip said. "She thinks the birth dad's black, but he's not in the picture."

"Mmm-hmm." Tasha frowned. "Y'all got any black friends in New York?"

"Hey!" Clay cried, fiddling with his phone. "Do y'all ever FaceTime with Aaron? I figured we're together, we could—" He studied Julian's face. "Or maybe y'all don't have that kinda thing going on. Never mind."

"Um." Julian set his cup down on the carpet by the couch. He turned to Clay in the chair beside him. "I don't know how to start. Aaron left me and my mom, too. Around the time you were born, I think. I was thirteen. I saw him two more times in my life, at my mom's memorial, and then a few years ago. He came to New York to tell us he was sick. He died. We found that picture of you and your mom when we were going through his—"

"When?" Clay asked. "When did he die?"

"Six years ago."

"Was he here in Houston?"

"Yeah. Over by Greenspoint Mall. I didn't know your name. If I'd known about you, how to find you, I would've. Tried. I'm sorry."

Clay sat still. Then he rose and went out a door off the kitchen, shutting it behind him.

"Rushhh," Vanessa murmured, looking at the door. "Dada rushhh."

"I am sorry," Julian said to Tasha, "to be the one to tell you. Our dad never had much online. I can see why Clay would've thought . . ."

Tasha shook her head and jiggled the baby on her knee. "He knew Aaron might be gone. I told him so many times: it doesn't matter what you find out, if you meet him or not, what matters is us, this baby, now." She looked from Julian to Philip, her eyes red behind her glasses. "We look like a mess. I know."

"No," Philip insisted.

"We fight or whatever, but we're so in love. He's a good man. A great dad when I stay on him. And smart, you wouldn't guess it, but—"

"Yes, I would," Julian said.

"He could do so many things. He's that romantic type, you know? Passionate. Like his mom." A pounding started on the other side of the door. "Could y'all watch the baby?" Tasha asked, hurrying her to Julian. "He's got his man cave in the garage, whenever he's feeling—" Something crashed. Tasha sprinted out the door and shut it. Muffled sounds of arguing floated into the house. Vanessa wriggled on Julian's lap.

"OK, baby," he said. "Where do you want to go?"

He put her down and held her hand as she toddled to the garage door. She lay both her palms on it and pressed her face against it. "Rushhhhh," she said. Then she toddled to the front door and looked out the window. Julian and Philip followed, finally hearing the tinkling sound that caught her ears.

"The ice cream man?" Philip said in his baby voice. "What do you think, Vee?"

Julian picked her up and they went outside. "Do you think it's OK?" he asked Philip. "Giving her sugar?"

Philip looked back at the house. "All relative, I guess."

Julian hoisted her up. She pointed at a Creamsicle. The three of them sat on the lawn and ate ice cream in the late afternoon sun, Julian helping Vanessa balance the stick in her tiny hands. He marveled at the lovely combination of her parents—her blue eyes, bronze skin, dark, tight ringlets jutting out joyously in all directions. Julian wondered about where she'd go and the things she'd see, the as-yet-uninvented tech that would be her given world and his glorious obsolescence. He kissed her cheek and told himself to hang on to this moment, which would end.

Clay and Tasha came outside, his left hand tucked behind him, and sat down. "Sorry," Clay said, looking around sheepishly. Tasha adjusted a bag of frozen peas on his knuckles. "Worked it out on the Sheetrock. Oop!" He leaned toward the baby in Julian's lap, wiped an orange dribble off her chin, and licked his finger. "She loves her some Creamsicle." His face softened as he watched his daughter. "We take care of her, and she just keeps growing."

Julian's phone buzzed. His heart shot into his throat. "A text from Marisol," he said soberly to Philip. "'I fucked up,'" he read. "'Sorry. Still wanna meet? Call me.'"

"Call her!" Tasha brayed and grabbed the baby.

Marisol picked up on the first ring. "Julian?"

"Hi, Marisol. I've got you on speaker."

"Hey, Philip," she said.

"Hi! We're here with Julian's brother and sister-in-law and their baby girl."

"You got a brother in Houston?" Marisol asked.

Julian looked at Clay. "Yeah. His name is Clayton. How are you?"

"OK. Um. Sorry about before. I musta freaked y'all out. I got scared and—yeah."

"I know," Julian said.

"Not about y'all. Y'all're funny and chill. It's, like, the world. This baby."

"We are too." He took Philip's hand. "Scared."

"But I wanna do this," she said. "If y'all do. It's the right thing."

"Yes," Julian said. "We want to too."

"My mom made food. Empanadas and chicken. Y'all wanna meet everybody?"

"At your place?" Julian asked.

"Yes!" Philip cried. "Of course! We need to know everything about you and your mom and sisters and everybody. We should know everything—for the baby, right, Jay? Everything."

"Yeah," Julian said, looking at Clay. "Or more than our parents did. Are you sure, Marisol?"

"Yeah, come over. We're gonna be family. And my sister thinks y'all're cute. Both y'all. But, like, Philip."

Clay giggled and rolled back onto the lawn. "He is cute," Julian said. "Text me your address. We're in Missouri City now."

"Hey, Marisol?" Clay cried, bolting upright. "Why'd you pick them?"

"Clayton!" Tasha shot him a furious look.

"Maybe now's not—" Philip began.

"She thinks we're nice," Julian mumbled anxiously.

"Like, me and Julian's dad? He was a real piece of—" Tasha swatted him. "Something," Clay continued. "But you get to pick your kid's dads. I know Julian's freaking amazing—he's my brother—and Philip too. But for you. Why them?"

The phone went quiet. "I don't know. I guess, the way they talk about each other, in the profile, like in love. And the pictures of traveling, where the baby'll go. Um. And Julian's work? That case helping the immigrants in Arizona? I googled him. You, Julian, sorry, TMI. There's all this news about it. They seem like good people."

"OK!" Julian interjected. "Great. Marisol, we'll be there in a half hour. Without Clay."

"OK. See y'all."

Julian hung up. Philip wrapped his arms around him while Tasha cheered.

"See?" Clay said as they struggled to their feet. "I knew she'd call. Things work out, right?" He thumped Julian's chest. "Sometimes?"

"Yes," Julian replied.

"So." Clay kicked at a dandelion. "Y'all coming back much after this?"

"For the delivery, which is any day now. And then however much Marisol wants. Once a year, maybe more, depending." Julian sighed. "A lot of memories, coming back here."

"More to come," Clay said timidly.

"Stay with us," Tasha suggested. "We got an air bed. And the cousins, you know."

"Thanks," Philip said. "It's nice to have somewhere you're welcome."

"Pictures!" Clay whipped out his phone. "Selfie alert, let's go." They took some group shots, and then Clay insisted Tasha take some of just him and Julian. "Look at that," Clay said, showing Julian a photo afterward. "Us. We look like, when you pull socks out of the drawer that don't match but close enough, so you wear them anyways?"

"That one's nice," Julian murmured. "Will you send it to me?"

"Yeah." Clay watched him. "Keep in touch. I got so many questions."

Julian nodded. "I don't know if I have answers."

"You're something. Say bye to Uncle Julian," Clay said, grabbing the baby and waving her little hand. "Bye-bye, Uncle Julian."

"Uncle Juuuu," she spluttered.

"That would be me," Philip said. "Uncle Jew's over here, Vee."

They hugged goodbye. Clay held Julian a long time when it was their turn. His grip was so firm Julian could feel it in his core, along with the waves of their breath combining, traveling down to his feet and anchoring him on the lawn. He squeezed Clay back.

Julian and Philip got in the car and buckled up.

"Do you want to see them again?" Philip asked. "Next time we're in town?"

"Yeah. Or this time. We've got another day."

"Yeah." Philip smiled. He looked up at the road ahead. "You ready for this?"

"No," Julian said. "You?"

"No."

They turned and waved one last time at Clay and Tasha and Vanessa standing in the street. Then Julian and Philip pulled down the block and drove to meet their birth mom.

Acknowledgments

Where to begin? I have such gratitude for so many people, so I'll start where everything starts—with my mother. Thank you, Sandy Deabler, for raising me. For teaching me that love is a strength, and faith is a struggle. For making me believe, through methods both clear and mysterious, that I have a voice worth hearing.

Thank you to Aileen Barry and the artists of Lynx Ensemble Theater—Bill Bowers, Joy Marr, Jen Wineman, Joy Besozzi, Brian McManamon, David Levine, Norm Lee, Devon Berkshire, and many others—who invested in me and gave me one of the first places I ever had to play and fail and discover as an artist. Thanks to Jessica Provenz and Dan O'Brien and Stefanie Zadravec, who treated me with the respect of a fellow writer before I knew if I really was one. Thanks to Timothy Ryan Olsen, Sara Katzoff, and Peter Wise at the Berkshire Fringe, and to Michael Goldfried, for the unforgettable experience of taking a show on the road.

Thanks to the Ensemble Studio Theatre, to which I had the privilege of trekking every week, rain or shine, on the western fringe of Hell's Kitchen, where I could be around artists who bring such unique beauty into the world—Amy Herzog, Lucy

Alibar, Annie Baker, and others—and where, in the process, I was humbled and became a better writer.

Thank you to the many friends who read chapters of this book at various stages, always with an encouraging eye: Michael Sendrow, Ida Rothschild, Jesse Cameron Alick, Doug Silver, Dale Heinen, Sara Fox, Sandra Pullman, Cher and Colleen Brock, Vandana Radhakrishnan, Lee Bailey, Rachel Dornhelm, Zoe Hilden, Terri Gerstein, Katie Rosman. Thanks to my friend Kasia Anderson, who sat with me on a sunny day in Central Park nearly two decades ago, a story of mine in her hands, and urged me to show not tell. Thank you, Matthew Sharpe, for your generosity and insight.

Thanks to my agent, Michael Carlisle, for taking a chance on me. Thank you, Michael Mungiello at InkWell, for your thoughtful feedback. And a million thanks to Elisabeth Dyssegaard at St. Martin's Press, for being an amazing editor, and sending me a handwritten markup, and for pretty much always being right. With your help I kept sculpting until I found the book I meant to write.

Thank you to my old friend Eliot Schrefer. This book sort of started with a wager over lunch one day as grown-ups, wondering how much we were willing to look back into our own pasts. But it also started earlier than that, with your unwavering support, of me and my dreams, practically and creatively, year after year, from the time we were in school. You are a true friend.

Where to end? That one's easy. Thanks to my amazing husband, Mark O'Connell. With your love and example, I became the person who could write this book. Sometimes I'll randomly think of meeting you as a teenager and I can't believe we're still here, alive, together. A teacher told me once to write what I know, and what I know is you. Thank you for being my partner in life, love, art, daddying, fur daddying, and whatever comes hurtling our way next.